LOST STARS

DONNY ANGUISH

ANOTHER PAGE PUBLISHING

For Will and Kathy Anguish. Since a million words couldn't fully express what I'd like to say, it's probably best to just use three: I love you.

CONTENTS

I

WORLDS APART

CHAPTER ONE

J on sat across from his best friend of six hundred years, devastated that he had to kill him. The man was unconscious, bloodied, and chained to a chair—a terrible contrast to the serene ocean below. Jon looked past the balcony railing and down to the jagged rocks. This wasn't how he wanted it to end. He took a deep breath and waited for Sargas to wake up.

Sargas eventually came to with a jolt and wrenched at his chains. His eyes flicked from side to side, then settled on Jon. He smirked. "So you finally figured it out. How long have you known?"

"Almost eighty years," Jon said, placing his hands on the table between them. "How long have you known about me?"

"Only a decade or so." Sargas turned and spat blood onto the stony floor. "Shutting them down was a mistake, you know."

Jon frowned and waited. Sargas couldn't know with any certainty that it was him who had shut down the gateways between worlds and caused the depression.

"Oh, stop that," Sargas said, waving the idea away. "It was you. Who else could have done it?"

"It wasn't a mistake," Jon said. "The war was killing millions. And besides, it's done. There's no going back."

"I don't care about the dead." Sargas's chains clinked against the chair. "You can't reach the planet of Jangali anymore. Not in time to find the organism, at least."

Jon bit the side of his mouth. How did he know about the entity on Jangali?

Sargas relaxed into his seat and laughed. "Six centuries of life and you still can't hide what you're feeling."

This organism on Jangali would change everything, and Jon couldn't let it fall into Sargas's hands. He focused. This would be his only chance to get the information he needed, but he had to know something else first. He had waited for so many years.

"Tell me," Jon said, leaning forward, "did you actually convince Ava to go through with it or was it her idea?"

Sargas cocked his head. "Does it matter?"

"Was it your fault or not?"

"Actually, it's always been *your* fault," Sargas said, pointing a bloody finger. "You made me do this. You could've just given me the extra years of life when I asked for them."

"You convinced her to kill herself so that you could have a *chance* at living forever. How can you be so selfish?"

Sargas let out a bellowing laugh. "You really don't have any idea, do you?"

Jon stood abruptly and the air seemed to bend around him. "Don't patronize me. I know exactly what you've done."

"Okay, sure, I nudged Ava over the edge, but she was ready to jump, wasn't she? Whose fault was that?"

Jon fingered the wedding band he couldn't bear to take off as she flashed across his mind:

Holding hands in moonlit water.

A warm spring day and a white dress.

Her laugh as she dragged him onto the dance floor.

"Why?" Jon asked, voice quaking. "How could you do that to her?"

Sargas suddenly lost his good humor. "How. Could. You?"

Jon stared at Sargas, then his gaze fell. He pulled out a thin syringe filled with a clear liquid and placed it on the table.

Sargas stirred in his seat. "You wouldn't," he said, eyeing Jon. "You're too noble for that. Too good—"

Jon quickly picked up the syringe and jammed it into Sargas's arm. The effect was almost immediate. Sargas's eyes went wide with surprise before his whole body deflated, like he were suddenly very drunk.

"Do you know the exact location of the entity on Jangali?" Jon asked.

Sargas writhed, trying to keep his body and mind alert. He clamped his mouth shut.

"You can't fight it," Jon said. "You might not tell me everything, but I'll get enough. You know I will."

Sargas sagged further and then appeared to fall asleep. Jon had never used the drug before but had read that this could sometimes happen. The passage he'd read recommended to get the subject standing. Jon walked around the table, unchained Sargas, and guided him to a standing position. He patted the man's face.

"Do you know the exact location of the organism on Jangali?"

"No..."

Jon sighed in relief. "Do you already have people on Jangali?"

"Yes," Sargas said, swaying to the side.

"Where are the other bodies?"

Sargas closed his eyes, and Jon thought he had fallen asleep again, but then his eyes suddenly snapped opened with surprising lucidity. Jon was so shocked that he took a step back.

Sargas's eyes flicked to the balcony. Jon followed his gaze, then looked back at him.

"No!" Jon yelled.

But it was too late.

Sargas lunged with an enormous effort, reaching the balcony railing and then throwing himself over it without any hesitation. Jon closed his eyes and was silent until he heard the body hit the rocks far below. He collapsed into a chair and kept his head bowed for a long while.

He turned to Treyges, who was waiting by the door, as unruffled in his black suit as he had ever been. "Contact the team and tell them to get ready. Raise the security level to red and prepare the ship to depart. Cut all communications with the core and dismiss everyone in the house. We're leaving."

Treyges bowed. "Where to, sir?"

Jon looked up at a particular patch of sky.

"Jangali."

CHAPTER TWO

S aiph was on his knees and praying when the only magic light in
the village went out. He stared up at the oddly shaped piece of
glass as a gust of wind sent it swinging. It creaked and produced an
eerie symphony with the crickets outside. Around him, other dirt-
smeared faces mirrored his shock.

"What does it mean?"

"Have we angered the gods?"

"Are the Fulgurians attacking?"

The crowded hut buzzed with anxious chatter, and everyone
seemed to have forgotten Saiph in the excitement. He couldn't get up
from a kneeling position on his own, not with his bad leg. He was about
to resign himself to a long, embarrassing wait when someone short and
dark-skinned knelt in front of him.

"Need a hand?" Ayanda asked.

"More like a leg."

She grunted as she put her arms underneath Saiph before lifting.
He grimaced in pain and then put his weight up against a beam, panting. Any exertion made his incompetent lungs work overtime, but the
pain in his leg always made it worse. He closed his eyes until it passed.

"All right?" Ayanda asked.

"Yeah. Good. What's happening?"

"Don't know, can't see anything," Ayanda said. She was too short to see over the others.

The pain was passing when Saiph saw a wooden bucket a couple feet away. He gingerly limped over to it and then turned it upside down before jumping atop it with his good leg. He peered over the heads of the others and saw a growing panic. He felt it too. The harsh light of the glass had never gone out before.

Saiph saw his father near the front, speaking calmly with Old Gillums. Even with all the commotion, he couldn't imagine his father being anything but calm. It radiated off him like a pleasant scent. Saiph breathed it in as deeply as he could and felt the rhythm of his heart slow.

"See anything?" Ayanda asked.

Someone suddenly fell from all the commotion and nearly knocked over the bucket Saiph was standing on. Ayanda quickly helped him down and they moved to the side. The yelling intensified.

"Quiet!" Gillums bellowed. "By the gods, settle yourselves!"

The space slowly calmed, and the yelling was replaced with nervous whispers.

"This is not the first time the Light of Tengrii has gone out," Gillums said. "It happened when I was a boy. The other villages lost Tengrii's light as well, but they came back!"

"Why's the light gone out this time?" someone yelled.

Gillums scanned the room of silent and frightened faces. The chorus of crickets outside was as loud as the villagers' fear.

"I don't know." he said. "In my experience, change like this has never been good for Altai. But if you let your Core Verses guide you and the Tenets anchor you, then nothing truly bad can ever happen."

Saiph and his father walked in silence, their breath steaming in the cold air. The dirt path leading their burrow was lightly illuminated by glowing green roots and the two moons high above. They had just set out, but Saiph was already shivering. He wished now that he hadn't cut his hair so short. Ayanda had said she liked it, though, that it suited his thin face and brought out the blue in his eyes. Saiph smiled and pulled his fur coat closer.

"What do you think happened?" Saiph asked.

"Don't know," Rosh said.

"Was it the Fulgurians?"

"No."

"Dad, do you know what the Light of Tengrii actually is?"

"It is the hope in the darkness. It is Tengrii's gift to the people so that we will not feel alone before we join the darkness."

"Yes, yes, I know that, but what *is* it exactly?"

Rosh sighed. "I've heard it called elec-tar-acity, but I haven't a clue what—"

Rosh stopped suddenly and held up a hand. He made a gesture, and they stepped off the dirt path and into tall grass. Saiph heard it now too, a distant pounding that was growing louder. At first, he thought that he was just shivering, but then he realized that the very ground was gently vibrating. They crept to the other side of the thicket and peered out across the next field. The noise intensified in equal measure with Saiph's pounding heart.

"What is it?" he whispered, trying to control his heavy breaths.

"Quiet."

Saiph saw its silhouette, and his eyes widened. It was monstrous. The two legs were taller than Gillums's two-story shop and so slender that Saiph wondered how they supported its fat, cylindrical top. It was moving faster than anything he'd ever seen. It didn't slow or move aside for anything in its path but dashed in a straight line, crushing everything underfoot. The grass swayed around them as the thumping faded into the distance. When it was gone, they turned to each other with identical expressions of bewilderment.

"What in Tengrii's name was that?"

Mornings were especially unpleasant during cold weeks. Saiph would sit on the edge of his bed in the quiet darkness, flexing painful sensation into his left leg and lungs.

Wiggle your toes. Breathe in. Breathe out. Close your eyes and think of running water.

That was what his father had said after the accident all those years ago. He would come into Saiph's room before everyone was up and pretend that his leg hurt, too. That his lungs were also frail. He did that every day for a year before leaving Saiph to do it by himself.

Saiph eventually grew out of the need to imagine running water, and nowadays he would usually just sit and contemplate life, the Verses, or some other interest instead. Today, his thoughts were so focused that it made the pain distant. He couldn't quite wrap his head around the fact that he'd never wake up to a festival morning in this house ever again.

Saiph opened his eyes and looked around. He had hated this room when he'd spent months lying in bed, recovering. He had sworn that when he got better, he would walk out and never come back. Now, though...

His gaze lingered on the display of costume masks from past festivals. He smiled at the one he'd made when he was eight, a terrible mockery of a fish. The idol of Tengrii that Ayanda had given him sat in his old rocking chair, comically small compared to its seat. The walls were painted with twenty-two stars, one for each of his years. Without his limp, Saiph could probably cross the width of the room in two strides. It wasn't much, but it was his, and it was all he'd ever known.

For a time, he was convinced that he'd live his whole life in this small bedroom. He was the last one of his age not to be married and have his own home. He understood why—he was crippled and feeble. Who would willingly burden themselves with him? He wouldn't wish that on anyone. It still made him sad, though.

He'd been glum when his friend William married, but he'd been ashamed and angry during the first wedding of a boy younger than him. Saiph felt a nearly overwhelming bitterness. It was as if his injury and asthma had also planted a seed within him, which was blooming into a thicket of poison ivy. He was so resentful that he nearly pushed the wedding cake to the ground. That's when he'd known that he had to do something to right himself. The very next day, Saiph had chosen his third Core Verse to live by and pray with each day:

If we cannot live to be happy, let us at least live as if we deserve to be.

He'd let go of his expectations after that. There were worse fates than his, and he was thankful for what he had. That painful but heart-felt acceptance of his lot in life was what had made his father's news so surprising. His own volt farm? Could he really handle that, despite leg and lung? It worried him and excited him at the same time. If he could only prove that he could do it on his own, then maybe someone would want him.

Saiph's thoughts were interrupted by the sound of whispers and a small laugh coming from the common room. He smiled. The younger children were always too excited to sleep before the Effulgence Festival, and Landon was no exception. After a few more minutes of deep breaths and a hard massage of his leg, Saiph stood up and limped toward the door.

Landon was sitting at his small wooden table, eating breakfast. Their mother was sweeping dirt off the floor. He didn't know why she bothered; dirt was a fact of life when you lived seven feet into the ground.

"Morn, my little beetle!" Milla said.

Saiph hugged her, resting his head on her shoulder. "Happy Efful-gence Eve, Mum."

She laughed. "May your light glow, Saiph."

He nearly fell asleep on her shoulder, despite the fact that he was a foot taller than her.

Milla rubbed his short brown hair with her fist. "What are you doing, boy! The Effulgence Festival isn't going to glow on its own this year, is it? Your father and sister are already out there. Roe was anxious to go, as you might have guessed."

"Roe, anxious?" Saiph said. "Roe, getting her way? Nonsense."

Milla laughed.

"And how's my hero doing today?" Saiph said to Landon. "Are you ready for the festival tomorrow?"

Landon stopped eating his porridge and gave Saiph a devious smile. "Party hard!"

Saiph quickly stumbled over and began tickling him. "Who's my hero? Tell me who it is! Tell me!"

"Me!" Landon said, laughing. "Me!"

Landon was short and chubby with a round face and slanted eyes. He spoke with a lisp and was always ready to dance, explore, or play a trick on Saiph. When Landon was very young, his father had told Saiph that he had met others with the Down before and that there was nothing to worry about.

Saiph dropped to one knee and squinted at Landon. "Remember, I get the first dance tomorrow, okay?"

"Okay," Landon whispered. "You're my favorite human."

"You're my favorite human," Saiph whispered back. Landon and Saiph gently put their heads together before Saiph stood up. He grabbed a chunk of warm bread from the table, wiped the flecks of dirt off, then stuffed it into his mouth. "See you at supper! Rest up for the big day tomorrow!"

The cold night had made for a cold morning, but the gods' divine wind had cleared the clouds, and Saiph was able to take in the last sunlight he'd see for four days. Trees seven hundred feet high stood at the edge of the field, pulsing veins of soft white light running from trunk to leaf. Saiph could just make out the large and hairy monikins swinging from the branches. As he walked, small orange flowers gently nipped at his feet, as if to say good morning. He took a deep breath and smiled. Ayanda always thought it was good luck to have a sunny festival eve. Thinking of her made him refocus, and he listened intently for any sign of her presence.

She always managed to scare the piss out of him on Effulgence Eve, but not this year. He was going to stop her. Maybe even surprise *her*. He was two miles out when the path bent to the left for the final mile to the family volt farm. Saiph's eyes scanned the path, and he was thinking on her impending failure when she dropped out of a branch fifteen feet in the air and landed on his back. The hit sent Saiph to the ground. Ayanda recovered quickly from her fall and put a knee on his back and her hand on the back of his head.

"You were thinking you'd make a fool of me this year, weren't you?" Ayanda said.

"Get...off..."

"Not until you admit it!" she said, laughing.

Saiph elbowed her in the side, but it was no use. He sighed. "Congratulations, you've once again succeeded in knocking a cripple to the ground. The Worst Person of the Year Award goes to you."

"Admit you weren't expecting the old fifteen-foot-tree-drop-onto-the-back maneuver," Ayanda said.

"Admit that you've been hiding there for more than three hours and have scouted that spot for over six weeks."

"Rubbish," she said. "Only just found it."

Saiph frowned at her lie, then laughed. He laughed so hard that he shook from it. Ayanda was the only person outside of his family who didn't baby him because of his condition. Though his leg throbbed and his breath was labored, he was happy.

"May your light ever shine, Ayanda."

She smiled. "Happy Effulgence Eve, Saiph."

Ayanda walked behind Saiph on the narrow path to the family's volt farm at the edge of the wood, speaking in masked excitement as he told her about what he'd seen with his father the night before.

"If this was coming from anyone else, I wouldn't believe it. What could it have possibly been? An animal?" she asked.

"I don't know, but I'm telling you I've never seen anything of the like. And it occurred not an hour after the Light of Tengrii went out."

"Do you think Tengrii is angry?"

13

"Seriously?"

"Oh, come on!" Ayanda said. "You know he's got to get angry every now and then."

"Tengrii is Lord of Blue Sky," Saiph said, "he isn't going to send a monster to terrorize Altai because we weren't praying hard enough."

"Oh, now I get it. Thanks for explaining that Tengrii doesn't actually give a damn about us. He couldn't possibly have the time for all that, being a god and all."

Saiph smiled and held his hands to the sky. "May Tengrii strike me down for my beliefs, then. Go on you wanker! Do it!"

Nothing happened. Saiph shook his fist at the sky for another few seconds before glancing smugly at Ayanda.

"It's your pyre," she said.

They approached the walls of the volt farm as the sun scaled the tree line. Made of stone ten feet high and two feet thick, the walls were the largest structures in the entire valley. Saiph didn't like to think about how long it must have taken his ancestors to build it. The volt farm was intimidating for most people in Altai, but Saiph had worked here his whole life. When they reached the first iron gate, Saiph took off his coat. He folded it neatly and laid it tenderly to the side.

"How can you care so much for that coat and then wear a shirt that has holes in it?" Ayanda asked. "I mean, I can't even tell what color it is anymore. And your pants...Tengrii help you."

"Now why would I need a fine shirt and pants when I have such a fine coat? Besides, your clothing isn't much better."

"At least I try to keep it clean! Not all of us can afford a coat like that!"

Saiph put one hand to his heart and the other in the air. "I solemnly vow to take better care of my non-coat clothing." He smiled. "Coming in today?"

"What? Of course not. It's way too cold to put that slop all over my body. I think I'll start spreading the word of your continued embarrassment on my way to mother's shop." She winked at him. "See ya at the morning feast tomorrow."

Saiph watched her go, wondering if she was going to ask him to dance. But no, it was still too soon. Her husband had died only a year and a half ago. But what if she did? He sighed, feeling guilty even considering the idea, and then entered the first gate.

To his right was the pool of yokai blood. He lowered himself to one knee, carefully filled his hands with the thick purple liquid, and then threw it over his torso. Once his body was covered, he dipped each of his fingertips into the pool and smeared ten lines from the bridge of his nose to his ears. He shivered as he put his clothes back on and went through the second gate.

"That you, Saiph?" Rosh called out.

"Yeah!"

"Need some help over here!"

Saiph frowned, grabbed the spear leaning up against the wall, and ran as fast as his leg and lungs allowed. When he got there, he saw three beetles the size of his hand latched on to his sister's right leg. They glowed with a soft white light.

"Stay still, Roe," Rosh said.

"Damn things hurt!" Roe shouted. She kicked again.

Rosh looked up at Saiph. "Hold her down, please."

Saiph rested one hand on Roe's ankle, one on her thigh, and then put his weight onto her leg. She struggled for a moment, then relaxed. Rosh grabbed a beetle's back with a gloved hand and used bronze tweezers to slowly pull its legs out from Roe's skin. The glove started to smoke from the beetle's heat and Rosh had to take a moment to let it cool off.

Rosh shook his head as he removed the last beetle. "This isn't a game, Roe. You don't follow my words. Anybody's words for that matter. I told you there wasn't enough blood to repel the voltbeetles. The volt animals aren't scared of you; they're scared of the scent of a two-thousand-pound yokai and its swordlike claws."

Roe stood up. "Well I'm fine, aren't I?"

Saiph looked at her leg and raised his eyebrows. Small holes leaked blood down her leg, and there were burns that were already blistering.

"No," Rosh said, "you're not. Go on home and get cleaned up."

"No!" Roe said, brushing her blonde hair out of her eyes. "It's my first time working the Effulgence Festival! You said at sixteen I could help!"

"And obviously you're not ready for it if you can't even put on enough blood to repel the voltbeetles. Get on home now and help your mum."

"But—"

"Now," Rosh said, "before I decide to lock you in your room for the ceremony tomorrow."

Roe looked like she was about to protest, but she finally turned and limped off.

"Should I help her home?" Saiph asked.

"Think she'd want your help?" Rosh said as if Saiph had just declared that he had invited a Fulgurian to supper.

Saiph involuntarily thought of the forest people that had made war against the Skyfallers, going against everything the people of Jangali stood for. He always pictured them as dirty, with fang-like teeth, though of course he'd never seen one of them before.

The iron gate slammed shut and brought him back to the present. "No, I suppose she wouldn't like that."

"You suppose..." Rosh shook his head. "Come on, there's still a lot to do before the feast tomorrow."

Saiph and Rosh spent the afternoon coating the seals of large glass barrels in yokai blood. If the voltbeetles got out because the glass wasn't properly coated, Tengrii himself may very well personally escort Saiph to a shallow grave. The white glow and comforting warmth that the voltbeetles gave off was at the center of the festival, and no one was going to brave the coldest, darkest day of the year without a few beetle barrels to keep them comfortable.

"Last night," Saiph said as he stuck his brush into the bowl of purple liquid, "you think it was the Skyfallers or something else?"

"Only a few stories have made it to our part of Jangali," Rosh said. "They speak of Skyfaller magic. And I mean magic beyond the healing potions they trade. Thunder that kills, flying wagons, that sort of thing."

Saiph nodded. "Then it was them?"

"I don't know. Maybe, maybe not. Though we can both agree we've never seen anything like that, yes? The others will want to know if it was some sort of beast."

"I suppose it could have been, but you're right, we've never seen anything of the like."

They continued to brush the seals as the sun arched through the sky, stopping only to sip water from their canteens, nibble stale bread, or throw meat to the big voltcats when they became distracting.

"They've built a city as well," Rosh said on one such break. "Ayanda's mother heard it from another hunter a few weeks ago. The man had an...interesting tale. Said there are buildings taller than the trees and that there are so many lights that the dark never touches it."

Saiph tried to imagine that amount of light without the sun and failed. The Skyfallers must have powerful magic at their command.

"Is that why the Fulgurians fight them?" Saiph asked. "To steal their magic?"

"I wish I knew," Rosh said. "I pray that they still live within the Tenets and find guidance in their Verses."

Dusk approached and they placed the last seal on the last barrel and loaded them into the wagon. Rosh covered the beetle barrels with a white blanket and sat next to Saiph on a log outside the gate. They rested their elbows on their knees, and Rosh pulled out a bottle and two cups.

"You know," he said, pouring pungent red liquid into one, "your mother and I are very proud of you." He handed him the cup and Saiph eyed it skeptically.

"Go on," Rosh said.

Saiph took a sip. They nodded at each other and drank quietly as the sun departed. The orange mixed with the blue sky, and Kayra began to eclipse the sun completely as Jangali entered its far orbit around the huge planet.

"You nervous, going out on your own?" Rosh eventually asked, not looking at him.

Saiph wasn't sure what to say. He looked into his cup as if the words were at the bottom, just out of sight.

"What if..." Saiph began, "what if I don't want to leave? What will Landon do? He won't understand."

"This is your life, not his," Rosh said. "Don't you want your own farm? Your own family?"

Saiph scoffed. "My own family? I doubt that will happen, Dad."

Rosh repositioned his large frame on the log and scratched his beard. "You're young. You never know where life might take you."

"I still don't feel ready," Saiph said. "Not ready at all."

"No one ever really is, I think. It's like jumping from the mother tree, terrifying when you let go but thrilling in the air before you hit the water."

They sipped their drinks.

"Did I ever tell you about my and your mum's wedding?" Rosh said.

Saiph shook his head.

"I had been trying to persuade your grandfather to let me marry your mother for over two years. Every time I asked him, he'd say, 'Prove that you're not a complete git, and I'll consider it properly.' Well, once I gave him a full beetle barrel of his own, he changed his mind. That and the fact that we were going to get married anyway, with or without his consent."

"You can do that?" Saiph asked.

"Anyone can do anything at any moment, Saiph. But my point is that, on my wedding day, after spending two years of convincing your grandfather, I sat on top of a beetle barrel because I was cold."

"Are you serious?" Saiph said, laughing. "How old were you?"

"A year younger than you are now."

Saiph laughed even harder. "I don't believe it."

"My point," Rosh said over the laughter, "is that no matter what you do, you're going to get your ass burned sooner or later, so you might as well let go and have the wind of your life rush by."

Saiph sobered and stared at his glass, which reflected the soft white glow of the barrels and the last remnants of orange sunlight. He couldn't remember anything quite so beautiful. "I'll miss this," he said, lifting his head to stare at the horizon.

Rosh looked at his eldest son.

"Me too."

CHAPTER THREE

J on sat in a sleek white room and tapped his fingers against a polished white table. His dark jacket matched his wavy hair and his mood.

"Shall I bring them in, sir?" Treyges asked.

Tokomoto was first, his wheelchair creaking with every other rotation. His youthful face and diminished stature were overshadowed by his partner, Russ, who was six and a half feet tall with shoulder-length blond hair and a white cowboy hat. Russ was closely followed by Ellie, her pale skin and lab coat off set by her spiky red hair and freckles.

Amira had dark-skin and was very short, but no one in a room ever missed her because of her size. The left side of her head was shaved and tattoos ran from her bare skull to her wrist, covering extensive scar tissue. It was mostly her eyes, though. People always noticed the wary intelligence within them.

Trailing behind was Silvestre. Jon had known her for her entire life, but he still found her striking. Her tanned skin and black hair made a brilliant complement with her pure red and glowing eyes. There were no visible pupils or irises. Only red.

"Please be seated," Treyges said.

Russ took his seat next to Tokomoto. "So!" he said. "What's the occasion, Jon? Thought we were done in these dark times! No pun intended, of course." He was the only one to chuckle. "Oh, I'm sorry, I didn't realize this meeting was supposed to be melodramatic. I'll pretend I'm furious about something important." He frowned deeply.

"You know people are watching us now," Silvestre said, her bionic left hand twisting in a manner that no biological hand could. She always did that when she was nervous. "Everyone is anxious about the latest blackout."

Jon nodded. "I understand the current social and political climate, Sil. I appreciate you coming."

"Then what has happened?" Tokomoto said softly. He looked even more frail than he usually did. Jon hoped he wasn't in one of his darker moods.

An antique clock hung on the wall and ticked loudly in the silence. Jon looked at each of them, making sure he had their attention. "I know you've struggled recently," he said. "These past few years have been hard on everyone. But I have a job for you. A big one."

"Might as well spit it out," Silvestre said.

Amira looked back and fourth as the others talked, the long black hair of her right side swaying with the conversation. Ellie pulled out a tablet and started taking notes.

"It's secretive in nature," Jon said, "but it will be dangerous and will require you to travel."

"Cool!" Ellie said. "Where we going?"

Russ leaned so far back in his chair that it looked like he'd fall at any moment. "Hold on there, Ellie. Just exactly how far are you planning to go?"

"Jangali."

"You're not talking about the Jangali at the rim?" Silvestre said. "Because that would take at least four years to get to."

"Five, actually," Jon said.

Russ and Tokomoto shared a look, and Russ voiced their question. "What in the hell is Jangali?"

"Seriously?" Silvestre said. "You don't even know all thirty-eight worlds? Not even the most recently discovered one?"

"I've been busy," Russ said.

"For the last forty years?"

Russ grinned. "Yep. And I don't look forty, I look thirty-five."

"But you *are* forty!"

"So you think..."

Jon shook his head, smiling slightly as he hit a button on the desk. The room went dark and a three-dimensional projection appeared above the middle of the table. "Jangali is the smallest moon in system 4.8.15.16.23.42," he said. "It orbits the fifth planet, Kayra, which is a gas giant with rings that aren't unlike Saturn and Andernach."

The projected image sprang to life. Three moons orbited a beautiful and colorful planet with a ring that seemed solid but was actually made of millions of rocks. The smallest labeled object in the simulation was tagged "Jangali." It revolved slowly around the bigger planetary bodies.

"What are those two red lights?" Russ said.

Tokomoto leaned over. "Those are Silvestre's eyes..."

"Oh, right. Apologies."

"Jangali orbits Kayra every sixteen days. Right now," Jon said, "Jangali is on its dark cycle because Kayra blocks ninety-nine percent of all sunlight from reaching it. As the moon rounds the planet, it experiences different intensities of light and heat. Its weeks are like Earth's seasons."

"Most unterraformed planets are dangerous," Amira said, her voice crisp and her Algerian accent soft. "What is Jangali's profile?"

Jon scratched his chin and shrugged. "It can be dangerous, I guess. It has a higher percentage of oxygen than planets like Earth and Mars. The plants and animals grow to huge sizes. Our analysis shows that it can easily support animals that are thirty feet tall and that weigh twenty tons, and the trees probably shoot up to nearly a thousand feet."

Russ whistled and Ellie's eyes widened. Even Amira looked impressed.

"If I'm being honest with you," Jon said, "I'm more worried about the two dynamics from Forhanastan that are currently administering the planet."

The projected star system winked out and was replaced by two people. They were clearly brother and sister, but what was most striking was their glowing, pupil less eyes that were similar to Silvestre's, only yellow.

"Why are two dynamics from Forhanastan running the place?" Ellie asked. "Aren't the people from there kind of...vicious?"

"I'm not entirely sure who they're working for," Jon said, "but they're not on Jangali for some sort of mission trip. They are Class D dynamics. They are very powerful and skilled and won't be friendly toward us."

Russ stood up, and Tokomoto looked as if he would have if he could. "Well, Jon," Russ said, "it's been right nice seeing you and Treyges, but Toko and I will have to decline. Five years is a lot of time nowadays, and those two dynamics don't look all that accommodating."

Silvestre stood as well. "You know there are a lot of things I'd do for you Jon, but flying half a decade through space to be killed by Forhanastan dynamics isn't one of them."

"Is Jangali a nice place?" Ellie asked.

Everyone looked at Ellie as if the Republican Guard had just marched in and started singing "All Hail the First Protector." Amira remained seated, tapping her fingers against the table.

"You haven't heard my offer yet," Jon said as Sil, Russ, and Toko began to leave.

"It is not a standard contract?" Tokomoto asked.

"It's not. I'll compensate you for your time and for the risk involved."

Russ squinted and lifted his chin. "How much?"

"Fifty extra years for each of you, which can be exchanged at the established rate of credit, three years for your subordinates. Years en route will also be provided."

While most eyes widened at the offer, Amira's narrowed. "Your offer is too generous for five years of travel. What else is there? What is happening on Jangali?"

"The energy crisis is getting worse, and if anymore stars are lost, there will be mass panic," Jon said. "And, well, a Class G dynamic has been traced to Jangali."

"Class G!" Ellie said. "Has that ever happened before?"

Silvestre's mouth hung open. "Only once," she said. "The organism died quickly, though."

"Think what we could do with that much continuous energy," Tokomoto said. The others nodded.

"What sort of organism is it?" Amira asked.

Jon sighed; it was always Amira who asked the right questions. "It's a human being," Jon said.

"My god," Russ said. "The first?"

"Yep. The first Class G human dynamic out of thirty-seven billion souls in existence."

Silvestre dropped her red eyes and shook her head, and Tokomoto fidgeted the controls of his wheelchair. Ellie even stopped smiling. Jon worried that they were seeing the fortune that a dynamic of that power could sell instead of the human being behind that power.

"As you can imagine," Jon said, "there are others that are going to be looking for this person, hence the danger."

"Do others know that it is a human being?" Tokomoto asked.

"No," Jon said. "It should give us an advantage."

"Hah, you would know," Russ said. "Compensation for mission success?"

Jon thought for a moment. "Sure. I'll leave it up to arbitration at the end. You agree to come then?"

Amira graced them with her first smile of the day and gave a curt not. Ellie yelled her assent. The others shook their heads.

"Really?" Amira asked in surprise. "People are so weird..."

Jon sighed. "You all know that the extra years are running out. This is nearly the last I have."

The others looked between one another nervously.

"I can't give you any more years, but neither will anyone else soon. Instead, I'll also pay you ten million credits each."

Everyone agreed, though the news that the extra years were running out somehow overshadowed the fact that they had all just made a fortune.

"When do we leave?" Amira asked.

"0800."

"0800!" Russ said. "We can't get everything ready by then!"

"You have to," Jon said. "Leave behind anything and anyone who's not ready in two days."

"Why are we in such a damn rush?"

"Because two days ago, the Grecian Empire, the Asura Republic, Cynix Corporation, and Houses Harain and Khumbuza departed for Jangali."

Everyone went silent.

CHAPTER FOUR

S aiph was sitting on the edge of his bed, massaging his leg, when he
saw a faint white light creeping through the seem of the door. Roe
was sitting around the family's small beetle barrel, wrapped in a
blanket.

"Morn."

Roe pulled the blanket closer. "Morn."

"Sorry about yesterday," Saiph said, grabbing a blanket and sitting
next to her on the uneven bench.

"Not your fault. Was more mad at myself."

Roe was always calmer in the morning. It was as if she knew the
whole world was against her but wasn't yet conscious enough to take
notice of it.

"What mask are you wearing this year?" Saiph asked.

"Mother helped me make a voltguar. It's shit."

"Best get used to seeing ugly voltguars. You'll be working with them
soon, I expect."

"You heard Father." she said, "I doubt he'll let me within a hundred
yards of the volt farm after yesterday."

"He only wants you to be safe. He knows you're ready, but the volt farm isn't a place to take risks, Roe. Have you ever seen a voltguar move? I mean, really move? They're so fast that all you'd see was a glowing blur before you died."

"I'm not like you and him," Roe said. "More can be done with the volt farm. I know it. All you two do is breed beetles all the time. What about the other volt animals? What about hunting for other, more powerful colors?"

Saiph moved his cold feet closer to the light. "I suppose you're right, but you've got to learn before you can innovate. If only to appease Father."

Roe slumped. "You're probably right."

"As usual," Saiph said, grinning.

Roe punched him in the arm. They sat and stared at the tiny balls of light crawling around the glass barrel.

"Mother and Father think it's time I start my own volt farm," Saiph said.

"What?" She looked at him like he had just slapped her across the face. "You can't leave!"

"It's not like I'm leaving the valley. I probably won't even leave Altai."

"You might leave Altai!"

"Well, no," Saiph said quickly, "I'm sure that won't be the case."

"Oh. You're sure. How very comforting!"

Saiph was taken aback by how quickly Roe accepted the idea of him running his own volt farm, as if his leg and lungs weren't even a consideration. He moved closer and put an arm around her shoulders. "Look, I don't want to leave. I want to stay close. You can come over to my volt farm and carry out your crazy experiments, if you'd like."

"Really?"

"Oh yeah, definitely. It will be spectacular. We'll die painful and young deaths, of course. But it will be a grand time before that, I'm sure."

Roe shook her head and smiled. "What about Landon, does he know yet?"

"No," Saiph said. "I don't think so."

"Gods, I don't want to see it when you tell him. He'll be devastated."

"Just try and help him out when I'm gone, okay? Play with him a little."

Roe sighed. "I guess, but I'm just not as good with him as you are."

"Try? Please?"

She nodded.

The whole conversation with his sister about his leaving, of how Landon would take it, how his mother and father believed in him—it stirred something within him. A Verse popped into his mind like it had been placed there:

All a person has in life are family and friends. If you lose those, you have nothing. So cherish them more than anything else in the world.

Saiph had never heard anything more true in his life.

A short while later, the whole family was seated around the table putting the final touches on their festival masks.

"You call that a yokai?" Roe said.

Rosh picked up his mask and studied it. "Not very frightening, is it?"

"Now, now," Milla said. "I think it's very fearsome, dear. Even if it is missing the horns." She winked at her children.

"Your yokai looks like it just heard an amusing joke," Saiph said. "I don't know if Tengrii's most fearsome beast is privy to jokes."

"Yours isn't much better," Rosh mumbled, setting his mask down on the table.

"Hah!" Saiph said, holding up his mask. "Maybe that's the joke you told the yokai? Very funny. Just look at this beautiful voltbear. Quite fierce. I dare say that it would strike mortal fear into even the bravest of souls."

Roe and Milla looked at the mask and then nodded placatingly.

"Whatever," Saiph said. "It's not quite done yet. A few more crucial adornments, and the children will run in terror."

Milla sighed. "A noble aspiration..."

Landon lifted his mask to his face and hissed. "I'm a voltbutterfly!"

"Oh my!" Saiph said. "Landon, that is incredible! I didn't know you were an accomplished artist!"

Landon nodded and splashed more paint onto his mask.

When they finished decorating, Rosh brought out a small bowl of voltbeetle blood. Saiph and Roe dipped their fingers in and smeared the blood across their masks, giving them a faint white glow. It would only last a few hours, but it had a mesmerizing effect. Only the masks of volt animals that glowed with Tengrii's blessing were marked with the blood. They were more rare than normal animals in the wild, but sometimes they glowed red, orange, or even yellow. Saiph had only seen one yellow glow in his life, the sytin, a giant bird that lived in the southern mountains.

"Father, have you ever seen a voltyokai? Roe asked.

Rosh chuckled. "Wouldn't be here if I had."

"Are they out there, though?"

"Not sure. It seems a thing of myth to me, but you never know. Yokai are rare, and volt animals rarer. It could be that we've just never seen one."

Milla urged them to hurry as they tied leather strings to the sides of their masks. When they were done, Landon helped Saiph stow the supplies they'd need for the day in a large basket by the beetle barrel. Roe and Rosh swept the stone floor and put away the blankets. When Milla finally gave her approval, they donned their coats and then loaded the wagon.

Though it was morning, it was still very dark, and Rosh held up a handheld volt orb to light the road for the two lembu pulling the wagon. Saiph and Landon sat in the back with the beetle barrels, their heads tilted up toward the sky. The stars shone bright during winter-week, and Saiph adored the dots of light. They were so beautiful and mysterious.

"What are they?" Landon asked.

"They're space butterflies, of course. Aren't they lovely?"

Landon nodded.

Nearing the edge of the forest, they could hear the festival before they could see it. Villagers chanted and played their drums, the rumble reminding Saiph of distant thunder. Landon laughed and sat up, trying to get a look at the village. When they passed the tree line, they could see the soft and glowing white light that emanated from Altai.

The town was set in a large, natural clearing in the forest, a dozen small buildings scattered within the area. Trees towered above the village on all sides, the foliage of every few glowing with white light. Saiph smiled and breathed deeply, taking in the smell of damp wilderness in crisp air. He looked to the right and saw other masks glowing along different paths that led to the village center. He laughed again, excited and happy.

People were milling about when they pulled the wagon into the town square. Roe, Landon, and Milla went to help set up copper plates and mugs on a long table.

"Look at me, Saiph!" Landon said, placing a plate neatly on the table.

Saiph gave him a thumbs-up. "Nice job, Lando!"

Next to them, a group of men were setting up an elevated stage while children played in the patches of tall grass. A small army of people were at the cook station, cutting, slicing, and tasting; Saiph could smell the stew even from a distance. The cook was turning a large wooden ladle through a giant pot, her face and apron spotted with mush.

"Did you fill the stew with opiates again this year, Tinsu?" Saiph called out. "You know I was just getting over my addiction from last year."

Tinsu turned her chubby cheeks toward him. "I did no such thing!"

"Then why have I been craving your cooking so much?" Saiph said, scrunching his face in confusion.

"Maybe my cooking is just good! Ever consider that?"

Saiph scratched his chin. "No...no, that can't be it."

Rosh rolled his eyes as he got down from the wagon.

Darakai walked up carrying an entire cask of wine by himself, his dark skin drinking in the glow of the beetle barrels. "Leave the poor woman alone, you monster. She's slaved all week preparing for today."

"You don't say?" Saiph said, gingerly getting down from the wagon. "Well, she certainly deserves a reward, then, doesn't she?"

He reached into his pocket and pulled out a small glass bottle usually used for holding Skyfaller healing potions. Inside, a baby volt-beetle crawled around, giving off just enough light to illuminate Saiph's palm. Tinsu giggled like she was twenty years younger.

"For me?" she asked.

"For you," Saiph said. He placed it into her hand.

"Thank you, Saiph. It's wonderful!"

"A beautiful present for a beautiful woman!"

Tinsu's chubby cheeks turned red. She hugged Saiph tightly, and gruel from her apron smeared his shirt.

Darakai laughed. "You're a slick one, Saiph. Not slick enough to get past Ayanda yesterday morning, I hear."

"Rubbish," Saiph said, releasing a latch to the back of the wagon. "I'm as strong as a bear, quick as a voltguar, quiet as a—"

"Screaming yokai," Ayanda said, striding up. "Smart as a dung squirrel, and agile as the moons."

They laughed and Rosh glared at them. "Stop fooling around and help me get these barrels."

With his injured leg, Saiph couldn't lift the barrels, so he tried to look busy as Darakai and Ayanda helped his father. As they worked, Saiph noticed that there was a tension beneath the excitement in Altai. He saw two scouts standing outside the festival circle, watching the tree line for anything suspicious. A small group was standing next to the Temple of Tengrii, speaking in whispers. Mothers were watching their children more closely than they usually would. The Light of Tengrii going out had everyone spooked. And they didn't even know about the monster yet.

"Have you told Gillums about what we saw the other night?" Saiph whispered to Rosh.

He nodded.

"And?"

"He went and looked at the tracks, but he didn't know what it was either. He's worried." Rosh glanced at Ayanda and Darakai. "But there's nothing we can do about it at the moment. We'll talk after the festival and decide what to do."

When they were done situating the circle of beetle barrels around the village center, the torches were doused, leaving only the glowing white light to illuminate the area. It was gentle and serious and calming. Soon enough, the final preparations were complete, and the first festival meal of the day was to begin. The villagers took their seats as Gillums walked to the raised platform.

"Welcome to the three hundred and nineteenth Effulgence Festival, may Tengrii's lightning live within your hearts!"

People cheered and clanged their copperware against their mugs.

Saiph leaned over and whispered to Roe, "Here it goes..."

"Either wake me when it's over or smother me in my sleep."

Saiph held in a laugh.

Gillums cleared his throat and smiled out at the crowd. "First, I would like to personally thank Tinsu for putting together such a wonderful feast and Rosh for providing the beetle barrels." Everyone clapped politely. "Before we get started with the day's festivities, though, there are a few announcements I must make. First is that a runner arrived from Polikville last week."

Saiph glanced quickly at his father, who was staring at Gillums in anticipation. Even Roe was alert. They had not heard from the outside world in half a year, Polikville being the closest town and nearly forty miles away.

"Their team that trades with the Skyfallers never came back from their journey, and now they're running low on healing potions after a bout of the pox and wish to trade with us. What do you say?"

The crowd was silent for a long moment before a woman in the back yelled out, "Give them the damned potions, you hateful old bastard!"

Everyone laughed but murmured in agreement.

Gillums put a hand to his forehead and strained to see the back of the crowd. "Who was that? You know very well that I have to put it up for a vote!"

"Vote's done, you fool! Give 'em the potions now before anyone else becomes sick!"

Saiph remembered his grandfather, red-faced and pocked, dying in his bed. The smell of him still made Saiph's stomach turn. No one should have to suffer like that. He'd limp the forty miles to Polikville himself if he had to.

Gillums smiled smugly. "I actually already gave it to them and sent them on their way, so I'm glad you all agreed."

"Corruption!" someone yelled.

The crowd laughed again.

"All right, all right," Gillums said, "enough of that. This incident has gotten me and some of the others talking. If the Polikville team doesn't come back soon, we might have to send someone out there to find out what's happened to them."

Roe leaned over. "Have we ever done that before? Sent someone out to look for the Skyfallers?"

Rosh eyed them. "We've always depended on the Polikville traders to get it for us. But these are odd times."

"It is just an idea that I want you all to think on over the coming weeks," Gillums said. "Now look, the Effulgence Festival always takes place on the coldest and darkest days that Jangali sees, but this festival is warm, illuminated, and joyous. It is through our own effort that this day is a time of celebration! We can overcome anything if we set out minds to it! Is that not right?" The crowd agreed enthusiastically. "This may be hard to hear," Gillums continued, "but there may be dark and cold ahead. Cold and dark beyond these next four days of the Effulgence Festival."

The crowd buzzed.

"But if we stay together and follow the Tenets, there will always be warmth, light, and hope."

Saiph nodded with the others.

"Speaking of the Tenets," Gillums said, "it is time to announce this year's special Tenet. Remember, it is not here to remind us of the words —we all know those—but to remind us of how these words make us feel and why that feeling is important."

Gillums pulled out a sheet of paper and untied the string around it. He smiled and then read what it said. "This year's special Tenet is the fourth Tenet: *Another day, another life.*"

For a long time, Saiph had been confused by the shortest Tenet. Now, he smiled. It was one of his favorites.

"Let us spend ten minutes in contemplation," Gillums said, "if you could please remain quiet."

Saiph considered this year's Tenet, but he also thought of the other nine. He liked to remind himself of them during this prayer. If he had them and his Core Verses on his mind, he could get through anything. Even the pain of being alone and crippled.

After the ten minutes were up, Gillums raised his mug. "To Jory Sellen, who passed away last month from a fall at the river. He was thirty-four. Another day, another life."

"Another day, another life," the crowd roared.

The day's feasting and celebrating began in earnest after that. People mingled together, showing each other their masks as they waited in line for food. There was roasted chicken, fried sytin eggs, roasted sigsig nuts, and dramain soup. The smell of it all was intoxicating.

Any lingering uneasiness over the last few days' events left Saiph as the wine arrived, and before he knew it, he was laughing and joking like it was a normal festival day. He even got Roe to lighten up when he began teaching a group of kids the lyrics to his made-up song, "Ode to

Grand Master Saiph," conducting them as if they were a group of master musicians.

The dancing started soon after the meal was over. Saiph and Landon were in the middle of the dance circle, moving and shaking their bodies with reckless abandon. Landon laughed the whole morning, and it filled Saiph with joy to see him having such a wonderful time.

Saiph took a break to get some food for Landon, and when he returned, he nearly spit out his wine. Darakai had picked up Roe like a sack of potatoes and had begun to dance. Roe's expression was the same as if a voltlion had just defecated on her boots. After a brief but futile struggle, she fell limp in Darakai's large arms, letting her limbs numbly sway with his movements as he smiled and laughed.

Those who weren't dancing were huddled around the many beetle barrels, keeping warm and enjoying each other's company. All were cheery for the morning celebration, and Saiph was both content and disappointed when the gong rang out to signal the afternoon break. Most people would go home and rest before the evening ceremonies.

Saiph was limping slowly toward the wagon, his leg throbbing from dancing and standing for so long, when Ayanda stopped him.

"What do you want, cripple hater? I'm very tired and crippled at the moment," Saiph said.

"You're not going home to nap with the rest of the old people, are you?"

"Um, yes, that's precisely what I'm going to do."

Ayanda smiled at him. "Not this year, my boring friend. Follow me."

Before he could protest, she grabbed his hand and pulled him into the darkness.

Saiph and Ayanda escaped the circle of barrels unseen and ran down the dirt path that led to the springs, a volt orb full of small beetles held out to light the way. A few minutes later, Ayanda grabbed his arm to stop him.

"Darakai, you out there?" Ayanda said in a raised whisper.

The branches moved. "Yeah, I'm here."

Three people stepped out from the trees. Darakai was so large that he was easy to spot, even in the darkness. As they got closer, Saiph saw that Liam and Nayara were with him. They were a couple years younger than Saiph and were getting married later that year.

"Were you able to get it?" Ayanda said.

Liam held up two large wineskins and smiled. "Wouldn't be here if I hadn't."

They walked quickly, glancing back every now and then to make sure they weren't being followed. It was dark without the moons, but they knew the way, and the volt orb and glowing vines provided enough light to illuminate the path directly in front of them. A few voltsparrows were even fluttering quickly through the trees, giving at least a little light to their surroundings. They passed around the wineskin as they walked, the sounds of nature echoing in the darkness.

"I saw you dancing with Roe a lot this evening, Darakai," Nayara said. "I'm not one to judge, but by the looks of it—"

"We are just friends!" Darakai said.

"That's right you are," Saiph said. "She's my sister!"

"Yeah," Darakai said, "and what you going to do about it, little man?" His chest swelled and he loomed over Saiph. Saiph wasn't short or overly tall, but he definitely didn't have Darakai's sheer mass. Or two good legs. Or two good lungs.

Saiph cocked an eyebrow at him. "Oh, look, you're large. Good job on that one, I know how hard you've been working on it. But don't think that I'm above poison, because I'm not."

They heard the sound of the waterfall, and Liam yelled and started jogging for it, taking off his shirt, despite the bitter cold. They all laughed and followed him.

When Saiph walked around the bend and came through the tree line, the volt orb became drowned out by other light, and he tossed it to the ground. No matter how many times he saw it, the Mukta Falls always took his breath away. Dual waterfalls fell from the cliff above, cascading a hundred feet before hitting the steaming water. Thousands of tiny voltminnows swam beneath the surface, giving the entire spring a soft orange glow. Liam was in the water first.

"By the gods, this feels incredible!" he said, immersing his body in the warm water.

Saiph took off his shirt. "The walk home is going to be horrendous."

"Will you stop worrying about the future for once," Ayanda said. "Just have a little fun!" She took off her shirt and jumped into the water.

Darakai glanced sideways at Saiph. "I'd do as she says, but that's just me."

The others splashed in the spring, making a racket that only people their age could achieve. Saiph got slowly into the water, and he trembled in relief as the warm water soaked his bad leg, banishing the stiffness and pain. He wanted to weep from the relief.

After a few more minutes in the heat, Saiph felt well enough to swim farther out. Ayanda joined him in the shallowest part of the spring, and together they dove for the bottom, trying to catch a voltfish. They never did, but it was even warmer near the floor, and the glow of the voltfish was so bright that the light shone through their closed eyes.

"When I die," Saiph said as they waded through the water, "I'd like to be buried at the bottom of this spring. I suppose that it will be a significant inconvenience, but I'll be dead and everyone will have to respect my last request."

"Why are you talking about dying at a time like this!"

"It was only a joke..."

"You're always joking!"

"Are you really hating on laughter? Come on. Besides, sometimes laughter is the best thing to hide behind."

"And what would you be hiding from?" Ayanda said, swimming closer.

"Oh, all sorts of things. Awkward silences, uncomfortable situations..." He peered at Ayanda. "Change."

"Change?" Ayanda said. "I suppose change can be scary, but what would life be like without it?" Ayanda was right next to him now, her usually curled and frizzled hair weighed down by water. Her black skin stood out against the orange light. She was beautiful. She was his friend.

"Wooo!" Liam yelled out from nearby.

"Ow, ow!" Darakai called out.

"Will you two shut up?" Nayara said. "You're so meddlesome. I can't believe I agreed to marry such a drunken child."

Ayanda broke away from him, smiling mischievously.

They swam and laughed and drank for another hour before deciding to head back to get more food. The walk home was as cold as Saiph expected it to be, but it was completely worth it. They huddled together for warmth as they walked, Darakai at the center because of his mass.

"You're not providing any warmth, Ayanda," Darakai said. He turned to the others and whispered, "I think we should cut her loose."

Ayanda punched Darakai in the ribs, but then snuggled in closer, grabbing Saiph's hand as she did so. Saiph squeezed it and smiled at her. She smiled back.

"What was that?" Nayara said, voice tense.

"What was what?" Liam said. "I didn't hear anything."

Saiph heard it, distant but unmistakable. "Quiet. Quiet! Stop walking."

Everything was still, and then they heard the pounding of what Saiph knew were giant footsteps.

"What is that noise?" Darakai whispered.

"We should go..." Ayanda said.

They took a step forward but stopped again as branches moved off to the side. Saiph was too terrified to react. He just stared at the spot where the branches had rustled together. A moment later, a man stumbled out onto the path, heading toward Altai. He didn't take any notice of them. After a few shaky steps, he fell to the ground.

Ayanda was the first to get over her shock. She rushed over to the figure, and the rest of the group followed. The man looked up at them with glassy eyes. His face was bruised, and there were small cuts running up and down his arms. Saiph thought he recognized the man.

"He looks familiar," Darakai said.

Saiph bent down and put a hand on the man's shoulder. "Are you all right? What's happened?"

The man's head bobbed up and down, and his eyes were unfocused. He was muttering something. Saiph leaned in closer to make out the words.

"Run. Hide. Run. Hide. Run. Hide. Run. Hide."

CHAPTER FIVE

J on had been so busy with preparations the last couple of days that he'd hardly been able to think about Sargas. Now, as he looked down on Mars through the shuttle window, he remembered his friend throwing himself from the balcony—then the mangled body upon the rocks. How had it come to that?

Jon rubbed his eyes, only now realizing that he hadn't slept since his encounter with Sargas. The tablet beside him chimed, and he glanced down at it. He sighed, realizing that he should have called earlier. He slid a finger across the glass and then flicked it in front of him. A projection of Theresa appeared.

She breathed in to speak, then stopped, squinting at him. "You look tired."

"I am."

She frowned. "Is it happening?"

Jon nodded, and her projection moved, as if she had collapsed into a chair. "I swear, at this age, I always think there's more time."

"Give it a few hundred more years," Jon said. "It'll turn back around."

Theresa was one of the last of the golden age to gain her agelessness. She was young compared to him but still older than many would even wish to be.

"Wait," Theresa said, concerned, "do you not know why I'm calling, then?"

"It's not for a friendly chat?" Jon said, rubbing his eyes.

Theresa shook her head. "Another star went dark. It was only fifty light-years from the Sphere's eastern edge.

Jon sat up straight, suddenly alert. "Show me."

"Computer," Theresa said, "bring up the latest projection of the Sphere of Humanity."

The projection in front of Jon changed into one of the Milky Way galaxy. In the bottom right was a small sphere of translucent white that surrounded the territory that humanity had colonized.

"Zoom in on section E0827.626.112829," Theresa said.

As the view moved toward the sphere, the detail of the projection became immensely intricate. The sphere, which seemed so tiny compared to the entire galaxy, was actually so vast it was beyond comprehension. It still amazed Jon how much they had left to explore.

Stars zipped past as they moved to the eastern side of the sphere. Then, right at the edge, was a digital tag for where the light of the star used to be. It was completely gone—now surrounded by trillions of energy-absorbing nano-bots called Essens.

"When did it happen in real time?" Jon asked.

"About eight months ago, we think."

Eight months? There wasn't much time left before the Essens reached stars within the Sphere of Humanity's boundaries. The panic would rise. Trade to the east would decline. People would leave for the core and the west. There would be pressure.

"Jon?" Theresa said.

He came back from his thoughts and focused on Theresa. She looked uncharacteristically lost. "What's wrong?"

Theresa's black hair was streaked with gray, and her face was lined, but she still somehow projected an innocent earnestness, even after all these years. "I bet when you were a child, it was easy to blame things on those who had come before you. They couldn't defend themselves. They were dead. But you're still here."

Jon sat back in his chair, attentive. He waited for her to go on.

"I don't blame you," she said eventually, "but how could you and everyone else from the beginning let this happen? How could you let one of the Great Technologies turn against us?"

Jon had expected this question for a long time and had already decided how he would answer it. It was what made the lie come out so smoothly.

"We weren't gods like some people today make us out to be, Theresa. We made our share of mistakes. The things that brought such prosperity were the very same that were our downfall. But I promise that I have a solution for the rouge Essens."

"Then why haven't you done anything yet?"

"They need to be closer," Jon said.

He could see the tension and frustration in Theresa's shoulders, though most wouldn't have noticed any outward change in her.

"Do you know what Emperor Phylas said to me this morning? When I asked him if he would send aid to the east? He said, 'The west is trillions of miles and eight years away. What do I care for the eastern-ers' problems?'" Theresa shook her head, but she wasn't done. "The Speakers will elect someone who is fluent in the language of war, and the computer system on Timios has initiated a search for a new president."

Jon sighed and tapped his fist on the shuttle window. Mars was all but a spec now, and he'd be arriving at the ship soon. "I know all of this, Theresa. Do you think I am holding off on purpose? That I don't care what happens?"

"No, of course not," she said, deflating. "I'm just worried."

"If I could ease your mind any further, I would." Jon took a deep breath. He hadn't been so exhausted in decades. "You and the rest of the Oligarchy will need to be a calming force while I'm away."

"Away? Where are you going?"

"To the northern edge," Jon said. "To Jangali. A Class G dynamic has been traced there."

Jon didn't see her reaction as he looked out the window at his ship, a massive sphere of glass and metal. From the silence, he assumed that she was as stunned as most people would be. Jon stood and began to gather his things.

"That's..." Theresa started. "That's remarkable. The implications are intriguing, to say the least, but how will this help us against the rouge Essens?"

Jon glanced at her projection as he leaned up against the wall next to the exit. "I'm not worried about the Essens, Theresa. I'm worried about something else."

———

Jon stood at one of the ramps to his ship and stared out at the thousands of soldiers in green and black as they bustled about, organizing munitions, machines, and manpower. Russ was nearby, bellowing orders and checking equipment.

"Get that battery in, boy. You want to die out in the black? We're space-side in twenty!"

The men and women around him laughed as a group of white coats caught Jon's eye.

"Jon!" Ellie said. "Jon!" She pushed past the crowd. "Jon, this is Missy, one of my students." A young woman stepped forward.

"Hello, Missy, it's a pleasure to meet you."

"Oh no, sir," Missy said, shaking Jon's hand, "the pleasure is mine. Most definitely all of mine. Definitely." Her breathing was labored.

"Missy, would you mind if I spoke to Ellie for a moment?"

Missy nodded frantically but kept staring at him.

Jon guided Ellie by the arm and stepped to the side. "How old is she?"

"Twenty-four."

"I can't press upon you enough how dangerous this job will be. People are going to get hurt. Killed. Missy shouldn't be there for that."

Ellie looked at her feet. "You don't understand," she said. "The latest blackout has people panicked. She's from the east. She has nowhere else to go."

Jon looked from Ellie to Missy and saw how the woman fidgeted and scanned the room. She wasn't just nervous—she was afraid of being left behind.

Jon sighed. "Who else are you bringing?"

Ellie gestured at the group behind her. "They're young but very talented. You won't regret bringing them, I promise. Please?"

"These people are your responsibility. If they're hurt, it'll be on you."

"They have nothing else..." Ellie said.

"I know, I'm just preparing you for the worst. Get them on board."

Jon hoped he hadn't just doomed a dozen more people to their deaths. He turned and found Treyges waiting to give him a status report.

"The ship's provisions have been fully loaded, sir."

"Were you able to get the specialty items I asked for?"

"Yes, sir."

"Thank you."

Treyges nodded. "The engineers have completed their third and final check. All systems are fully operational. The scouting craft outside have given the all clear, and the push-pull drive has been through its power-up procedures and diagnostic tests. There is also a message for you from..."

Treyges trailed off, and Jon followed his gaze. The preparations around them had stopped, and silence had seized the loading dock. Jon heard the creak of a wheelchair, and Tokomoto emerged, parting the sea of soldiers like Moses parted the Red Sea. Each man and woman bowed as he passed, causing a wave of silent respect."

"Why are they bowing?" Missy asked Ellie.

"Don't let that wheelchair fool you," Jon said. "That man is considerably more dangerous than all these soldiers. He's saved all of them more than once."

Missy and the other young doctors glanced among one another skeptically. They were probably thinking that they'd be the ones saving lives on this mission, and no doubt they'd save a few. But Jon wondered how many of their lives would be decided by Tokomoto's attention before this was all over.

"All right, all right!" Russ yelled. "Freedom to worship tiny Asian men has been revoked. Back to work."

Tokomoto wheeled up the ramp, and the chaos resumed as quickly as it had ceased. "When will the full briefing take place?" he asked.

"Two days," Jon said. "Once we are fully out of the system and everyone has had a chance to get settled. Is there anything I can do to make your trip more comfortable?"

"No." Toko wheeled past him without another word.

It must have been one of those days where he couldn't banish the gloom, no matter how hard he tried. Jon hoped he'd get those days out of the way on the trip over.

The last of the gear and soldiers entered the ship. Jon knew that this loading dock would look similar to the other twelve that existed along the ship's four-mile circumference. In less than ten minutes, the dock would fall away and *Stargone* would power its engines to escape any remnant tug of Mars's gravity.

"Sir, may I venture a question?" Treyges asked. Jon nodded. "What exactly do you expect to happen once we get to Jangali and find this being?"

Jon shook his head. "I've no idea."

"Very good, sir."

"Are Silvestre and Amira on board?"

"Yes, sir. Amira embarked on dock eight. Silvestre boarded from dock four."

"Sarah?"

"I tried to keep her away, but I suspect she made it on board," Treyges said.

"She's a force of her own, isn't she?"

"Unstoppable, some might say."

Jon scoffed. "Come on, let's get on before they leave us behind."

CHAPTER SIX

"That man is from Polikville," Gillums said. "I recognize him. He's one of their foragers."

After they'd found the man, Saiph and the others brought him back to the village as quickly as they could. Ayanda had run ahead to let people know. Gillums and some of the other elders now stood in a circle, discussing what to do. Rosh was among their number, so Saiph stood off to the side, trying to listen in. Ayanda was beside him.

"I haven't told the rest of you yet," Rosh said, "but my son and I saw something the night Terngrii's light went out. Something huge and powerful running across the fields."

"Was it a yokai?" an older woman asked.

Rosh shook his head. "It was taller and slimmer. It moved in an odd manner as well, unlike any animal I've ever seen."

Ayanda's mother, Jantia, frowned at Rosh. "Something has happened to Polikville. You think it was this thing?"

"I don't know," Rosh said. "Possibly."

"We need more information," Gillums said. "And the people of Polikville may need our help."

A few in the circle grunted their assent.

"My daughter and I can lead a group," Jantia offered.

"I will bring six members of the watch," Gillums said.

Rosh nodded thoughtfully. "My son and I will also come."

Saiph's stomach dropped and he felt his breath pick up speed.

The others in the circle all looked at Rosh uncomfortably. Nobody spoke for a moment as they glanced between one another. They all thought that Saiph couldn't make a trip that far but didn't want to tell Rosh that. Saiph glanced over at Ayanda, who caught his eye, but she quickly looked away. That hurt more than all the other bowed heads combined. Gillums eventually stepped up.

"Um, Rosh, Polikville is a nearly forty miles away, and we'll need to get there as quickly as possible. If—"

"I know how far Polikville is. If this thing really is an animal, though, Saiph will know how to deal with it. You've seen how he is at the volt farm."

Gillums hesitated, considering, then nodded. "Yes, you're right, of course. Meet on the north edge of the wood in twenty minutes with as much food and water as you can carry comfortably. The rest of you, get the town prepared."

"Prepared for what?" a man said.

"Anything."

Rosh walked quickly away from the group, and Saiph struggled to keep up with his father's long strides.

"Why'd you do that?" Saiph asked. "You know full well that you could do whatever I could if it's an animal, and I *will* slow everyone down."

Rosh stopped suddenly and spun on Saiph, grabbing him firmly by the shoulders. He looked him in the eye. "You were better with the volt animals at twelve than I have ever been. You are smart and strong, and your Core Verses show much wisdom. You are *not* a burden. Do you understand me?"

Saiph nodded, filled with a strange mixture of alarm and pride. He'd rarely seen his father so intense, but the words made him feel light as air.

Half an hour later, the group was walking down the narrow path through the forest. Saiph made certain that he was at the back, so that he wouldn't hold others up when he inevitably fell behind. The hot spring had helped ease the pain in his leg for the moment, but his breathing was already the most audible sound in the forest. He felt embarrassed at what the others must be thinking of him—what Ayanda must be thinking of him.

Saiph distracted himself with the sights of the forest. He loved this place as if it were the sixth member of his family. The largest of the trees were so high and expansive that they blocked out most of the sky, but they also pulsed with veins of green light that twisted through the bark and ended within the tips of the leaves. They gave off just enough light to see by but also cast the forest in a mesmerizing puzzle of shadows. Saiph tilted his head upward, as if to look at the stars, and saw a dozen orange glowing voltbirds fluttering about, chasing one another.

"Hey, we're falling behind."

Startled, Saiph brought his gaze back down. Ayanda was looking at him, and the group had indeed gained some distance. "Right. Sorry. You can go on, I'll catch up."

She smiled at him, flashing her pearly white teeth. Her frizzy black hair was pulled back for the hike, and the sleeves of her shirt were rolled up to her shoulders. She made Saiph wish he were better.

"Come on," she said, "we'll catch them now, then hang back a little bit so we can talk without Gillums shushing us every ten feet."

Saiph nodded and smiled back. "You know, I was just letting the others get ahead so that they didn't feel too terrible when they got passed by a cripple."

"Oh, my mistake."

"No need to apologize," Saiph said.

"I didn't."

"Look, I said it was all right. You're forgiven."

Saiph started walking and caught Ayanda rolling her eyes as he went around her. It took nearly twenty minutes for him to make up the fifty feet he'd lost while staring at the trees.

"What do you think we'll find?" Ayanda asked quietly.

"I'll freely admit that I'm frightened to find out," Saiph said. "What if it wasn't some sort of animal? What if the ninth Tenet has been broken?"

"That seems to be obvious."

Saiph took a quick drink form his waterskin. "Probably, but we shouldn't jump to conclusions. Perhaps that's what the Fulgurians did, and now they find themselves in some unholy battle." Saiph shuttered at the thought of it.

Ayanda was quiet for a moment before saying, "But, Saiph, what if the Fulgurians are still following the Tenets? What if they *did* forgive after they were harmed the first time? What if they *did* only defend themselves after a second offense? What if they attack now only because the Skyfallers intentionally hurt them for a third time?"

The group ahead stopped to rest and refresh themselves. Saiph stopped too, then turned and handed his water to Ayanda. "I'm not sure if I want that to be true or not. I'd be happy to see the Fulgurians still abiding by the Tenets, but I hate the thought of Skyfallers being so terrible."

Ayanda finished taking a drink of water. "The whole thing reminds me of your first Core Verse."

Saiph nodded. *"The truth is rarely pure and never simple."*

It had been the very first Verse he'd chosen when he'd turned fifteen, and it was still his favorite.

Gillums called out from the group ahead, and they set out again. It was hard to tell what time it was during a winterweek, when the sun didn't show itself for four days, but it must have been late. Saiph could feel the exhaustion of the miles they walked accompanied by a drowsiness that had little to do with it.

His leg throbbed terribly after another hour of walking. As always, his heart rate and breathing picked up from the pain. It wouldn't be long now before he lagged behind. How much farther was it? At least another eighteen hours.

I can do this. One foot in front of the other.

Ayanda glanced back at him, then at the group ahead, worried. He tried to hide how out of breath he was, but that only made it worse. If he didn't rest, he'd have an attack, which wouldn't help anyone.

Saiph was saved any more humiliation by his father, who came striding back down the path. "Ayanda, go and help your mother scout ahead. We'll be leaving the forest soon."

Ayanda looked back at Saiph and gave him a sad smile before running off.

"Thanks," Saiph said.

"You've done well. I'd have guessed you would have needed a rest over an hour ago."

Saiph sat heavily on the ground, breathing more deeply now that Ayanda was gone. His father was quiet while his lungs sucked in the oxygen they needed to catch up. They were both accustomed to such breaks.

Saiph nodded that he was ready to go after half an hour, and they estimated that the group was a couple miles ahead at that point. They wouldn't reach them again until they made camp to eat and sleep. Saiph noticed that the trees were getting progressively smaller and less dense. He hadn't been this far away from Altai since his accident, but he thought that it wouldn't be long now before they hit the plain. He was excited to see it once more—a seemingly endless grassland that glowed purple and swayed with the wind like water.

Unfortunately, he'd never get the chance.

Ayanda's mum came running down the path. She was a hard woman, which is what made Saiph so concerned by the alarm in her expression.

"Something's happened. We're turning back."

"Back?" Rosh asked.

She nodded grimly. "We have one of the Skyfallers."

The Skyfaller was tall. Even taller than Saiph's father, who stood four inches above six feet. He had strange blond hair that stood up on its own in an unnatural way and clothing that was unlike anything Saiph has seen before. The shirt, pants, and boots were completely black and made out of some alien material that was smooth and sleek. He was intimidating, even unconscious as he was.

"Is the woman from Polikville going to be all right?" Saiph asked Ayanda.

"She better be," Ayanda said, venom in her voice. She stared at the tied-up man as if he were Erlik Ata himself, come to take her away to the underworld. "How could he *do* such a thing?"

A part of Saiph was glad he hadn't been there to see it. Apparently, the man had been on top of the woman, forcing himself upon her. It was an act that was denied much of the leniency that the eighth Tenet granted. It was so horrible and shocking that it hadn't truly sunk in yet.

Gillums and half of the group had taken the woman ahead to Altai. She told them that there was nothing in Polikville to go back to and that they needed to prepare. She said all of this with a distant look, as if she weren't entirely there.

"Go back with the others," Rosh said, coming up to them.

"What are you doing with him?" Saiph said, pointing at the Skyfaller.

"We're going to wake him up and question him."

Ayanda folded her arms across her chest. "I'm staying."

Saiph looked between her and his father and then nodded, as if to say, *me too.*

His father sighed. "Do not interrupt while we speak to him. Remember the eighth Tenet: *Forgiveness does not change the past, but it does enlarge the future.*"

Ayanda didn't flinch or soften, but Saiph nodded at the words and calmed himself. He silently repeated other Verses of forgiveness to himself. Despite the wretchedness of the situation, it helped.

Ayanda's mother and two men of the watch were also with them. They had agreed that Rosh would do the talking, and once they were all in position around the man, Jantia splashed water on the Skyfaller's face. He came to with a groan.

"What the fuck?" he said, squinting and looking down at the ropes that bound him. His eyes adjusted to the dim light of the forest and he looked at them. "Who the fuck are you? Untie me!"

He struggled, but the rope was as unforgiving as Ayanda appeared to be. Nobody said anything as the man continued to fight at his bonds, anger contorting his face. After he wore himself out, he looked around again, then abruptly started laughing.

"Y'all are so fucked," he said. "Do you have any idea what you're doing?"

His accent was strange, and Saiph had to concentrate just to understand what he was saying.

"My name is Rosh Calthari. What is your name?"

"Untie me first, then we can talk. I promise to go easy on you if you do. This is all just a misunderstanding."

"I apologize," Rosh said, "but I wouldn't feel comfortable with that. The neighboring town has been attacked, and you were forcing yourself upon a woman who did not want you. Will you at least explain why you and your people have done these things?"

"This is so ridiculous," the Skyfaller said to himself, limply straining against the rope. He looked Rosh in the eye. "Let. Me. Go."

"No."

The Skyfaller yelled in frustration, making Saiph jump. So much anger. Did the man not understand why they had tied him up? Did he have no guilt for what he'd done?

Rosh took two steps forward and knelt down before the Skyfaller. "Do you have Core Verses where you are from?"

"I don't know what the hell you're talking about."

"Jangalians choose Core Verses at different stages of their life, to help guide them through it. My fourth Core Verse says that there is no revenge so complete as forgiveness."

The Skyfaller stared at him blankly.

Rosh looked back at him for a long time before saying, "If you cooperate, we will forgive you and let you go."

"You're serious, aren't you?" the Skyfaller said, frowning.

"As serious as the crimes you committed."

The Skyfaller swallowed and licked his lips. "What do you want to know?"

Rosh stood back up, towering over the young man. "Why did you attack the last village?"

"Look, we were fine at first, letting the locals worship trees and fairies and shit, you were no good to us. But others are coming now. We need more energy and laborers."

Saiph didn't have much of an idea of what the Skyfaller was saying. Apparently his father didn't either.

"Others? Energy?"

"Shit, you people have been on your own for too long. How the hell did you even get here?"

Rosh shook his head in confusion. "We walked here from our village."

"No, how did you get *here*, to this moon? How long have you been stranded?"

"This is our home," Rosh said carefully. "It's always been our home. How long have you been here?"

"Ten years," the man said, leaning his head back against the tree. "Ten miserable fucking years. I was one of the first ones off the ship. There were only a few hundred of us back then..." He trailed off, as if lost in a memory.

"And how many of you are there now?" Rosh asked.

"About twenty-five thousand," the man said absently. "They practically brought a city with them this time. The twins think this place has real potential, I guess. Can't imagine the cost of it all."

"What's your name?" Rosh asked.

The Skyfaller looked up at him. "Brint."

"Is our village in danger, Brint?"

"Nah, not if you just surrender. XO will make ya pay if you resist, though. He ain't a very patient man... Damn, he's going to have my ass for this."

"What sort of magic will you bring against us?" Rosh asked.

"Magic?" Brint said, chuckling. "*Magic?* Please tell me that you're joking right now?" When no one said anything, he laughed. He laughed so hard that his whole body shook. "I knew you all were odd from our fights with those forest people, but this is too much. I thought you were just some hippie refugees who stumbled upon this place or something!"

Saiph wouldn't have liked Brint even if he hadn't known what the man had done. Though he was tied up, Brint didn't seem to be as concerned as he should have been. He acted as if they were children who didn't quite know what they were doing. Yet Saiph would bet the volt farm that the man couldn't quote a single Verse.

"I know y'all don't get it yet," Brint said, "but this world don't belong to you no more. It belongs to the Harain family. Sooner you accept that, the easier it'll be."

Rosh stared at Brint for a long moment, then looked to Jantia. "Make sure he is secure for the trek back to Altai."

She nodded.

"What?" Brint said. "Hey! You said you'd let me go if I answered your questions!"

"And we will," Rosh said, gathering his pack together and slinging it over his back, "but I still have questions. And there is another you must ask for forgiveness. She will be harder to convince than I was."

Brint scowled. "You're making a mistake. Our battle droid has already scouted your village! It's as good as gone. Let me go right now, and I promise to speak with the XO about how you're treated. I may even be able to get him to take you all to the same work camp. But if you take me back to your village, I swear it'll be worse for you."

Rosh cocked his head and looked down at the man. "I'm sorry for whatever made you this way. Truly. You are consumed by your anger, violence, and pain—everything we strive not to be. You will come with us to Altai, and you may continue to laugh at my questions there. Until then, I would recommend silence via prayer."

They hurried back to Altai as fast as they could, adrenaline propelling Saiph through the pain of his leg. He no longer cared how loud he breathed compared to the others; he only cared about inhaling as much oxygen as he possibly could to keep going. He had a terrible feeling about all of this.

When they had almost reached Altai, Saiph signaled to his father, who dropped back to speak with him. Saiph caught his breath for a moment before asking, "What are we going to do?"

"What do you think we should do?" Rosh asked.

Saiph shook his head. "We should get everyone out of Altai. Run or hide like the man from Polikville suggested."

"You would have us run away?" Rosh asked.

"We'll stand no better chance than Polikville. And better to run than to willingly participate in such a conflict."

Rosh nodded. "I agree with you, though others may not. We will have to convince them."

They quickly caught up with the group as they reached the clearing of Altai proper. Most of the town was at the center, eating a meal at the tables that had been set up for the festival. They were still illuminated by the beetle barrels they had placed in a circle around them. A nervous tension permeated the entire area.

"Did you see the Polikville woman?" the blacksmith asked.

"Looked like she'd been beaten," his wife answered.

Saiph didn't hear any more as they passed. Roe came up to him with Landon in tow. She handed him a cup of water. Saiph nodded in thanks and then sat down at a table to rest.

"What the hell is going on?" Roe asked.

"Nothing good," Saiph said. "We were on our way to Polikville when we found—"

Saiph stopped speaking as Gillums walked on to the platform. The Altainians quieted and looked to him.

"As most of you have heard by now, something has happened in Polikville. We left as fast as we could to see what had happened to them and if they needed help. Sadly, we were too late. They were attacked by Skyfallers. The entire town has been burned to the ground and its people carried away or killed."

The crowd muttered in shock and concern.

"We apprehended one of the Skyfallers, and Rosh found out that they are planning to come to Altai and do the same here as they did in Polikville."

"We should fight!" a woman called out. "The ninth Tenent has been broken, and we are allowed to defend ourselves!"

Others yelled their assent.

"That is one option. The other option is to run and hide, as Rosh has suggested to me." People grumbled in frustration, and Gillums held up his hands in a calming gesture.

"I've lived my whole life in this town, and I love it more than I can put into words. But this town is not the buildings we take cover in or the tables we dine at—it is the people who inhabit it. I cannot stand the thought of losing a single one of you to the Skyfallers. I cannot stand the thought of any of you having to battle through the emotional consequences of purposely killing another human being.

"I know it is distasteful, to abandon our homes, but I believe the alternative is worse. My sixth Core Verse is: *All my life I have had a choice of hate or love. I chose love and I am here.* Let us choose love this day and save not only ourselves but the Skyfallers as well. If we don't wait for them here, then they cannot commit any more crimes."

Gillums speech had done it. Saiph could tell from the murmurs of ascent, the way the crowd shuffled, the look of resolve on the faces around him. He raised his glass in salute and was thinking about how much he respected the man when he felt a soft vibration shake the ground beneath him.

CHAPTER SEVEN

Jon walked with purpose through the sleek white hallways of the ship, nodding to the crew as he went. *Stargone* was like a miniature city, and it took him twenty minutes to get from the dock to the control sphere at the center. He submitted to a retina scan, fingerprinting, and a subtle blood test upon arrival and was cleared to enter. He stepped through the large sliding doors and into a massive sphere. There was a platform in the middle of the room that seemed to hang in midair. Atop it were the men, women, and computers that controlled the ship. Jon strode down the thin walkway, which had a fifty-meter drop on either side. But it didn't faze him, at least not like it did the young man who was staring at the ceiling in the middle of the platform, unmistakably overwhelmed and out of place. He was young, baby-faced, and overweight.

"Vincent," Jon said, "thanks for accompanying us. Your talents will be most appreciated."

"This is *awesome*," Vincent said. He pushed his glasses up and stared around at the sphere's walls, which projected a three-sixty view of the space outside the ship.

Jon smiled. "I like it too."

Vincent's posture went rigid, and he stared at Jon. "I am so honored, Mr. Foster," he said, vigorously shaking Jon's hand. "So honored."

"Please, call me Jon. Have you been aboard a dreadnught-class ship before?"

"No, Jon, sir, I have not, sir, though I have always wished to, sir."

"Would you care for a tour?"

"From you?" Vincent said. "Aren't you busy or something...sir?"

"Vincent, this trip will take five years. We'll be busy, but we won't be working all day every day. Come on, I'll introduce you to your new home."

Jon led Vincent out of the sphere and into the large hallway that led to the Grove. The interior of the ship was mostly white, but different-colored control panels and signs were interspersed throughout. There weren't any cornered objects; everything was smooth and rounded.

"*Stargone* is the sixth dreadnought of the twelve in existence," Jon said, "but it's the third largest overall. I like to think of it as our own little floating city. It was constructed in orbit, since it was too large to ever escape a planet's gravity, but in open space, it can travel vast distances at amazing speeds using the latest latch-and-pull technology."

"What's the latest latch-and-pull do?" Vincent asked as he ran his fingers along the wall, feeling the material.

Jon smiled. A lot of people had trouble talking to him the first time they met him. It was unfortunate, but he had accepted it a long time ago. Vincent, however, was such a curious young man that he already seemed to have forgotten his nervousness.

"You understand how the drive warps space in front of it and behind it?"

Vincent nodded absently.

"Well, the newest tech uses the energy of our passage through warped space to extend the push-pull effect. It almost acts like a contained wave now. They say that a ship can reach speeds up to thirty times the speed of light."

Vincent nodded at the concept, then stopped and tapped a fist against the wall. "What's it made of?" he asked.

"What you just tapped is reinforced carbon fiber, but the interior is mostly titanium 712. She has a few other superconducting metals strewn through her body, though." Jon pointed to the right, and they turned through a door and entered the largest space within *Stargone*. The Grove always elicited a gasp from those seeing it for the first time, and Vincent was no exception.

"How tall is it?" he asked, mouth agape.

"Forty stories." Jon pointed to the balconies that surrounded the courtyard. "The upper levels are filled with apartments, a couple restaurants, research labs, and fitness facilities, but the main attraction is the park."

Vincent brought his attention back to Earth—or what seemed like Earth. The large area was covered in grass, trees, and dirt paths. People walked about as if they were in the woods and not hurtling through empty space at an unimaginable velocity.

"It's amazing," Vincent said.

"I'm glad you think so."

Jon let him take in the sight a while longer.

"Jon, you have minute?" Amira said.

She wore her customary black, and the half dozen earrings and piercings on her left ear had been swapped out. Jon flicked his eyes toward Vincent, who was still staring off in wonder. "Is it important?"

She shrugged. "I suppose not. Just wondering when you're going to assign our travel duties?"

"Probably in a couple days. Try and enjoy yourselves and get settled for now. Oh, how rude of me. Amira, this is Vincent Cross. He'll be working with me on a special project."

Amira nodded at him, which was about as good as Vincent could hope for.

"Hi!" Vincent said, ignoring the less than warm greeting. "This is all so crazy, right?" He gestured around at the park.

Amira softened at that. She was accustomed to people looking at her in a certain way. It was as if they needed a moment to take all of her in, but Vincent appeared not to notice anything unusual. She liked that. "Oh yes," Amira said, "very crazy. Remember to come here at least once a day to fight off any claustrophobia."

Vincent titled his head in thought, then nodded. "That's a really good idea. Thanks for the advice."

Amira actually gave him a smile and Jon was even more impressed with the young man.

"See you in a couple days," Amira said, then turned and walked away."

"Are all the places on this ship as incredible as the control center and the Grove?" Vincent asked.

"Not exactly. There are some less savory places too. Speaking of, let me show you to your quarters."

Vincent's expression fell and he took a deep breath.

"I'm only joking," Jon said. "Well, sort of. You see, private rooms are a lux—"

A ping interrupted Jon.

"Sorry to disturb you, sir, but I believe I found her," Treyges said through the comm.

"Where is she?"

"In the cargo bay, buried beneath a few thousand oranges."

Jon sighed. "I'll go get her. Would you please show Mr. Cross to his quarters?"

"Of course, sir."

Jon excused himself and left for the lower floors.

———

The cargo bay was housed with the air revitalization system, water reclaimer, waste oxidizer, and other life-support systems at the bottom of the ship. Jon looked down at his device, which displayed a green line, leading him to the crate he was looking for among the thousands within the bay. He slid between them, and the arrow became larger as he went. He stubbed his toe against one of the pods and cursed, thinking how ridiculous it was that he was down here.

The path stopped at an innocuous-looking box. He knocked on the side of it as if it were a small housing pod instead of a crate full of fruit.

"Come on out. I know you're in there."

He heard a rustling not unlike the sound of the plastic ball pools he'd played in as a child.

"Ow! Damn it!"

The side of the pod fell open, and oranges rushed out and scattered everywhere. A woman came out with them, hitting the ground and crushing a few oranges beneath her. She made a disgusted face as she touched her citrus-drenched pants.

"How'd you find me?"

"Didn't. Treyges did."

"Ugh, that stuck-up little shit," Sarah said.

"Don't blame him for doing his job."

"I don't *blame* him, I just don't *like* him. There's a difference." Sarah stood and brushed herself off. "So where we going?"

"You don't even know where we're going?" Jon asked.

"Not a clue, which means it must be juicy. No pun intended."

"I guess I'll take that as a good sign to the secrecy of the trip and ignore the fact that you would jump on board a ship without considering where it is going or how long it will take to get there."

"Wait," Sarah said, "how long will it take to get there?"

"Five years."

Sarah's eyes went wide. "Which edge are we going to and why!"

"I'll tell you about it at the meeting in a couple days. Your room is already made up." Jon began to walk away.

"Hey. Everything okay?" Sarah said. "You look down."

"Just tired."

Sarah took a step closer and stared at him. "You sure you're all right?"

"I'm fine. Promise."

Jon went to his room. It was different than the other dwellings on board. It was much larger and included a kitchen, dining room, and office. It had an expensive security system too, but most distinctive was its furnishings. While most of the ship was made of metal, plastic, and intermittent patches of green, Jon's home away from home was made of dark woods and brick. There were antique bookshelves filled with real books, and a fire crackled next to a rocking chair and grandfather clock. It smelled like a forest breeze after a thunderstorm. Separated by an eight-inch-thick sliding door from the hall, it seemed an entirely different world.

He walked in and sat on the bed, his posture rigid. The clock ticked in the background as he rubbed his hand over the bedding. He eventually pulled out a photograph that showed a smiling man in a tuxedo sitting next to his daughter in a wedding dress. The clock ticked louder in Jon's mind as he thought about what Warren and Ava would think of him now. Would they disapprove?

He thought they might, and it broke his heart. Water welled up in his eyes, knowing that this would be the only time he would show his uncertainty. He didn't sob, but he let a few tears fall down his face for the first time in 258 years—the last time he saw his wife.

CHAPTER EIGHT

The people of Altai fell silent as copper mugs and plates rattled on the tables. Saiph thought of the creature he'd seen from the other night, gauged its leg span, and started to count.

One...

Thump.

Two...

Thump.

Three...

Thump.

Rosh came running over to him and Roe.

"What do you think?" Saiph said. "Half a click?"

"Closer," Rosh said.

People screamed. They stood up from their benches and looked at their food as if it had insulted them. Not even a yokai could shake the ground like this.

"Everyone stay calm!" Gillums yelled.

They didn't. People ran in every direction, leaving the circle of beetle barrels for nearby huts and holes. Men picked up spears, and women scooped up their crying children.

"What's happening?" Landon asked. He was scared. Saiph grabbed his hand and pulled him closer.

"Get your mother, Landon, and Roe outside the circle and then get our bows from the wagon," Rosh instructed.

Saiph barely heard him. He stared off in the direction of the footsteps, imagining what horrors awaited.

Thump.

"Saiph!" Rosh yelled.

Thump.

"Now!"

Saiph blinked and then picked Landon up and ran for his mother. He found her gathering up a group of frightened children.

"It's time to go," Saiph said. "Take them away." He handed Landon to his mother.

"Where?" Milla asked.

"I don't know, Mum! Anywhere but here!"

"We'll head for the western wood," Roe said.

Saiph ran for the wagon in the field as if the Skyfaller horde were directly behind him. There was no moonlight from Ay or Fay, and the light from the beetle barrels was dim from this distance. Saiph tripped over a rock and fell hard to the ground, but adrenaline propelled him back to his feet. After searching in the darkness for a moment, he found the wagon. Saiph slid under it and loosened the leather straps that held the bows and quiver to the belly. He slung them over his shoulder and turned to see the white light of the village center mixed with the yellow light of a large fire.

"No..." Saiph whispered.

He ran recklessly through the dark, dimly aware of how dangerous it was to be running with a pouch full of sharp objects and a bum leg. Saiph stared at the ground in front of him, trying to see every rock or stump that sought to slow him. He finally looked up when the light of the beetle barrels illuminated the terrain directly in front of him. He stopped dead in his tracks. The monster was within the circle, standing thirty feet tall. Firelight shone off a body made completely of metal.

Below the monster stood a dozen men in uniforms like Brint's, but one man wore a black uniform that was adorned with polished badges and colorful cloth around the edges. He was speaking to the villagers gathered in the circle. They were staring up at the giant, mouths opened and spears gripped tightly.

"...don't want to hurt you," the man in black was saying, "but you must tell us where our man is right this instant."

"Your man was apprehended while committing an intentional act of violence against a woman," Gillums said, stepping forward. "The Tenets allow his detainment, for his safety and for ours."

The other man muttered something to himself in frustration. "I am Sergeant Pierce of House Harain. Your village is under my jurisdiction and subject to our laws. Hand over our soldier or consider yourselves enemies of the state."

Gillums frowned. "Juris-what? Who are you really, and what is *that*?" Gillums pointed at the giant.

"You will address me as 'sir' or 'Sergeant Pierce.' This is your final warning."

Gillums frowned. "My name is Gillums Markeet, and I'm one of the elders here in Altai. I have worked the dirt my whole life and have followed the Tenets with honor. You have no right to demand—"

Gillums was cut off as Sergeant Pierce raised an object in his hand to eye level and squeezed. There was a flash and a small clap of thunder, then Gillums's chest exploded in blood. Saiph inhaled sharply and dove behind a barrel. He could hear the others yell in anger, and a few of them dropped to Gillums's side as he died with gurgling and ragged breaths. Others took a step forward, an anger to their eyes that Saiph had never seen before.

"Don't!" Sergeant Pierce yelled. "Not unless each and every one of you wants to die today!"

The Altainians hesitated.

"Don't move," Rosh said to those around him. He gestured to one of the younger members of the watch. "Go and get the Tenent breaker. Bring him here." Rosh raised his hands before Sergeant Pierce, palms out. "You've come here on a sacred day and killed a good man. Please, tell us what it will take for you to stop shedding blood, sir."

Sergeant Pierce shook his head. "I require all of your Essen harvesters to come with me. They are being requisitioned for the good of House Harain."

"Our what?"

Saiph could see the lines of Pierce's mouth grow taught. Saiph had never seen so much anger in a man.

"Who put together those barrels?" Pierce said.

"I...I did," Rosh said.

"Who else farms as you do?"

"I'm the only one."

Pierce shook his head and raised the object in his hand.

"There was one other," Rosh said quickly, "but you just killed him."

Sergeant Pierce narrowed his eyes. "You expect me to believe that you and that old man harvested and collected enough beetles for all these barrels?"

"We are talented...Asen...farmers, sir."

"*Ess*-en," Pierce corrected.

"Yes," Rosh said. "That."

"It's unbelievable how little you know about your own profession."

Rosh stared at him, expressionless.

Pierce sighed. "All right, well, *you* are definitely coming with me. But I don't believe you and this old man were the only Essen farmers. Tell me who the others are or I'll start killing until you do. The rest of the people here will be transferred to other camps nearby."

The huge metal creature took a step forward.

Saiph glanced at Gillums, who was unnaturally still and covered in blood. There wasn't a chance that he'd hide here while someone else he knew died. "I'm the other farmer, sir! Don't hurt anyone!"

Sergeant Pierce gestured to the soldiers behind him, and they rushed over and grabbed Saiph. His hands were thrust roughly behind his back, and something was placed on his wrists, binding them. He looked over at his father, but another man had bound him and was throwing a mask over his face. A moment later, Saiph's vision was blocked by black cloth.

"Only way you'll live through this is by being obedient," Sergeant Pierce whispered to Rosh's and Saiph's covered faces. "If you didn't have that idiot, Brint, then I would have leveled this place and claimed you attacked first. No one would have blinked an eye. No one."

Pierce paused, as if thinking, though it was hard to say without seeing him. Saiph could hear muttering and the sound of clicks and bursts of air from the metal monster standing nearby. His mouth was dry and his leg throbbed, but it was hard to feel anything other than fear.

Sergeant Pierce spoke again, but louder. "Round up the rest. If anyone resists or runs, shoot them. We're not wasting any more time here."

"No!" Saiph yelled.

He felt as much as he heard the footstep of the monster as it stepped forward. There was that sound like a sharp clap of thunder again and people started screaming. Saiph was dragged in the opposite direction. He struggled.

"Stop! Let me go!"

He lashed out with an elbow and felt something connect. The grip loosened, then broke. He stumbled forward, but he only got a few steps before his leg gave out and he fell hard to the ground. He tried to get up and run, but he couldn't. He was too weak—too feeble. Saiph yelled out in frustration, but it only made his breathing heavier.

"Little shithead," the soldier said from behind. "Know how easy it'd be to kill you, limp dick?"

Saiph was hauled to his feet, and then something hit him *hard* in the face. He fell back down. A boot struck his ribs. Once. Twice.

"Don't kill him, Hant. He's why we're all the way out here."

Saiph was lifted back up, and though he couldn't see, he swore that he felt it coming. Something hard hit his head, and everything went dark.

Saiph woke to a river of pain, but a pounding head, a parched mouth, and a throbbing leg stood out most. Wind was blowing hard against him, whipping the excess cloth of his mask around his face. There was also an unnatural and repetitive clanking sound and a pungent smell of smoke and fumes. It was overwhelming. Saiph's head sagged, and his mouth watered before he vomited into the black cloth. He shook, trying to let the sick slide through the cracks of his mask and onto his chest. Someone grunted and kicked, hitting his bad leg. He grimaced in pain.

Saiph felt tears in his eyes. What had they done? Who had they killed?

"Dad?" He said, stifling a sob. "Rosh?"

No one answered.

"Dad!"

But the wind and silence persisted.

CHAPTER NINE

The important members of Jon's crew entered the dining room where Jon was eating. An alluring aroma wafted around as Treyges passed out coffee and pastries. Jon knew why he insisted on always serving the others, but it was odd that they didn't question it. Maybe it was because he looked like the quintessential butler: thin gray hair, perfect posture, meek, unceasingly polite.

Russ unceremoniously stuffed food into his mouth as the others politely waited for everyone to be served. Silvestre stared at him in open disgust.

"Wha'?" Russ said through a mouth full of food. "I hunkry!"

Sarah smiled and decided that she wasn't that polite either. She began to eat.

"So," Amira said, "what are our duties for the duration of the trip? I am curious to hear."

Jon put down his cup of coffee. "I guess we'll start with you, then. Think you can customize one of the landing pods to survive an intense electrical storm?"

"How intense?" Amira asked.

"About an average of sixty thousand volts per centimeter over a ten-mile radius."

"Really? This exists on Jangali?"

Jon nodded. "Can you do it?"

Amira scratched her scarred and tatooed temple. "I have a few ideas, but it will be expensive."

"Don't worry about the cost. It's important, so give it your top priority. Your other minor duties have been sent to your inbox." Jon turned to Russ, who sat up straight. "Russ, I need you to begin training your troops for forest-based guerrilla warfare and how to use gasoline powered weapons. There are going to be places in the fight where Tokomoto won't be able to help. And his attention will be spread thin as it is. Are your Andhaka charging?"

"No problem, boss man. I'll get to it. And yeah, they're charging. A quarter of them are already fully powered up."

Jon nodded. "Toko, please prepare as you normally do; I've sent you the maps you'll need. If you could come up with a few creative plans to deal with multiple battlefronts, that'd be useful. And study the land around the forest I marked, please.

"Ellie, I'll need you to assist in a complex surgery when we arrive at the planet. The procedure outline has been sent to you, and I'll welcome any recommendations you have. Train your doctors to treat diseases native to Jangali, and they'll need to refresh themselves on how to treat injuries without a fully equipped medical facility."

"Aye-aye, Captain," Ellie said.

"What do you need from me?" Silvestre asked.

"Try learning some of Jangali's customs and traditions. You'll have to train the Class G dynamic if we get to them."

"We're going to train this thing?" Silvestre said.

"It's not a thing, it's a person. And no, I'll not automatically train him or her, not until we've become acquainted," Jon said. He turned to Sarah. "Can you study the biosphere of Jangali and get back to me on any potential problems?"

"Already started," Sarah said.

"I also wanted to let you all know that I will be busy working with Vincent Cross on a special project. If you see him around the station, try and make him feel welcome. He is a bit—"

Jon was cut off as the room went dark and then was bathed in red light. Sirens wailed.

"Treyges?" Jon said.

"There has been a station-wide power outage and emergency power has been activated. Sir, it does not look like a system failure to me."

"Well, what is it then, Trey?" Sarah said. "A system success?"

"It's been tampered with."

Jon closed his eyes and made a quick decision. "Ellie, Toko, and Sarah, stay in this room. You'll be safe here. Don't open the door for anyone but us. Amira, go with Treyges to the control sphere and direct emergency crews from there. Russ, take a squadron and start doing sweeps of the lower levels. Guard the life-support systems. Send a second team to the backups. Silvestre, you're with me."

Sarah started to protest, but was interrupted by another loud siren. Jon looked to Treyges.

"There are twenty-two fighters inbound to our position," he said calmly. "They will arrive in fourteen minutes. They look like scythes to me."

"Twenty-two scythes!" Sarah said. "Who can afford that many in this day and age?"

"We need to restore power and get out of here," Jon said.

He walked quickly down the hall, Silvestre trailing behind him. People ran past them as the red lights continued to flash. Treyges was on the ship-wide comm, asking everyone to remain calm and report to their stations. The man had one of the most soothing voices Jon had ever heard.

"Where are we going?" Silvestre asked.

"Data and networking hub. Sixth floor."

"Why? Can't we check the network afterward?"

Jon glanced at her with a raised eyebrow and kept walking. "This attack isn't going to kill us. If they knew when we were going to be leaving and where we would be now, then they know that too. This is a distraction."

"No way twenty-two scythes are a distraction."

Jon shrugged. They reached a corridor and took a sharp left that led to a stairwell.

"You know who is behind this, don't you?" Sil said as they jogged down the stairs.

"Yep."

"And you're not going to tell me, are you?"

"Nope."

They reached the sixth floor and burst through the door. The hallway and adjacent rooms were empty. There were no screams or sounds of hurried footsteps.

"What information could they possibly want that is worth twenty-two scythes?" Sil asked.

Jon glanced around the deserted hallways, then walked toward a side panel and punched in a code. The small storage door slid open, and he pulled out two clear masks.

"Do you have your aura suit with you?" Jon asked.

"Negativa, Amira is upgrading it for me."

He handed her one of the masks.

"Why?" she said.

Jon strode down the hall and heard Silvestre follow. He stopped at the entrance to the networking and data center and stared into the darkness.

"What can you see?" he said.

Silvestre peered inside, her red eyes glowing brightly. "The entire staff is on the floor. It looks like they're breathing, though."

"Look lower, at the station equipment. Is there anything there? Anything disturbed?"

Sil's eyes narrowed. "No, I don't...wait. There is some ripped-up paneling near the back."

"Damn rats," Jon said.

"Excuse me?"

"There are these modified rats that have been altered to bite through wiring and other technical infrastructure."

"I thought you said they wanted info? Do these rats have little rat computers and little rat keyboards to rat hack their way into the system?"

"I think they're hoping that the rats will destroy some security systems that would allow them to access our internal network."

Silvestre rubbed her forehead. "Okay...so are these things dangerous?"

"Um, a bit, yes. Don't let them bite you."

Jon received a ping. "What is it?"

"Eight minutes until the scythes are in firing range, sir," Treyges said.

"Copy that." Jon turned to Silvestre. "A light, please?"

Silvestre held out her bionic hand, palm up, and a sphere of red light that matched the color of her eyes popped into existence. It hung there and pulsated softly as it floated.

Jon held up a hand to cover his eyes. "Turn down the heat a bit?"

"Sorry."

"No problem. The rats are attracted to heat, so they'll be coming for you."

"Great..."

They walked into the room, the soft red light illuminating their path. Jon reached down to each person they passed and placed two fingers on their neck. Everyone was alive. They passed a row of large servers, and Silvestre held up a hand. Jon looked at her, and she motioned them down the row. They came upon three holes that were about six inches in diameter. Jon stared at them as he received another ping from Treyges.

"Sir, the system is trying to repair itself, but there's something that is stopping it. If this persists, we will not have power back in time."

Jon switched the link off and turned to Silvestre. "We're running out of time."

"What do we do?"

Jon shook his head. "You're not going to like it..."

She waved for him to go on.

"So the rats are attracted to heat, right? We don't have time to ferry them out one by one, so we need something very hot and very bright that will make them come running."

"Come running and try to kill that heat."

"Yes, exactly. Very sharp."

Silvestre sighed. "You better stand over there."

Jon retreated to the back of the room, and Silvestre closed her eyes and scrunched her face in concentration. The sphere of light began to glow more intensely, and Jon could feel the heat even from the back of the room. The rustling below the floor ceased for a moment, then became frantic.

"They're coming!" Silvestre said. "What do I do?"

Jon popped his head out from his hiding spot below a desk. "Kill them!"

Jon watched as the rats came scurrying out of the three holes like cockroaches. They were at least two feet long with thick black hair, beady eyes, and sharp claws. Foam dripped from their mouths. Silvestre recoiled and took an instinctive step back. For a moment, Jon thought she was going to turn and run, but she steadied herself. She bent her knees slightly as the first of the rats leapt at her chest. With one hand steadying the ball of energy, Silvestre stepped to the side and sliced through the air with one of her knives.

When had she gotten that out?

She moved so fast that Jon could barely track her movements. It was rare to see a dynamic in attack, but it was always impressive and, in this case, disgusting. The rats were quickly reduced to blood and hair in less than half a minute.

"Nice work," Jon said. He stood up and walked toward her.

Silvestre stared at him, covered in black blood and other rat matter. "That was, unquestionably, the most disgusting thing that has ever happened to me."

"At least you had a mask on, right?"

"Like you knew..." Sil mumbled.

Jon pinged Treyges.

"Sir?"

"Send all the repair bots to level six. Send a medical team too."

"Yes, sir."

"What's happening with Russ?"

"His team encountered several agents attempting to sabotage critical systems. They were neutralized. No survivors."

A few minutes later, the lights blinked back on and the ship lurched forward. Jon almost lost his footing, but Silvestre reached out and steadied him.

"Thanks."

She nodded. "What the hell just was all this?"

"The first shots of a war."

"War?"

Jon nodded.

"Lovely."

CHAPTER TEN

Time faintly registered as Saiph was carried away by some magical vehicle that he couldn't see. He had no idea where he was or how far he had traveled. Distantly, he recognized that it was still winterweek, though, since no sunlight seeped into his black world. In between bouts of unconsciousness, he thought of his family and friends and how many of them were now dead and gone forever. Were his mother, Roe, or Ayanda among them? He couldn't even consider something happening to Landon.

Eventually, the rushing of wind in his ears and the odd mechanical roaring ceased. Saiph sat upright. There were sounds of metal on metal, and the vehicle he sat on shook slightly.

"Here's what's gonna happen," came the voice of Sergeant Pierce. "We're taking you off the truck and handing you over to the Department of Labor. You will not speak during this process. You will not cry. You will not smile. You will not whistle or hum. You are to remain silent. Those who do not comply with this will receive three lashes and their masks back. Is that clear?"

No one answered.

"Good. Hant, Brint, take their masks off and get them off the truck before they can stink it up any worse."

Saiph heard footsteps slowly coming down the length of the truck. A hand roughly grabbed the back of his neck and forced his head down. He heard a click, and then the mask was ripped off. A guard stood above him.

"Bet you wished you hadn't taken a swing now, huh?" The guard lifted Saiph to his feet and shoved him toward the exit.

Saiph looked around and concluded that he was in some sort of large metal container. There were about thirty-five other dirty and tired prisoners, but none he recognized. Who were these people?

They stumbled out one at a time, the others hopping the three feet down to the ground. When Saiph got to the end of the container, he hesitated. He couldn't jump down like that with his leg. How would he get down? Saiph looked to the side for something to hold on to, but before he could do anything, he was shoved. He tried to keep his feet, but as soon as his leg touched the ground, it gave way with a jolt. For a moment, he couldn't move or think. There was only an intense pain in his side and in his leg. Saiph was hauled to his feet and forced into line. They stood there like that for a while, and Saiph was able to ease his breathing and wait for the pain to ease to a deep ache.

When he recovered, Saiph scanned his surroundings. It was unbelievable. Though the sky was still dark, huge lights were attached to tall poles, illuminating the clearing. They weren't like the beetle barrel lights but were harsh and bright instead, like the Light of Tengrii, only much larger. People were everywhere too. More people than Saiph had ever met in his entire life. The noise was deafening, and Saiph was happy to stay quiet, not wanting to contribute to it.

"Group 2342 from the Enil Valley!" A voice boomed out above the commotion. "2342!"

The guard leading the group raised his hand and walked up to the platform. An overweight woman with long hair bent down to hear him, and she nodded several times. The woman held a thin metal slab that projected light from one side, and several times she would stare at it before putting her finger to the light.

Magic, Saiph thought.

"The transfer of group 2342 from the army to the department of labor is complete. Will the prison guard please step forward and relieve the army."

People in black uniforms were replaced with others wearing similar dark-blue uniforms. They all carried one of those thunder-making weapons that had killed Gillums. Once Sergeant Pierce and the other men in black left, the heavy woman spoke again.

"Men and women of the Enil Valley, welcome to labor camp sixty-two. The government has requisitioned you for your unique skill set. In return for your labor, you will receive food, lodging, and safety from the Fulgurian threat. You will not speak back to your superiors. You will not become lazy in your duties. You will not run. If you're caught out of your bunk at night, you'll receive ten lashes. Any escape attempt, and you'll be sold to the coliseum for the diarchy's pleasure."

Diarchy's pleasure? What is she talking about?

The woman gave her whole toneless speech without looking up from the slab of light. After making several marks, she turned to a man in uniform and waved him away.

"Where's my daughter?" a woman cried out.

The organizer at the front shook her head and turned away. A large guard grabbed the woman who had called out and shoved her to the ground. Two other guards grabbed her arms and dragged her to a wooden pole as she struggled. They bound her hands around the beam and tore her simple dress, revealing her back. Anger boiled within Saiph, and he had to bite his lip to keep from yelling out.

"What are you doing!" the woman said. "Let me go!"

The large guard pulled a whip from his belt and, without warning, lashed the woman. A brutal red line of torn flesh spread across her back. The woman's cry of pain was still echoing when the man struck her again. The woman collapsed, her bound hands the only thing keeping her up. She dangled close to the ground as the third lash scarred her.

"I'm Captain Worthington, your master here at sixty-two," the large guard said as he holstered his whip. "Anyone who does not follow the rules will receive the same as this woman. It is true that we need you for your labor. But we do not need you as much as we need order."

Worthington walked down the line of prisoners, staring into each of their eyes for a moment. Saiph met his stare. He was an ugly man, but Saiph couldn't decide if it was because of his actual characteristics or because of his perpetual grimace.

"This compound is more than five miles in diameter. It has walls fifty feet high with a guard tower every twelve hundred feet. We patrol the wilderness beyond every hour of every day. Even if you manage to get over the walls, past the patrols, and through the woods, we have other tools beyond your comprehension that will find you immediately. There is no escape. This is your life now. Accept it."

Saiph and his cohort were led away from the towering lights and deeper into the camp. He could barely take in his surroundings, he was so out of it. Eventually, they came upon their barracks. Each person was assigned a small, dirty cot, a thin blanket, and a pathetic-looking uniform. They were told to change without an ounce of privacy. Saiph had never felt so humiliated in all his life. He was so tired that he was having trouble holding back tears of frustration. He wanted to scream and kick and rage, but he thought about the woman's limp body dangling from the whipping pole and forced it down.

When the lights were shut off, he lay down on his cot and tried to calm himself. He thought about his family again, and a terrible ache engulfed his very being. He muttered the words and prayers that always calmed him.

There is no revenge so complete as forgiveness. There is no revenge so complete as forgiveness. There is no revenge so complete as forgiveness.

No Verse had ever felt so empty.

A loud gong jolted Saiph from his dream. It was still dark outside.

"Get up!" a voice called out. "Get up, you swine! Stand in front of your cot and prepare to be counted!"

Saiph stood at the edge of his bed and waited as guards came down the aisle, reading numbers on the slaves' uniforms and comparing them to their notes. After Saiph's number was checked, he was handed a portion of stale bread and a cup of cold soup. He ate it greedily as he looked around.

The barracks was large and made of wood, although there was no flooring, which made Saiph worry about summerweek's rain. Altogether, eight torches lit the room, leaving little to see by. However, Saiph noticed that there were no bars, gates, or locks. It was quite open, and the space would even seem inviting after a few days out in the wilderness.

"Count complete," the voice called out. "Fall in!"

Saiph finished his bread and lined up with the other prisoners. They were led outside and into the pitch-black morning. He had no idea where they were going, but the walk was surprisingly long, and he began to believe Captain Worthington's boast about the size of the enclosure.

The land here was more barren and flat then it was back in Altai. There were only a few plants, and none of them even moved when he walked past. It felt odd to Saiph, not having any tall trees within sight. It was unnatural.

The path eventually began to narrow, and the blazing lights from the center field faded noticeably. He welcomed the darkness. It comforted him and helped him forget where he was.

A couple miles later, they came upon a smaller enclosure, demarcated by eight-foot walls. They walked through an iron gate and to the familiar pool of yokai blood. The purple liquid bubbled quietly while they waited for direction. Captain Worthington stormed through the gate like an aggravated voltguar ten minutes later.

"Your daily supervisor is this old sack," Worthington said, pointing at an old man in a slave's shirt. He had big round glasses that made his eyes bulge like an insect's. "Listen to him and the other guards and work hard. If you don't, I'll hear about it and come back here. You do not want me to come back here. Understood? Good."

Worthington and the other guards left, leaving the prisoners alone.

"What, they're just going to leave us here? All on our own?" a teenage prisoner said.

"What's ya name, boy?" the old man asked.

"Nico. Son of Nicado."

"You see that tower, Nico, son of Nicado? Just beyond them last walls there? That there is a guard tower, and from that impressive vantage, they be watching our every motion. Step outta this volt farm without permish, and they be on you like a sytin bird on a lonesome calf."

Nico stared at him with open skepticism but didn't disagree. "So, do I call you Old Sack Supervisor, then?"

"Name's Chet. Prefer if you called me Chet. Chet's a good name, you see. Yes it is. Chet's thinkin' that you're thinkin' of your old life, ain't ya? Mistake! Now's the time to swallow ya pride a smidge, yes'm indeed."

"How long will we be here for?" a woman asked.

"You ain't gettin' the picture, are ya, sweetums? You're here 'til the ground separates ya from the air."

"Oh Tengrii..." a man groaned.

"Tengrii won't help ya! Chet might, though! Ya could try praying to him."

Saiph raised a hand. "Can they listen to us out here with their magic?"

"Magic? Nah. They don't care what you lot are saying, as long as you're working. Now enough questioning. You'll have the rest of ya life here to be pondering the answers. Everyone here volt farmed 'fore, yes'em?"

Most people nodded weakly, but some were too distraught for even that.

"These first few weeks are 'specially tough for newcomers. Best thing ya can do is work your tail off and be submissive to your betters. So that's what we're gonna do. Four quadrants to this volt farm, each bigger than any of your small-timing farms from 'fore, so it needs some organizing, which good old Chet is gonna do for ya. You may thank me however you see fit. I'm counting you off into fives now. Ones be feeding and watering beetles. Twos and threes got the voltguars and bigger critters. Fours be painting yokai blood and upkeeping the enclosure. Fives be digging new beetle ditches."

Saiph received a five. He glanced around as he walked with the other fives to the northwest corner. Saiph was amazed at the sheer size of the volt farm and knew he couldn't even see it all in the darkness. Roe would have liked it. The thought of her almost made him miss a step. Then he thought what she would do and realized she wouldn't take any of this crap. He straightened his spine, even though he ached everywhere when he did.

"Well, we've had a turn of bad luck, wouldn't you say?" a man said from behind him. He was tall, gangly, and in his late thirties by the look of him. His brown hair was thin and wispy.

"Bad luck?" Nico spat. "Bad luck! This is more than a bit of bad luck, mate. We're slaves! Just yesterday I was celebrating my mum's birthday, now I'm digging ditches in a foreign land."

"We could spend the rest of our lives in this five-mile enclosure," a tall woman with blonde hair said weakly.

"What's your name?" the tall man asked.

"Charlotte."

"Well, Charlotte, my third Verse is: *A of turn of bad luck is like the turn of the world. Give it time and the sun will rise.* With that, I promise to let you come with me when I escape."

"You're escaping?"

"Of course! Not right away, mind you. But eventually. I'm not spending the rest of my days digging beetle ditches and eating stale bread."

"Me neither," Nico said.

Saiph turned to face the man. "It's encouraging to find that I'm not the only one thinking along this line." Saiph offered him his hand. "Saiph Calthari."

"Name's Alistair. Pleasure to have you along, Saiph. You're the one who asked if they could hear us?"

Saiph nodded.

"Smart."

"Smart?" An older woman scoffed. "Have you seen their magic? There's no escaping something like that. They had a monster thirty feet tall at my village. Made fully of perfect metal!"

"Same at mine," Saiph said.

The group went quiet as they relived their enslavement.

"Where there's life, there's hope!" Alistair said, shattering the silence.

"By the gods, are you going to be quoting Verses at us all day?" Nico asked.

"And night, likely," Alistair said.

Charlotte shook her head in confusion. "How can you be so cheery?"

Alistair scrunched his face in concentration. "I expect it has something to do with being dropped on my head as a child. Yes, that's definitely it."

They dug large pits for the remainder of the day, and Saiph had nothing to do but dwell on where he was. He couldn't get over how barren the ground was here, like it had been trampled by a herd or something. There were no moving plants or vines at all. Back home, their volt farm had been its own little world of life, but this volt farm was just as much a prison as the camp itself. Voltguars were in large metal cages and the voltbeetles were grouped together much too closely. It was as if someone had seen a volt farm in a painting and then tried to build the largest one there ever was.

Saiph worked in silence, choosing to focus on the work and his thoughts. Where was his father? Was everyone all right? He couldn't help but see those he loved gazing sightlessly up at Tengrii's sky. It was overwhelming. Saiph's muscles strained as he moved dirt from one place to another. He focused on the movement, and the familiar routine calmed him. He had to think—devise a way to escape this nightmare. It didn't take him long to realize that he didn't have enough information. He needed to watch, listen, and wait.

Saiph worked himself hard, despite his injuries, and was only half conscious on the walk back to the barracks. He was certain that the only reason he didn't sleepwalk back was because the pain of his body would jolt him with every step. Charlotte, Nico, and Alistair all wore similar expressions of exhaustion. When Saiph reached his thin cot, he fell onto it, foregoing his self-made promise to take a better look around the barracks. The only thing that kept him from instantly falling asleep was a small prick in his side. He rolled over and felt around his blanket. His hand brushed a thin stick of metal about the size of his index finger. He held it up, puzzled. It hadn't been there the night before, had it?

He looked closer and saw a small engraving of some strange leaf. He ran his fingers over it, feeling it in his hands. The pen-like item suddenly moved on its own, expanding and creating a thin sheet of glass surrounded by metal edges. Saiph dropped it in alarm and then covered it and his head with the blanket. Then, astonishingly, the sheet of glass magically lit up and conjured words out of light:

Are you Saiph Calthari?

CHAPTER ELEVEN

The first year went better than Jon expected. No mishaps, technical failures, unexpected violence, or additional wire-eating rats. He spent most of his time in the tenth-floor lab with Vincent, Sarah, and Ellie, which had one of the best views of the park. He was surprised how absorbed he was in his work and also at how much he got along with Vincent, who was so young. The boy was truly a technical genius.

Jon sat at his work desk and tinkered with a metallic arm. Vincent was to his right, a line of waving electricity fluctuating between two nodes as he adjusted virtual knobs on his tablet. Ellie and Sarah were distracted by their own studies but were there in case they had a question for the other two.

Vincent abruptly stopped his experiment and looked at Jon. "How did you do it?" he asked.

"Do what?" Jon said, continuing to work.

"Create the Essens?"

Ellie's and Sarah's fingers stopped typing, and Jon put down the mechanical arm.

"Really, Vincent?" Sarah said. "You know he can't tell you that. I doubt anybody else knows but him."

Jon raised a hand. "It's okay. He's been patient for over a year now. I think that you would have asked far sooner at seventeen."

"No I wouldn't have!"

"Oh, I'm sorry, I must be remembering a different seventeen-year-old who stole an electron microscope."

Sarah blushed. "*Borrowed.* I brought it back, didn't I?"

"What exactly do you want to know?" Jon said to Vincent. "I can't tell you everything, not only because some of it is still confidential, but because it's very complex."

"I know!" Vincent said. "I know, but...it changed everything, and I don't know how you did it. Did you ever think it might not happen?"

Jon laughed. "Plenty of times. I can't tell you how many nights I went to sleep thinking that it was impossible. I would say that the hardest part was merging the biological and mechanical systems. You know that Essens are partly biological?"

"Yeah, I read that somewhere, but I have no idea why."

"Creating a single Essen to fly into space and absorb power from a star wasn't the problem. We had the tech to capture light and turn it into energy efficiently for a while, even at the molecular level. It was the replication that was the issue. I needed one to become millions. Millions to become billions. The replication process just didn't work the way we wanted it to. So we took examples from nature and used similar processes that could create a nearly metal and glass exterior but still have some biological maintenance centers."

"I still don't see how that could work."

"Neither did I. For many years, in fact. I thought it had failed completely until the test stars started disappearing from view. The massive amount of energy followed shortly after that."

"Then what?" Ellie asked.

"Really?" Sarah said. "Don't they teach history in school anymore?"

Jon shook his head. "Funny that things I lived and remember are now considered history."

"Don't blame us for that," Vincent said, "just tell us what happened."

"Well," Jon said, "the Essens started surrounding other stars and capturing their energy too. We had all the power we needed to build the things we did, like the gateways between planets."

"Man, what I'd give to see a gateway up and running..." Vincent said.

Sarah pulled her stool closer. "What happened when the gateways shut down?"

"I thought you knew all this!" Ellie protested.

Sarah nodded at Jon. "I want to hear it from him. You know what's happening with the blackouts, right?"

"Of course. Everyone does."

"It's all connected," Sarah said. "One event leading to another, then another, then another."

Their eyes bore into Jon, eager. They would wholeheartedly believe whatever he told them, not even stopping to consider the possibility that he would lie to them or that he could be wrong. It made him uncomfortable. He'd try to give them as much truth as possible.

"The Sphere was a different place when we had enough energy to maintain the gateways," he said. "Imagine waking up on Earth, having lunch on Tau Ceti, going for an afternoon swim on Nero, then ending the day by gazing up at the rings of Andernach. The Sphere was one place, under a single leadership. Trade was on a scale that makes today's market laughable. More importantly, we all *thought* of ourselves as one people. Now we all identify with our type of government, world, or religion, like we did during the time of my birth."

"You sort of sound like one of the Banded," Sarah said. "They would be excited to hear that you're joining him."

Jon chuckled bitterly. "The Banded's ideas about uniting humanity again aren't entirely misguided, but no, I'm not a member."

"But how are the gateways connected to the panic about the blackouts?" Ellie asked.

Jon swiveled his seat toward Ellie. "People are scared that the

Essens will cover their world's star, not because it would kill them but because they would have to go live with someone else. Someone different. Someone not *them*. They don't want to do that."

Sarah shook her head. "So badly that they'd fight to make sure they didn't have to."

Jon nodded. "The very fact that people are speculating about the worst is making the worst happen."

Vincent moved his equipment to the side and put his elbows on the desk. "What are you saying? That there will be a war?"

"I am," Jon said. "It's already begun."

The keypad lock to the front door beeped, and everyone looked to see who was entering. The door burst opened, and Russ, shirtless and dripping sweat, quickly entered and slammed the door behind him. He put his palms on the door and breathed heavily as he stared out a peephole. Outside, they heard at least a dozen people run by. Russ breathed a sigh of relief and turned around. "Oh, hey guys! That was a close one!"

"Russ, you can't use this room to play your games! There's some outrageously expensive equipment in here!" Sarah said.

"No kidding?" Russ said, taking a look around. He picked up a gadget, stared at it for a moment, then threw it back on the table.

"Hey!" Vincent said. "Careful with that!"

"Apologies," Russ said, "apologies. What are you four working on in here anyway?"

"Top secret," Ellie said, smiling. "No one can know. Not even you."

"Jon!" Russ said. "Do you not trust me? Am I not your dearest friend? Tell me, brother!"

"No can do, Russ," Jon said. "I trusted you to only use that code for emergencies, and now you're using it to play games."

"First of all, they ain't games. It's *training*. Second of all, that was an emergency. They were going to catch me, and if they did that, they might start thinking they're better than me. And if they think they're better than me, I might start to resent them. And if I start to resent them, I might not train them anymore, which means they might not be ready to cover me in a fight. And if they're not covering me in a fight, I might die. Do you want me to die, Jon?"

"I really don't know? We'll have to leave it up to the people. All in favor of Russ dying..."

Jon, Ellie, Vincent, and Sarah raised their hands.

"No respect!" Russ yelled. "I can tell when I'm not wanted." He walked to the door and peered out the peephole again. "I'll take my chances on the outside."

He slipped out the door, closing it silently this time. He took off running in the opposite direction his soldiers had gone. The group looked around at each other.

"That actually kind of looked like fun," Ellie said.

Jon walked the deck as preparations were made for the one-year celebration. While he had been content over the last year, many others living on board found life in space boring and repetitive. He wasn't sure if it was being around the same people all the time, not having any natural sunlight, or that claustrophobic feeling that most people experienced at some point, but long periods in space often lowered morale. When Jon announced a one-year-anniversary party full of drinks, fruit, and meat, the passengers nearly went crazy with excitement.

The rooms near the park were transformed into booths that people could rent out to sell their favorite recipes and specialty items. Games were set up for the children, and there was even a small swimming pool. For a short while, everyone would forget they would be on this station for another four years and enjoy the party like they would on their home planet.

A few hours later, Jon strolled through the park in his nicest suit, a glass of red wine in his hand. Amira walked beside him wearing an elegant dress. Even she needed a break from the monotony of life in space sometimes.

"Tell me," Amira said, "do you ever get tired of this?"

Jon laughed. "Do you? You're, what, one hundred and fifteen now?"

"Fourteen," Amira corrected. "And one hundred and fourteen is much different than six hundred and seventy-two."

"I suppose that's true," Jon said. "Word of advice... Taking pleasure in the everyday joys is more important than the memories of life's great moments."

"To the small joys," Amira said. "Something I need to get better at."

Jon clinked his glass against hers with a laugh. "Yeah, you really do."

"I doubt I'll ever make it anywhere near six hundred though. Especially with the years running out."

Jon shrugged. "You may not want to."

They continued to walk the small path through the park, saying hello to others as they went. When they emerged from the trees on the other side, they spotted Tokomoto staring gloomily at a crowd of people. He wore his usual loose trousers and T-shirt.

"What's all the commotion?" Jon asked.

Toko nodded his head toward the center of the group. "You will see."

A moment later, the crowd parted enough to reveal Russ in a white tuxedo and cowboy hat. He was staggeringly drunk. Not that this was surprising to Jon, but it was startling to see Ellie and Vincent following Russ's lead. Russ handed Vincent a small glass of a red liquid and slapped him on the back. When Vincent threw it down in one gulp, Russ cheered and lifted him off the ground in a bone-crushing hug.

"At least they know how to enjoy the small things," Amira said.

"That man," Tokomoto said, "is the stupidest man I have ever met."

"I kind of like him."

They turned to see Sarah and Silvestre walking toward them. Silvestre wore a long black dress that contrasted brilliantly with her eyes. People stared at her as she walked by. Sarah wore a white skirt and somehow still managed to look regal.

"You can't be serious?" Silvestre said to Sarah, straight-faced.

"I know, right? I'm not even sure why."

"I am thinking," Toko said, "that you are stupid too."

Sarah ruffled his hair. "Whatever, I'm going to join them." She walked over to Russ, Vincent, and Ellie, and they greeted her with an enthusiasm that suggested they hadn't seen each other for many years, rather than a few hours.

"To be young," Amira said.

"I am young," Tokomoto said.

"So am I," said Silvestre. "And Sarah is older than you, isn't she?"

Amira scowled at the mention of Sarah's name. "Yes, but she was born to forever be a child. You two have the souls of a grumpy old man."

Tokomoto nodded like this was a compliment of great worth, but Silvestre looked uneasy.

"You could go over and join them," Jon said. "You're only young for a short while, after all."

"But you've given me a load of extra years," Silvestre said. "I won't start to age again for at least another seventy-five years."

"Youth is determined by the mind and heart, not the amount of gray in your hair."

Silvestre hesitated.

"Go on," Jon said, giving her a push. "I promise Tokomoto will not judge you as an idiot. Isn't that right, Tokomoto?" Tokomoto looked up at Jon from his wheelchair as if this was not going to be the case at all. "See! Judgement free zone. Off you go."

"Is that an order?"

"Yes."

Sometimes it was hard to tell when Silvestre rolled her eyes, but this wasn't one of those times. She left, though, and walked over to the other group. Jon, Amira, and Tokomoto retired to a table near the trees, and a waiter brought them wine, bread, and cheese. They talked of their projects, both official and unofficial, and enjoyed the people watching while it was still early. Jon and Toko were discussing some of the new software that Toko was writing for his robotic army when Jon received a call from Treyges. Jon held up his hand in apology to Tokomoto.

"Everything all right?"

"Yes, sir, but you have a new message."

"Can it wait?" Jon asked. "I'm at the anniversary party right now."

"It is from Jangali, sir."

Jon sat up straight. "And?"

"It says: 'I found him.'"

CHAPTER TWELVE

T he Book of Light was an object of pure fantasy, like a genie lamp or the weapons of the Old Gods. The light came and went as he commanded without fail. All Saiph had to do was run his finger across the surface of the metal and the book would expand. The first night he'd gotten it, nearly a month ago now, it had written to him:

Are you Saiph Calthari?

Saiph had brushed his finger across the glass, and a streak of white had appeared and then slowly faded. Using his finger, he wrote: *Yes.* It faded gently into the background, as if sinking into nothing.

On this device is a book. I suggest you read it, the Book wrote back.

The glass changed, and the cover appeared. Saiph had been reading late into the night ever since, and today, it left him feeling supremely tired.

"I don't understand why we've got to fix somebody else's farm," Nico said.

"We ain't fixing a farm, we're getting it ready. For newcomers," Chet answered.

They walked as a group in bright sunlight. Saiph hadn't been to this part of camp sixty-two before, but it all looked the same to him anyway. Flat ground. Small trees. Walls in the distance.

A nightmare.

"More slaves, you mean," Charlotte said.

"You should call them what they are, Chet," Alistair said. "'Newcomers' almost makes it sound welcoming."

Chet didn't turn around as he led them farther away; he merely waved a hand and grumbled some nonsensical response. They passed other groups of slaves as they walked. Some farmed normal grains and fruit trees, but many others were cleaning, cooking, or melting down old metal. Eventually they came upon a truck occupied by two men. Saiph had learned that word from Chet. Apparently a "truck" was what had brought him here, and it was what the Skyfallers used to move quickly from one place to the other. Saiph still hadn't figured out how it moved on its own, though. Just another magic he didn't understand.

"You Chet?" the guard called out.

"Yep!" Chet said, raising a hand in greeting. "You another guard?"

The Skyfaller actually chuckled. "We'll be your minders for today. Guess the boss wants this farm up and running as quickly as possible. It's over this way."

The two guards turned and walked toward a half dozen squat buildings off to the side. Beyond them, Saiph could see the smaller enclosure of the volt farm they'd be working. He glanced over at Alistair, who was already looking at him. They both nodded and then made their way to the front of the group so that they were only six or seven feet away from the Skyfallers. The guards peered back at them but didn't pay them much mind.

"But they look *old*," the chubby guard said.

The other guard, who had spoken to Chet, was muscular and broad shouldered. "That's exactly what I'm saying. They must have built them."

"You really think that the locals, who don't have a pot to shit in, built fifty-foot-high, four-feet-thick stone walls? How would they have even moved stones that big?"

"Hell if I know, Smithy! Those Egyptians did, didn't they? I mean, do you think the beetles built them, then?"

"No, of course—"

"Then shut up about it already, you're giving me a headache."

If the Skyfallers hadn't built this place, then who had? Saiph didn't think it was the people of Jangali, though he couldn't be certain. He and Alistair shared an intrigued look as they approached the smaller walls of the volt farm.

The guards unlocked the first gate, then the second. Inside was ground even more barren than the rest of the camp. There was nothing to this volt farm. No beetle rows, ditches for yokai blood, or shed for tools. It would be a long couple of weeks to get this going, even with the entirety of their barracks working. This thought emphasized just how tired Saiph felt and how badly his leg hurt. Unsurprisingly, the guards never gave him time to massage it in the morning before walking on it.

"And here we are," Broad Shouldered said. "Off to work! We'll be watching for any idleness."

Chet assigned them tasks based off their number. The fives were to plant small fruit trees on the eastern side, which would feed and attract voltbeetles. Alistair, Nico, Charlotte, and Saiph were near a cracked section of the wall with a small sack of seed.

"So the Skyfallers didn't build this place," Alistair said. "That's something."

"Not something that will help us get out of here," Nico pointed out.

Saiph wasn't so sure. He knelt to plant a seed and grimaced in pain before saying, "Have any of you ever seen something like this place on Jangali? Could our ancestors really have built this?"

Alistair shook his head. "Not even close."

Nico laughed at the idea.

"I have," Charolotte said.

They all looked at her, surprised.

"Really?" Saiph asked. "What is it?"

Charlotte looked away and shrugged. "There's a place about twenty miles from my village, tucked into the mountains. It's a building of some sort, built right up against the rock. It's... Well, it is something of the Old Gods."

Saiph leaned forward. "What is it? What's inside?"

"It's forbidden to enter. Anyone who has gone inside hasn't returned. My people, they are—" Charlotte swallowed. "They *were* happy to leave the Old Gods and their things alone."

Alistair put a hand on Charlotte's shoulder. She was trying not to cry. Saiph opened his mouth to ask more questions, but Alistair shot him a look.

"It's all right," Alistair said. "It's okay to mourn for them."

Saiph inwardly cursed himself. Curiosity had gotten the best of him, and he'd upset his friend without even noticing. They hadn't spoken much of their homes since they'd been brought here. It was too painful. Too fresh. Their inner wounds were still bleeding, and they didn't know how to stitch them up. Saiph searched for wisdom within the Verses and the Tenets, but it was hard to find these days.

"There was a man in my village, Hycol, who used to let his pigs sleep in the house," Alistair said.

Saiph frowned with the others and stared at Alistair. What was he talking about?

"Right in his bed with him, actually," Alistair continued. "Five fully grown pigs, just snoring away with their owner. He loved those pigs. Took them everywhere. He even had a little carriage that he rode in, pulled by the pigs."

Nico scoffed. "A pig carriage?"

"Swear to Tengrii," Alistair said. "That's how he got to town."

"So he was...off, right?" Saiph asked.

Alistair looked at him like *he* was the crazy one. "Seriously?" he said. "Of course he was! He talked to the pigs like they were his family. He would bring them to Core Verse ceremonies. Speaking of, want to know his Core Verse?"

They were all smiling now, and they nodded for him to go on. Alistair cleared this throat and held up a hand for silence. "*I like pigs. Dogs look up to us. Cats look down on us. Pigs treat us as equals.*"

Saiph couldn't help but laugh. "That's not one of the Verses!"

"Oh yes it is!" Alistair said, pointing at him. "It's one of the throw-aways! Check it out for yourself!"

Charlotte's tears mixed with laughter, and Nico was actually rolling on the ground in amusement. Saiph's laughter grew when Nico wouldn't stop. The Verse wasn't even that funny, but the sound of his laughter was contagious. He hadn't truly felt this relaxed since before that horrible day in Altai. It reminded him of home.

"My brother has the Down," Saiph said, "and he's the happiest person I've ever met. He dances all the time. Doesn't matter what time it is or what's going on. He'll just break out into moves you've never even dreamed of. It's as if he's listening to music that no one else can hear." Saiph chucked again, picturing it. "I miss him."

They quieted. "You'll see them again," Alistair said. "We must believe that."

"I believe it," Nico said, "but we seriously got to start thinking of a *plausible* way to escape this place."

"So you still don't think that luring a sytin bird and flying away on its back is plausible, huh?" Saiph asked. "I'll be sure to give you a salute as I fly away on my giant bird. You'll remember it for all the rest of your miserable days here at camp sixty-two."

Nico squinted in the bright sunlight. "I promise not to laugh when the sytin turns over and I see your helpless form fall from the sky."

"Hey!" They turned to see the chubby guard calling out to them. "Back to work over there!"

They hurriedly went back to planting. Saiph put seed after seed in the ground, but his mind was turning. Should he tell the others about the Book of Light? Anyone caught with Skyfaller magic was punished severely. If they told... But no, he would have to trust someone. He couldn't do this on his own.

"I have a Skyfaller device," Saiph whispered. "It may be able to help us."

"What?" Nico asked. "How?"

"It was underneath the blanket of my cot. I don't know if it was left there on accident or what, but it knew me."

Alistair kept working but whispered back, "What do you mean, it knew you?"

Saiph covered another seed with dirt and moved up the line. "Light appeared on glass, and it spelled out a message. It said, *Are you Saiph Calthari?* I was able to write back and tell it that I was. Then it gave me a book. It's called *The Big Bang to Boundless: A Cumulative History of Humankind.*"

"A book?" Nico said scathingly. "How is that going to help us?"

"We have to learn, Nico," Alistair said. "We'll never get away if we don't understand what we're up against." He turned back to Saiph. "What does the book say?"

Saiph saw Nico roll his eyes but could tell that he accepted Alistair's argument. "The book is...odd. It doesn't read like a story, but the chap who made this up must have had quite an imagination. It says that everything, everywhere, came from one tiny dot, smaller than you can even see and that everything is made up of...*atoms*...which are tiny pieces of stuff that come together to form bigger stuff. He even thought that people descended from monkeys."

"Monkeys?" Charlotte said, brushing her dirty-blonde hair out of her eyes. "Really?"

Saiph shrugged, reflecting her skepticism. "I suppose it doesn't matter how fantastical it is, as long as we know that the Skyfallers value it."

"Any magic in there?" Nico asked. "Like spells or something?"

"Not that I've seen. The book is massive, though, and they work us all day. I've barely had time to look at it."

"Maybe you can skip around," Alistair suggested, "rather than reading the whole thing?"

"I suppose we'll have to."

Five weeks later, Saiph was reading about something called the Roman Empire. It was late, and the only sounds in the barracks were the snores of the other slaves. He wanted to join that chorus of slumber, but he also couldn't put down the Book of Light. These Romans were horrifyingly interesting. An entire people who spread death and *gloried* in it. Their whole way of life was shaped around competing and conquering. It was no wonder the Skyfallers were so violent, if they enjoyed stories like this.

Yet, the Romans were wonderful too. The author had magic pictures that showed people in gleaming armor, animals called "horses" that people could ride on, and buildings that left Saiph astonished at the author's imagination.

The Colosseum was the most impressive looking. Saiph remembered the Skyfaller administrator speaking that word the day he'd arrived at camp sixty-two. *Those who try and escape will be sent to the coliseum for the diarchy's pleasure.* The Skyfaller coliseum was where they sent the most disobedient slaves, so Saiph suppressed his desire to visit.

Saiph was reading about the Roman's most famous emperors, nearly falling asleep, when something caught his attention. He sat up with a jolt, suddenly alert, heart pounding. A man named Marcus Aurelius was quoted, and Saiph knew the words—had recited them thousands of times:

When you arise in the morning, think of what a precious privilege it is to be alive—to breathe, to think, to enjoy, to love.

It was his second Core Verse.

CHAPTER THIRTEEN

It's a him, Jon thought, *and only a handful of years older than Vincent.* He was still coming to terms with that. The Class G dynamic, with enough power being sent to his body to warp gravity itself, was a twenty-two-year-old boy who didn't know anything beyond his own backworld, backcountry village. When Jon heard about the boy's circumstances, though, he decided to act.

His team stumbled into the ship's bridge early the next morning. The sphere was dark, and the only light came from the ship's computers and the Virgo system that was projected on the far side of the dome. Russ, Vincent, Ellie, and Silvestre walked down the narrow path looking as if they had forgone sleep and had instead spent the night banging their heads against a wall. Treyges handed them coffee when they arrived at the center platform.

"Sorry to bring you in so early after the party last night, but something has happened," Jon said.

"Tell me that the cure for hangovers has finally been developed," Ellie said.

Jon looked at Ellie, unamused. Everyone quickly got the message and stood a little straighter.

"Things are moving faster than anticipated. We'll be jumping to Jangali in three days."

A chorus of protest erupted from the group. Jon closed his eyes and raised a hand. "Stop."

The room went silent except for the creaks of chairs from the crew flying the ship.

"How do you have the stored energy to make a jump?" Sarah said. "I didn't realize anyone had that much energy these days. The last jumps stopped only days after the Essens stopped sending power."

"I'm one of the few who has the resources to make a jump like this, but I'm not the only one."

"Well shit," Russ said, "we should have asked for more money!"

Jon laughed, and it released some of the tension in the room. "I paid you as much as I could, Russ. *Stargone* doesn't have enough energy to make a second jump. This is a one-time deal. There is a lot more going on, and I promise that most of it will be explained soon."

"So why are we jumping?" Tokomoto asked.

"My source on Jangali has located the dynamic. It's a twenty-two-year-old boy from a small village in the northern reaches. He lived in one of the most isolated places in all the worlds. He knows almost nothing about technology or human history. He's a farmer of some sort. We think that his forebears must have crash-landed there or something. Either way, they've been living there ever since."

"Seriously?" Amira said. "How long have these people lived there? How have they survived?"

"I honestly don't know," Jon said, "but I get the impression that it's been at least a few hundred years."

"Well isn't this great," Silvestre said, stone-faced. "Our payday is an ignorant farmer who doesn't even know what a toilet is."

Russ and Vincent laughed.

"Don't judge him so quickly," Jon said.

"That doesn't explain why we need to jump there. He sounds pretty safe to me, hidden in isolation," Sarah said.

"You said that he *lived* in an isolated place. Past tense. Where is he now?" Ellie asked.

"That's why we're jumping. The twin dynamics in control of Jangali have implemented"—Jon stumbled for a moment—"vile practices. The man we seek has been a slave for ten months now."

The others looked as if Jon had just vomited on the floor.

"A *slave?*" Sarah said. "There is slavery still in existence? How is that possible?"

Jon shook his head. "I don't know, but we're not going to let it continue."

The others nodded, their eyes conveying a resolve that had not been there before.

"We jump in three days," Jon said. "I need you to finish your projects as quickly as possible. Amira, how close is the shuttle to being ready?"

"I thought I would have several more years to work," she said. "It is not ready."

"We've got to have that shuttle."

Amira sighed. "It will be done in three days. Not very safe. But done."

"Vincent," Jon said, "you know how close we are. I need you working around the clock with Ellie. You can sleep when you get there. Understood?"

Vincent nodded.

"Tokomoto, Russ, Silvestre, we are hitting the ground as soon as we reach orbit. Prepare yourselves. We'll talk more about the details tomorrow."

"What can I do?" Sarah said.

She asked with a vigor Jon had not seen in her since she was young.

"I know we don't have a lot of info, but find out everything you can about the Fulgurian people. They are a woodland tribe that resists the twins and their capital city. I have no idea how, but I want to know."

"Fulgurian," Sarah said. "Got it."

"Everyone here also needs to read up on Grecian, Asura, and House assets."

"Ah, come on, Jon," Russ said. "Can't you just tell us? I don't have the patience for reading right now, not with all the excitement."

Jon sighed. "Fine. I'll give a brief overview for those who are incurably lazy."

Russ smiled like a kid who had just gotten his way.

"The Grecian Empire is ruled by Emperor Phylus. He's been in charge for close to ninety years now, and nobody's sure how many years he's purchased. The contingent they've sent should be formidable, though a bit outdated. Their resources are stretched thin, since they always have to keep an eye on the neighboring Free Worlds."

"What about Khumbuza?" Amira asked. "Is Aoko personally seeing to this?"

"Yes," Jon said, "but she's gotten better. I spoke with her not ten years ago."

Vincent grunted. "You say that like it was yesterday and not more than half my life."

"I think Khumbuza is our best chance to form an alliance with. Do you still speak with Farah?" Jon said.

A cloud of anger passed over Amira's face. "No. And why would you make an alliance with a House over a government? That is not like you."

"This is a special situation."

Sarah cleared her throat. "I've been working with the Cynix Corporation for the past eight years or so, and though they look healthy from the outside, I think they're on the way out. Not one of those peaceful-die-in-your-sleep deaths either. More like indiscriminate violent death throes that will strike anyone near."

Jon nodded. "I suppose this is their final gambit to get back in the game, then. Their desperation might be dangerous. As for the Republican Guard and House Harain, we're disturbingly in the dark. They've been quiet, but have been gaining power for the last twenty years."

"How can a whole House with billions of people under its umbrella be secretive?" Ellie asked.

"Just read up on what I send to you, Ellie. It'll make more sense."

Russ looked up from a report he was glancing at. "Is the Oligarchy sending anyone?"

"No, Russ. They're not even on the list you're looking at."

"Well, I know, but I just love the toys they bring. Have you tried out the MP-48? Kicks like a mule, but the sheer power is Russ-approved."

Silvestre was absorbed in the report, but she spared a moment to ask, "What is the Asura Republic doing? They never leave their planet unless it's an emergency."

Jon shrugged. "They're closest to Jangali? They like being apolitical, but with every year that passes, they realize that their isolation will be their downfall. They even elected a new president. He's ambitious."

"What about Queen Isabella?" Russ asked. "She's a fox!"

Jon rubbed his eyes. "All right, that's enough questions. Read the rest on your own. Let's get to work."

The others left the command sphere with a sense of energy and purpose. Jon was disgusted by the idea of slavery, but he knew that the others would be as well, and he used that fact to get them fully on board with his cause. Their full and undivided participation was needed if he was going to pull off everything he had planned. As the last of them left the sphere and the door slid shut, Treyges stepped into view. The others always seemed to forget about him.

"That was well done, sir."

Jon shrugged. "It was necessary." Treyges was staring off with a peculiar look. "What is it?" Jon asked.

"There have been several oddities since we departed. I'm beginning to wonder if one of them is the cause of that," Treyges said. He gestured at the door.

Jon frowned. "Do you really think so?"

"It's possible."

Jon stared long and hard at the door, his face deeply concerned. He looked back to Treyges. "You'll keep an eye on them?"

Treyges bowed his head in assent.

CHAPTER FOURTEEN

en months. Ten demeaning, miserable months. Nearly every day
there'd be a moment where his enslavement would hit Saiph and
make him feel empty, like his soul had just vacated his body. He'd have
to forcibly grab it and put it back in through the power of positive
thinking:

*Where there is life, there is hope. The world will turn, and tomorrow
will be different.*

But tomorrow never seemed to come. He watched for any opportunity—waited for the smallest opening. He had listened and asked questions, but in reality, he was no closer to escaping than he was on his first
day at camp sixty-two. He was only better at keeping his head down,
pleasing the guards, and avoiding trouble. Even with Alistair, Charlotte, and Nico's, combined effort, he still thought that their escape was
improbable, if not impossible. Charlotte was beginning to lose hope. He
didn't blame her.

"I can't go on like this," she said, breaking down into tears over her
breakfast. She often cried these days, but Saiph understood her frustration. He constantly thought about Altai and his family. Not knowing
their fate pained him like a physical wound. The chance of seeing them

again was what kept him going, yet if he thought of them for too long, it became too painful to bear.

He had to get out.

"Chin up, Charlotte," Alistair said. "We'll find a way yet. We just need to take bigger risks."

"That's a good way to wind up with a few scars across your back," Nico pointed out.

They spoke quietly at the edge of the cafeteria. They had learned the hard way that the other slaves were just as dangerous as the guards. Most of them were criminals, brought here to work for violent offenses. They were cruel and opportunistic, willing to sell out a fellow slave for an extra loaf of bread.

"So we get a few lashes," Saiph whispered. "We've come to an impasse. We either try something new, or we stay here for the rest of our lives."

The others nodded hesitantly.

Though he was no closer to escape, Saiph was learning. After he'd seen his Core Verse in the Book of Light, he'd become even more interested in it, if that was possible. At first, he thought that the Skyfallers actually had knowledge of the Verses and that they weren't beyond hope. For months, he was convinced that their best chance of escape was to remind the Skyfallers of the Verses. To have them see the light and set them free.

What a waste of time. The Skyfallers didn't care about the Verses, and they never would. If anything, it made the whole situation worse because it had left Saiph feeling so hopeless and disappointed.

After Saiph had spent those first months scanning *The Big Bang to Boundless* for more Verses, and not finding a single one, he gave up and started reading again. Nothing he read was as exciting as finding a Verse, but it *was* interesting. He felt like he was close to understanding something, but he didn't know what it was, and he wasn't willing to wait any longer.

"Three more weeks," Saiph said, "then I'm going for it, one way or another."

All his life, Saiph had stayed comfortable in his village, taking no risks, understanding nothing of the outside world. He'd always thought that he couldn't, because of his breathing and leg problems. All that didn't matter now, though. If he wanted to see his family again, he would have to run through the pain and without the air he needed. It was time for risk. It was time for a little exploring.

When he brought the topic up with the group, Nico and Alistair immediately agreed. Charlotte needed a bit more convincing, but she was on board after a couple hours of persuasion. They would wait until the last night of the next winterweek, when everything was at its darkest, then take a closer look at the forbidden areas around camp sixty-two. During the next few days, they made sure that their shirts and pants got an extra splash of dark-purple yokai blood, thinking it would help hide them during the night. They talked quietly about the plan during the day. When the night came, they felt ready.

"One last time," Alistair said. "Saiph and Nico are going west and then heading south. Charlotte and I are going east and then swinging north. Caution is more important than territory scouted, but too much caution and it's all for nothing. If anything happens, rendezvous at the well next to the barracks. Everyone got it?" They nodded. "All right, let's light this beetle barrel up."

"You stole a beetle barrel?" Nico said. "I thought we were going for stealth!"

Alistair sighed. "It's an expression, Nico."

"Well, I don't get it. What is that even supposed to mean? If a beetle barrel—"

"Erlik's breath, Nico," Saiph said, "just let it go. We're leaving." Saiph nodded at Charlotte and Alistair. "Good luck."

Saiph and Nico set out, sticking to the brush as much as they could. They had both grown up near the woods, and they crept with enviable quiet. They mostly passed other barracks, and three times they saw that those barracks were watched over by guards with thunder sticks. Only once did they see guards on the road, and the roar of their vehicle announced them so boisterously that Saiph and Nico had plenty of time to hide. They had traveled just over two miles when they came to the wall they had been told about on their first day. It was massive and built of solid, smooth stone. Where stone like that came from, Saiph didn't know.

"Will you look at that," Nico whispered. "Ever seen anything like it?"

Saiph shook his head. "Should we check it out?"

"I don't know; one of those guard towers is right there. I think we should head south."

Saiph nodded, relieved.

They followed the curvature of the wall and eventually crossed a small stream where an eight-legged creature Saiph had never seen before bounded through the bushes and startled them. After another half mile, they came upon a building that didn't look like a barracks. They waited for ten minutes, but there didn't seem to be anyone else around.

"Ready?" Nico asked.

"Ready."

They ran across the open ground, then hid behind a large metal container near the building. It smelled awful. When nothing happened, they moved to the door and, as quietly as they could, opened it. A small light barely illuminated half the room, but it was enough for them to see that no one was there. They slid inside and closed the door behind them.

"What do you think this is?" Nico asked.

"No idea. It's not a bedroom or a kitchen, right?"

"Let's take a look around."

Without disturbing anything too much, they sifted through papers and books that were sitting on a large wooden table. None of the writing made sense to Saiph, but he grabbed a stack anyway and put it to the side. He opened one of the drawers and found a small black thunder stick inside. Saiph took a step back, remembering what it had done to Gillums.

"What is it?" Nico asked.

"It's a thunder stick. You point it at someone and thunder erupts from it, leaving whomever you were pointing it at bloody on the ground, dead."

"Let's take it! With magic like that, we could definitely make it out of here. Think it might work on a tower?"

"I don't know," Saiph said. "I don't really like it."

Nico lifted it out of the drawer. "I'm taking it."

"Be careful!" Saiph said. "And don't point it at me."

"I won't, I won't. Calm down, mother dearest."

They heard a roaring sound outside, and lights came shining in through the window. Saiph and Nico dove to the ground and crawled over to the door. The roaring cut off. A truck door slammed shut. Footsteps approached the front door and Saiph and Nico looked at each other in terror. They frantically scanned the room, and Saiph pointed to another door. They quickly crawled to it. The room was absurdly tiny, and was filled with pleasant-smelling clothes hanging from a horizontal pole. They shut the door as someone entered the front room.

There was no sound, and Saiph tried not to breathe, but fear was making his heart pound in his chest. If he didn't get enough air, he'd have an attack. The footsteps started up again, followed by a light that shone through the seam of the door they were hiding behind. Saiph and Nico drew their feet back, not wanting any of the light to touch them. The person on the other side coughed, and Nico flinched. They waited there for several minutes in sheer terror.

A strange ringing sound suddenly permeated the room. Once. Twice.

"This is Lieutenant Lyons," a woman said. Silence for a moment. "How many were caught? Two? Just whip them and get it over with."

Saiph looked at Nico, but he was just as confused. Who was she talking to?

"No. No. Fine. I'll be there in five minutes." There was a click. "Imbeciles and incompetents, that's all they give me."

Footsteps again. Light off. Door opening and closing.

Saiph and Nico waited for several minutes before slowly opening the door and creeping out. The truck that the woman had come in was gone and there was no sign of anyone else.

"I think we should head back now," Saiph said.

They made it back to the barracks without incident, the thunder stick and papers jammed into their pockets. They were back at least two hours before dawn, yet Alistair and Charlotte had yet to arrive. They assured themselves that they would be back soon.

An hour later, they heard one of the loud vehicles pull up to their barracks. Someone was sobbing outside. The door was thrown open, waking up everyone who wasn't already up.

"Everyone outside!" Worthington boomed. The barracks scurried to obey. Alistair and Charlotte were on their hands and knees, their clothes ripped and their backs bloodied. Alistair had a bruise the size of an apple forming over his left eye.

"These two," Worthington said, "were caught outside of the barracks after hours. Not only did they break the rules, but they embarrassed me in front of my superiors. This is utter horse shit! I won't have it! Since none of you deemed it necessary to tell us that these two had left, you will all receive two lashes. Turn around."

Saiph was terrified, but he turned anyway, scared of more punishment if he didn't. A few people sobbed quietly. The first crack of the whip lit the air like a bolt of lightning and was follow by a yell of pain instead of thunder. Saiph couldn't see it, facing away as he was, but he could hear lash after lash, closer and closer. When he heard it once more, and the woman beside him cried out, he purposely tried to relax himself.

He felt it before he heard it. A searing pain across his back that burned like fire. It hurt, but he was no stranger to pain, and he remained silent. The second lash hurt even more when it intersected with the first lash. Still, Saiph didn't flinch or make a sound. If anything, he stood straighter. The rest of the whipping went by in a haze, and Saiph collected himself as it did. A few minutes later, it was over.

"Turn around," Worthington said. He glared at them, nostrils flaring. "You will never leave this barracks without permission again. If anyone does, the rest of you will alert me immediately. Half rations today. Get to work."

That next night, when the torches were doused and the barracks was quiet, Saiph reached into the hidden nook of his cot and pulled out the small stick of metal. His back hurt fiercely with every movement, and his leg was a constant discomfort nowadays, but he got as cozy as he could. Once settled, he ran his finger over the edge of the metal, and it expanded into the Book of Light. As usual, *The Bing Bang to Boundless* appeared on the glass, but he didn't feel like reading at the moment. He wanted to speak with it again.

He tried writing on it, but it only made marks on the book. He tried shaking it, but that didn't do anything either. Running his finger across the leaf symbol again would only close it. He tried every movement he could think of. Twisting it, flicking it, tapping it... When he tapped the leaf symbol three times, the book suddenly disappeared and was replaced with a blank gray background. Saiph placed his finger on the glass and a bright mark appeared, then slowly faded away. Saiph wrote, *Help*, then watched it vanish.

He waited for over a minute before a reply came. *Are you all right, Saiph Calthari?*

Saiph's heart lurched, and he quickly wrote back. *I am trapped as a slave in a big camp and must escape with my friends so that I can find my family. Can you help me?*

The response came quicker this time. *No, I cannot. Not yet. Stay put. Read the book I have presented to you.*

Saiph frowned; the book was doing him no good. The Book of Light clearly didn't understand his situation. *What good is a book when I am a slave? My family needs me. My friends need me. Please help me.*

It is not just a book. The Big Bang to Boundless *is the truth of the past. It is real. You* must *keep reading. You need to understand. I am sorry, but camp sixty-two is the safest place for you right now. The twins are looking.*

The safest place for him? This book didn't know what it was like. Not knowing if he'd be whipped the next day for some trivial infraction or docked a food ration for giving someone the wrong look. And claiming that the book was real? That men actually came from monkeys? That the universe exploded outward from something smaller than he could see? Utter rubbish.

I do not believe you, Saiph wrote back, *I will do this on my own.*

He ran his finger over the leaflike symbol and closed the Book of Light. All magic had done for him so far was take him away from his family and friends. He would do this his own way.

Pain and despair kept Saiph from sleeping, so he went outside and sat down on a log against the side of the barracks. He gingerly put himself into a position that was the least painful, but it was difficult. His leg had gotten worse since he'd gotten here, and he worried that his body was taking too much abuse. Saiph closed his eyes, and took deep breaths to allow his lungs a reprieve.

After a few minutes, Saiph opened his eyes to the sky and its thousands of glittering stars. Kayra dominated the horizon. The planet was mostly a soft orange, but it was smeared with lines of white and red, as if it were painted by the gods when they were children. A large hurricane was forming on its southern pole, a vortex of white cloud. Saiph had always enjoyed watching Kayra and its shifting color. He could stare at it for hours at a time and not get bored.

One of the worst conditions of camp sixty-two was the lack of distractions. No games of find the yokai or stories around the dinner table. His mind was consumed by work, plans of escape, and thoughts of his family. That's why he liked the Book of Light so much. For a little while each night, he would be absorbed by the tale and forget all about his troubles. But the book was letting him down. Kayra might not be as good of a distraction as the Book of Light, but it was more dependable.

Saiph heard footsteps on the path leading up to the barracks and tensed. Guards hardly visited in the night, but maybe they would after a few slaves had been caught sneaking around. He tried to stand, ready to hide, but he couldn't get up. The figure popped his head around the corner and held up a hand.

"Only Chet, boy. Keep ya underclothes from spottin'."

"Chet?" Saiph said. "What are you doing here in the middle of the night? They'll catch you!"

"Nah, they won't be catchin' old Chet. Sneakier than I look! Hah!" Chet sat down on the log next to him. "What ya be doin' up in the middle of the night, Saiphy? Somethin' be botherin' ya?"

"You mean other than being a slave for the people who abducted me, murdered my people, and destroyed my home?"

"Still harpin' on that, are ya?"

"I've got to get out of here, Chet. I know you'll try to talk me out of it, but I can't take it any longer."

Chet was silent. The crickets sang in perfect harmony around them, and a howl of wind made the leaves dance.

"Ever hear the tale of Heron of Alexandria?" Chet asked.

Saiph shook his head.

"He was a man who was livin' many a thousand years ago in a place called Egypt. He was a smarty, this Heron. His brain was stronger than a yokai's arm. With only his mind, he created new *technologies*. Ya knowin' this word?" Saiph shook his head again. "Ya knowin' what an invention is?"

"Yes," Saiph said, eyeing him. "I'm not an idiot, Chet."

"Just checkin'!" Chet said. "Well, technology is sort o' like an invention. Like the makin' of a new tool. Except the tool is crazy smart and can do incredible things! Incredible, I tell ya. Like flyin' through the air or talkin' to someone from a hundred miles away like they were right next to ya."

"So Heron of Alexandria created these tools?"

"Well, no, not those exactly. He created somethin' called a steam engine. You know how steam be rising from the pot when ya fire it? Well, imagin' you got a whole heap load of steam. More steam than you can hold in your mind. All that steam gots to go somewhere, right? Least, that's what Heron was thinking. He trapped the steam in a box and had that steam push on something, like a wagon wheel. You catchin' what I'm throwin'?"

Saiph sat and thought about it for a moment. He didn't truly understand how steam could move a wagon, but the idea was interesting, so he nodded. "What did Heron do with it?"

"Nothing," Chet said. "The library where he worked burned down and he was killed. The great steam engine invention was lost and was not thought of again for over a thousand years."

"That sounds sad. The world might have used a steam-moving wagon," Saiph said.

"You'd think that," Chet said, "but it may have worked out for the best. Some think that people weren't ready for that kind of power. That they might of used technology in all the wrong ways. That sound familiar to you?"

"Not really," Saiph said.

Chet sighed. "Think on what I told ya before you go all Monte Cristo on me, yes'm?"

"You know, I don't understand half the things you say, Chet, but you're not half bad."

Chet laughed. "Think on it," he said, grabbing Saiph's shoulder. Chet stood up and walked into the darkness. He was so quiet, Saiph barely noticed him leave.

CHAPTER FIFTEEN

"The jump through space will commence in approximately twelve hours. Please know your point of stability. The jump through space will commence in approximately twelve hours. Please know your point of stability."

Jon was so focused, he barely heard the ship-wide announcement. It had been playing once per waking hour for the last day and a half. He stared at his tablet, looking at the diagram of the human form.

"This isn't going to work!" Vincent abruptly said, dropping a piece of equipment on the table and throwing his hands up. He looked crazed and his breathing was heavy. He hadn't slept since Jon had told them about the jump.

"What's not going to work?" Jon asked, keeping at his task.

"We're going to need more points of extraction for the suit."

"Didn't we agree that six would be enough?"

Vincent ran his hands through his hair. "It won't work."

Jon sighed and picked up his comm. "Silvestre, it's Jon. We need you in lab twenty-three as soon as you get here. Bring your aura suit."

"On my way," she said.

Jon walked over to a counter in the corner and poured more coffee into a mug. He extended it to Vincent. "Don't worry, we'll get it. We're close. Deep breaths, all right?"

Vincent closed his eyes and nodded. Jon patted him gently on the shoulder before walking back to his seat. Silvestre came in a few minutes later, a small rectangular box attached to her hip.

"Everything all right?" she asked, looking around.

"Yeah, everything's fine. We just have a couple questions about your aura suit."

Silvestre frowned. "My aura suit? Why?"

Jon glanced at Vincent, then back to Silvestre. "Vincent and I have been building one for the dynamic on Jangali. It's...an unorthodox model, to say the least."

Silvestre's cheeks puffed out, and she sat heavily into a chair. "You're really going to give this person a suit? You know that once you give it to him, there's nothing you'll be able to do to control him?"

"I don't want to control him, Sil," Jon said. "If this person turns out to be a crazed lunatic, then I won't give it to him. But I want it to be ready in case I do."

Sil shook her head, unconvinced. "What do you want to know? To be honest, for how much I depend on this thing, I don't have a great understanding of how it works."

Vincent cleared his throat. "Most dynamics don't know it, but the energy within you that gets transferred to the suit comes from multiple points."

Silvestre looked taken aback. "Really?"

"Put it on. I'll show you."

Silvestre looked to Jon, who nodded at her. The box at her side suddenly exploded into motion, unfolding and covering her body in a hurricane of complexity. It kept unfolding until she was encased entirely in silver metal. When the last piece slipped into place, a low thrum of power emanated from the suit, and her red eyes glowed brightly through slits in the mask.

"Wow," Vincent said, "I've never seen one unfold like that. Which company built yours?"

Silvestre pointed at Jon. "He made it for me."

Vincent looked over, impressed. Jon winked at him, then turned back to Silvestre. "If you focus, you can feel specific points where the energy is transferring from your body to the aura suit."

Silvestre went still as she tried to feel the points of transition. Jon had given the suit to her when she was only ten years old. He'd seen her do incredible things while wearing it, and it had gotten him out of trouble more than a few times. It had also cost her a hand.

"There," Silvestre said, "I feel it. There are...three?"

"Very good," Jon said. "One on the small of your back, one on your naval, one on your upper chest. Sil, what's the greatest amount of energy you've ever had to use at once?"

"I think it was about twenty-eight percent."

"And how did it make you feel?"

"Horrible, actually. How did you know that?"

Jon looked back at the aura suit schematic on his tablet. "Because when a dynamic tries to force too much energy through the conduits, there's some kickback. I don't know why it's uncomfortable for you all, but that's what's happening."

"You still think six is going to be enough?" Vincent asked.

"I really don't know," Jon said, "it might be. We don't know exactly how much energy this dynamic is going to command. Still, you're probably right. We should air on the side of caution and put more points of extraction. Ten?"

Vincent nodded tiredly. "Ten," he agreed. "But where do we put them?"

Jon thought for a moment. "Let's have them augment the flight systems. Two on the upper back, two near the heel."

Silvestre's aura suit broke apart and started to fold back into the box at her side. It was done in less than ten seconds. "I still don't think you should give—"

She was cut off as a caution light on the ceiling flared to life. Jon picked up his comm and opened a line to Treyges. "What's happened?"

"House Harain, the Grecian Empire, and House Khumbuza have

all jumped to within a three-week journey of Jangali. Sir, someone must have told them we were going to jump..."

"Prepare the ship for an immediate jump. Get everyone to their points of stability as quickly as possible."

"Yes, sir."

Jon frantically issued more orders to get the ship ready. Though most of his attention was focused on this task, there was also a part of his mind that couldn't keep from wondering who the mole in his inner circle was.

CHAPTER SIXTEEN

No matter how hard he tried, Saiph couldn't keep away from the Book of Light. He was angry with it for not helping him, but not angry enough to stop reading. The stories he read were fascinating. He read about great leaders like Alexander the Great, Queen Elizabeth, Genghis Khan, and Joan of Arc. He loved the idea of a horse. The drawings of the fairy-tale animal were incredibly lifelike, and he would have given his left pinky finger to ride one. They seemed so real to him that he began to doubt that the book was purely fictional. It didn't read like a bedtime story, and while some of it was obviously made up, other aspects made sense.

He thought long and hard about what Chet had told him, how technology and tools could be used to accomplish incredible feats. While reading through the book, he started to see what Chet was getting at, and it finally dawned on him that the Skyfallers might not be magical at all, but just had better tools than they did.

He tried to read as much as he could in the brief snippets of time he had at night before bed, but the book was far too long. Instead, Saiph skipped around, absorbing as much as possible. He never turned to the end, though. He hated knowing the ending of a story before it was finished. Ayanda would always jump straight to the last page and then taunt him with her knowledge, threatening to tell him if he didn't do as she said. The memory made him smile, but it quickly soured. He prayed she was alive. He would have suffered everything he'd endured a hundred times over just to know that his family was still breathing. But he would never find that out here. He would not—could not—stay any longer. It was time.

Charlotte stayed away from them after the whipping. Saiph, Alistair, and Nico attempted to coax her back into their schemes, but she wouldn't even speak to them. They could only hope she'd change her mind when they made their escape. They had lost sleep for weeks while they formulated a plan, but Saiph was proud of what they'd come up with. Its success relied heavily on distraction, since they all agreed that escape by force was as useless as it was stupid.

Though it was Nico's fiendish idea, it was Alistair and Saiph who were able to think of a way to pull it off. They decided to use the thunder stick and a fire to cause the most confusion possible. To do this, Saiph and Alistair stole four boxes from the volt farm and chiseled tiny holes of equal size into the bottom of two of them. They stacked the boxes in pairs and filled the top boxes to the brim with water and counted to see how long it took the water to drip from one box to its pair below it. Then they repeated the experiment, except this time, they placed the bottom box on a small ramp. As it filled with water, the box would slowly gain weight and start to slip down the incline. They tied a thin length of rope to each bottom box, once connecting to a thunder stick, the other to a candle. When the first box slipped far enough down, it would pull on the thin piece of metal on the thunder stick, hopefully causing the weapon to produce its thunder-like boom. Saiph had seen a few pictures in the Book of Light, which made him fairly certain that this was how the thunder stick worked. The second pair of boxes was easier; all they had to do was rig the rope so that it would knock over a candle into kindling.

Altogether, it took an hour for the boxes to trigger the thunder stick and start the fire. On the night of their escape, they would place the distraction, make their way to the other side of camp, and then scale the wall as soon as the thunder stick and fire went off. It took them the entire week to prepare.

"How do we know that one of the others won't go running to Worthington? None of them want to get whipped again," Nico said.

"We be as quiet as possible," Alistair explained. "When we're outside, we wait for ten minutes to make sure nobody comes out after us. When it's clear, we tie off the door so that no one can leave."

Saiph nodded. "We've added an hour to the timeline to account for any unforeseen problems."

"And Charlotte?" Nico asked.

"I'll talk to her," Alistair said. "Try and convince her one last time."

Saiph tried to get a couple hours of sleep before they were meant to leave, but he was too nervous. Instead, he pulled out the book and stuck it into his shoe to take with him. He couldn't leave it behind. It was the only magic he had, and as much as he hated to admit it, he had come to love it.

Saiph sat on the edge of his cot in the dark and sifted through his thoughts. He *had* to get home. At first, he'd sworn that he wouldn't go home without his father, but he had no idea where his father was. He wasn't in camp sixty-two—of that, Saiph was sure. He thought that his father would have wanted him to find his mother, brother, and sister first anyway. Saiph wouldn't give up on him, though. He would go home to check on his family, but then he would find him, even if he had to walk all of Jangali on his bad leg to do so.

In the barracks, when the snores grew loud enough, Saiph glanced outside and up at the stars. It was time. He walked to the front door where Nico was crouched.

"Alistair here yet?" Saiph whispered. Nico shook his head.

It was another couple of minutes before Alistair showed up, Charlotte trailing behind him. Saiph and Nico smiled. Charlotte shook her head and smiled back.

"Let's get the hell out of here."

When no one followed them out, they tied the double doors together and went to get their supplies. They had hidden the boxes containing everything they needed in the brush a quarter mile up the road. Everyone quickly grabbed their assigned items and started to move quietly to the eastern wall.

They hadn't been able to leave the barracks since they were caught a couple weeks back, but Alistair and Charlotte had come across an abandoned section of wood on their first outing that would work perfectly for their fire. It hadn't rained in days, and Saiph touched the brush and trees when they arrived; they were as dry as they could have hoped for.

"Pour the water in ten minutes?" Saiph whispered.

"Ten minutes," Alistair said.

Saiph and Nico snuck off to the nearest guard tower.

"This close enough?" Nico asked.

Distant laughter came from one of the towers.

Saiph breathed out. "Yeah, think so."

They set up the two boxes and ramp in a small tree that was covered by a much larger tree. Then they tied the rope from the sliding box onto the trigger so that it would fire once the box had slid far enough down.

"You got the time?" Nico asked.

"Yeah, fifteen seconds left."

558. 559. 600.

Saiph and Nico poured the water into the box above, checked to make sure it was dripping, and then hurried back to Alistair and Charlotte.

They reentered the wooded area to the soft sound of dripping water. Alistair raised his eyebrows and both his thumbs, and Saiph nodded to him. They gathered the remaining rope, food, and water, and made the trek to the wall. Several vehicles went speeding by, but they were heading south, which they could only hope was a good sign. Maybe there was some sort of banquet this evening? Saiph prayed they were all stupidly drunk. Perhaps every guard at the camp would accidentally and simultaneously fire upon one another, killing their entire staff in one fell swoop. Yes, that would be ideal.

When they reached their rendezvous point, they sat and waited for their distractions to spark.

"I just wanted to say," Alistair said, "that no matter what happens, it has been a privilege to scheme and plot alongside you. Perhaps not you, Nico, but definitely the rest of you."

Nico cuffed Alistair on the arm. "I hope you all won't blame me for tripping Alistair when the dogs are on our tails."

"Thank you," Charlotte said more seriously. "Thank you for convincing me to come. I don't want to live and die here."

Saiph nodded. "When we get to the wood..."

"*If* we get to the wood," Nico said.

"No, *when* we get to the wood, split up in different directions. Not too far, mind you, but just enough so that they can't get us all in one go. Run like Erlik Ata himself is about to put you in the ground, because that's essentially what will happen if we're caught."

The others looked between one another, and then Alistair said, "How's your leg?"

Saiph shook his head and looked at the ground. "Don't wait for me. Just go, okay?"

"Saiph..." Nico said.

"No, Nico. This is the way it has to be. Promise me you'll go."

They agreed in the end, though Saiph could tell they didn't feel good about it. They were good friends.

"Anyone have an appropriate Verse?" Alistair asked.

They thought for a moment, then Charlotte said, "*And the day came when the risk to remain tight in a bud was more painful than the risk it took to blossom."*

Saiph nodded. "Well chosen."

They readied their packs and hid a bit closer to the wall. They had chosen this particular section because it was equidistant between two guard towers and, most importantly, had a very large volt tree whose branches easily surpassed the height of the wall. Its bark had blackened marks and scars of white lines around its base where the Skyfallers tried to cut it down, but a volt tree this large was unnaturally tough. They'd probably given up, thinking it was too much work when no one ever escaped anyway.

"Any second now..." Charlotte whispered.

The wood caught more quickly than expected, and they could see it burning even from this distance. Flames rose forty feet into the air. Not thirty seconds later, the thunder stick went off, booming into the wind five times. They could hear guards to either side of them shouting and pointing to the fire.

Saiph ran.

He watched the others sprinting in front of him as he hobbled behind, gritting his teeth in pain. When he got to the tree, Alistair was already throwing a rock with a rope tied to it. He hurled it as high as he could, aiming for a thick branch. He missed and it fell to the ground. He tried again, missed again.

"Come on, Alistair, you've got this," Saiph said.

Alistair hurled the rock a third time, and it soared over the branch and down the other side. The long rope now sat atop the thick branch. Saiph quickly grabbed the rock end of the rope and tied it to the trunk of a smaller tree. Niko tugged on the dangling part of the rope to make sure it was secure.

"Here goes nothing."

Nico was off, climbing the rope with surprising alacrity. Saiph was next, followed by Charlotte, then Alistair. This was perhaps the most nerve-racking part of the plan. Not only were they unreasonably high off the ground, but if the guards from the tower to the north looked this way, there would be nothing to hide them from view. Saiph climbed as fiercely as he prayed. He forcefully made himself look up at the branch and not down at the ground or at the guard tower.

After an intense few minutes, they made it to the branch. No one had noticed them.

Keep moving. Have to keep moving.

They climbed farther up the tree to a branch that sprawled over the wall. They moved across it, grabbing the branch with hands and knees and sliding themselves forward inch by inch. The bark was scratching Saiph's skin terribly, but adrenaline made it feel small. He reached the top of the wall and straddled it, letting go of the tree. The others did the same.

Alistair had tied the end of the rope to his foot so that it followed him up. He quickly untied it once he was settled on the wall. The other end was still tied to the trunk of the tree below. Charlotte pulled out another long rope and tied it to the first, doubling its length, then threw it down the other side of the wall. It would still be a bit short, but they hoped it would be long enough for them to jump the rest of the way to the ground without breaking any bones. Nico climbed down first. They heard a thump hit the ground without a scream, and then Saiph followed him. It was easier going down than up. He put his legs against the wall and descended a few feet at a time. When he hit the ground, Nico grabbed his shoulder, hope radiating across his face. Saiph peered up at Charlotte descending. She was going slow.

"Come on," Saiph whispered. "Come on."

"Hey!" They heard someone shout in the distance. "Look!" A larger light came on and centered directly on Alistair, who had taken the hint and was now descending quickly.

"We've got runners!" An incredibly loud shriek filled the air, and Saiph knew that it couldn't mean anything good for them. Thunder sticks boomed from the guard towers around them, and stone began to fall from where Alistair was climbing.

"Jump!" Saiph screamed.

Alistair didn't hesitate. He let go of the rope and fell to the ground with a sickening thud. The thunder sticks were still going off, causing the dirt to stir up around them. Saiph dove at Alistair and pulled him from the light and into the surrounding forest. The weapons were still firing, but once they were twenty feet into the trees, Saiph felt that they weren't in imminent danger any longer.

"You all right, Alistair?"

He winced. "My ankle..."

Saiph bent down to touch it, but Alistair grunted in pain. "Go," he said.

"We're not leaving you," Charlotte said.

"You'll never make it with me in tow. Didn't we agree to do the same because of Saiph's leg? I'm going to walk and then hide; it's our best shot. Now go, there's not much time."

Saiph bent down and pulled Alistair into a hug. "If you don't make it out, I'll come looking for you. I promise."

"Me too," Nico said.

"I'm going to stay with him," Charlotte said.

"No!" Alistair said, pushing her away. "They'll just send you to the coliseum too."

More of the weapons went off, closer this time. Saiph could hear dogs barking in the distance. He ducked his head, gave one last look at Alistair, Nico, and Charlotte, and then disappeared into the woods.

Saiph's heart pumped out of control, and sweat poured from every pore in his body. He had no idea how deep the woods went, but he was far in now. He hadn't caught sight of Nico or Charlotte since they'd split up, and he could only hope they were still free. Saiph saw a clearing up ahead and limped toward it. He stopped in the middle and looked up at the sky to get his bearings. Tengrii's brightest was still in front of him and he pushed onward, confident in his direction.

Saiph stared at the ground as he jogged, then walked, trying not to trip over anything. He knew that he needed to look up and check his surroundings, but he was going for speed—though the guards would probably laugh at his progress. He didn't care, though; he was getting as far away from camp sixty-two as possible. After several hours, Saiph finally burst through to the other side of the forest and into the most beautiful sunrise he had ever seen. The sun had just crested the horizon and was reflecting across a river that sparkled like a thousand baby voltbeetles.

Saiph had never been so thirsty in his life. He dropped down to his knees and rapidly scooped water into his mouth. It was cold and clean and he could have slept for weeks on the bank of that river, but he couldn't linger. He took deep breaths of desperately needed oxygen, then forded into the water. About halfway across, Saiph heard something in the distance, but he couldn't make out what it was. All he knew was that it was getting louder. He picked up the pace.

The sound was coming closer, but there was nowhere to hide now that he was out of the forest. The only thing he could do was keep going. Still, the sound got closer. Then Saiph realized why he couldn't see where the noise was coming from. He looked up and saw the impossible. A metal container was flying through the air with several men inside of it. Like a sytin bird, it swooped to the ground with a steady grace. Guards jumped out of it, and Saiph knew it was over.

He fell to the ground, exhausted beyond mere physical tiredness. He turned away from the flying monstrosity and toward the sunrise. He looked at it with the utmost envy. No one could catch the sun or the stars. He took a deep breath of cool air and closed his eyes. He heard footsteps and then felt a stab as an intense shock rippled through his body. He fell into unconsciousness.

CHAPTER SEVENTEEN

S aiph awoke in a place he didn't recognize. This time, his prison did have bars. He sat up and tried to scrub away the pounding in his head.

"You awake?"

"Who's there?" Saiph said.

"It's Alistair." A figure limped over from the corner and put a hand on his shoulder. "Are you all right?"

"I think so. You?"

"Ankle is a bit troubled, but I'm okay."

They sat in silence for a moment, stewing over their failure.

"Have you seen Nico or Charlotte?" Saiph asked.

"No. I hope they made it."

"Me too," Saiph said, managing to smile. "Any idea where we are?"

"The coliseum," Alistair said. "They transported us in a truck. You were out for nearly the whole day. Your breathing has been...bad."

"I'll be fine. What's the coliseum like?"

Alistair limped to the side of the barred cage and gingerly lowered himself to the sandy floor. "I saw it when they were hauling us in. It's huge, Saiph. I wouldn't have believed it if I hadn't seen it for myself. A huge circular building with thousands of seats surrounding a clearing in the middle."

Saiph couldn't see much beyond their cell, but he could hear coughs and muttering every so often. They were there for nearly twelve hours before they saw another person. A guard brought them a bowl of soup and a cup of water. Saiph tried to ask him what was going to happen to them, but the guard acted as if they didn't exist. Saiph ate his soup and slept. He must have still been exhausted from his escape, because when he woke up, there was another person in the cell. Saiph skittered back and shook Alistair.

"Hello there," Alistair said to the stranger. "What's your name, friend?"

The woman had short hair, was well muscled, and was missing her right eye.

"We're not friends," she said, not even bothering to lift her head.

"Right," Alistair said, "but if we're to be roommates, it might be best to get on good terms, wouldn't you say?"

She chuckled without humor. "Oh, don't you worry, we won't be here for long."

"Why do you say that?" Saiph asked.

She finally looked up and frowned. "You're serious?" When she saw that Saiph wasn't joking, she said, "Where are you from?"

"Altai, in the Enil Valley."

"Don't know of any Altai, but the Enil Valley must be a thousand miles from here."

"A *thousand*?" Saiph said.

"You don't even know where you are?"

Saiph and Alistair shook their heads.

"Well, I'm sorry to be the bearer of bad news, but you fellas have received death sentences."

"I'm sorry," Alistair said, "but is that a threat?"

"Nope," the woman said, "just a fact."

Her name was Lorena. Maybe she pitied their ignorance or wanted to think of anything but her current predicament, but she became very talkative, giving them the information they had craved for so long. She explained that Jangali was ruled by a brother and sister, Elean and Aulan, the fire-eyed twins. They were brutal and unforgiving and had built the coliseum on the doorstep of the Fulgurian wood in order to send a message to the locals resisting there. Every captured Fulgurian fought in the arena as the crowd and twins watched. All of them eventually died. If not the first match, then the second, or very rarely, the third.

Funny how quickly a life could change. Even so, Saiph was surprised at how well he took the news. It was like he'd known that he was going to die all along and the revelation that it was actually happening was all according to plan. He asked Lorena when they'd be forced to fight, and she told them that, before she was caught, she'd heard that there was a match scheduled for the third day of springweek.

That was today. This could be his last day to breathe the air. To feel his heart pump blood through his veins. To look upon the world and shake his head in wonder.

He thought of his family. His mother, stern but gentle at the same time. She did everything for them, never tiring or complaining. His father, who taught him everything he knew about volt farming, hunting, and tracking. Saiph remembered how his father had sat with him every morning after his accident, teaching him how to live with the pain of his leg. Saiph was proud to be his son.

Stubborn Roe. Saiph prayed for the man who married the fireball that was his sister. He found himself imagining her as a bride, dressed all in green under the trees and Tengrii's shrine. Then he saw himself there, Ayanda dressed in green herself, a tiara of thorned vine wrapped around her black hair...

Saiph put his head in his hands and tried not to weep for all he would never do.

What would they tell Landon? He wouldn't understand, would never know what had happened to his favorite human. All Saiph wanted to do was to hug him one last time and tell him that everything would be all right—tell him to keep dancing to his own song.

"Don't give up," Alistair said.

"You heard her, everyone dies in the arena. The captives have to face impossible odds. We don't even know how to fight. We're volt farmers, Al, not warriors."

"True, we may fight and we may die. But Erlik take me if they crush my spirit before that happens. I'll fight. I'll try and escape again. I'll do whatever it takes. Tell me you're with me, Saiph. I know we can get out of this."

Saiph smiled sadly. "With you to the end, no matter what that end may be."

Alistair slapped him on the back. "Where there is life, there is hope. Another day, another life, right?"

And then Saiph remembered. How could he have forgotten?

"I am Jangali's biggest idiot!"

He frantically reached into his hidden pocket and felt for the Book of Light. It was right where he'd left it. He pulled it out and tapped the icon to unlock it. Alistair stared at it with opened amazement.

"That's incredible!" Alistair said. Even Lorena was looking at him curiously.

Saiph tapped the icon three times, and the blank gray screen appeared.

Hello? he wrote. *Is anyone there?"*

He waited.

Saiph? Where are you? Are you well?

The words faded gently as hope blossomed.

I am at the coliseum near the Fulgurian wood. I fight very soon. Can you help us?

I cannot arrive in time. You must hold on. You must stay alive for another couple of hours. Try and escape to Fulguria if you can. Help is coming. Stay strong. STAY ALIVE.

The writing faded away. Help was coming. They just had to survive the first fight and then everything would change. Saiph was clinging desperately to this tiny thread of hope when the door to their cell opened.

Saiph, Alistair, and Lorena were roughly ushered out of their cell and into a larger room with a tall ceiling, stone walls, and a massive wooden table with dozens of weapons on it. There were five other prisoners already there, picking through the swords, clubs, and spears. By the way they all resembled each other, half starved and rugged, they were obviously part of the same group. Saiph was trying to place them when he realized they were Fulgurians. For so long, he had seen them as a group who disobeyed the Tenets and started a war. Now that he knew what the Skyfallers were capable of, he envied the Fulgurians' willingness to fight. Saiph had no doubt that they followed the Tenets before committing violence.

Saiph glanced at Alistair, who shrugged and walked over to the table. Saiph followed him, and they started picking through the weapons. Each one felt awkward in Saiph's hands, which only emphasized his ignorance. Lorena walked over and picked up a spear, swinging it twice through the air with an easy grace. Alistair grabbed a spiked club. Saiph decided on a sword, grabbing it with both hands and feeling the weight of it. It would have to do.

"Two minutes," an amplified voice said from somewhere above.

Saiph took a seat on a bench to try and settle himself, but he couldn't stop shaking. He tried counting, tried thinking of something pleasant, but the awareness that he was going to die was smothering. He opened his eyes to see one of the Fulgurian girls looking at him with a sad smile. She must have been about Roe's age, but she didn't look nervous at all. Saiph straightened his back and forced his hand to stop moving. He could be brave too. The girl winked at him as a door opened at the end of the room.

"Make your way up the gangway and onto the platform. Anyone who stays in this room will be subject to extermination. You have one minute."

"No matter what's up there," Alistair said, "we stay together."

Saiph nodded. "Together."

Halfway up the steps, Lorena turned her head to the side and vomited. Saiph's stomach roiled, but he focused on Alistair's back and kept going. When they neared the other door that led into the arena, Saiph closed his eyes and thought of one of his favorite Verses on death:

Life is dream walking. Death is going home.

The doors opened, and a cacophony of sound washed over him. A thousand people screaming all at once was exceptionally disconcerting, but it was one sound in particular that made the breath catch in Saiph's throat: a roar.

Saiph was pushed out into the sunlight, and there, a hundred feet away, stood a fully grown yokai. It was twenty-five feet tall with at least four thousand pounds of pure muscle hanging on its bones. Its light-blue fur was a tangled mess of knots and dirt. The claws protruding from its eight fingers were as large as some of the short swords the others were carrying, and its horns would have been double that length if they weren't curled.

The yokai pounded the ground, confused and angry at the audience that he couldn't reach. It would only be moments until the yokai realized that there were people inside the arena and come charging at them, intent to take out its anger.

"Oh fuck," Lorena said. "Oh fuck!"

Above the yokai, Saiph couldn't help but notice that a section of the crowd was partitioned off. Two people sat on raised, throne-like chairs in a booth. It was difficult to make out their faces completely, but their eyes were unmistakable. They *glowed*. Just like a volt animal's. Saiph had never seen or heard of a volt human, but apparently they existed.

The roar of the yokai brought his attention back to the fact that he was about to die. The Fulgurians only hesitated for a fraction of a second before they began to run at the yokai instead of away. Saiph thought that their bravery stepped beyond the line of stupidity and right into the realm of insanity. The yokai noticed the charging humans, and it and turned to face them, letting out another ground-shaking roar before running at them with blinding speed. Saiph didn't understand how something so large could move so fast.

The yokai was on the Fulgurians in seconds. Three of them immediately rolled to the ground, staying as close to the dirt as they could. The other two jumped into the air, swinging their swords at the yokai's arms. It was like the blades weren't even there. The yokai's claws ripped through the first Fulgurian, and a balled fist smashed a second, his body bursting into blood. The yokai's foot lashed out, kicking one of the rolling Fulgurians hard enough to send her flying forty feet through the air.

"Come on!" Lorena yelled. "It's now or never!"

Saiph wouldn't have responded at all if Alistair hadn't started running with her.

Together.

He would stay with Alistair until the end. Saiph heard the yokai roar again, but it sounded different. It was a roar of pain. The other two rolling Fulgurians had stabbed the yokai's feet and ankles. The yokai jumped away from the two Fulgurian women and directly toward Alistair. He wasn't fast enough, and Saiph didn't even have time to scream. The yokai knocked Alistair to the ground with a backhanded slap and then tore into his shoulder with his teeth. Alistair's arm was ripped from his body, and his blood soaked the coliseum floor. The yokai threw Alistair's corpse across the arena like it was nothing at all. His detached arm lay only feet from Saiph.

Saiph stood there dumbly, repulsed and paralyzed. Alistair. The man who was always ready with a smile. Who schemed and joked with him. Who had been through all the same hardships as he had, was gone in less than a second.

Together.

Glowing yellow eyes filled with wry amusement looked down on the scene from the booth above. They were clapping. Saiph barely saw Lorena die as a claw took her in the neck but his shock was beginning to turn. The frustration and sadness that he had come to live with these past ten months were transforming into pure hatred—a divine rage. Something burst inside of his chest, like a dam releasing all the oceans of the world. It flooded him. The feeling was so incredibly overwhelming that he barely noticed the crowd go absolutely silent, or how Elean and Aulan had stood up to stare at him, their mouths agape. Even the yokai had stopped killing for a moment.

Saiph felt like the sun and the stars, like the untouchable body of a god. For the first time in years, he didn't feel the pain in his leg. Now the idea that he'd had in his cell, that his death was already written in the stars, made sense. He had not died; he just had never truly been alive.

Saiph took a breath and looked up at the waiting world with eyes that glowed a deep and vibrant blue.

CHAPTER EIGHTEEN

Saiph slowly realized that the people around him had not fully paused to look at him like he'd first thought. They were actually moving, only slower somehow, but not even that description was entirely accurate. It wasn't that they were moving slower, it was that Saiph perceived them differently. He could track even the tiniest and fastest of movements. He took it all in at once.

A yokai charging him.

Metal unfolding around the Twins.

Teeth marks around Alistair's body.

He wasn't sure what he was capable of now, but he didn't want to find out it wasn't enough. It was time to go.

The yokai swung at Saiph, but Saiph easily stepped inside its reach and, with an open palm, hit the yokai in the chest. He'd punched the animal with such force that it flew above the high walls and into the crowd. Saiph was as shocked as everyone else. The yokai lay in the stands for a few long seconds as people scattered away, screaming in terror. Finally, it shook its head and realized where it was. It immediately ran from the stands, chasing people down and causing havoc. Saiph looked up at Elean and Aulan. Only a few seconds had passed since they'd stood, but their bodies were almost completely covered in metal. Saiph sprinted to the last remaining Fulgurian girl, moving with mind-boggling speed. He reached her in a blink. It was the young woman who had winked at him below.

"If we reach the Fulgurian wood, will we be safe there?"

The woman nodded. Saiph didn't have time to worry about propriety; he heaved her over his shoulder and sprinted away from the twins and toward the far end of the arena. He reached the locked door and ripped off its metal hinges with a single pull. He ran through a tunnel with the Fulgurian woman bouncing on his shoulder. They came out the other side and into an opened space with a crowd of people. They stared at him fearfully.

"Which way?" he asked the girl. She didn't answer. "North, east, south, or west?" Saiph asked.

"North."

Saiph flew by people and dodged around their slowness. He overtook the vehicles that had carried him hundreds of miles from his home. Skyfallers were everywhere, their large buildings all around. When he reached the outer walls of the small city that housed the coliseum, he jumped. He easily cleared the twenty-foot height. The guards just stared as he soared past them. Even in his panicked state, Saiph still felt a sense of wonder and euphoria he was feeling mixed with an ache over Alistair's departure. It was overwhelming. Once on the open plain, he picked up speed, and the wind roared in his ears.

"How far to Fulguria?" he yelled.

"Twenty miles!"

He didn't tire. He didn't struggle for every breath. He didn't collapse from the pain of his leg. Ten minutes into his run and the woods became visible. Had he always been able to see this far? The world around him seemed crisper. He could hear sounds that he'd never noticed before. One of those sounds, however, was unnatural. He chanced a look back to see what could only be described as two balls of fire flying toward him. As quick as he was, Saiph couldn't fly. He willed his legs to move faster but feared he might fall, which could hurt or kill his passenger. For all he knew, it would kill him.

They were only a half mile from the trees when Elean and Aulan fell like shooting stars from the sky, landing in front of him and blocking his path. Saiph could see their burning eyes through the cloud of dust. As it settled, their bodies became visible. They were both wearing suits of yellow-and-silver armor, gleaming and unmarred. The taller one had spikes riddled across the body and helmet, strange symbols written in between them. Saiph would have guessed that the man would sound like a bear, but his voice was surprisingly high-pitched.

"Now where have you been?" Aulan asked. "We've been looking all over for you."

"We've been worried sick," Elean added. She was shorter than her brother, but only by a couple inches. Her yellow armor had a wavy and elegant design. It had the same strange symbols, but they were larger and appeared less often. The shape of her faceplate made it look like she was perpetually smirking.

"What are you talking about?" Saiph asked as he set the Fulgurian girl down.

"Do you think he knows, Elean?"

"No, I don't believe he does, Aulan."

They took a step toward him.

"Stay behind me," Saiph said quietly. "Then run for the forest when there is an opening. I'll join you if I can."

Saiph wasn't expecting Elean to lunge so unexpectedly and quickly. Her movements were not nearly as slowed down as the rest of the world. As she attacked, Aulan lifted his palm up and jumped into the air, a yellow beam firing from the center of his hand. Saiph jerked to the side, but the beam still grazed his shoulder, painfully burning him. Elean slammed into his side, knocking the wind out of him and throwing him twenty feet backward. Saiph's body slid against the dirt. Luckily, he had landed on his back, because if he hadn't, he would never have seen Aulan come hurtling down at him, knee first. Saiph rolled out of the way and jumped into the air. Elean was firing yellow light from her hand now. Saiph rolled in midair, twisting and turning to avoid the fire. Two more blasts grazed him, one on the leg, the other on the top of his shoulder.

He clenched his jaw as he came back down. He kept one eye on the twins while he glanced down at his hand. It was burned, but Saiph could see that the skin was very slowly reforming. It reminded him that he was not a farmer anymore. These people had taken Alistair from the world, killed his family and friends, enslaved him for months. Saiph would show them exactly what he thought of Skyfallers.

When Aulan righted himself and came sprinting toward him, Saiph let his anger run wild. He made sure to keep Aulan between Elean and himself. Aulan must have expected him to turn and flee, or to jump again, because he seemed surprised when Saiph ran toward him. Aulan raised a hand and fired, but Saiph pivoted a shoulder and dodged the light. Ten feet from Aulan, Saiph slid to the ground, letting his momentum carry him while dodging more beams of light. With five feet left, he slammed his hands against the ground, propelling himself back to his feet. He took two steps and then threw his legs out in front of him, slamming both feet into Aulan's chest. The perfect metal bent slightly inward and sent Aulan flying through the air.

Elean laughed as her brother hit the ground. "You let him hit you!"

Saiph used this second to look around. The girl was gone. At least one good thing came out of this mess. The sun was setting to the east, and Saiph thought that if he could survive a while longer, he might lose them in the darkness of the woods.

"He's fast," Aulan said, rising.

"He doesn't have a suit!"

"I bet he'll get you once before we grab him."

The twins turned their attention back to Saiph and then lifted into the air as if gravity didn't apply to them. As they circled, Saiph had trouble keeping an eye on both at the same time. They lifted their palms to the air and started to fire yellow streaks of light at him. He dodged, barely comprehending how fast he was moving.

Two pieces of metal rose from Aulan's shoulders, and something else came rushing at Saiph. He dodged left, but this new weapon caused fire to bloom from it after it hit the ground. The force of it threw Saiph to the side, which ultimately might have saved him from the other tiny fireball weapons. Saiph rolled and sprang back to his feet, taking a step and then jumping at Elean. She moved back just in time to keep Saiph from grabbing on to her. Saiph growled in frustration.

He ran toward the woods, weaving from side to side. He had to get them out of the air. Better yet, he had to make it into the woods and disappear. Light and fire were all around him. He dodged left and right, glancing back every few steps to see where the twins were. They were still out of reach, too high for him to get to. One of the burning beams hit his shoulder and went straight through the back and out the front of him. He screamed in pain.

"Don't kill him, you idiot!" Aulan yelled.

"Is he dead? Is he?"

"Too close."

"Superb accuracy shouldn't be criticized."

Saiph got to his feet and started to run, but another beam went through his left leg, sending him to the ground.

No! Not my leg!

"That, my dear, is accuracy. You see how he is unable to run but is in no mortal danger?"

Saiph heard the twins land, and he struggled to get to his feet. He was halfway up to standing when he collapsed back to the ground. When they got close enough, Saiph lashed out with his good leg, sweeping the feet out from beneath Elean. Saiph bounced on top of her, hitting her with all his strength. The metal was beginning to give way when a fist hit the side of his head, sending him to the side and leaving the world blurry.

Elean screamed in anger.

She returned to her feet and walked angrily over to Saiph, striking him across the face. Saiph's head snapped to the side, and he spit blood onto the ground. The blows to his head left his thoughts confused, but the feeling of panic remained and he desperately crawled to get away. Elean kicked him in the side, and Saiph heard something break. His breathing became pained. Elean flipped Saiph over and raised another fist. Over her right shoulder, Saiph saw something very curious. A floating red light was in the air, getting larger with every microsecond.

Before Elean could land her punch, Saiph sat up and pushed her in the chest, not so much to do any damage but to give him space. Elean flew several feet into the air and was about to come back down when she somehow sensed movement and quickly turned.

Too late. The red blur smashed into her with all the momentum of a planet. Saiph tried to get up again, but the pain was too great. He lay down and tried to keep from passing out. He watched the skirmish and gave thanks to the Book of Light.

Help had come.

CHAPTER NINETEEN

J on traveled in Amira's enhanced shuttle and watched the fight from one of Tokomoto's scouting drones. What he saw was nothing short of miraculous. The twin dynamics fired upon the unarmored man, sending laser after laser, missile after missile. Yet Saiph Calthari moved with unimaginable speed and grace. Fire erupted all around him, but nothing seemed to hit. How a person could do that without an aura suit was beyond Jon's understanding.

"My god," Amira said from behind him. "That is impossible." Vincent sat next to him, shaking his head in wonder. The ship was silent with awe for a moment as they watched him.

"He can't keep this up forever," Jon said. He tapped a button on the console. "Tokomoto, what's your status?"

Tokomoto's voice came over the intercom. "Silvestre is thirty seconds out. I am thirty-seven. Russ and his men should touch down in the forest shortly after that."

Jon watched the screen, and his stomach lurched when a laser shot went through Saiph's shoulder as he tried to reach the protection of the woods.

"No!" Sarah yelled. "Come on, just hold on a little longer!"

They cringed as the smaller twin beat Saiph. Ellie stifled a sob, and Amira put an arm around her shoulder. Somehow, Saiph remained conscious, and Jon saw when his eyes flickered over Elean's shoulder. Saiph sat up and pushed his assailant off him. Silvestre was there a second later, colliding with Elean before she could attack Saiph again.

"That a girl!" Sarah yelled.

"Boom!" Vincent cried.

Amira flashed her teeth and pumped a fist.

Jon stared at the screen. Silvestre was not nearly as powerful as either one of the twins, and she would need help fast. It came. Tokomoto's drones swarmed the air like locusts, moving with the precision and speed that made him infamous. The coffin-like pods landed next, striking the ground and opening up like flowers of death. From the inside, his metal soldiers emerged, forming a perimeter around the taller of the twins. The man tried to leap into the air, but the drones hammered him back down with a plethora of tiny lasers.

Jon turned his attention back to Silvestre. She was on the retreat. She stumbled from a quick attack, and Elean stuck her hand to Sil's chest and released a wave of energy. Silvestre flew through the air, and before she could even hit the ground, Elean was hurtling toward her. Before Elean could finish her attack, a wave of armor-piercing bullets slammed into her, not puncturing her armor but considerably slowing her momentum.

Elean turned to the forest. Russ and his men were firing from the cover of the trees. She fired indiscriminately into the wood and sent out shield pulses to melt the bullets before they could hit her. Jon noticed that there was light in the woods near where Russ hid. A moment later, eight glowing panthers broke the tree line, followed by their dirty and half-starved handlers. Elean fired at the animals, but they dodged and inched closer with every second. Jon could see the confusion in Elean's body language; she'd clearly never fought an animal like this.

Aulan was pinned down, but he was destroying drones and bots at an alarming rate. Still, he was not unharmed—Jon could see holes in his armor.

"I can't tell what's happening!" Ellie said. "It's too fast!"

"We'll win," Jon said. "They need reinforcements."

Not a moment later, the smaller dynamic disengaged Silvestre and the Fulgurians and flew toward her brother. She attacked the ground bots long enough for Aulan to escape the encirclement. Together, they left the ground and rocketed back toward the city.

"Do you want me to follow?" Tokomoto asked.

"No," Jon said, "let them go. We don't want to fight their entire army. We need to get out of here before they come back with help. Silvestre, are you all right?"

She was breathing hard. "Yeah, think so."

"Russ?"

"Uh, yeah, all clear...I think."

"What does that mean?"

"Well, there's a whole bunch of angry-looking forest folk giving me the crazy eye."

"Don't engage," Jon said. "Ask for Tasaday."

"Roger."

Amira guided the shuttle down to Jangali. When they touched ground, the ramp lowered and Jon strode down it. Soldiers were all around now, setting up a perimeter. One of Ellie's doctors was seeing to Silvestre. Jon glanced at her, and she gave him a pained thumbs-up. He looked over and saw Saiph Calthari sitting in the grass with an expression of unadulterated exhaustion. Even from here, the boy's eyes burned like the stars of old.

———

Saiph sat on the ground, only half aware that he was in shock—not only from the pain in his leg, shoulder, and ribs, but of from his wondrous delivery from a terrible fate. A large flying vehicle touched down nearby and lowered a ramp. A man walked down it, striding with a magnetic confidence through the grass. The surrounding people stared at him as he passed, and the whole scene seemed to bend around him.

The man made a beeline toward Saiph, not taking his eyes off him. He stopped about five feet away and stared at him with a calm sort of sadness, like he had seen everything a man could see and concluded that life was not worth the trouble after all. His presence was palpable. He took a few more steps forward and dropped to one knee.

"Are you all right?" he asked, his voice smooth and deep.

Saiph bowed his head and shrugged. "I don't know. Probably not."

"I am so sorry for what has happened to you. Truly."

Saiph looked up and saw the man's eyes filled with genuine sorrow.

"Who are you?" Saiph asked.

"My name is Jon Foster, and I have traveled the stars to find you."

II

BEGINNINGS

CHAPTER TWENTY

To those who risk everything for me, who have put their trust in me
without knowing the whole story, I leave this account.
—Jon Foster

Entry 1:

My life has been so long, and the war has destroyed so much, that most
of what people think they know about me is fiction. People are always
asking me where I was born and where I'm from, but the truth is, my
life began the day I met Ava. The day of my parents' funeral. My
sweet, beautiful, amazing Ava, bringing light to the darkest day of my
seventeen years. I had only seen her a couple times as a child, but I
remembered her instantly. She was wearing all black and looked
thoughtful and sad.

After some man spoke about my parents as if he knew them well, I
walked without direction, not knowing what else to do. The world

appeared hazy and my body was numb. I couldn't recall the last time I had eaten, but it didn't seem important—nothing did.

I eventually came across the tallest oak tree I had ever seen and, without thinking or knowing why, sat down at the trunk and stared out across landscape. I don't remember how much time passed before I heard her voice.

"Jon?" Ava asked. "Shouldn't you be back there?"

Her hair was brown and her skin almond, which made her eyes a strikingly bright blue.

"I don't know," I said.

Ava was silent for a long minute, watching me. She then walked over and sat next to me. I looked up at her.

"I—" Ava began, but she stopped. Her diamond eyes were magnified by the thin sheet of a coming tear. I looked into those eyes, and for the first time since my parents died, felt that maybe the world wasn't as cruel as I thought. I shakily nodded at her, knowing that she had lost her mom some years back. I tried to hold back tears of my own as she squeezed my hand and brushed her fingers across mine.

I didn't know what was going to happen to me. I didn't know how long and winding my life would become. But I knew that I was looking at something so lovely that it quieted the roaring emptiness inside me. It is a feeling I have not forgotten these past six centuries.

You may be wondering why I'm telling you this, but to understand me, the ebb and flow of my life, and how humanity has come to be where it is, you must first understand Ava Winters.

CHAPTER TWENTY-ONE

S aiph was wary of strangers who fell from the sky, but he had a feeling that he might be able to trust Jon. These people had saved him, after all, and if they wanted to kill him, they would have already. Saiph couldn't stay awake for another moment anyway. He passed out in the middle of the plain as the day faded away.

Sometime later, Saiph was shaken awake. He felt like he'd barely slept, but he could see a gray sky through the roof and hear patters of rain. He was in a small hut.

"Saiph," Jon said, patting him on the side of the face. "Saiph, wake up."

"Water." Jon handed him a cup, and Saiph drank it down. "Am I home?"

"We're in the Fulgurian Forest."

"Fulguria," Saiph said dreamily. The day before came rushing back to him. "I was with a Fulgurian girl. We escaped together. Is she well?"

"Yes," Jon said. "Her name is Hekura. She told us what happened."

Saiph's head bobbed back down, and he was about to nod off again, but Jon gently shook his elbow. "I'm sorry to wake you, but you can go back to sleep in just a few minutes, I promise. It's urgent that I speak with you. You're not in the best of shape."

"What's wrong?" Saiph asked.

"We have several doctors here. People who tend to the sick," Jon clarified when Saiph looked at him, confused at the word. "And one of them says that she needs to repair your shoulder and leg, and set a few bones in your rib cage. We'd like your permission to do that."

"Will it hurt?" Saiph asked.

"We'll keep you asleep during the repair, but there will be some discomfort afterward."

"Worse than the discomfort I feel right now?"

Jon chuckled. "No. Definitely not."

"Then you have my gratitude," Saiph said.

"There is something else..."

The man looked uneasy, which made Saiph nervous and brought him further into consciousness. "What is it? Are Elean and Aulan back? Are they coming?"

"No," Jon said. "No, you're safe. It's just that I have an offer for you that I don't feel either of us are quite ready for. Time is short, though. I assume you don't have the most trust in people after everything that's happened to you?"

"Not exactly," Saiph said.

"Well, understand that I don't know you either, Saiph, though I've heard nothing but good things. I want to give you something, but it is very powerful and very dangerous, depending on how you use it. Either way, though, it would allow you to defend yourself against people like Elean and Aulan."

Saiph's attention was now fully upon Jon. He was tired of being the victim. Tired of Skyfallers dictating the terms of his life. Rain started to pour in earnest. "What is it you want to give me?" he asked.

"I've built you a suit of armor like the ones Elean and Aulan wore."

Saiph narrowed his eyes. "What do you want for it?"

"Nothing. It's yours if you'd like it."

"You want...nothing?"

"I won't lie to you," Jon said, "I need your help against the people who have wronged you. But I won't force you to help if you don't want to. Hell, after I give you an aura suit, I couldn't even if I tried."

Saiph eyed him suspiciously but then tried to remind himself that this man had done nothing to earn his distrust. He had saved Saiph's *life*. Even after everything he'd been through, the Tenets and Verses were still with him, and their collective intention whispered to him— guided him. The sixth Tenet was the loudest of them all:

Witty, funny, smart, brave, beautiful, ambitious, diligent, passionate, resourceful: These are all secondary. There is no greater quality than kindness.

Was this man not compassionate? Saiph could see it within him. There was patience and sympathy in his eyes and threaded through his words. Whether he followed the Tenets and knew the Verses or not, Saiph would wager that this man was good.

"Thank you for saving me," Saiph said, "and for being so kind."

Jon looked at him curiously. "Of course."

The overwhelming blanket of exhaustion was coming over him again. Saiph couldn't help but close his eyes. "I'll take the suit, and in exchange I will help you."

"You can decide that later," Jon said. "There's one last thing, though... Giving you the suit will make your surgery more complicated, since we'll need to put some equipment inside of your body."

Saiph didn't care about anything but sleeping at that point.

"Do it," he said. Then he slept.

Saiph hadn't believed them when they said he'd been unconscious for a week. Supposedly the surgery alone had taken *nineteen* hours. The pale, redheaded doctor said they wouldn't have been able to do it if he wasn't a dynamic—whatever that meant. All he knew is that it made him a little nauseous when he thought about them tinkering around inside his body for that long.

When he awoke, he asked for Jon.

"Hey," Jon said, walking into Saiph's hut a few minutes later. "How are you feeling?"

"Strange. I hurt, but also feel kind of good."

"That's not unusual. Most people would be either dead or in a coma after a surgery like that, but you'll probably be walking in a few more days."

"Why?"

Jon took a breath. "Why don't we go for a stroll?"

He came back a few minutes later with a chair on wheels, an ingenious contraption that let Saiph roll around without having to walk. He just pushed a small lever, and the thing moved.

"What is this?" Saiph said excitedly.

"It's an automated wheelchair for people who are unable to walk properly."

Saiph closed his eyes and touched it, feeling the stirring of unbelievable relief mixed with a dash of excitement. "This is incredible." He looked at Jon. "I could use this when my leg is bothering me. I hate to ask anything more of you, but please, it would be so wonderful."

"Saiph," Jon said, "Dr. Ellie reset the bone during your surgery. It must have been terribly painful when you broke it, but it healed very badly too, which is what caused you so much pain."

Saiph blinked, confused. "Wait, what are you saying?"

Jon put a hand on his shoulder. "Once you've recovered from the surgery, it won't hurt like it did before; you'll be able to walk and run like normal."

The first couple of years after the accident, Saiph would spend hours thinking about the day his leg would be fully healed. He imagined himself running through the fields or carrying Landon on his shoulders. Those little daydreams eventually became unhealthy, though. He was never going to get better, and it was naive to think otherwise. Accepting that had nearly been as painful as the leg itself.

"Are you sure?" Saiph asked, unembarrassed of the crack in his voice. "I'll be normal again?"

"Normal?" Jon said. "Oh no, you'll be anything but normal, but I promise you it's in a good way."

Saiph bowed his head, and his breathing suddenly got heavier as he tried to force down the tears of happiness. He didn't dare hope for more, but he had to know about the other thing that had held him back his whole life.

"My lungs? Are they..."

"They'll be better too. Your new condition takes care of most of that. We have medicine for it as well. You just have a severe case of asthma."

What a stupidly blissful dream this was. It couldn't sink in—not completely. But the idea of it, the hope of it, was overwhelmingly euphoric. More than anything else, he felt *relief*. He hadn't realized it until that very moment, but there had always been a part of him that wondered if he'd always be able to take it. If one day the burden of his condition would just become too much and he'd give up on life.

What a change a few days could make. A week ago, he had been in a slave camp. Now, his leg was healed, his lungs worked, and he was free. *Another day, another life.*

Saiph was eventually able to compose himself. He was sure that the feeling of euphoria would come again when he actually started running, but Jon told him, quite firmly, that he wasn't to try until he was fully recovered. So instead, Saiph rolled beside Jon as they traversed the Fulgurian village. It was comprised of a series of small huts, with a few larger structures interspersed between them. The forest trees towered high above the buildings, and ropes and ladders were strung between them. When Saiph glanced up, he could see Fulgurians high above, sitting on platforms and running across rope bridges that were sometimes draped in glowing purple vines. Many of the Fulgurians were attending to volt animals, and Saiph was surprised at how many they had. They even had small glass spheres that contained volt insects he had never seen before.

The Fulgurians were mixed together with Jon's people, and the contrast was shocking. The Fulgurians were half starved, dirty, and had an intensity to their eyes that the newcomers lacked. Jon's people were almost chubby by comparison. They laughed more too. The only thing they had in common was that both groups openly gawked at Saiph as he rolled by.

"Why are they all staring at me?" Saiph whispered.

"You haven't seen yet?"

"Seen what?"

Jon ushered him to the side and took out a mirror. He was about to hand it to Saiph but pulled it back at the last moment. "This might be a bit shocking."

Saiph gestured for Jon to hand it over. "Seriously, I'd probably believe anything right now."

He looked at the sheet of glass and into his eyes. They burned blue. His pupils and irises were gone; there was only a blank sheet of glowing light where they use to be.

"What... How..."

Jon nodded down the path, and Saiph numbly followed. "It's to my understanding that you received a book, correct?"

"Oh yeah!" Saiph said. "The Book of Light!" He reached down into his pants pocket, but he was wearing a different pair than usual. He panicked.

"Don't worry," Jon said, "it's back in your hut. It's fine."

Saiph relaxed. "What is the book? It's not magic, is it?"

"It's not. It's only another tool that we have. The things you read in that book, what Chet told you about technology, and about machines, is all true. It's the history of humanity."

"You know Chet?" Saiph said.

"I've known Chet for a very long time. He helped me find you."

"But he's a slave!"

"He's many things, but a slave...I don't think so. He was just trying to find you and look out for you."

"Well, he did a shit job at the latter."

Jon laughed. "He'll be glad to see you're all right. He's on the way here now. Charlotte is with him. They just dropped Nico off at his village."

Saiph was so happy to hear they were all right, but then he remembered Alistair and he grew quiet. Jon let him glide along the forest floor for a while in silence. Like in Altai, the flowers tried to nip at him as he passed. He made sure that the wheels of his chair didn't hurt them.

"My family," Saiph said. "My village. Do you know if they're all right?"

"I'm sorry, but I don't. I have one of my people looking for the survivors, though. We need to find them before Elean and Aulan do."

Jon pointed to a side path, and Saiph guided his chair down it. They went a little farther before the track ended at a fast-moving stream. Beyond the water was nothing but untamed wilderness. It was dark, save some of the glowing plants, and Saiph could hear forest animals howling in the distance. Jon propped himself up on a stump and sat so he was eye level with Saiph.

"The story in the Book of Light...it's all real?" Saiph asked.

Jon nodded. "Jangali isn't the birthplace of humanity. We come from a different planet entirely. It's called Earth."

"Earth," Saiph said, trying it on his lips.

Jon let him sit to think about it, allowing him wrap his mind around impossible ideas.

"I still don't understand what tech-*no*-logy is?"

"Technology," Jon corrected. "And it's going to take time. That's partly why I had Chet give you the book. While you recover over the next couple of weeks, I want you to read. It will help you comprehend everything that's going on. I'll help you learn too, but I can't be here all the time. Others will have to teach you as well."

Saiph nodded. "I want to learn."

"Good, because you've got a lot to absorb."

Saiph put a hand up near his eyes and shook his head at the blue light that covered it. "Can you at least tell me what's happening to me?"

Jon rocked gently back and forth, puffing his cheeks and breathing out. "I can try." He walked to the stream, cupped water into his hands, and splashed his face.

"This is going to sound crazy to you, but I'm going to ask that you just take my word for it, okay?"

Saiph nodded and Jon sat for a moment, thinking.

"Do you have money in Altai?"

"We have copper coins that can be exchanged for goods, if that's what you mean."

"I do. Well, for a while now, the people of Earth have valued everything in terms of energy. So if a loaf of bread cost one copper coin in your village, a loaf a bread would cost one credit of energy in our society."

Saiph shook his head. "I'm not quite following the energy part."

"You see, all of our technology and machines are powered by energy we harvest from the sun. Our machines can do nearly everything in our day-to-day lives, *if* we have the energy to afford it." Jon pulled out something that looked like the Book of Light, but smaller. He pushed a button and it lit up. "You see, we are basically capturing the light from the sun and using it to power this little machine. It's where the light comes from."

"Okay..." Saiph said. "I'll pretend to fully understand. Go on."

"About five hundred years ago, all of Earth's problems stemmed from a limited energy supply. We couldn't capture enough of the sun to meet all of our energy needs. So, we created different machines to do this for us. They are called the Essens."

"How do the Essens capture light from the sun?" Saiph asked.

Jon shook his head again and looked like he was searching for the right words. A butterfly fluttered past, and Saiph smiled at it while Jon thought. Eventually, Jon said, "It's really quite complicated, but what you need to know is that we launched this machine into outer space. You see, all the stars in the sky are actually suns; they're just too far for you to see them properly."

"No kidding," Saiph said.

"A single Essen is so small that we were able to speed it out to the stars. Once it arrived, it multiplied, using the energy of the star to duplicate itself over and over again. Within a few years, Essens surround the star completely, absorbing incredible amounts of energy. Then they sent that energy back to Earth and other planets so that we could use it for ourselves."

Saiph rested his elbow on the side of the chair and shook his head. He had barely noticed the sky darkening, but now realized that a storm was brewing. He could smell it on the air.

"What does this have to do with what's happening to me?" he asked.

"Well, the Essens are not purely machines," Jon said. "They also have some biological aspects to them. A few centuries ago, some sort of virus or sickness infected the Essens, both its computer brain and its biology. A strange hybrid virus we'd never seen before. They began to use the energy they absorbed in unpredictable ways, and we weren't able to control them. They spread to other stars without being told to. But most importantly, the biological part of the virus spread to other living beings."

"The volt animals?" Saiph said.

"Yes, exactly. Most of the organisms that contract the virus simply die, but many have also adapted to live with it. The Essens with the same viral strain send their energy to these organisms, and the organisms are able harness that energy to make themselves...better."

"That's what's happened to me? I have some sort of virus?"

Jon nodded. "Yes, and it's infusing your body with the energy from a star."

"But how did I contract a virus from something that lives among the stars?"

"The Essens are extremely small. Some of them get blown away by solar winds, or even when a star explodes. They've been dispersed throughout our part of the galaxy. Especially to here on Jangali, for whatever reason."

"And what about the suit that you gave me?"

"Your body is able to use the energy to improve your senses and make you faster, stronger, and able to heal quickly, but it is pretty inefficient and limited. For instance, no matter how much energy your body is imbued with, you wouldn't be able to fly. The suit changes that. We call the suits 'auras.' The aura is able to tap in to your body's power reserve and use it in incredible ways. You saw only a fraction of what Elean and Aulan can do, but flying and firing lasers are two of the more useful ones."

"I'll be able to fly?" Saiph asked, unable to keep the excitement from his voice. "First you tell me I'll be able to run again, then that I'll be able to *fly!*"

"You'll be able to fly," Jon said, grinning.

"So where's my aura? Can I try it?"

Jon suddenly looked uncomfortable. "You were sort of out of it before, and I didn't have time to fully explain. I'm sorry for that. But if we had waited, you would have had to go through another painful surgery instead of just this one."

"Look, I just learned that there are many planets, that Jangali isn't where people are from, that I can fly, and that I have burning blue eyes that everyone stares at. Honestly, what's one more thing?"

Jon shrugged. "If you say so. Well, your aura is...inside you. We installed it into your body."

"What?" Saiph said. "How the hell do I get it out?"

"We'll teach you how to summon it, but you absolutely should not do so yet. Not in your condition."

"*How* does it come out?"

"Well, you know how your book unfolds and expands when you touch it? It's the same sort of process. The...unfortunate...part is that it will have to come out of your body somewhat violently."

Saiph took a deep breath. "How violently?"

"Small metal tentacles will have to puncture the skin to get out. It will hurt a bit, but it won't do any lasting damage and your body, and the aura will heal those wounds within a few seconds. From there, your aura will expand rapidly and encase you."

Saiph wasn't nearly as disturbed as Jon obviously assumed he would be. He considered it a small price to pay if it gave him the ability to fly and defend himself from Elean and Aulan and fly. Hell, he'd lived with a constant pain for the better part of twelve years. A few seconds of pain was nothing in comparison.

"Sounds good," Saiph said. "I think I saw that happening to Elean and Aulan when I was at the coliseum. They didn't attack me right away but stood there as metal unfolded over their bodies."

"That's right," Jon said. "Except their auras are a bit different. You're actually the first person to have an aura installed into your flesh. The rest of the dynamics carry around a device to do it for them. You'll have several advantages having it inside you, though. It's much more difficult to damage it, since it's protected by your body. It will summon four times faster, since it will unfold from several different points. And it will always be charged and ready for use, since it is as much a part of you as anything else."

Saiph shook his head. "And you're absolutely sure it's not magic?"

"Pretty sure. Unless I was unknowingly casting spells on it while it was built." Another clap of thunder sounded overhead. "Saiph, the aura is good for many things, but it is ultimately a fighting machine. I won't ask you to fight if you don't want to, but there is a war coming to Jangali. We could use your help."

Saiph thought about all the humiliation and pain that the Skyfallers had inflicted on him and his family and was almost frightened of how angry it made him. He had also given Jon his word.

"I'm in," Saiph said. "Whatever it takes."

Lightning struck in the distance, and they started back. Jon told him to read and rest and that he would do everything he could to find the people of Altai. Jon said he was going to be busy over the next few days, but he invited Saiph to a meeting next week to introduce him to his friends and colleagues. Saiph accepted.

Not a moment after he wheeled back into his hut, the rain started to come down again. A minute after that and the storm intensified. Flashes of lightning lit Jangali every few seconds, and thunder roared across the sky. Saiph had heard of the infamous storms that formed over the Fulgurian woods, but it was quite different experiencing it first-hand. He lay on his bed, listening to the storm and dwelling on Jon's words, trying to come to grips with what was happening to him.

CHAPTER TWENTY-TWO

E ntry 2:

After my parents died, I lived with my uncle Dave on the other side of town. He had a drinking problem, but he was a happy and boisterous drunk. He never hurt me or anything like that, but he couldn't be relied upon either. I don't think he was ever meant to be a parent.

I don't know what I would have done if I hadn't had Ava. She was kind and generous to me. Maybe because she understood what it was like to lose a parent. Maybe it was because she was just that good of a person. Either way, we became friends.

"I'm heading over now," Ava said.

I put my phone between my head and my shoulder and slipped on a shoe. "Is this one of those 'I'm leaving now but am really not even dressed yet' comments?'"

"I'm getting into my car here in just a second."

"All right," I said, smirking.

I was sitting on the curb outside my house when Ava pulled up in her sleek little white car an hour later.

She was grimacing and smiling at the same time. "Sorry. Bad traffic. Really bad traffic."

I went to the passenger side and hopped in. "Two or three times?"

"Two or three times what?" she said, starting to drive.

"Did you change your outfit two times or three times?"

"How dare you! The traffic. Oh, it was bad, Jon. Like, apocalypse bad."

I looked at her and raised my eyebrows.

She sighed. "Three times. But don't I look nice now?"

She did.

The sun was starting to dip below the horizon, and the end-of-summer air was cooling. We drove past Stanford University with the windows down, heading for Lin's house.

"Why are her parents out again?" I asked.

Ava shrugged. "They're at a charity event, I think."

A few minutes later, we pulled into the driveway of a large and beautiful house. It had a neatly manicured lawn with tall trees and thick bushes. The house itself was brilliantly lit with dozens of ornamental lamps. The front door was built for royalty, but we didn't bother with it; we walked around the side and to the patio, where we knew we'd find Lin, Omar, and Tim. We could hear music playing.

Lin was in the pool, buoyed by a large, inflated yellow duck. Her bikini was pink with flowers and somehow made her already model-like body look even more alluring.

"Aren't you cold?" Ava asked.

Lin's head flopped to the side to face them. "Yeah. Gotta get in my pool time before winter, though."

"She's been in there for over an hour," Omar called out. "I can see her goose bumps from here." He was sitting at a massive marble table, playing chess with Tim.

Omar was a large boy who was heavily muscled for his age. He would have been intimidating to anyone if it weren't for his baby face and easy smile.

"Come help me, Jon. I'm getting walloped again," he said. "At least I think I am..."

I walked over and stared at the board. Tim had an elbow on the table and was leaning his face into his hand, bored. He was the shortest of our friend group, but we kept telling him that he had yet to grow into himself. He'd have been better looking if he ever looked a little happier.

"You are indeed being walloped," I said. "You're actually about to lose in two moves. Nothing to be done about it."

"Damn," Omar said. "At least I'm getting better, right, Tim my boy?"

Tim raised an eyebrow. "Better? You lost in seven moves."

"Yes, but I'm beginning to recognize that I'm about to lose. That's progress."

I laughed. "Hey, I'm proud of you. Only two weeks ago you were calling the knights 'horsies.'"

Lin was getting out of the pool and Ava was handing her a towel. They were both very pretty. Omar, Tim, and I were aware of the girl's attractiveness compared to our own, but it never mattered when it was just the five of us.

"What are we even doing tonight?" Omar asked.

Lin sauntered over, picked up some keys from the table, and jingled them.

"What's that?" Ava asked.

"Keys to happiness."

"Will you stop calling it that?" Tim said. "It's called the liquor cabinet."

"Same difference."

Omar roared with laughter at something Ava said, but I didn't hear what it was. I could only chuckle at Omar's endless howls of high-pitched amusement. We were in the media room, sitting in a circle on the floor, floating on a sea of pillows and blankets. A bottle of vodka was being passed around.

"My god, Omar, will you quiet down a bit. My parents will hear you from Palo Alto," Lin said.

"I'm sorry," Omar said through tears, laughing still, but quietly. "It's been a while since I've lost it like that."

"Everything been all right at home?" Ava asked.

Omar sat back against leg of a couch. "You know how my parents are. Get good grades, Omar. Work a part-time job, Omar. Fast for Ramadan, Omar. Uphold the family honor, Omar. Watch your sister, Omar. Cook dinner, Omar. It never ends."

We sat there, staring at him for a moment. Omar hardly ever complained, though we knew how smothering home life could be for him.

"It's shit to realize that you hate your parents and that, when you leave home, you won't call them. Won't speak to them. That will be it."

I was taken aback at his confession. "They love you, though," I said. "You know that, right?"

"I'm not so sure. I think they love the person they want me to be, rather than who I am." Omar looked up and glanced at Tim, Ava, and me. "I'm sorry. That must seem so petty to you guys."

It was difficult for me to be objective about Omar's life at home. I was still recovering from my own grief. The scariest part was that I wasn't sure if it would ever get any easier, or if I even wanted it to.

"Hey, perk up now," I said, overly bright. "You always have your next life in heaven, right? That's something."

Omar laughed. "Not if I keep hanging out with you infidels, tempting me into sin. Pass the bottle."

Lin handed it to him. "Can't we all be like Jon's uncle Dave and enjoy our alcohol?"

"To Uncle Dave!" Ava said.

"Here, here!"

"All right, Tim, it's your turn," Ava said. "If you could have anything you wanted, what would it be?"

Tim cocked his head thoughtfully. The drinks never seemed to affect him very much, but I assumed that it was only his quiet nature winning out against the alcohol's effects.

"If I could have anything in the world, let's see... Yes, I know. I'd wish for Omar to stop calling the pawns in chess 'my children.' It's not only stupid but inaccurate. Oh, I'd also be six inches taller."

"The one wish in this room that may come true!" Omar said.

"Wait, wait, Lin hasn't gone yet," I said. "What would you want, Lin?"

"I wish that I had the most wonderful and beloved singing voice in the world," she said. "And everyone would love me for my talent!"

"What?" Ava said. "The male gender fawning over you all the time isn't enough?"

"And female gender," Tim added.

"Who wants to be lusted after like that? It's gross," Lin said.

"I know, right?" I said. "It's just so hard sometimes, all these women lusting after me. It's like, can't they stop staring at my body for just one minute? Don't they want to get to know me?"

Tim pretended to throw up.

"Next question, next question," Omar boomed over the laughter.

Ava reached for the pile of tiny ripped sheets of paper and pulled one out. "What is your biggest fear?"

"Oooo," Lin said, "getting real deep here, lady and gents. You're first, Ava."

Ava didn't hesitate. "Clowns."

"Clowns?" Tim said.

"Clowns," she confirmed. "Their big creepy smiles hidden beneath layers of makeup and...and war paint! And their laughter. The ha-haha-ha-haha. There is nothing creepier than a fully matured, wild clown."

"All right, you've convinced me enough to not write you off as completely nuts," I said. "What about you, Omar? Biggest fear?"

"Torture," he said. "Specifically with knives and stuff. My gran used to tell these awful stories of people being tortured back in the homeland. Gave me nightmares for weeks."

We shuddered at the thought of it.

"Who wrote this fucking question down?" Lin said. "This isn't fun at all! I'm thinking about clowns torturing me!"

"Respect the question!" Omar said. "You're up."

Lin took a sip of vodka and passed it over to Ava. "I fear that I will die an ordinary person, who lived an ordinary life and who never did anything special or unique."

We nodded in what we thought was a sagely way, then everyone looked at Tim.

"I don't know," Tim said. "Hyenas, I guess."

We all knew there was more, but if Tim didn't want to talk about it, we weren't going to make him. He helped move it along.

"What about you, Jon? Let's get this question over with."

"Honestly, I'd be afraid of losing this like I lost my parents." I gestured around at our circle. "I mean, what's the point of life if you can't get drunk with your friends, right?"

"Here, here!"

"Well," Lin said, "that was real uplifting. No more shitty questions like that. I'm picking the next one."

Lin picked up a piece of paper but didn't even read from it. "Who is your celebrity crush! How exciting."

The only time I ever felt normal was when I was with my friends. It is impossible to describe the pain I felt when I thought about my parents. They weren't oppressive like Omar's. They didn't occasionally hit me like Tim's father did. They didn't ignore me like Lin's. They were wonderful.

I could tell you everything about them, even after all these centuries, but this isn't their story. Their story ended much too soon to have an effect on what was to come. Their passing did bring me to my friends, though. I can't say exactly why the five of us became so close. Maybe it was a combination of shared suffering and a similar sense of humor that did it. Maybe it was because we didn't have anyone else. I suppose it doesn't matter. They became my new family.

We sat and drank late into the night, getting sillier as the hours ticked by.

"I don't even know what you're saying right now!" Omar said. "What am I familiar with?"

"No, no, no," Ava said, "you're my familiar. Like my demon servant that follows me around."

"If anything," Tim said, "you are all *my* familiars. Reluctantly."

I laughed. "Oh my gosh, I am definitely referring to you guys as my reluctant familiars from now on. It's perfect."

Lin nearly spit out her drink. "It's so witchcrafty. I love it!" She leaned over and put a finger under Tim's chin. "You are my most reluctant familiar, I think."

Tim jerked his head away and we all laughed.

My Reluctant Familiars.

I realize now that we had no idea just how apt that name was.

CHAPTER TWENTY-THREE

I f Saiph was being honest with himself, he didn't actually mind being bedridden for a week. He slept most of the time, and all his meals were brought to him. Not soup-and-bread meals either, but exotic meats and cheeses. Dr. Ellie even brought him something called a "cookie". It was the most delicious thing he'd ever tasted.

When he wasn't sleeping or eating, he read, distracting himself from more unpleasant thoughts. He went back to the beginning of *The Big Bang to Boundless* and read from the perspective that it was all real, paying close attention to the details. He still skipped ahead occasionally, but only to read the science portions of the book. His thirsty mind drank in the wonders of physics, biology, and chemistry.

Sometimes the claims were so outrageous that he got dizzy and had to put the book down. He tried to wrap his mind around the fact that the universe was 14 billion years old and that if he wanted to travel from one end to the other, it would take him 93 billion years, and that was if he was traveling at 186,000 miles per second. It seemed just as absurd as any fairy tale.

A week after his surgery, Saiph woke up feeling energized and healthy. He decided almost immediately to get out of bed and walk.

His leg didn't hurt at all—at least not in the way it used to. It was the most surreal feeling. Eventually, Saiph found a ridge that overlooked a stretch of the giant kola trees and sat down to learn about the ancient Sumerian people. He read about Mesopotamia—the cradle of human civilization—and the Tigris and Euphrates rivers. He enjoyed the story of the ancient hero Gilgamesh and liked the pictures of the clay writing tablets. What he found most interesting, however, was their religion. They also believed in Tengrii, but they called him Anu instead. They had gods not only for nature, but for things like sleep, writing, and wine. It probably should have bothered him that there were so many other gods and religions, but it didn't. The gods had always just been embodiments of nature to him. His real religion was the Tenets and the Verses.

But what else didn't he know? He had always been so content in the Enil Valley, never having any desire to venture beyond. But now he'd do just about anything to know more. His ignorance was part of the reason he had been enslaved. He'd never let that happen again.

Saiph was taking a break from reading, basking in the sunlight on a rare clear day, when he heard footsteps. He sat upright and looked at the path behind him, but no one was there. His improved senses were still going to take some getting used to. He closed his eyes and focused on the sound of the steps. He guessed that his visitor was still a quarter mile away.

Hekura stepped out of the woods and into the clearing a few minutes later. Saiph was glad to see her well. She was a mousy girl, with oversized ears and a large nose. Her long hair was matted with dirt and more twisted than Elean's and Aulan's sense of humor.

"I sit with you?" Hekura said, her words choppy and heavily accented.

"Yes, of course." He gestured beside himself and she sat down. For a while, they just sat there, looking out over the landscape.

"I want to give thanks," Hekura said. "For life saving."

"I might have died if you hadn't attacked the yokai first. I should be thanking you."

Hekura shrugged. "Maybe. We force to attack. You not force to save me." She clapped him hard on the back. "Maybe I pay you back someday, eh?" She laughed and stood up. "Come, Chief Jon gather the leaders to speak."

Saiph had been so absorbed in his book that he had forgotten that the meeting was today. They were probably waiting on him. He got to his feet and walked as quickly as he could back to the village.

The gathering was being held in a small metal building that Jon's people had erected in a clearing a half mile from the village center. Saiph stepped through a door that slid open on its own, and the conversational chattering ceased as everyone turned to look at him. Saiph counted ten people around a large oval table, noting how awkward it was to have all these strangers staring at him. What took him back most however, was the woman with eyes like his, only red. He had seen her once, but she had been in her aura suit. They didn't have people like her where he was from. She had brown skin and flowing black hair that brilliantly complemented her eyes. For the first time, Saiph was glad that people had a hard time telling where he was looking. Something else was bothering him though. "It's..." he started, "cooler in here."

Jon smiled. "We have machines that can control the temperature of enclosed spaces."

Saiph raised his eyebrows and nodded appreciatively. "That's absolutely brilliant! How incredible." The group smiled at his enthusiasm, and he got more serious. "I apologize for my tardiness. I lost track of time."

Dr. Ellie giggled. She said before that she liked his accent, but Saiph couldn't see what was so funny about it.

"No problem at all. Take a seat wherever you'd like."

There weren't many open seats left, but Saiph walked over to the one closest to Jon and sat down.

"So," Jon said, clapping his hands together, "introductions. Saiph, the man on your right is Russ Henson; he's in charge of our human ground troops and the Andhaka, which you'll learn about soon."

The large yellow-haired man reached over and stuck his hand out toward Saiph. "I'm also head of the party planning committee and the sultan of good times and merriment for this little shindig."

Saiph wasn't sure what he was supposed to do, so he hesitantly stuck out his hand like Russ was doing. "Pleasure to meet you, Russ." Russ grabbed his hand and shook it up and down.

"Next down the line is Vincent Cross, our resident baby genius. He helped me design your aura suit and is going to be teaching you about it."

Vincent scowled at Jon but then smiled and waved at Saiph.

"Speaking of aura suits," Jon continued, "the woman with the red eyes is Silvestre. She'll also be teaching you how to use your aura suit. She'll explain more about your abilities and how to use them."

Silvestre nodded curtly to Saiph, and he gave a small and awkward wave back.

"The woman next to her is Amira Béringer. She's our lowly mechanic."

Amira scoffed. "More like your everything," she said in a strange but lovely accent. "But I'll show you of our machines and how they work."

"Looking forward to it," Saiph said.

"You've already met our chief doctor, Ellie." Saiph smiled and nodded at her, and she gave an enthusiastic smile back.

"That," Jon said, pointing to a man in a wheelchair, "is Tokomoto Tagawa. He's our outlier and controls an army of fighting machines. He'll tell you what he does, and it'll be important that you listen. You'll be working together a lot."

Saiph nodded, and Tokomoto remained expressionless.

"Next is Sarah. She'll be teaching you about politics and government." The woman nodded at him.

"The gentlemen to Sarah's right is Tasaday, chief of the Fulgurians and our most gracious host."

"Thank you," Tasaday said, "for saving Hekura. You are most welcome in Fulguria." His pronunciation was much clearer than Hekura's had been.

"Lastly," Jon said, pointing to a man standing in the corner, "is Treyges. If you need absolutely anything when I am not around, please see him." The man politely bowed to Saiph, and Saiph returned the gesture even though he was sitting.

"Everyone, this is Saiph Calthari, volt farmer, son, brother, and the most innately powerful person in the universe. Anyway, on to business." Jon motioned for everyone to open the folder in front of them. Saiph watched the others and looked at Jon, confused. Jon passed him a folder. Saiph opened it and inside was a small note among the papers.

You're probably not going to understand a lot of what we're about to say, and we're not expecting you to. Feel free to interrupt at any time and ask questions. If you're uncomfortable with this, write your questions down, and I will answer them for you later.

Saiph mouthed a thank-you.

Everyone flipped through their papers with efficiency, even Tasaday. Saiph found it amazing how quickly he was able turn his childhood fear of the Fulgurians into esteemed respect. He wondered how they had resisted the twins all these years, but then he remembered the ferocity of their voltpanthers.

"Tokomoto, have you seen anything happening in the capital with your spy drones?"

"The military is mobilizing. The camps on the outskirts are outsourced to mercenary groups and have been given twenty-first-century technology to keep the countryside under their control. A few of them have some antique battle droids. Harain's military, on the other hand, is very modern. They have a fleet of drones, plasma tanks, antiair flaks, and, of course, the twin dynamics themselves."

"What about the other Houses?" Jon asked. "What's their status?"

Treyges cleared his throat. "The Republican Guard and House Harain reinforcements didn't have enough energy to jump directly to Jangali, but they're only two weeks out. The other parties jumped with their remaining energy as well and will arrive successively over the coming weeks, ending with the Grecian Empire in approximately six weeks."

"Has anyone tried to contact us yet?"

"No, sir," Treyges said.

"Well, that gives us some time to plan and prepare. I think our first priority should be to liberate the countryside and free as many people as we can. Start thinking of the most effective and least violent ways to do this. You know what the camps are like, Saiph, so any suggestions you have will be welcomed."

Saiph nodded.

Jon and the group discussed other matters such as supply, logistics, arms manufacturing, and the maintenance of something called *Stargone*. Saiph took it in as best he could and wrote down the topics he didn't understand. When Jon ended the meeting, he asked Saiph to stay behind.

"How are you feeling?" he asked.

"My leg is a bit sore, but other than that, I feel wonderful."

"If these were normal times, I'd have you rest for another week just to be sure, but we're being pressed. Are you ready to start your lessons?"

"Yes. Very."

"Good. I want you to meet with Tokomoto first, he'll be waiting for you in a separate building just past the shuttle." Jon noticed Saiph's excitement deflate. "You'll spend all day with Vincent, Silvestre, and your aura suit tomorrow. I want you to visit Tokomoto first, though. You need to see what he sees."

Saiph took a moment to eat a lunch of traditional Fulgurian porridge, which consisted of nuts and berries strewn about a thick, milk-based substance. He wasn't sure if it was the dynamic virus or if it was because he was recovering from his surgery, but ever since he'd woken up, he'd had an abnormally ferocious appetite. After he finished shoveling down his food, Saiph made his way to Tokomoto's pod.

At first, Saiph couldn't see where another of the metal buildings stood. He looked closer and off to the side. Next to a large tree, the building he was looking for stood covered in brush and vines. Why had they deliberately covered it? The door was especially difficult to find, but a few minutes later, he was knocking gently. The door slid open. Saiph stepped inside and into almost complete darkness. Saiph could just make out Tokomoto sitting in the center of the room. It was eerie.

"Mr. Takagawa, sir, it's Saiph Calthari. Jon sent me to see you."

Tokomoto turned and faced him. "Put this on," he said, holding out something Saiph couldn't see. Saiph cautiously walked over and took a pair of thick black goggles from Tokomoto's hand. Even in the dark, Saiph could see the frailness of Tokomoto's wrists.

"Where do I put them?" Saiph asked. Tokomoto pointed to his eyes. Saiph slipped them on and was immediately overwhelmed by a hurricane of light and movement, Tokomoto the eye of the storm. He was in a different room from the one he'd just been in.

"This is a virtual command structure," Tokomoto said flatly. "I control my army from here."

Saiph peered around in disbelief. He lifted one eye of the black goggles up, and half of the room returned to darkness. He put it back down, and the room of flashing light was there again. Incredible.

"Where are your goggles?" Saiph asked.

"I wear contacts," Tokomoto said.

"I don't understand."

"Thin pieces of glass that fit over my eyes. They don't work for dynamics. Your eyes give off too much heat."

Saiph stared around the room. A half dozen boxes of light appeared on the walls, each showing one point of view, and then flashing away, showing another. A map of what could only be Jangali was hovering to Tokomoto's right, red pins marking certain locations. Numbers and statistics were scrolling near the ceiling, and a checkered grid lay directly in front of Tokomoto.

"This is the most magical thing I've ever seen," Saiph said.

Tokomoto gave him a sideways glance. "You like it?"

"Oh yes," Saiph said. "I wanted to go and use my aura suit right away, but I'm glad I came here first."

"Really? Now you want to see what I do more than using your aura suit?"

"Are you serious? Look at this place, it's brilliant!"

Tokomoto warmed to Saiph after that. He was not a talkative man, but Saiph could tell he was trying to explain it to him the best he could.

"And those boxes," Tokomoto said, "are video feeds of my scouting drones, so that I can see what's going on directly, rather than from data or satellite."

"How many scouting drones—I think I'm saying that right—do you have out there?"

Tokomoto glanced up at a box of light that projected statistics. "At the moment, seven hundred and eighty-two."

Saiph's mouth fell open. "That many!"

Tokomoto nodded, pointed to the map, and flicked his wrist. The map came to the center of the room and expanded. "We are here," he said, pointing to a patch of green. "The Harain city is over here. The red arrows are all of the settlements and camps that my drones have seen so far. The tiny blue dots that are moving are all of my active drones. All I have to do is focus my attention on any of these blue dots, and a video feed will appear, allowing me to see what it sees."

"By Tengrii," he said, "you're like a god!"

"Who is Tengrii?" Tokomoto asked.

"You don't know Tengrii?"

Tokomoto shook his head.

"Tengrii is Lord of the Eternal Blue Sky. God of Lightning."

"I see..." Tokomoto said.

"Tokomoto, sir, what have you seen so far? My family and friends are out there somewhere. I must find them."

"Yes," Toko said, "Jon told me to look for them. It is difficult, though. I do not know what they look like, so I must have my insect scouting drones listen in on conversations. They are programmed to recognize words, such as 'Altai' or 'Saiph,' and to alert me when they come up, but they haven't heard anything yet."

"What if those key words just weren't uttered while you were there?" Saiph asked.

Tokomoto shrugged. "Then I would have missed them."

Saiph bowed his head and rubbed his eyes. "I have to find out what happened to them."

"If you'd like, we can go through the video feeds I've complied so far, see if you recognize anyone."

"You'd do that for me?" Saiph asked.

Tokomoto nodded. "Can you draw?"

"Not very well."

"Try drawing their faces anyway. We'll plug it into the computer, and the face-recognition software will be able to narrow it down for us."

A light ding filled the room, and a red message appeared in front of Tokomoto. He pushed it with his finger, and a voice spoke from nowhere.

"Tokomotozuma-san, this is Russ Henson, lord commander of the best fighting force on Jangali and seven-time champion of the *Stargone* Beer Olympics, please come in."

"What do you want?" Tokomoto said.

"Thank you for responding, Tokomotorcyle-san, Russ Henson would like to request a full drone scout of the eastern woods. Believe there is some movement out there."

Tokomoto looked at his map. "There is another electrical storm coming in, you'll have to scout on your own."

"Roger that, Toto-san. Russ Henson out."

The connection cut off.

"Why can't you scout the eastern woods?" Saiph asked, drawing on a virtual sheet of paper.

"The reason the Fulgurians are still here, and the reason we're hiding here, is because these woods have abnormally intense electrical storms."

Saiph grunted. "Tell me about it. It's like a hurricane every day."

"The storms overload electrical systems, especially the mobile ones. Drones and other fighting machines aren't reliable in the woods. And the Fulgurians have their trained volt animals that can fight against human troops."

"Ah, so that's how they keep the Harain Skyfallers from ruling them. Very smart."

After Saiph finished drawing, he tried to describe his family to Tokomoto, hoping he might be able to narrow the search further.

"My sister, Roe, is sixteen. She's short for her age and has shoulder-length blonde hair and blue eyes. Her skin paler than mine. She's like a taller version of my mum. Her name is Milla. My father's name is Rosh, and we have a similar complexion, but he's taller by a good four inches. More muscular too. My younger brother's name is Landon. He's short and squat for his age, and his eyes are a bit different. He has something we call the Down."

Tokomoto was nodding as he looked down at a screen. His fingers flew across the controls as he entered the information Saiph was saying into his machine.

"Okay, I have added their names and description into the program. Anyone else?"

"Yeah," Saiph said, "there is also my friend Ayanda. She's short, has black skin and a full head of curly black hair. And then there is my other friend Darakai. He's dark and is as big as a bear. You can't miss him."

After that, Saiph looked at images for hours. He felt numb as faces flashed across the screen, the novelty that so many people existed on Jangali having long worn off. He had no idea how long he'd been at it, but he was very tired. His eyes kept closing, and his head would dip down before he would quickly bring it back up to stare at the screens.

"Saiph," Tokomoto said. "I think that is enough for today."

"I have to find them," Saiph said, slapping his own face.

"We will," Tokomoto said, "but not today. If they survived the attack on your village, then they are, in all likelihood, still out there somewhere. One more day won't matter much."

Saiph thought about his own captivity and disagreed, but he couldn't keep his eyes opened any longer. "Thank you, Mr. Tokomoto, sir. It means"—he yawned—"so much. To me."

"Please, call me Toko. Go rest now."

Saiph slept poorly that night, images of faces still flashing across his mind, but none of them the people he wanted to see. If Tengrii was looking down upon him, he would have heard Saiph's riotous dreams, and seen the worry for his family in his restless sleep.

———

Saiph was groggy and tired the next morning. Jangali was in the middle of a summerweek, and the air was heavy with moisture. Sweat clung to his shirt, telling him that he maybe slept a bit longer into the day than he should have. He sat up and swung his legs off the side of his bed. He took a deep breath and reached for the cup of water on the ground beside him. Leaning against the cup was a note:

Meet me at the river.

—Silvestre

The river? Saiph thought. *That's two miles away!*

It was still his first instinct to associate distance with pain, but then he remembered that it wasn't an issue any longer. He took a deep breath and smiled.

Saiph's next thought was that he was going to see and use his aura suit. In just a few hours, he could be flying. If he wasn't awake before, then he was now. He grabbed his pack and set out.

The Fulgurians were already up and moving about, tending to the day's chores. The lane to the river was the largest and busiest path, since it led to the only large source of clean water. People of all sorts stared at him as he hurried past. He remembered the way he had gawked at Silvestre's eyes when he'd first seen her and decided not to let other's stares bother him. In the shadowy woods, Saiph could see the faint blue light that his eyes gave off. That would take some getting used to.

He reached the river that the Fulgurians called Tengrii's Vein and bent down to drink a handful of water. He looked about for Silvestre but didn't see her. He approached an older woman. "Excuse me, have you seen the woman with the red eyes?"

She pointed south. "At big rock downstream."

Saiph found Silvestre sitting on top of a boulder that was nearly ten feet tall. She was staring out past the river, waiting. Someone else was there too. *Vincent,* Saiph remembered. The pudgy boy looked tired and unhappy.

"Morn," Saiph called out to them.

"Good morning," Vincent said with a yawn.

Silvestre jumped off the rock and landed on her feet with a thud. "Let's get one thing straight," she said, "I don't know you and I don't think Jon should have given you the aura suit. They're dangerous, destructive, and difficult to control."

"Uh, okay..." Saiph said.

"If you try to do more than I tell you, I'm done," she said. "If you fall behind, I'm not waiting for you. If you fuck up, you're cleaning up the mess. Got it?"

After nearly a year in a slave camp, Saiph was tired of being treated cruelly for no reason. He didn't care how beautiful his insulter was. "Well, aren't you a ray of sunshine. Before we begin, I'd like to express my sincere and undying gratitude to have you as my teacher. As you can tell by my tone, I wouldn't want anyone else."

She narrowed her red eyes. "Just try not to kill yourself on the first day. Jon would be displeased if you did."

A few minutes later, Saiph found himself sitting in a small circle with Silvestre and Vincent. A small ball of red light hovered in the middle, something Silvestre had created. He hadn't noticed it before, perhaps because he was staring at her eyes, but Silvestre was missing a hand. In its place was a metal prosthetic. The ball of light originated from that palm.

"You may have noticed," Vincent said, "that the color of your eyes is different from that of Silvestre and Elean's and Aulan's."

"Wait," Saiph said, "are you sure?"

Silvestre grunted in amusement.

"Do you want to learn this or not?" Vincent said. "I'm trying to keep it simple. 'Cause I'm telling you, you don't want me to go complex. Even wise Silvestre here would be begging me to stop."

"Sorry," Saiph said, "please continue. Simply."

"The color of a dynamic's eyes is dependent on what kind of star their energy comes from. Silvestre's base Essens surround a red dwarf star. Elean's and Aulan's Essens are sending power from a main sequence yellow star, which is much more powerful."

Silvestre frowned at him.

"What, do you actually expect me to be *inaccurate?*" Vincent said, looking disgusted. He shook his head and turned back to Saiph. "Ignore her. Anyway, the color and power of your star is what gives you your aura, hence, your aura suit."

"How many colors are there?"

"From weakest to strongest: red, orange, light orange, yellow, yellow green, white, then, of course, blue."

Saiph grinned. "So you're telling me that I'm the strongest color and Silvestre is the weakest?"

"Well, that's not what I was trying to say, but yes, that's technically true."

"This is exactly what I'm talking about," Silvestre said. "You don't get it, Saiph. You are the only human being ever to have a blue aura. You're the reason everyone has come to Jangali."

"Why would that make them all want to come here?" Saiph asked.

"It's complicated. Sarah and Jon can explain it to you better than I ever could."

Could this really be all his fault? Had his family and friends died because of what he was? The thought made him sick. Silvestre must have seen the look on his face, because her voice was a fraction softer when she told him to quit daydreaming and pay attention.

She spent hours explaining the feel of the aura suit and how difficult it was to control the energy in his body. Vincent told him how his aura was built, oblivious to the fact that Saiph had absolutely no clue what he was talking about. It was nearing dusk when Silvestre finally asked if he'd like to try and summon his aura.

"Really?" Saiph said. "You're not worried I'm going to explode or something?"

"Oh, I'm worried," Sil said, "but time's short. Sink or swim, little fishy."

Vincent set up a few devices that would record and measure the summoning of Saiph's aura suit. Saiph stood in the middle of the area that Silvestre had cleared for the trial.

"With more powerful dynamics, a small wave of energy sometimes releases when the aura suit is summoned, but don't be alarmed by it. It's not enough to hurt anyone."

"Okay," Saiph said. "So what do I do again?"

"Focus on your pass phrase. Picture it in your mind's eye and then repeat in your head. You have to really focus on it. It might be hard at first, but it'll become second nature after a while."

"Right," Saiph said. "Sure. Got it." He shifted back and forth.

"Remember, it might hurt a bit," Vincent said. "We don't really know how much, though. You're kind of the first person to ever do this..."

"Great," Saiph said, "thanks for the soothing words, Vince."

Silvestre waved away his complaints. "Oh, come on, you big baby. Just get it over with."

Saiph closed his eyes. *Here goes nothing.*

In his mind, he pictured the sunrise he had witnessed before the guards of camp sixty-two had recaptured him. He pictured its majesty and felt the wonder combined with the staggering hopelessness that he felt. He thought of the fourth Tenet, his pass phrase:

Another day, another life.

He repeated it in his mind. *Another day, another life— Another day, another life— Another day, another—*

A burst of blue mist ejected from where he stood, making Silvestre and Vincent take a step back. Pain erupted over his body, and he dropped to his knees and screamed. He felt as if he'd been stabbed eight times simultaneously. His breath was heavy with shock, but the pain began to fade almost immediately. He opened his eyes and saw the world like he had never seen it before. Everything was crisp like it was on a cold and cloudless day, except exponentially more clear. There were symbols and numbers neatly placed near the edges of his vision. Silvestre and Vincent approached him slowly, wide-eyed.

"Are you all right?" Silvestre asked.

"Talk to us, man?" Vincent said. "Oh god, I hope we didn't kill him."

"I'm fine," Saiph said. His voice came out deeper than was normal. He looked down at his body. He was enclosed in sleek black armor that had veins of pulsating blue energy twisting around it in a seemingly random pattern. He reached up and touched his mask. The eyes were slanted, and he could see the blue glow on the palm of his hand.

"Dude," Vincent said, "you look *awesome*."

"How do you feel?" Silvestre asked.

Saiph stumbled. "In-incredible." He felt the energy of his body fused together with his aura suit.

"All right, that's good, I guess..." Silvestre said. "Now, a dynamic can control where the energy in his body will flow to. You should be able to feel the different systems of your aura suit; it's almost like sensing a new limb. It is extremely difficult to control for most dynamics, especially the first few times."

Saiph didn't feel this way at all. He felt one with his aura. Like it was part of him. Which, in a very real way, it was. He could feel the energy in his body and move it like his own fingers and toes. He stuck out his hand, palm up, and let a slither of energy release from it. A ball of deep-blue light emanated from his hand.

"Whoa there," Silvestre said. "That's really good, Saiph, but don't go too fast. You need to be careful."

"I can feel it, Silvestre. I can feel it very acutely. I can control my aura like my own body. I know it."

"Okay, just—"

Saiph didn't wait, he took a step back from Silvestre and Vincent and then sent a burst of energy to his back and feet. A crack filled the air as he shot into the sky. He streaked upward toward Kayra, which was titanic in the western sky. He was moving incredibly fast, but the energy lifting him was nearly silent, giving off only a soothing pulse. He went higher. Then higher. He flew through cloud after cloud, and when the mist cleared, he stopped, then hovered.

Saiph tore his gaze away from the giant planet above and looked down at Jangali. The sun had begun to set, and it bathed the land in orange and shadow. The edge of the Fulgurian forest was perfectly straight from this high up, like a line had been drawn and the trees were told not to pass. A vast mountain range was visible to the east, emerging so abruptly from the flat ground and towering so high that it looked as if it had a desperate desire to reach the stars. And there, could he actually see the curve of his world?

Saiph stared at the point on the horizon where the ground nearly met the sky but never quite did, and a new plane of reality opened to him; his old way of seeing was erased but rapidly filling up with a new perspective. It left him breathless with awe. He hovered in the air like a god and saw the world anew. He would never be the same.

CHAPTER TWENTY-FOUR

E ntry 3:

"What was your mom like?" I asked.

Ava and I walked down a long boardwalk that carried us over a sea of green marshland. She wore a white scarf and knit cap, and her hands were tucked underneath her arms for warmth. Several puffs of air emanated from her mouth before she answered.

"She was the happiest person I ever met. And the most caring. Never shut up, though." Ava laughed. "She could talk a million miles an hour, and interspersed between her rambling, she would say things like, 'Oh, I'm talking too much, aren't I? Aren't I? Oh dear.' It was either hilarious or annoying, depending on my mood. Out of all her words, though, she never had a mean one for anybody. Always saw the good."

I adjusted my coat and watched the birds, waiting for her to go on. Ava stopped walking and stared off in the same direction I was, lost in memory.

"She was the world's most dedicated and worst cook. Couldn't bake a cake to save her life, bless her. For some inexplicable reason, my sweet and gentle mom loved the most violent and scary television shows. She spoke three languages, worked five charities, and would have wanted six kids if she were healthy enough for it. I loved the way she brought me hot chocolate whenever I cried and would rub my back until I fell asleep. It was the only time she was ever silent."

Ava and I had been friends for over a year now, and I wasn't sure if she knew that I was in love with her or not. Some young people might not understand love, but I did. I absolutely did.

"She sounds lovely," I said.

"What about your mom and dad?" she asked.

Their faces instantly appeared in my mind, clear as the day I last saw them. "They were quiet people. My mother was an English lit professor at a community college. My father was an engineer who taught the micro-electro-mechanical systems class at Stanford. They were academics to their core."

Ava smiled. "My dad said that your dad was one of the only 'Iron Pilers' he ever respected."

I chuckled. "He would have thought that funny, even if his other engineering colleagues wouldn't have. My parents liked to read a lot. And they never said no when I asked for a new story. We used to go to Florida every year for the Fourth of July. We'd sit on the beach and eat hamburgers and watch the fireworks going off for miles in either direction. I don't know why, but memories of them always hits me when I am least expecting it. Like the smell of coffee that my father used to drink, or someone wearing a similar dress to what my mom would wear."

We walked for a while in silence. We eventually came upon a small bench that looked out over the lake. I pointed to it and we sat down.

"Have you ever thought that, since we can't get to know our parents anymore, we won't ever really know ourselves?" I asked.

Ava stared at the ground. "I don't know. Maybe sometimes. Other times, I think it just messes with our heads, gives us an excuse for the way we are. We all have to make it on our own, in the end."

"I'm in love with you," I blurted out, instantly horrified at my words.

She looked at me, surprised, but with a small smile on her lips. Her lips. I couldn't stop thinking about what it would be like to kiss them.

Without thinking any further, I leaned toward her. She put her hand on my chest, and I thought she was about to push me away, but she grabbed my coat and pulled me closer. My stomach tingled, and the bitter cold suddenly disappeared. Those few seconds seemed to have eternity wrapped within them, and I could hear the pounding of my heart, whispering to me in a sort of Morse code: *She is your perfect.*

I instantly knew this was true, and it was the most wonderful feeling.

You may have heard of Ava's father by now, the infamous Warren Winters, the man who changed the world. Yet, when I met him for the first time, he was still a genetics professor at Stanford. Ava and I had been together for two years, and even though her father taught in the building over from where I attended many of my classes, I had never met the man.

"I don't know, Ava. I've seen him from a distance, and even then he looked intimidating."

"You do realize that one day you will actually have to have a conversation with him."

"Not if we elope and go live among the uncontacted tribes of New Guinea."

Ava giggled. "I'm not entirely convinced that would stop you from meeting him. I'm his baby girl after all."

"Exactly my point!" I said. "I'm dating his baby girl!"

She rolled her eyes. "Just come to dinner tomorrow night. He can be sweet, once you get to know him a bit."

Ava had been working on me for weeks, and when she wanted something, I could only resist for so long. The next evening, I shelved my signature shorts and flip-flops and put on my nicest button-down. Ava squeezed my hand as we walked up the driveway to her father's house and assured me that everything would be fine. She opened the front door.

"Ava? That you?"

"Yeah, Dad."

"I'm in the kitchen," Warren said.

Ava led me through a living room that was stark and undecorated. The coffee table was filled with papers, journal articles, and graphic data. In fact, every surface had a book or some manner of reading material on it. I found it a bit odd, but he was an academic widower.

"Dad," Ava said, "this is Jon. Jon, this is my father."

Warren Winters was a tall, stick-thin man in his midfifties. His pale skin was unlike Ava's, but their other characteristics firmly established that they were father and daughter. He smiled and removed an oven mitt from his hand. "Please, call me Warren."

We shook. "Thank you for having me over, sir."

"It's my pleasure," he said with a smile. "I can't believe we've never actually met before. It's like you've been avoiding me or something."

I laughed and he smiled at me knowingly.

"I hope you don't mind spaghetti," he said. "It's my specialty."

Ava scoffed. "Specialty? It's the only thing you know how to cook."

"That's not true. I cook peanut butter and jelly sandwiches almost every day."

"That's not cooking."

"But I toast the bread!"

Ava and I stood in the kitchen and helped Warren with whatever he needed while the pasta softened. Warren opened a bottle of wine he had bought for the occasion and poured us all a glass. The night was going much better than I had expected, and the wine helped me relax. I suspected that Ava had had the same stern talk with her father that she'd had with me earlier in the day.

Behave yourself. Be nice. He's important to me.

When the food was ready, we refilled our glasses and sat down at the small kitchen table. I dutifully scooped pasta onto three plates and passed them around.

"So, Jon," Warren said, "Ava tells me that you're going to get your PhD in nano-engineering? Any idea what you'll be specializing in?"

"I'm planning on researching how nano-technologies can work with biological structures."

"Wow, very interesting," he said.

"I think so, though I'm not sure many would agree with us."

"Ain't that the truth," Ava said, winking at me.

Warren rolled his eyes. "Psychology majors..."

"What are you working on, sir? Anything new?"

"Oh, you know, little of this, little of that."

"Tell him the truth, Dad," Ava said.

Warren looked puzzled.

"Fine, I'll tell him," she said, turning to face me. "When he achieved his goal of becoming tenured, he set a new, loftier goal of breaking into the top one hundred worldwide Candy Crush rankings. He's currently in the twenty thousands, but a few more years of hard work and he'll be in the ten thousands for sure."

"Wow," I said, "that's quite the aspiration, if you don't mind me saying."

He frowned at us, but there was humor in his expression. "What the hell is Candy Crush?"

I suddenly forgot why I had been so worried and stressed. Warren seemed perfectly hospitable to me, and it got easier as the night went on.

"How's the rest of the crew?" Warren asked. "How's Omin?"

Ava stared daggers at him. "*Omar* is doing just fine. He's still over in San Jose, going to school."

"But it's like he never left," I added. "He's the most active group texter I've ever met. It's a little overwhelming actually."

Ava smiled. "Lin is working in San Francisco as a waitress."

"Wasn't she in school?" Warren asked.

"Yeah, but she didn't like it much. Never liked school, actually."

Warren shook his head disapprovingly. "And what about Tim?" he asked. "How's good old Timmy Boy doing?"

Warren knew Tim the best because he and Ava had been friends the longest. Tim's mother had died of cancer around the same time that Ava's mom had. They'd met at the hospital when they were thirteen years old.

"Good question!" Ava said. "We see Tim the least, even though he's at Stanford too. He's really busy with school. He's trying to start med school a year early."

"Is he still seeing Dr. Thompson?"

Ava glanced over at me, then back at Warren. "Dad, that's private."

I looked at Ava, confused, but she didn't meet my eye.

"I was just asking," Warren said. "Always liked Dr. Thompson. One of my favorite mind healers."

I went ahead and changed the subject for Ava, even though I was curious about why Tim was seeing a "mind healer," as Warren put it.

The rest of the night went as well as I could have hoped for, and I told Ava as much as we walked down the driveway to her car.

"I think he likes you," she said, a huge grin on her face. "Honestly, he's not usually like that."

"Not usually like that? How often are you bringing guys over to meet your dad?"

"Let's see, you're the four...five...five hundred and twenty second? Wait, do male prostitutes count?"

"Doubly so."

"Well, gosh, I didn't know I had to keep track of stuff like that. You're so high maintenance sometimes."

We began having dinner with Warren once a month, and I came to know him better. He had two aspects to his life: Ava and work. Everything else was distant and trivial. As far as I could tell, he only had a few friends, and even those few sometimes fell into the acquaintances zone. At first, I didn't understand why; he could be positively charming when he wanted to be. Supposedly, Warren hadn't been the same since the death of Ava's mother and was becoming more eccentric with every passing year. Ever since she died, he had been researching something very secretive. Rumors spread among the faculty that he had gone off the deep end, but he was so brilliant in his field that they wouldn't dare do anything to him. Warren didn't seem to mind the gossip, though, so neither did Ava or I.

We should have paid closer attention.

CHAPTER TWENTY-FIVE

Saiph spent the next week reading *The Big Bang to Boundless* and training with Silvestre and Vincent. There was so much to learn and so little time. Vincent taught him how to use his onboard computer and radio. Saiph called Tokomoto to try it out, and the man laughed at Saiph's outright excitement at being able to talk to him from so far away. Vincent also explained all the numbers scrolling in the bottom of his vision and what they meant. It gave him directions, the weather forecast, incoming messages, and video feeds. He could even open up his book and read if he wanted. Vincent was explaining all of this to him from the shuttle.

"So all dynamics run out of energy, then?" Saiph asked.

Vincent leaned back in his chair and put his hands over his large belly. "Yep. The lower-class dynamics can run out pretty quickly, actually."

"So how do we get our energy back, exactly?"

"It's complicated, and every dynamic is different," Vincent said. "For now, just think of it like a beam of energy flowing into you at a constant rate. You use your energy, then the beam slowly fills you back up."

Saiph nodded. "And my aura suit knows how much I have left? That's what the percentage in the right-hand corner means?"

"Yes and no. We still aren't sure exactly how much energy you control. The bar will get more accurate with time, but it could be way off. You could have a lot more or a lot less, so you'll need to be careful."

"Why don't I just try and use all my energy so that I know?"

Vincent sat up and held up both hands. "Don't do that!"

"Whoa, I wasn't going to do it right now. Calm down, Vince."

He relaxed. "Sorry. It's just that it might take you a day or two to recharge, and we don't have time for that. What's more, if you lose all of your energy quickly, you'll get sick."

"Sick?"

"Yeah, it's like having a really bad flu. It happens to all dynamics."

"And nobody thought to tell me this before?" Saiph said.

"I just told you, didn't I?"

"Yeah, after I brought it up!"

Silvestre's lessons were much different than Vincent's. She taught him how to shape the energy and how to let it go. They practiced for hours so that Saiph could get the hang of how much energy he needed to release to accomplish certain tasks. Too much and he would waste energy and potentially harm someone or something that he didn't intend to. Too little and what he meant to do would have little to no effect. She also showed him how to release a wave of energy that would act like a shield for a few seconds, protecting him from projectiles and other forms of energy.

Most intense was the arms training. Supposedly, it was very difficult to injure, capture, or kill another dynamic with lasers and other projectiles, the armor being too strong and the dynamic too fast. The best way to hurt them was with hard, blunt-force trauma, which is why all dynamics carried a premodern weapon of some sort. Silvestre carried daggers. Saiph was given two swords that Vincent had made for him. He was able to send energy into the weapon and heat it to incredible temperatures, making it easier to slice through thick armor. Silvestre trained him how to use his new blades, but it was slow going.

Saiph learned things other than the workings of his aura suit too, like the fact that Silvestre treated everyone with a general rudeness and not just him. He wasn't sure if this made his opinion of her better or worse. They bickered frequently. Silvestre was unnecessarily scathing in her critiques, and Saiph's cutting sarcasm never led to a peaceful resolution. He genuinely disliked her for a while, but he soon found their exchanges almost comical, more so since it was clear that Silvestre didn't find it funny at all.

He was by the river, arguing with Silvestre about what he was and wasn't ready for, when he heard a pleasant ring in his ear.

"Hello?"

"Saiph? It's Toko."

"Toko! It's nice to hear a friendly voice. You see, I'm with Silvestre right now—"

"Saiph. I think I have found your family."

Saiph arrived at Tokomoto's pod five minutes later. Jon was also there, staring into the darkness. Saiph slipped on a pair of goggles and saw that Toko and Jon were watching a large video feed.

"Is that them?" Tokomoto asked. He pointed to a group of people on the screen.

Saiph nearly collapsed from the soul-wrenching relief he felt. They were there. Right in front of him. Darakai, Milla, Roe, and Ayanda. They were surrounded by a few strangers, but there were also other people from Altai. They were dirty, bruised, and wore the familiar Skyfaller slave uniform. Saiph couldn't see Landon.

"Where are they?" Saiph asked.

"Camp eighteen, sector forty-two. It is about fifty miles away from where Altai use to be," Tokomoto said.

"What do we do?" Saiph asked.

Jon looked at him with a frown. "Go get them, of course."

"When?"

"Now," Jon said. "Right now."

Jon left the room, and Saiph heard him speaking orders into his comm. Saiph turned to follow him but then walked back to Tokomoto. He put a hand on his shoulder. "Thank you, Toko," he said. "I will never forget this."

Tokomoto nodded. "I will be out there with you through my machines. Go."

Saiph reached the command pod and saw that Russ was already lined up with three dozen soldiers. Their faces were streaked with black, and they wore different shades of green and brown. Landon was dominating Saiph's thoughts, so he tried to focus on the task at hand.

"Where's Silvestre?" Jon asked.

Russ grabbed a strap and tugged it tight. "Should be here any minute."

"Get your people on board Amira's shuttle."

"Beta Squad, fall in!" Russ yelled. "We're going to get Saiph's mama!"

The men and women cheered, and Saiph colored in embarrassment. A pulsing sound filled the air, and a moment later Silvestre dropped from the sky in her red-and-silver aura suit.

"Where are they?" she asked.

Saiph was surprised by the urgency in her tone. "Work camp a few hundred miles north of here."

She cracked her knuckles. "We'll get 'em back, Saiph. Make those bastards pay for what they've done to you."

Saiph was too stunned to respond. He had thought that she didn't care.

"What's your energy level at?" Jon asked her.

"I'm at seventy-eight percent," Silvestre said.

"Do you want to save some energy and ride with us?" Jon asked, gesturing toward the shuttle. It was powering up, kicking dirt into the air. A strong wind emanated from underneath it, making Saiph's clothes press hard against his body.

"No, I'll go with Saiph," Silvestre answered. Jon nodded and walked up the ramp of the shuttle. It slowly lifted into the air as he walked up it.

"Wait!" Saiph called out. "How am I getting there?"

Jon smiled. "How do you think?" The shuttle door closed and lifted into the sky. Silvestre waited for him.

Another day, another life.

His aura erupted from the eight points of his body, and a burst of blue mist was thrown outward. Pain. Darkness. Light. Strength. He flexed his hands and rolled his shoulders. The feeling the aura gave him was intoxicating. He wanted to scream in delight. A red glow pulsated under Silvestre's feet, and she lifted into the air. Saiph sent energy to his aura and shot upward like an arrow of shadow.

He had never really done an extended flight before, and even though he was anxious to get there, he couldn't help but feel amazed as the land passed beneath him. Jangali felt much smaller than it had before. The lakes were dots and the trees melded together into a blanket of green.

"We're going to make this quick," Jon said over the comm. "We don't want any reinforcements to arrive and we don't want any hostages. You're authorized to use deadly force. These people have killed and enslaved, and if they don't want to give that up, then we must do what we have to."

Saiph didn't want to kill anyone. The mere idea of it sickened him. But then he thought of Worthington, Sergeant Pierce, Elean, and Aulan and the unthinkable things they had done. The image of Alistair being ripped apart by a yokai flashed across his mind. The way his arm had come off so easily... Then he heard the screams of people he loved as the metal monster strode toward them. He imagined Landon, scared and alone, being confronted by the monster and then killed.

It made him so angry. How could people do such things? Never in his life did he imagine himself wanting to hurt people like he had over this past year. It frightened him. This wasn't what the Tenets and Verses were about. Growing up, it had been easy for him to do his Verse studies, morning prayers, and ceremony preparations. Some kids thought it was boring or stupid, but Saiph had always loved them and wanted to embody them. Studying the Tenets and Verses had never been a chore. The only time they had been was in camp sixty-two, when things were hard. But what good were the Tenets and Verses if he only adhered to them during times of ease?

The fifth Tenet said that if you accepted the strangeness within yourself, then you would accept the strangeness within others. He had always thought the Skyfallers to be strange, but not once did he think to accept or understand them. How could he not have considered that? He didn't know where they came from or what made them this way. What if there was more to their story than he realized? What if some of them were forced to do this and then Saiph killed them? His stomach turned.

But the alternative was even more distasteful. Was he supposed to let his family rot away in a slave camp? Was he suppose to let thousands of others suffer the same fate? The ninth Tenet made it clear that Saiph was allowed to do what was necessary—he'd suffered a thousand pains at the hands of the Skyfallers. Then he remembered the tenth Tenet, the one that had always seemed the least meaningful to him:

If you must temporarily lose your conscious, at least hold on to your humanity.

He'd never truly known what that meant. He saw it now from a whole new perspective. He didn't want to kill people. It was wrong, and he didn't want any part in it, no matter what had happened before. But he couldn't just let the Skyfallers keep hurting others either. He would have to temporarily lose his conscious. But no matter what happened, he couldn't lose the other part of him—the human part that didn't want to hurt others. He would do only what he had to, and he would keep the tenth Tenet close to his heart while he did so. It seemed the only solution.

"Everything okay over there?" Jon asked through a private channel.

Saiph shook himself and looked over at the passenger seat of the shuttle he was flying next to. Jon was looking right at him, as if he could see through the mask and the light of his eyes and know exactly what he was thinking. How could Saiph explain? Did he even want to?

He settled on a Verse. *"If everyone is the hero of their own story, then who am I?"*

Jon was silent for a moment. Then he said, *"Ideals are like the stars: we never reach them, but like the mariners of the sea, we chart our course by them."*

Saiph was almost too shocked to take in the meaning of his words. "You know the Verses?" he asked.

"I suppose I do," Jon said.

A pocket of air made Saiph suddenly drop a dozen feet, and his stomach lurched. Instinct brought all of his attention back to the moment, and he righted himself before flying back up to the shuttle.

"ETA two minutes," Russ said over the group comm.

The green arrow that bobbed in Saiph's vision and pointed the way to the camp was getting bigger by the second. It was all about to happen.

"It will be all right," Jon said. "There's nothing wrong with setting your family free from a captor that took them from their homes in the middle of the night for no better reason than greed. It's good that you keep your ideals, even if you never reach them, but sometimes you have to take action for the benefit of others."

Saiph nodded, Jon's words reaffirming the conclusion he had already come to. It helped to hear someone else say them, though. Saiph clenched his jaw and steeled himself for the task to come.

"The camp is surrounded by large stone walls with only one entrance gate. Silvestre, Saiph, we'll need you to take care of the guard towers that surround the perimeter. Avoid using missiles or lasers; no need to light up the night. Tokomoto, try to sneak in as many drones as you can. Protect the prisoners when the chaos erupts. Russ and your ground bots will do the heavy work until Saiph and Silvestre are finished with the towers. Understood?"

They sounded off in agreement.

"Stay close to me for now," Silvestre said in a private channel. Saiph looked over and nodded to her.

"We're setting down now," Russ told them. "Get close to the wall and wait for the go-ahead."

Silvestre and Saiph glided to the trees below and crouched behind tall grass. The motion reminded Saiph of his father, who was always so quiet in the woods. Saiph checked his energy level and saw that he was at 97 percent. Not bad for a long flight.

"I'll go left," Silvestre said quietly, "you go right. We'll meet on the other side."

"How am I supposed to take out the towers without firing?" Saiph asked.

"You have a star's power at your disposal," she said. "Are you really so incompetent that you can't take out a few stone towers?"

"Oh, my apologies, warrior princess, I didn't realize—"

"Go," Jon said.

Silvestre immediately left her feet and flew toward the left tower. Saiph sent a flow of energy through his aura and rocketed toward the right tower in silent flight. He crashed through the glass window of the first tower like it was paper and cut the flow of energy to his flight systems. The four guards in the room stared at him, terrified and unmoving. If they were paralyzed with fear, then Saiph was paralyzed with indecision. He could easily kill these men, but they looked so scared.

One of the guards came to his senses, lifted his gun at Saiph, and pulled the trigger, spraying bullets everywhere. Saiph could see the bullets as if they were in slow motion. The attack shattered his confusion. He knew what he had to do, but actually doing it would be one of the most difficult things he'd ever done.

Saiph sent extra energy to his legs and arms and threw himself to the side. He hit the inner wall and bounced off it as if he could choose the direction of gravity. He grabbed the attacking guard by his uniform and hurled him toward the window. The man barreled through the glass and flew thirty feet before he plummeted to the ground. Saiph had barely put his strength into it. He did the same to the other guards without even the slightest resistance. They were too slow, too weak. Saiph burst through the other side of the tower like a bullet and into the next one in only a few seconds. He went from tower to tower, tossing people aside like pebbles. The whole ordeal took less than two minutes. An alarm hadn't even gone off yet.

"I'm done here," Saiph said in the group comm.

Don't think. Just act. The tenth Tenet is with me.

"Give me a minute," Silvestre said, breathing hard. "I can't keep this up. I'm at nineteen percent power."

Saiph checked his own energy levels: 97 percent. "Do you need any help?" he asked her.

"No, ass face, I don't."

Russ laughed into the comm. "Should probably leave that alone, Saiph. She's like a pissed-off hornet during combat."

"Only during combat?" Saiph asked.

"Well, maybe when she talks too. And when she eats or drinks or walks or breathes. Other than that she's quite pleasant to be around."

"Done," Silvestre said.

"Tokomoto," Jon said, "what's the ground looking like?"

"They know that something is wrong, but they aren't sure what it is yet."

"All right," Jon said, "Silvestre, take the back side. Saiph, meet up with Russ for this one and follow his lead."

An icon appeared on Saiph's mask that indicated Russ's location. Saiph ran along the top of the wall. If anyone were to look up, he'd be a black streak in the night. His reflexes were unworldly; anyone else trying to run along that wall, even at a normal speed, would have lost their footing and plummeted to a quick and easy death, but Saiph barely had to think about it. Most of his thoughts were elsewhere. Saiph opened a private comm to Jon.

"Do you know where my family is?" he asked.

"Tokomoto has a few insect drones watching them," Jon said.

"When the fighting erupts here in a second, a nav point will show you where they are. Help Russ for a moment and then head for your family. Tokomoto will accompany you with a dozen or so drones."

"Thank you."

"Don't forget to retract your aura before you see them. You look like a demon in that thing."

"Right. Good call."

"Good luck."

Saiph was almost to the end of the wall when an intense pain suddenly engulfed his body. It felt like his every cell was on fire. His vision blurred and he fell, barely managing to hang on to the top of the wall. After a long moment the pain vanished and he felt normal again.

What the hell was that? What's happening to me?

He was scared, but he'd have to worry about it later. His family was depending on him.

Saiph found Russ outside the entrance, hidden in the bushes with his soldiers. As soon as Saiph arrived, he nodded to the gate. "Take care of that for us?"

"How?" Saiph asked.

Russ clicked his tongue in disappointment. "I'm gonna explain to you a little philosophy I live by, Saiphy Poo. It's called the Path of a Thousand Flames and it has one tenet: when in doubt, blow it up with fire."

Saiph was incredibly nervous, but he couldn't help but laugh. Russ clapped him on the back. Saiph's stuck out his hand like he was holding an imaginary melon and started to flood his palm with energy. He wasn't sure how much he'd need for a thick metal gate like that, so he made sure to put a lot into it, which turned out to be a bit of a mistake. He let the energy loose, and a stream of blue light shot at the gate. A ground-rattling explosion lit up the night for a few moments, and debris flew in all directions. Russ and his men dove for cover.

"Holy shit!" Russ yelled. "I hereby promote you to high priest of the Path of a Thousand Flames! Let's go, boys, move in! Move in!"

Beta squad swarmed in, wearing heavy green battle suits that augmented their strength and defense. Inside, fifty guards fired machine guns at the entrance. Russ and his men were forced to take cover and fire back. Saiph rocketed high into the air, far above the camp, and looked down at the defenders. He shot back toward Jangali and landed behind them. He stuck out his hands again, sending energy to all of his fingers. A small laser fired from each of them, sending seven guards to the dirt. He did so again, and another six dropped. Russ and his soldiers moved forward and spread out.

Saiph focused on the nav point. Twelve drones flew up to his side, and he sprinted toward the green arrow. A couple of guards popped up along the way, but the drones peeled off from him to address the issue. He made it in under a minute. He stopped outside the small, pathetic barracks, unsure of how to proceed. The adjacent area was clear and quiet. Gunshots and explosions rang out in the distance. Saiph focused, and his aura came apart and folded back into his body. It hurt. He took a breath to steady himself and then went to the barracks door. The drones stayed behind.

The barracks was dark and seemingly empty. It would have been pitch black for anyone else, but Saiph could see people hiding in various places. Someone tensed next to the door. They were swinging something at him, but Saiph reached up his hand and caught the club right before it hit his face. The man yelped in surprise as another came up behind Saiph.

"Stop!" Saiph yelled. "I'm here to help! Is Roe Calthari here?"

A short girl with blonde hair stepped out from her hiding place just beyond the door, a chair leg in her hand. "Saiph?" Roe whispered. "Is that you?"

Saiph rushed up to her. "Roe, oh god, Roe. You're okay. Thank Tengrii." She fell into his arms and squeezed him tightly. He hadn't seen Roe cry since she was a little kid.

She pulled back from him. "Saiph," she said, reaching for his face, "your eyes. They're—"

"There's no time to explain," Saiph said. "I'm here with friends.

We're getting you out of here. Where's Mum? Where's Landon? Is he okay?"

"He's okay, don't worry."

Milla came running up from the back. "Roe? What's happening?" She saw Saiph and broke into tears. She enveloped him in a hug. "My boy, my sweet boy."

A man walked up from the back. "You're a smooth one, Saiph. You know I had everything under control here, right?" Darakai's large form came into view.

"Darakai!" Saiph said with a laugh. "I would never presume to steal your thunder like this. I just came to witness your grand escape!"

He laughed and grasped Saiph's forearm before pulling him into a hug. "I don't know what's happening, but it's damn good to see you. Even if your eyes are glowing like two voltbeetles."

As Saiph shook Darakai's hand, his eyes roamed the room. Others from Altai were smiling at him and nodding. Where was she?

He heard it and laughed before she could even land on him. She'd been hiding in the rafters, of course. He turned around, and Ayanda landed on his shoulders, knocking him to the ground.

"Everyone saw it!" she yelled. "Got him again!"

She looked down and smiled at him. "Took you long enough."

"Stop playing," he said, forcing a grin. "Where's Landon?"

"What's happening out there?" a man cried out.

"My friends are taking the prison and freeing everyone," Saiph said loudly, "but we have to leave before more guards come."

"Where will we go?" another said.

"We've been hiding in Fulguria. We're taking you there."

"Fulguria! That's hundreds of miles away!"

"They're barbarians! I'm not going there!"

Others yelled their agreement.

"Listen to me!" Saiph said. "It's not what you think. Now, where the hell is Landon!"

"Saiph?" a small voice said from the back of the room. Two people moved out of the way, and Landon appeared. When he saw Saiph, he rushed over on his short legs. "Saiph! Saiph! Saiph!" he yelled, running toward him with tears running down his face. Saiph bent down on one knee and hugged him fiercely.

"Saiph, Saiph, Saiph," Landon kept muttering.

"It's all right, buddy, I'm here. I'm here..." Saiph rubbed his back how he liked it and felt a bump. "What's this?"

Saiph lifted the back of Landon's shirt and peered down it. A scar ran from the top of his left shoulder to the bottom of his spine. They had whipped him.

A rage unlike anything he'd ever felt before gripped Saiph. His vision blurred because of it. He hadn't even known it was possible to be filled with this much anger, this much burning hate. He was shaking.

"It hurt real bad. Real bad," Landon said through his tears.

The ground shook slightly beneath Saiph's feet. He ran to the door and peeked outside. Two huge battle bots loomed there.

"Oh Tengrii," A woman cried. "We're doomed."

"Stand back," Saiph said.

"What are you doing?" Roe said in a raised whisper. "You can't go out there!"

"Do you trust me?" She nodded. "I promise to explain everything when we're safe. For now, step back. Stay with Landon."

She took a step back, and Saiph waved the group back another step.

Another day, another life.

The black armor sprang from his body and covered him in under four seconds. Everyone cried out in alarm.

"Witchcraft!"

"Black magic!"

Saiph's already magnified senses were compounded in the aura. He filtered out the cries of alarm and heard the battle bots stop and swivel their heads toward the barracks. Saiph burst out of the door and bounded toward the two killing machines. They reacted quickly, shooting an array of lasers at him. Saiph hit the ground and slid under them. He used his momentum to pop back into the air. The machines adjusted their aim at a frightening speed, much faster than Saiph had anticipated. Saiph raised a hand and sent a ball of energy at one of the bots. It exploded in a heap of metal. The shot also threw him to the side, allowing him to dodge the other beams that were streaking toward his chest.

Saiph landed on the ground near the bot and surged energy into his right leg. He kicked the machine, and its legs flew out from underneath it. As Saiph kicked, he simultaneously sent energy to the jets in his back and lifted into the air. Before the ten-ton bot could even hit the ground, Saiph clasped his hands together and brought them down hard on front of the machine. The metal folded inward, and it hit the ground so hard that a large cloud of dust rose from its lightless corpse.

Saiph turned around to see the others standing outside. They stared at him, mouths agape. Roe slowly walked up to him, thought about speaking, but then quickly shut her mouth.

"Follow me," Saiph said.

———————

They made it back to Fulguria with minimal losses: six injured and two killed by a lurking battle bot. When they landed, Milla and Roe hugged him again. Landon clung to his leg wherever he went, probably scared that his favorite human would leave him again. Charlotte and Chet had also arrived a few hours earlier. Saiph was filled with happiness, but the reunion with family and friends also served as a reminder of who was still missing. He was bombarded with so many questions by the other Altainians that he could hardly catch his breath. Jon came to his rescue.

"Everyone!" he said. "Everyone, may I have a moment of your time, please?" The frantic group turned to him and quieted. "Thank you. I know you've been through a great ordeal and that you have many questions. I promise that we will do the best we can to answer them for you, but it will take time. For now, I recommend taking in this moment and celebrate the fact that you are out of that dreadful place. I'm so sorry for what has been done to you, but we will try to make Jangali a better place. Please see my friend Treyges here, and he will show you a place to put your belongings and sleep."

The crowd's energy died down, and the weight of the last eight months surfaced. They shuffled over to Treyges, and he sent them with a Fulgurian escort to show them to an empty hut or pod.

Saiph gestured to his mother, Roe, Ayanda, Darakai, and Charlotte. They barely fit in his small hut, but they also didn't want to be apart. Saiph told them everything that had happened to him since the attack on Altai. When he laid it all out at once, even he found it hard to believe. The others didn't interrupt him, but Charlotte cried quietly when Saiph told them of Alistair's death.

"It's been a long night," Milla said. "Let's rest now."

Everyone found a spot in the small hut and began to settle in. Darakai and Roe took the back corner and leaned against the wall and small table. Milla laid on the bed after Saiph insisted she take it. Charlotte lay down at the foot of the bed, wanting to be alone.

"I'm going to go get some water," Ayanda said, looking meaningfully at Saiph.

"I'll show you where it is."

Landon clung to Saiph's leg and pulled on his sleeve like he did when he wanted to whisper something to him. Saiph bent down. "What is it, Lando?"

"I'm scared," Landon whispered.

"Want to come with Ayanda and me to get water?"

Landon nodded.

The three of them left the hut and followed the path down to the river. It was late and hardly anyone was out.

"I'm sorry," Saiph said, "but I have to ask. Where's your mother?"

Ayanda grimaced and shook her head, unable to say the words. Saiph stopped walking and wrapped her in a hug. Landon couldn't understand what was happening, but he hugged them both as well. When Ayanda was able to collect herself, they kept walking.

"What about you?" she asked. "Are you okay?"

Saiph shrugged. "It's been a hard year."

They got to the river, and Saiph held Landon's hand and guided them toward a sitting area near the bank. Ayanda gestured to Saiph's eyes. "What's happened to you? And your leg...it seems better."

Saiph smiled every time he thought about his leg. "They healed it. I can walk and run like everybody else. And my lungs are better too."

"That's not all that's new," Ayanda said, gesturing toward his eyes.

"Right. That's a bit harder to explain."

Two older Fulgurian men came down the path, speaking quietly. They nodded at Saiph and Ayanda as they passed.

"What about these people you're with, then?" Ayanda asked. "Do you trust them?"

"We can trust them," Saiph said firmly. "They could have done anything they wanted to me after my escape from Elean and Aulan. I was completely helpless. But you know what they did? They fixed me up, protected me, taught me, and helped me get you and my family back."

"Still," Ayanda said, "what do we really know about them?"

"I admit that I don't know the details, but I know enough. I know that they're good people. Not everyone can be bad out there." Saiph paused. "And there is something about Jon, the man who leads them. You'll see it when you talk to him more, but there is something there. It's difficult to describe."

Ayanda put a hand on his knee. "I don't know them, but I trust your judgement."

Saiph placed his hand on hers. "Are you doing all right, though? Really?"

Ayanda sighed. "No, not *really*. But I'm just so glad to be out of there and to see you're alive and well. It's been a while since any of us had something good happen."

Landon had been leaning his head against Saiph, and now he was softly snoring. They sat together quietly with only the sound of the river flowing gently by. Had he done right? It felt like he had, sitting here with Ayanda and Landon. But then he remembered one of the guards he'd thrown out a tower window. He could see her terrified face as she fell to her death. Guilt washed over him.

"What are you thinking?" Ayanda whispered, not wanting to wake Landon.

Saiph swallowed hard. "Yeah. I just...I killed people back there at the camp. Lots of people."

"Wish I could have." Ayanda scoffed. "The ninth Tenet was broken, Saiph. They were the worst people I've ever met. Why do you feel bad?"

"I just do," he said, shrugging.

"Fine. Feel bad for tonight, but seriously, don't get hung up on it. They *whipped* Landon. They killed my mum. For what? Why? So they could have us farm?" Her disgust and hatred for the Skyfallers was palpable.

"Hey," Saiph said, "you won't believe what else I've learned. All people come from a place called Earth. And we were once monkeys."

Ayanda looked over with a cocked eyebrow, the darkness in her eyes subsiding. "Did you hit your head? It's okay if you did. I just need to know the truth."

"Nope. Head is as incredibly sharp as it has always been. You see, it all started with a bang..."

They probably should have gotten some rest, but Saiph didn't care. They stayed up half the night talking. After all, it wasn't often that one got to explain the history of everything to their best friend.

As Saiph recounted what he had learned, an idea began to form. He should have seen it before, but he had been so worried and busy.

"The camp you were at," Saiph said, "did you know the Skyfallers that captured us didn't build those?"

Ayanda frowned. "Really? How do you know that?"

"A few things. One: I overheard two of the guards at my camp talking about the walls and wondering where they came from. Two: The walls are *old*. Remember the Skyfaller we captured in the woods? He said they'd been here for ten years. Three: Jon said that Jangali was only recently discovered." Saiph stood up and started pacing, the idea injecting some adrenaline into him.

"Do you think our ancestors built those walls?" Saiph asked.

Ayanda considered it, but then slowly started shaking her head. "No. There's no way we built them. There's not enough of us."

"Exactly. I don't think the others realize that yet. I think they assume that we built them. But if we didn't, then who did?"

As if the gods had heard his question, just the person he needed to see came strolling down the path. "Stay with Landon for a second," Saiph whispered. "I'll be right back."

"Where are you going?"

Saiph didn't want to lose the figure in the darkness. He jogged to catch up but slowed as she bent down to the water at the riverbank, sipping it and splashing her face.

"Hey," Saiph said, "how you doing?"

Charlotte turned around sharply but relaxed when she saw who it was. "Doing fine, I suppose." She went back to cupping water in her hands.

Saiph was so excited, he wanted to just blurt out his question. He held back, though. "What will you do now?" he asked instead.

Charlotte shrugged. "I really don't know. Probably stay here for a while. If you all are freeing the camps, then maybe I can find some survivors from back home."

Saiph nodded. "I'll help you, if I can."

"Thanks."

Charlotte sat on the ground and then placed her feet in the water. She looked tired and beaten down. She was probably still grieving about Alistair. First, she'd lost her entire village and home; then, the very next person she cared about was killed. She must feel cursed. They sat quietly together for a time, but Saiph couldn't keep it in any longer.

"You know I can fly now?" Saiph asked.

"Good for you."

"Well, I was thinking that maybe I could fly to your village. See if anyone is there?"

Charlotte perked up. "That's a good idea. Why didn't I think of that?"

"It takes a while to get used to the idea that we can travel hundreds of miles in under an hour," Saiph said.

She chuckled. "Yeah, I guess you're right. You'd do that for me?"

"Yes, of course." He licked his lips. "There's something else though too..."

Charlotte eyed him. "What?"

"You know the building of the Old Gods near your village? The one built into the mountain's side that no one ever came back from?"

"Yeah..." Charlotte said.

Saiph smiled, the light of his eyes glowing brightly in the night. "I want to see what's inside."

CHAPTER TWENTY-SIX

E ntry 4:

I graduated from Stanford in the spring of 2026 and would start my graduate program that upcoming fall. To celebrate, Ava and I had everyone over to our apartment.

"Nano-engineering," Omar said. "I always knew you were dim, Jon, but this is crossing a line. Might as well study the art of bobblehead manufacturing for all the good it will do you."

"Nano-engineering is the future!" Ava said, coming to my defense.

"You, my dear, are a parrot who has bought in to Jon's elaborate lies."

I laughed. "What's your major again, Omar? Isn't it, let's see... Muggle studies?"

"Humanities!" Omar said. "What's more important than that!"

I clapped him on the back. "You're right, you're right, I'm sorry!"

Omar laughed. "Congratulations, Jon, can't wait to see what you do next!"

"Thanks, Omar."

He wrapped me in a bearlike hug.

"Where's Lin?" I asked, pulling away. The room was crowded with friends and people from my graduating class, but really, all I wanted was to see my Reluctant Familiars.

"Linsanity has arrived," Lin said, carrying a bottle of liquor under her arm and holding glasses. She wore a black leather jacket and had gotten her nose pierced since I had last seen her.

"What is that!" I said, pointing to her nose.

"It's a manifestation of my rebellious nature," Lin said. "Now shut up, we must drink to your success. Where's Tim? Tim!"

Tim slid between a couple of people and joined our little circle. "I've been summoned?" he said. He eyed the shot glasses in Lin's hand. "Oh no, no way, I'm not doing that. I've got class tomorrow."

"Come on, Tim!" Ava said. "You've always got something tomorrow. Live for the now!" She smiled at him. "Come on, you can do it. Say yes..."

Tim sighed. "Yes, fine..."

"Just like old times!" Omar yelled.

Lin poured our shots, and we threw them down with a grimace.

"That was horrible," Ava said.

"Round two?" Lin said.

"No!"

"Absolutely not."

Lin shrugged. "It was just a suggestion, be cool, be cool."

"Where's Chris?" I asked. "Was he able to get off work?"

Lin poured herself another shot and then lifted it in a toast. "To cheating assholes," she said, tipping it into her mouth.

"Ah man," Omar said, "say it ain't so."

"I swear, I am only attracted to the worst people."

Ava took a step over and wrapped an arm around Lin. "Why don't we talk shit about Chris until you feel better? You always like that."

Lin nodded shyly. "Yeah, okay."

Ava looked up at Tim and me, and we glanced between each other.

"Um," Tim said, "um...Chris was a very stupid man. Yes, very stupid. I brought up the radicalization of Colombia once, and he went on for thirty minutes about how he hated Columbia University because some chick who went there never called him back."

Lin laughed.

"I'd like to stay on the subject of Chris's subpar intelligence," I said. "Once, we were watching television and a picture of Mount Rushmore came up and he said, 'Crazy, how nature made that.' Like erosion and weathering just happened to carve four United States presidents into the side of a mountain."

Lin laughed even harder. "How could you not have told me these stories before!"

"We couldn't!" I said. "He was your boyfriend!"

The apartment was loud with music and people, but we stayed in our little circle for over an hour, talking and catching up. No matter how much time had passed between the five of us, we always fell right back in to our old rhythm. Omar was loud and laughed at everything everyone said. Lin was sultry and beautiful. Tim was quiet and sad looking but always exceedingly witty whenever he spoke. And Ava was always the sweetest, always taking care of everyone.

"So, Timothy," Lin said, "or should I call you Dr. Timothy? Have you been hanging out with all the cute med-school girls?"

Tim was expressionless. "Please don't call me that."

"What? Timothy or Dr. Timothy?"

"Any form of Timothy. You know I hate it."

"Are you avoiding the question, Timothy? Is a cute girl with you here right now or something?" Lin started scanning the room.

Tim breathed out and then walked away from the circle.

Ava shot Lin an annoyed look.

"What? What did I say?"

"You know how he is. Can't you just leave him be?"

Ava left the circle and went after Tim.

Lin rolled her eyes. "He can be so sensitive. I'm one of his best friends, for crying out loud. And he does need to find a girl!"

Ava disappeared into the crowd without a response.

"Whatever," Lin said. "I'm getting a beer. You guys want one?"

Omar and I nodded and Lin left. We looked at each other, not knowing what to say after the sudden departure of the rest of our circle.

"And then there were two," Omar said.

"Yeah...didn't see that coming. Did you see that coming?"

"No, no, definitely didn't see that coming."

Some drunk guy we didn't know fell down nearby and spilled his drink everywhere. We both took two steps back to avoid the mess.

"Omar," I said, "do you think Tim is too sensitive?"

"Oh yeah, definitely. Can't talk to him about anything important without him running off like that."

"Why do you think he does that?"

"Don't know," Omar said, "but I figure we should just be here for him when he needs us. If he wanted to talk, he'd talk."

I nodded. "How long do you think Ava, Lin, and Tim will bicker?"

Omar's face scrunched up in thought. "I'd give it a little over an hour."

"Great! That should be enough time. Don't leave this party without speaking to me first!" I said, beginning to walk away.

"Why's that? What's going on?" Omar called out to me.

"You'll see!"

"Great, thanks." Omar shoved his hands in his pockets and rocked up on his toes and then back down. "I'll just stand here alone. Alone and awkward." He trailed off, glancing at the drunk guy still trying to get to his feet. "At least I'm not as embarrassing as you."

The man looked at him, a stupid sort of grin on his face. "Yep!" he said.

The party was already thinning out a bit, so I made my rounds and talked to some of my other classmates for a while. I found that I couldn't concentrate on their conversations, though, and went to find Ava. She was speaking with one of her friends from...somewhere. She had so many that they were hard to keep track of. I grabbed Ava's hand

and pulled her away. "Sorry!" I said to her friend. "Gotta borrow Ava for a minute."

I pulled her out the door.

"Jon, where are we going?"

"To the roof, of course! No more whining!"

She laughed and ran with me up the stairs. Waiting for us were two chairs, a blanket, three candles, and some hot chocolate.

"I thought we could wind down the night up here," I said.

"Aw, you did this? It's perfect!"

We sat down in the chairs and covered ourselves with the blanket. The night was so crisp and clear that we could even make out a few stars in the sky.

"If you found a genie lamp and had three wishes," I asked her, "what would they be?"

It was late now, and the music from downstairs had stopped. Only the sound of distant cars carried on the wind.

"Altruistic wishes or selfish wishes?" she asked.

"Selfish, of course."

"I'd want to be able to speak every language in the world!" she said, throwing her hands in the air.

"Oooh, that's a good one."

"Your turn," she said.

"I'd wish for the ability to time travel."

"What, and mess with the space-time continuum, dooming us all?"

"And there would be no negative consequences!" I tacked on.

She smiled and wagged her finger before bringing her hot chocolate to her lips and drinking.

"I'd wish to have a magical cell phone that would let me talk to my mom whenever I wanted."

She rarely spoke of her mother, but I knew she was in her thoughts often enough.

"I'd request one too, just in case yours broke."

She blew me a kiss and rocked back in her chair. I caught it and slapped it to my cheek.

"Oh, and of course I'd ask for ten billion dollars," she said.

I laughed. "What would you even do with that much money?"

"What anyone would do," she said. "Hot strippers and copious amounts of cocaine, Scarface style."

I got up and walked over to her footrest to sit down. "I'll have you know that my premium rates can only be afforded by the billionaire class. And it's extra if you want a little action."

She laughed harder than she usually would have. "You have one more wish," she said, still smiling.

I reached into my pocked and pulled out a small black box, dropping to a knee beside her. "I would wish for you to marry me, to agree to have your story intertwined with mine. I love you, Ava, more than most people can comprehend, I think."

She cupped a hand over her mouth and nodded. "Yes, Jon. Of course, yes."

It wasn't grand and romantic, but that was never our way. We spoke the same language and saw the world through the same lens, only in a slightly different shade. We were happy with each other, and that was all that ever mattered.

A little while later, we went downstairs to break the news. We walked inside, and everyone had gone but Lin, Omar, and Tim.

"Where have you two been?" Lin said. "We're not cleaning up this mess ourselves."

Ava broke into a huge smile and lifted her left hand for them to see.

"No!" Lin said, sitting up like she had just been electrically shocked.

Omar's eyes lit up and his mouth dropped opened. "Are you serious right now! Are you serious!"

Lin got up and ran over to Ava, hugging her and screaming in delight. My gaze found Tim, and he was sitting there with a frown on his face, his mouth hanging slightly open. He was staring blankly at the floor.

"Tim," I said.

He looked up and broke into the biggest smile I had ever seen from him. "Congratulations! Wow! I can't believe it."

I shook hands with Tim and Omar, and Lin gave me a huge hug. I wrapped an arm around Ava and smiled at her. I couldn't believe that I had gotten so lucky. I had a family again, and it was one of the happiest moments of my life.

We were married at a small vineyard on May 14 of the following year. All of our friends and family attended and told us repeatedly how happy they were for us. We danced as the sun set behind the California mountains and drank the wine that the very earth we walked on had provided. I knew that it would be one of those days that would stick out in my memory for the rest of my life, and it still does, even after all these years.

"Don't stop spinning me!" Lin cried out.

Omar's muscles bulged out of the dark suit he was wearing as he spun Lin around and around.

"You're going to throw up!" he said.

Lin had her eyes closed to keep from getting dizzy. "At least I'll be spinning!"

Ava and I were dancing more conservatively, but we laughed at Lin's enthusiasm. I put my hand on the arch of Ava's back and pulled her in closer.

"Oh!" she said. "Watch it there, mister."

"Oh, wife, don't be so dramatic."

Ava smiled at me. I couldn't stop saying "wife" ever since the ceremony.

"Have I told you how beautiful you look yet? I didn't forget to mention that, did I?"

Ava rolled her eyes. "Only like a million times. But you can keep on saying it if you want. I don't mind."

I kissed her.

"Where's Tim?" Ava asked, looking around.

"Last I saw, he was walking off with his date. Can you believe he brought a date? She's pretty too!"

Ava kept scanning the area for him.

"He's really come out of his shell this past year," I said. "I'm proud of him."

Ava brought her attention back to me. "I am too. I hope he's happy and having fun."

The song ended to applause, and I escorted Ava off the dance floor and to our table to sit and take a break.

"Have you noticed that Omar seems a bit down?" Ava said.

I frowned and looked over at him dancing with Lin. He was smiling. "He looks perfectly happy to me?" I said. "Look, he's smiling and dancing."

"I know," Ava said, "but it just seems a bit forced, is all. Sometimes, I think he feels like our lives are moving faster than his or something."

I wasn't sure how Ava had come to this conclusion, but I had learned to trust her instincts on this sort of thing.

"What do you mean?" I asked.

"Well, you're really smart and successful in school. I'm going into my own PhD program. We're married now. Tim is going to be a doctor. Lin has traveled all around the world, but what's he done?"

"He's done lots of stuff! He graduated college and teaches high school. I could never be as good a teacher as he is."

"I know, but I don't think he sees it that way. I think he feels a little left behind."

"Oh..." I said lamely. "Will you talk to him?" I said.

She shrugged. "I'll try."

I was silent for a while, thinking about what Ava had said, when Warren approached us.

"Jon," Warren said. "Son!" He laughed drunkenly. "That'll take some getting used to."

"Warren," I said, laughing. "Father!"

We both laughed much harder than was appropriate, and Ava shook her head at us. This was the first time I'd ever seen Warren intoxicated, and it was a sight to behold. I only saw him drunk a few other times throughout his life, but this was the only time it was for a happy reason.

"I want to give you two your wedding gift now, if that's all right. I can't wait any longer."

Ava and I stood up, and we followed Warren past the bar and band and over to an elegant gazebo. The first crickets had begun to sing, and a pleasant breeze was making the vines sway around us.

"Right, so I wanted to give you your wedding gift," he said. "The first part of it anyway." Warren pulled out a small box and handed it to Ava. "I had them specially made."

Ava opened the box, revealing two identical rings. They were each shaped like an infinity symbol or double helix, two strands of gold weaving around each other. A small inscription was written in Latin on the outside of them.

"Wow," Ava said breathlessly, "they're stunning. What does it say?"

"Yours says, 'to see a world in a grain of sand and heaven in a wild flower.' And Jon's reads, 'hold infinity in the palms of your hand and eternity in an hour.' It was one of your mother's favorite William Blake poems."

"That's very beautiful. Thank you."

He waved a hand. "This is only the first part. The second half I'll give you in a few years. I'd hoped to give it to you today, but it's not quite ready yet."

"You don't have to do anything else for us, Dad. You've done more than enough. We're just grateful to have you in our lives."

I nodded along at Ava's sentiment.

"It's not just for you, it's for me too. I want you to have it. Don't worry, you'll see."

Ava hugged her father and then Warren stepped forward and embraced me as well. The gesture surprised both Ava and me. When I think of Warren now, I try to think of him the way he was on that day.

CHAPTER TWENTY-SEVEN

Saiph caught up with his family over the next couple of weeks, trying to make up for lost time. They explained to him that, after Altai was destroyed, they had made their way south, hoping to find refuge in the next town over, but it was already burned to the ground as well. They sheltered in the forest, scavenging and hunting, too afraid to go out into the open. Two weeks later, a group of ragged-looking soldiers came by and rounded them up. They were too weak and afraid to resist, and they were sold to camp eighteen for food and booze.

The others asked him an endless number of questions, learning the truth the same way he had. Most of them accepted it readily enough, though many of the older folk, including his mother, refused to believe much of what Saiph told them about technology, machines, and Earth. When Saiph was off helping to free more slave camps, he gave the group *The Big Bang to Boundless,* and they read parts of it together, discussing ideas and fleshing out the details. They learned quickly.

He and Ayanda kept their ideas about the age of the camp walls and the building of the Old Gods to themselves for the time being. In this new world he'd entered, knowledge was like a currency, and they were bankrupt. He wanted to find out the secrets of Jangali for himself, before anyone realized there even *were* secrets.

One early morning during the first day of a winterweek, Roe approached him in the dark as he carried water back from the river. "Darakai and I are joining the army," she said without preamble.

"What? Roe, you realize that the army engages in war, there is a war on our doorstep, and that people die in wars, right?"

"Thank you," Roe said, straight-faced. "I'm glad you told me all that before I did something stupid."

"Why are you doing this?"

"How did you feel when you became a dynamic and were able to fight back?"

"I wasn't eager," Saiph said.

Roe crossed her arms. "I bet it felt incredible. Do you know how long I've dreamed of ripping them to shreds? I may not be powerful like you, but I can still fight. I want to kill the whole lot of them for what they've done. I hate them."

Saiph tried to think of what his father might say to her. "*If you are patient in one moment of anger, you will escape a hundred days of sorrow.*"

"Don't you throw Verses at me. They're just words. I've already suffered well beyond a hundred days of sorrow."

There was no stopping her. The world would change direction before Roe would change her mind. "I only worry for you."

"I'm doing this," Roe said. "I want to learn how to defend myself."

"Then I hope you learn well."

Roe put a hand on his shoulder. He held it for a moment before she left, and then he headed in the direction of the command pod. Saiph tried to order his thoughts as he walked. He'd been so focused on learning and getting his family back that he hadn't stopped to think about how quickly everything was changing. What did the projection of his life look like now? A year ago, he was going to be a volt farmer, but now... His father was still gone, and his mother was having trouble adjusting. Roe's life was about to change as drastically as his had. And what of Jangali?

How had his life become so complicated? It used to consist of working with the volt animals, learning his Verses, and spending any spare time with his friends and family. The most exciting thing he did was walking in the woods with Landon.

Walking.

Gods, how he loved walking now. At least a dozen times a day, it would hit him: *I'm not in pain. At this very moment, I don't hurt.* The lack of pain was pleasure. It was joy. It was freedom. It was indescribably wonderful. Nearly as good as flying...

So not all the changes had been bad. Everything just moved so fast on Skyfaller time. It was complicated and messy, and that was something he would have to get used to. He reminded himself of the second Tenet: *Remember what you have before you desire what you haven't.* Saiph arrived at one of his favorite spots that overlooked Tengrii's Vein and sat down. The sound of the running river helped sooth his anxiety, and he thought about all he was thankful for.

"Hey Saiph."

Saiph jumped in alarm, spinning around, but it was only Sarah. "By gods, you scared the volt out of me. How'd you do that?"

"I've been around a lot of dynamics. I know how quiet you have to be to sneak up on them." She smiled and sat down next to him.

She was a tall woman with long blonde hair, high cheekbones, and green eyes. She had an almost regal way of holding herself.

"What ya doing out here?" she asked.

"Oh, you know," Saiph said, "attempting to come to grips with the vastly complicated problems that plague my existence. Yourself?"

"Was on a run."

"What were you running from?" Saiph asked, concerned.

"Nothing, I was just running. For exercise."

Saiph looked at her like she was wearing a voltbeetle for a hat.

"All right, that's enough of this," Sarah said, "your first lesson starts now. Where I come from, people don't have to do any physical work and so they become unhealthy and possibly overweight. So some of us go running just to help move our bodies. Make sense?"

"I suppose..."

Sarah took off her shoes and put one leg over the other to stretch it out. "So, what grand problems were you meditating on out here?"

"I guess I'm wondering what's going to happen. To me, to my family, to Jangali."

"Can't say what's going to happen to you and your family, but I can tell you about what's going to happen to Jangali."

"I'll take that," Saiph said.

"The Grecian Empire, Cynix Corpartaion, and the Asura Republic will be here within weeks. Harain and the Republican Guard should be here tomorrow, and Khumbuza a few days after that. When all parties have arrived, alliances will be made, deals will be cut, contracts signed, all that good stuff. Then we'll fight it out."

"But why are they coming here?" Saiph asked.

Sarah shook her head. "That's a bit more complicated. You see, they were always going to come to Jangali at some point, because Jangali has some special properties. Not every planet has so many volt animals. And I've never even heard of a volt tree. Before, when the Essen power influx was still functional, nobody needed the extra energy, but now Jangali is like a gold mine. They could make a fortune off the volt organisms here, and the trees could be even more valuable, if we learn to grow them commercially."

Saiph kicked a pebble off the edge of the ridge. Sarah waited patiently for him to think it through. "You said that they were always going to come. If Jangali is so rich in energy, why haven't they come before?"

"Jangali is really, really far away, and it's expensive to get here, now that the gateways are gone. They were making preparations to come, but not for about fifty years or so. It was you that prompted them to come early."

"Why would they wait *fifty* years," Saiph said. "Who has that kind of patience?"

Sarah laughed. "You should see the patience Jon has. One time, he waited thirty years on Mars just to watch the first ocean fill up inch by inch."

"That can't be right," Saiph said. "Jon must be, what, thirty-five years old? Forty tops."

Sarah leaned forward, blinking rapidly. "Nobody has told you how old Jon is?"

Saiph shook his head.

"Jon is six hundred and eighty-seven years old. He's the third oldest person alive. He's the creator of the Essens and the son-in-law of Warren Winters."

Once again, Saiph felt his stomach drop at the arrival of impossible information. Like usual, he rejected it at first, then, slowly, came to accept it. No wonder the man had such a presence. He'd had over six centuries to practice, and he must have been a great man even when he was young. Saiph wasn't sure how long he sat there in stunned silence; it was sometimes hard to tell the passage of time during a winterweek.

Sarah took a deep breath and closed her eyes. "There's something about this place," she said. "We all feel it. Maybe it's the clean air and water, or the wildlife. And the trees! They're so big, I feel like I'm in a fairy tale." She paused and took another deep breath of air. "It's like Jangali is an echo of our own past, whispering to us, reminding us where we came from. It's been a while since I've felt this way."

"Where did you grow up? What's your home like if it's not like this?" Saiph asked.

"I'm from New Los Angeles, one of the largest cities in all the worlds. It has thousands of buildings that are at least six times the size of your trees here on Jangali. Fifty million people live within its boundaries, and it's a colossal mess of noise and chaos. When I was a kid, we had to wear masks outside because the machines we'd built had produced so much pollution that the air was poisonous." Sarah shook her head and chuckled. "I haven't thought about New Los Angeles in a long time."

"Sarah," Saiph said, "how old are you?"

"Where I come from, that's a highly rude question to ask."

Saiph smiled. "You're on Jangali now, and here it is terribly rude to not immediately state your age when questioned."

"Bah, fine. I'm two hundred eighteen years old. Maybe two nineteen; I have it written down somewhere."

"No way!" Saiph yelled, laughing. "My, Sarah, you've aged so gracefully!" Sarah let out a full-bellied laugh, but Saiph was fascinated and excited now. "How old is Tokomoto?"

Sarah thought for a moment. "Thirty-six, I think."

"Oh," Saiph said, disappointed. "What about Russ? Amira? Ellie? Silvestre? Vincent? Treyges?"

Sarah laughed again. "Oh god," she said. "Let's see, Vincent is only nineteen, Silvestre is twenty-six, Ellie is forty-five, Russ is forty, Amira is 114, and Treyges... Well, I don't know Treyges's age. Never bothered to ask the sniveling suck-up."

Saiph narrowed his eyes. "What about Chet? Jon said he'd known him for many years. At the time, I thought that meant something different."

"Hah!" Sarah said. "Old Chet. I have no idea, but he's at least two hundred years older than I am. I was doing research for my dissertation on the twenty-second century Wars of Unification and saw a picture of the guy. Looked exactly like he does now!"

"This is all completely ludicrous," Saiph said, wiping tears of laughter from his eyes. "I think I may be going slightly insane..."

Sarah and Saiph spent the rest of the afternoon together. She did most of the talking, explaining everything that was *currently* going on in the Sphere of Humanity. He had spent so much time on ancient history that he didn't really have a good understanding of what was happening now. Later on, Saiph admitted to Sarah that he'd never heard the name "Warren Winters" and "Boundless" was just a part of the title. So much for not skipping to the end of the book.

Sarah started with the history of the different Houses and their founders and how many of the leaders were still alive.

"How have they not killed each other after all these years?" Saiph asked as they sat down to a lunch of sandwiches and fruit. "Surely there must have been dozens of battles and assassination attempts over the years?"

Sarah swallowed the food in her mouth and took a drink of water. "The richest of them have this sort of unspoken agreement. They don't try to kill each other, and they don't fight all-out wars. It's too expensive —too risky. Most of the fighting occurs on small planets like Jangali. Thousands of others die, but not House heads or government leaders. They try and win incremental victories instead, building their power over time. Eventually, they hope to be able to control more of the power influx than their rivals and be able to subjugate them through economic and political means."

"These old fossils are rather dastardly, aren't they?"

"They didn't get to be hundreds of years old by being the hero."

"So which type of government is the most popular now?"

"Republics are probably the most common, but they're on the decline. More planets are considering the computer candidate search, surprisingly enough."

"What's that?" Saiph asked. He didn't care so much, but he could tell that Sarah loved talking about this sort of thing.

"Okay, so there's a small planet in the shallow southwestern part of the sphere that designed a computer to pick their leader. Whoever agrees to live on the planet also agrees that they will serve as dictator if the computer selects them. It has actually worked out well for them so far. We'll see what the computer does next, though."

"Why do you say that?" Saiph asked. "You make it sound like something else is happening."

"Jon explained how the Essens work?"

Saiph nodded.

Sarah shook her head, looking like she still didn't quite believe what she was about to say. "The virus that made us lose control of the Essens happened during the largest war ever fought. A war so terrible and devastating that it set us back hundreds of years. So when the Essens stopped sending energy, no one really had the time, inclination, or resources to look at what had actually happened. All we knew is that they stopped sending energy and the gateways shut down."

Sarah played with the crumbs of her sandwich as she thought about what to say next. "But the Essens stopped moving away from the core of the Sphere of Humanity and started moving back toward it. You see, we sent the first Essens very, very far away from Earth, just in case something went wrong. I mean, if the Essens covered up the sun around a planet, well, that would be it. All life would end on that world."

Saiph nodded in understanding, urging her to go on.

"So it has taken a while for the Essens to reach the outer edges of the Sphere, but they're close now. People are starting to panic. The eastern edge of the Sphere is in danger. Jon isn't concerned about it, which leads me to believe that he has a solution. Still, it's scary..."

What a mess. So the very machines that had given humanity a nearly limitless amount of energy, which had given them the ability to expand, which had made him a dynamic, were now on a rampage that could end all human life. Great.

"So what's everyone doing about it?" Saiph asked.

"Freaking out," Sarah said with a bitter laugh. "The computer selected this horrible politician guy for some reason. The Askan Empire released a statement that pretty much told the east to take care of themselves. And the Speakers—wait, did I tell you about them?"

"Nope. Missed that lesson."

"I'm sure you'll meet one eventually. It's the fastest-growing religion in the Sphere. Have their own planet and everything. They're a bit nuts, if you ask me. But anyway, they just selected a speaker of war to be their primary translator." Sarah breathed out and closed her eyes in frustration. "What I'm trying to say is that things are escalating quickly."

"Right, of course. I totally get what you're talking about..."

They finished their lunch and then walked down to the river. Sarah kept talking about the political climate of the Sphere, and Saiph felt that he was beginning to grasp the situation, but it was a lot to take in at once. How was he supposed to understand how the Grecian Empire checked the Free Worlds in the deep western quadrant of the Sphere while the Enlightened Oligarchy and Earthly Senate anchored the center? The ideas were like the stars; he could see them, but they were so distant that they didn't feel real. He dreaded the day they did become real for him, but for now, he had other questions.

"Sarah, do you know much about the Essens?"

"I know more than most, but they're really complex."

Saiph smiled. "That's okay, since my questions are probably pretty simple."

"Well, then," Sarah said, "what would you like to know?"

"Jon told me that I contracted a viral strain of the Essens virus that acted like a biomarker, which then made the Essens send power to me instead of somewhere else. But how did I even get this virus? If the Essens are so far away, how could I have possibly been exposed?"

Sarah sighed. "That is definitely not a simple question."

Saiph pursed his lips and put his palms together like he was praying.

"Oh fine," Sarah said, "I'll try my best." She thought for a moment as they continued to walk. "All right, so, an individual Essen is extremely small. Much smaller than you can even see, right?"

Saiph nodded.

"They're so tiny that they are sometimes blown off course, either by solar winds or gravitational pull or whatever. The Essen software doesn't know how to handle it, so they will move to areas of lower energy density and repel each other, which often gives them an even distribution over a very large area."

Saiph rubbed his forehead and frowned. "So if the viral strain I have is all around Jangali, why haven't more people become like me?"

"Coming into contact with the virus isn't enough," Sarah said. "The person needs to be genetically compatible with that strain of the virus. It takes a very specific mutation for someone's body to be able to contract and then use the virus, and most of the time, that mutation isn't even compatible with the strain of Essen they come into contact with. It's why dynamics are so rare."

"Okay...but if there are Essens on Jangali, then why isn't our sun in danger of being consumed?" Saiph asked.

"Well," Sarah said, "the Essens here have no hope of escaping the planet's gravity. They're stuck here. As for your sun being in danger, it takes a certain amount of Essens to reach critical mass. There aren't enough around these parts to start to multiply enough to cover an entire star.

"The Essens' strength are in their numbers. Individually, they're very small and fragile. A few Essens here and there always die off before they can multiply enough to sustain losses. Besides, the Essens that have accidentally come here don't know that they should be looking for a new star. They're still tied to the host star they've come from."

"Gods, this is confusing. I'm pretty sure I picked up exactly one percent of everything you just said."

"It's only because you're not used to the terminology. You've got to keep reading your book."

"I will," Saiph said.

They were just about to ford the river to check out one of the Fulgurian outposts when they both received a ping from Jon.

"They're early," he said. "Better come see."

Saiph and Sarah looked at each other and then started back toward the command pod.

———

Jon, Amira, Tasaday, Treyges, and Tokomoto were staring at a large projection on the wall when Saiph and Sarah entered. Saiph moved closer to get a better view, but he wasn't sure what he was seeing. Enormous flying vessels hovered over the Skyfaller city, and thousands of drones circled the larger ships. It was hard to tell how big anything was. Saiph glanced around and saw worry etched across the others' faces.

"I'm not quite sure what I'm seeing here," Saiph said.

Amira pointed to the screen. "The bigger of the flying vessels are transport ships for human and robotic troops. They carry five thousand people each."

Saiph counted four of the big ships. "Gods, that's a lot of people. How many do we have?"

Everyone looked at Jon.

"Russ has about two thousand. Toko has maybe eleven thousand."

"How are we going to fight that number plus the capital?" Sarah asked.

Saiph looked at the swarming mass uneasily.

"Others are coming," Jon said. "Maybe we can sway a couple to our side. If not, well, there are other options. Either way, we need to slow them down." Jon pointed at the screen. "House Harain and the Republican Guard ignored my hails."

Amira leaned up against the wall. "How has this happened, Jon? Didn't you used to control the Republican Guard?"

Jon laughed without humor. "I never controlled them. They've been on their own for a long time now."

They all sat in silence for a minute, thinking.

"So what are we going to do to slow them down?" Saiph asked.

"Sabotage, of course," Jon said.

Tokomoto shook his head. "Russ will be pleased. Sabotage is his favorite."

"Call him and Silvestre in, we need to act fast."

"Why?" Sarah asked.

"Because," Amira said, "tomorrow they will level the Fulgurian forest to drive us out."

The others left to prepare, and Jon explained to Saiph and Tasaday that House Harain would want to end the fight before the Grecian Empire, Cynix Corporation, the Asura Republic, and House Khumbuza arrived on Jangali and complicated the situation. The forest was a strong defensive position, so House Harain would have to drive them out of it in order to win a quick and decisive victory. The only way to do that was to level the forest with a pulse cannon.

"Is the pulse cannon in the Harain city?" Tasaday asked. "We have never been to the city, for it is very dangerous."

"The pulse cannons can't be kept in a city; they're too unstable. But I thought something like this might happen and asked Tokomoto to set up insect drones in a fifty-mile radius around the city. Harain landed one pulse cannon thirty miles east of the capital and another forty miles south. They set up a light heat shield that keeps out insect drones, but we were already inside the perimeter, so we know where they are and what they're doing."

"How long before the cannons will be able to fire?" Saiph asked.

"Twelve, maybe thirteen, hours."

"How long will it take to get there?"

"Two-hour flight time," Jon said. "Tasaday, these cannons are capable of destroying huge portions of the forest. The Fulgurian people will need to evacuate."

Tasaday frowned. "The wood is our home. We are not Fulgurians without it."

"If we fail to destroy the cannons, then everyone here will die."

Tasaday thought for a moment. "We will help destroy the cannons and get the others away from the forest. We cannot lose the wood. Our way of life depends on it."

"I agree. We cannot let that happen. Start organizing your people and volt animals. They will need to leave soon."

Tasaday bowed slightly. "*I no doubt deserve my enemies, but I don't believe I deserve my friends.*" He turned and left.

Jon's face was the same as it always was, but Saiph was starting to read him a little better.

"It's a Verse," Saiph said. "We live by a set of guidelines and ideas that are laid down in the Ten Tenets and by the Verses. All people on Jangali know them."

"Interesting..." Jon said. "I would like to know more about this, if you'd be willing to tell me."

"Of course!" Saiph said. "I've been trying to tell Skyfallers about the Tenets and Verses for a year now!"

Jon scratched his chin, thinking. "Now that you know that *The Big Bang to Boundless* is true, do you understand where your Verses come from?"

Saiph was taken aback. How had he not made the connection?

When you arise in the morning, think of what a precious privilege it is to be alive—to breathe, to think, to enjoy, to love.

His second Core Verse was something a Roman emperor had said. "Are all the Verses quotes from ancient people?"

"I don't know," Jon said, "but the ones I've heard so far have been."

Saiph felt weak for the first time since he'd become a dynamic. All of their beliefs were based on Skyfaller sayings?

"And the Tenets? What are they?" Saiph asked dazedly.

"Why don't you tell me one?"

Saiph picked the first one to came to mind. "*Remember what you have before you desire what you haven't.*"

Jon walked over to the corner of the command pod and grabbed a rolling chair. He moved it over to Saiph and offered him a seat. Saiph collapsed into it, his mind whirling. Jon got another chair and sat in front of him.

"That is no saying I've ever heard. That's all Jangali. Tell me another."

Saiph nodded, feeling better. "*Accept the strangeness within yourself, and you will accept the strangeness within others.*"

Jon smiled warmly. "I like that. I've also never heard that before. The Tenets are something of Jangali, I think."

Saiph relaxed. That was good.

"Your Verses," Jon said, "they embody some of the greatest ideas of the greatest people who have ever lived. You shouldn't be ashamed of where they came from. Wisdom is wasted on those who don't listen. It seems to me that Janglians listen very closely."

Saiph chuckled. "That should be Verse."

"What?"

"Wisdom is wasted on those who don't listen."

Jon smiled.

Saiph knew he was right. Knowing where the Verses had come from didn't really change how he felt about them or their wisdom. It didn't change anything. He would still say his Core Verses every morning and evening. He would still quote Verses at Roe, even though she hated it. And one day, he would still go on long walks with his father, discussing the Verses and their meaning.

Jon stood up. "I've got to get the wheels moving on this thing, but go and talk to Amira; she needs to brief you on what you're going to be dealing with out there."

Saiph nodded and began to leave the command pod when Jon called out to him. "Wait, there's something else you need to know." Jon looked concerned. "One of my people has betrayed us."

"What?" Saiph asked. "How do you know this?"

"Treyges was able to work it out. Someone is sending messages to House Harain, which is how they knew where we were and jumped early to get to Jangali. You're the only one in the group who I definitively know isn't the traitor. Keep your eyes open out there. Be careful."

Saiph left the command pod worried. Who could it be? He put the thought aside for the moment and pinged Amira. She was at his workshop a few pods over. Saiph knocked on the door, and Amira yelled for him to come in.

The pod was partitioned off into areas of unnecessary filth and compulsively clean. Metal parts lay everywhere, and screen readouts were filled with technical information. Amira was strapping on a protective vest and loading a type of gun Saiph had never seen before. She looked even more intimidating than she normally did.

"You're coming with us?" Saiph asked.

"Somebody must disable the pulse cannons, and I personally do not have enough trust in Russ to do this. He will leave a crater behind. I used to be with the special forces anyway."

Saiph laughed. "Is there anything you can't do?"

She shrugged off the compliment and Saiph let his eyes wander around the workshop.

"Okay," Saiph said, "I'm sorry, this may be terribly rude, but I've got to ask where your accent is from. It's brilliant."

Amira smiled and when she did, she looked like an entirely different person. Saiph liked both of them. "I am from Algeria, which lies on the northern part of the African continent on Earth. We speak the French language in my country, which gives me this accent. You know, your accent is very interesting as well. It's almost like's Earth's British accent but changed slightly. I have heard several of the soldiers speak of how attractive it is."

Saiph blushed, and Amira let out the first real laugh he'd heard from her. "So you can tell me about what we're going to face out there?" Saiph said.

"Right," Amira said. "So far, you have only fought technically inferior forces using twenty-second and even twenty-first-century technology. Now that House Harain and the Republican Guard reinforcements have arrived, that will not likely happen again." Amira must have noticed his nervousness, because she kicked an oil-stained chair over to him and gestured for him to sit down.

Saiph nodded, and Amira continued to fiddle with the large and odd-looking rifle in her hands.

"Obviously the most dangerous thing you can face out there is another dynamic, but we're not expecting any to be guarding the pulse cannons. What you'll really have to watch out for are the Andhaka."

Amira put down the rifle and picked up a large-screen tablet, manipulating it to pull up a photo and showing it to Saiph. It showed a tall, slim-looking machine that had six armlike appendages with blades on the end. Surrounding it were eight drones that looked very different from the ones Tokomoto usually used.

"The Andhaka are one of the deadliest fighting machines that you will ever face. They are extremely powerful, and they take half a year to fully charge. Their machine brains use the same quantum entanglement we use for long-distance communication to control their limbs and drone complements. Their reaction time is as fast as yours. The drones are not nearly as fast, but they are built to support an Andhaka's main body. They use thin lasers that are extremely potent and are able to cut through nearly anything, given time. If you come up against an Andhaka, don't let the lasers touch you for too long and don't let the main body grab you."

"How many of these things do they have?" Saiph asked.

Amira shrugged. "I do not know, but it shouldn't be more than two hundred in the whole army."

"Two hundred?" Saiph said, shaking his head in disbelief. "What do you do against that many of those things?"

"At once?" Amira asked. "Run. But you won't see them all together. They're incredibly expensive."

There was a knock at the door, and Amira glanced down at his screen to see who it was. "Come in!" she called out.

Chet stepped inside with a slight limp. "Oy!" he called out to Saiph. "Good to see that you are *Saiph*. Hah! Double-meanin' joke. Had me worryin' my tail off, yes you did."

Saiph smiled. "Wasn't that your job, Chet? To keep me out of danger?"

"Indeedin' it was. Did a damn fine job too. You Altainians are jus' too thick-brained to get through to. Couldn't be helped." Chet wandered over to a small table covered in tools and started going through them like they were his own.

Saiph leaned over and whispered to Amira, "So he really does talk like that, then? I thought it was part of his cover."

"He doesn't always sound like that," Amira said. "Not all the machinery is working upstairs, if you know what I mean."

Chet threw a small metal ball onto the floor in irritation. "I'm needin' an electrical stabilizer! Where you hidin' 'em, Amira?" he said, pointing at her accusingly.

Amira fumbled through a few tools next to her and picked up a small metal cube and tossed to Chet. "Are you coming with us to the pulse cannons?"

"To get myself killed?" Chet said. "Hah! No, I be engagin' in some other, safer, subterfuge."

"What else do you—" Saiph started to ask, but Chet stared at the cube in his hand and limped out the door without saying thank you or goodbye. He slammed the door so hard behind him that it made Amira and Saiph flinch.

"He's quite an odd man, isn't he?" Saiph asked.

"I believe that 'odd' is too weak of an adjective to describe him," Amira said.

Saiph laughed. "Is there anything else I need to know?"

"There are many, many things that you need to know. Forgive me, but you are still very ignorant. Unfortunately, we do not have time to go over it all right now. My only advice is this: In the countryside, you have faced nothing but outdated and obsolete technology. And the suit makes you feel invincible, I am sure. But, Saiph," Amira said, "you are not invincible. If you are not careful, the Andhaka will kill you."

Sobered, Saiph nodded. "Do we have any Andhaka?"

"Yes, we do. Russ has one of the largest privately owned stockpiles in the Sphere. He buys them all secondhand, though, and they are constantly in need of repair." Amira rolled her eyes in frustration, then shrugged. "He is very good with them, I must admit."

Saiph felt a little knot in his stomach unwind. "Good. I'm glad we'll have some of our own with us."

"Oh no, they will not be coming with us today. Russ will save them for when he truly needs them."

And just like that, the knot was back, tighter than ever.

"I will need you to accompany me during the excursion," Amira said. "You'll have to cover me while I disable the cannon."

"Who else will be with us?" Saiph asked.

"Russ, Silvestre, and a few techs will be attacking the other cannon. Tokomoto will be helping both teams, which leaves us with a few of Russ's soldiers and the Fulgurian contingent."

"Will it be enough?"

"I believe so. They will not be expecting us."

CHAPTER TWENTY-EIGHT

"Where are we being taken?" Ayanda asked.

Fulgurians, Altainians, and soldiers moved about them with a sense of urgency, packing items, organizing children, and loading them onto shuttles.

"A place in the mountains," Saiph said. "We'll hide there if the forest is destroyed."

She shook her head. "I don't understand the Skyfallers. Is there nothing they will not do?"

"They're monsters, plain and simple," Roe said, kicking the dirt.

Saiph didn't know what to say. Maybe she was right.

Landon tugged on Saiph's shirt. "Where you going?"

"Not far," Saiph said. "There's no need to worry; I'll see you soon."

A shuttle lifted off through the trees a little way in the distance and then flew north. The noise was dimmed by a deep roll of thunder. The rain would fall soon.

"It's time to go," Saiph said.

His mother came up and cupped his face. "Please be careful."

"I will."

Saiph watched their shuttle fly away and then left for the command pod. If the rest of the village was frantic, then the command zone was in chaos. Russ's soldiers, who called themselves Blackhawks, were being outfitted in their enhancement suits; techs fiddled with equipment; and the Fulgurian's volt animals were roaring and clawing, their bodies steaming slightly when the rain hit them. Saiph noticed that many of the others were wearing coats to protect them from the rain and cold. He didn't feel either, though, at least not in the way they did. He could sense that it was there, but it didn't bother him. If anything, he felt hot.

Many nodded at Saiph as he passed, looking at him almost as if they were in awe. Not knowing what else to do, he nodded back. At the center of the clearing, he found Jon speaking with Russ and Silvestre.

"There's my high priest!" Russ shouted with a laugh. "Not even cold, you see that!" How he could be so buoyant before a battle like this astounded Saiph. "Remember the Path of a Thousand Flames while you're out there, no matter what Amira tells you otherwise. Those special forces, man... Too sneaky for my liking."

Russ walked off and started barking orders to his soldiers as Silvestre finished speaking to Jon. She turned to Saiph. "Try not to do anything beyond your normal stupidity out there and get yourself killed. We still have to train you in hand-to-hand combat."

"As always, the grace of your wisdom leaves me in a state of peace. Thank you." She scoffed and walked off. Saiph actually managed a smile.

Jon looked serious as he faced Saiph. "If anything happens while you're out there, fly back to the mountains. Listen to Amira and don't bite off more than you can chew. Remember who you're coming back to."

"Where will you be?" Saiph asked.

"With the others, but beside Tokomoto. I'll be watching, but ping me if you need to."

Saiph watched Jon board the last of the shuttles leaving for the mountains. It lifted off the ground with a roar and escaped the tree line, the engines bright in the black sky. All that remained were the teams heading to the pulse cannons. The chaos had died down, and a quiet nervousness pervaded the camp as people made their final preparations. The emptiness of the surrounding village was eerie, and Saiph could hear the wildlife more clearly than he ever could before. It reminded him of the home he had lost.

Amira stepped out of a pod wearing dark-purple armor. She walked into the light and called out to the soldiers.

"Alpha Team, let's load up! Shuttles one, two, and three are for us. Blackhawks, separate yourselves into groups of five and intersperse yourselves with our Fulgurian friends. Introduce yourselves on the way over."

Russ called out similar instructions and led Beta Team onto their shuttles. Within a few minutes, they were in the air, flying south.

———

Saiph flew a hundred feet to the right side of the shuttle, his black form nearly invisible in the night. Flashes of lightning were periodically lighting up the world before it plunged back into darkness. It didn't do anything to help calm his nerves.

"Two minutes," Tokomoto said into Saiph's ear. "We are going for speed. Get Amira to the cannon as quickly as possible. As soon as the cannon is deactivated, retreat. I estimate that capital reinforcements will arrive within twelve minutes of initial contact."

Saiph pinged his confirmation.

Amira contacted Saiph. "I will only need a minute or so to disable the cannon, but I will be defenseless and vulnerable while I do so. The control panel I have to access is on the rear left side."

"I'll stay near you," Saiph said, "but you may want to have Tokomoto do most of the protecting. I don't have any experience with this sort of thing."

"Staying near me will probably be enough. You've been working on your shield bursts?"

"Yeah, I can manage that much."

A nav point indicated a clearing that was coming up fast. Saiph readied himself. He drifted to the rear of the shuttle and hid himself behind it. They wanted to keep Saiph's presence secret until they hit the ground.

"Incoming," Tokomoto said.

An explosion of noise came from the clearing, and balls of light streaked toward the shuttle. The shuttle banked left, then right, and Saiph followed behind it as if he were the exhaust. The shuttle sent out a succession of shield bursts, and explosions rippled the air.

"We just used half our shield energy," Amira said. "We need to land."

The shuttle dropped precipitously and skimmed the top of the trees. At the first sight of the clearing, the shuttle dipped even lower and then landed hard on the ground. The shuttle doors flew open, and Tokomoto's robotic ground troops leapt out and his drones filled the air, shooting down missiles that were heading for the shuttle. Amira, the Fulgurians, and the Blackhaws were barely out of the door when a ball of plasma came hurtling toward the ship.

"Saiph!" Amira shouted, pointing to the plasma.

Saiph leapt from behind the engine and flew at the ball of fire. He consolidated energy into his core and then flung it out in an even distribution. It struck the plasma, and it exploded with a tremendous force. The ground troops from both sides were thrown to the ground, but Saiph was already flying toward a bunker full of automated sentry guns. He shot a hole through the top with a missile from his shoulder and then entered it, ripping the sentry guns apart with his bare hands. Everyone else was so slow, like they'd all just woken up from a coma while he was already sprinting. It was too easy.

He threw himself out of the bunker and emerged to see the two sides recovered and firing at each other in earnest. Lasers lit up the night in flashes.

"Where's the cannon?" Saiph shouted into his comm.

"We landed too far away," Tokomoto said into his ear. "It is a few hundred feet up ahead. We need to get Amira to that cannon right away."

"So what do we do?" Saiph yelled as he shot bursts of energy into the sky like a moving mortar cannon.

Tokomoto took a moment, then said, "The Fulgurians are taking the left; I will take the right. You go down the center. I will call you if one side needs help." The comm cut out.

"Amira, where are you?" Saiph asked.

"Twenty feet behind you, hiding in a ditch. I heard Tokomoto. I will follow you."

Saiph watched as the Fulgurians and the Blackhawks parted to the left and Tokomoto's drones and droids went right. He flew down the center, firing slivers of energy from his fingers with inhuman precision, felling the Harain's human defenders. He was called several times to the left side to deal with the bigger battle bots that the Fulgurian animals and Blackhawks were incapable of handling. The forces on the right was progressing far more quickly, and he was finally understanding how dangerous Tokomoto could be. His robotic troops and drones darted in and out as if they were a single organism. How Tokomoto managed it, he had no idea. And he was doing the same thing with another group of units at the other pulse cannon. Incredible.

Saiph burst through a dense section of trees and saw the cannon sitting in another clearing. It was much bigger than he'd expected, at least sixty feet long and ten feet in diameter. Its casing was clear, and he could see its innards of entangled wiring.

"It's here, Amira."

She came up beside him, and they crouched behind a tree. "It seems quiet," she said.

"Maybe they're distracted elsewhere?"

"Maybe... Be ready. On my go, run for the back of the cannon." Amira held out her hand, then looked around and listened for a moment. "Go."

Saiph ran into the clearing, the blue veins in his suit pulsing with energy, his eyes ghostlike in the darkness. They reached the back of the cannon without incident, and Amira pulled a panel off and began pushing buttons. Saiph scanned the perimeter. He caught movement at the tree line, and when he listened closely, he heard a faint buzzing.

Thirty drones burst from the cover of the trees, and the ground shifted in two distinct spaces twenty feet away from the cannon, like two giant moles digging up to the surface. Saiph lifted off the ground and let marble-like bursts of energy shoot from his hands. Like a machine gun, the lasers fired in a large radius and kept the drones at bay. At the same time, he brought energy into his core, ready to release a shield.

"Saiph, watch out!" Amira yelled.

Saiph turned just as two Andhaka burst from the ground, their specialized drones firing their thin and deadly yellow lasers. Saiph released his shield burst, saving both him and Amira. Saiph was just steadying himself when something slammed into him with the force of an avalanche. His head whipped back, and pain flared through his body. A pounding reverberated through his back. Alarms were blaring over his vision.

Saiph sent a huge burst of energy into his feet and back to get away from the blows. He turned around to see Aulan hurtling toward him, his yellow-and-silver aura bright against the night. Saiph brought his hands together and fired a thick beam of energy, but Aulan curled into a ball and spun like the wheel of a truck. When he reached Saiph, he unfolded and kicked Saiph in the chest. As Saiph flew back, he gathered energy into his hands and feet. He caught movement out of the corner of his eye and flung his hands into the air, sending beams up and forcing his body down. A metal blade cut through the tree next to him and sliced through it like it wasn't there. Saiph was reeling at the machine quickness of the Andhaka.

"You *are* fast, aren't you!" Aulan said. "Oh well, more fun this way."

"Toko!" Saiph said into his comm.

"Get out of there, Saiph! I am doing all I can to save Amira."

Saiph spared a look at the cannon and saw drones and bots getting torn apart by the other Andhaka. Amira had stopped trying to disable the panel and was firing her strange gun at the enemy, but nothing seemed to hit.

"What about the cannon?" Saiph asked.

"Forget it," Tokomoto said. "Get out. Now."

The Andhaka prowled behind Aulan like it was some sort of wild predator. It moved in such a fluid way that it seemed alive.

"Your suit is rather impressive," Aulan said. "I'll need to have it reverse engineered when I take it out of your body."

The Andhaka darted forward at a blinding speed, and Saiph shot tiny lasers at its drones and torso. It spun in the air and twisted perfectly to avoid his shots. Saiph flew up to get away, only to find Aulan above him. Saiph fired lasers and missiles toward Aulan, but Aulan had a shield burst ready and blew up his attacks. Saiph was forced back to the ground where the Andhaka waited.

His heart pounded in his chest as he frantically thought about what to do.

Saiph looked around and then ran into the nearby trees, hoping they would cover him from Aulan's projectiles while he fought the Andhaka. The forest was dark, but Saiph could hear the machine stalking him. It emerged from behind a tree and scuttled toward him. Saiph jumped back and fired lasers, but the Andhaka dodged them again. It closed the distance in a flash and began swinging its blades at Saiph from several directions at once. He dodged two and deflected another, but a fourth blade buried into his side. He screamed in pain. A fifth and sixth blade were coming down to finish him off when a series of lasers forced the Andhaka to retreat.

The machine looked around like a confused animal and then charged Saiph again. A woman darted out from the brush, as fast as the Andhaka. She jumped in the air and touched the machine's head before it could react. The Andhaka fell over, completely lifeless. Saiph looked in amazement at the woman with tan skin and brown hair. She didn't have an aura on, and her eyes didn't glow like a dynamic's. How did she move like that?

"Who are you?"

The woman smirked and then ran deeper into the forest. Saiph followed her, but when he rounded a tree, she was gone.

"Saiph," Amira said over the comm, "I need help."

Saiph grimaced at the pain in his side, then left the cover of the trees and flew toward Amira. The other Andhaka and Aulan had gone after Amira when they weren't able to reach Saiph in the forest. Fulgurians and Blackhawks had arrived to help, but they were dying at an unthinkable rate. Soldiers had limbs cut off by Andhaka or were blasted off their feet by one of Aulan's lasers. Wet patches of blood spotted the ground, and screams filled the night. It was the worst thing Saiph had ever seen.

Suppressing his nausea, he rocketed toward the Andhaka. It turned toward him like it had eyes in the back of its head, and all its attention focused on Saiph. The drones circled it like flies around a horse. The Andhaka even kept dodging bullets and lasers that were coming from behind it.

"Amira, get the Fulgurians and the Blackhawks back to the ship! I'll be right behind you!"

"Roger that!" she yelled. With Saiph engaging the first Andhaka and Tokomoto occupying Aulan's attention, the human remnants of their force ran for the shuttle.

The Andhaka's drones fired their lasers, and it took all of Saiph's focus to keep dodging them. The Andhaka's main body twirled its blades and moved back and forth, waiting for Saiph to come into range. Saiph was thinking that his plan wasn't going to work when he heard the blast he was waiting for. Saiph flipped in the air and poured energy into his feet and back, sending him abruptly in the direction of the ground right as tiny missiles and lasers came from Aulan behind him. Saiph's body had obscured the shots, and he hoped that the Andhaka wouldn't have time to calculate its evasions. It moved with unthinkable speed and precision, but it wasn't fast enough to dodge the entire attack. A laser cut through two of its legs, sending it tipping to one side.

Saiph saw his opening and darted for the Andhaka's main body, dodging its lasers as he went. The machine's blade-like arms still came for Saiph, but he threw out a large enough shield burst to slow them down. He jumped and landed on the Andhaka, sending energy into his right arm. He punched through the body and ripped out its parts. The drones and body fell limp to the ground.

"Amira is down," Tokomoto said in his ear.

"Dead?" Saiph yelled.

"No, but she is not in very good shape. She took a blade to her left leg. I'm sending in every drone I have in the vicinity to buy you a minute from Aulan. Get Amira and the crew to the shuttle."

A swarm of drones and droids came to his aid, and he could see Aulan fighting to keep them away. Saiph flew toward the shuttle and found Amira on the ground, her left leg lying in a pool of blood. For a moment all he could think is that she would have another scar on that side of her body.

"This," Amira said, wincing, "is why I do not go out in the field anymore. I am too old for this shit."

"What do I do?" Saiph asked.

Amira sat up with an enormous effort and cut the leg of her pants away, revealing a grueling cut that was eight inches in length. "I need you to cauterize this."

"Cauta-what?"

"Use a tiny laser to burn my flesh together."

"What!" Saiph said. "I can't do that!"

"I will die otherwise," Amira said. "Do not worry, I have had worse." Her eyes flicked up to the tattooed and disfigured skin of her skull.

Tokomoto rang in his ears. "I am running out of drones. Hurry."

"Okay, okay," Saiph said, lifting a shaky finger and pointing it at Amira's leg.

"Wait," Amira said. She fumbled around in the brush, pulled out a stick, and bit down on it. She took a deep breath and nodded.

Saiph sent a sliver of energy to his index finger and formed it into a thin and soft beam of energy. The whole process only took ten seconds, but Amira's cries of pain made it seem like ten hours. After he was finished, he picked up the now-unconscious Amira and flew her to the waiting shuttle. A minute later, the shuttle was flying toward the mountains, Saiph following beside it.

Once Saiph was sure that Aulan wasn't following, he fully realized that they had failed. The Fulgurian forest, the only place he'd felt safe since he'd been abducted, would be wiped from the face of Jangali. The Fulgurians' entire way of life was over. Saiph could practically hear Tengrii crying out in sorrow.

CHAPTER TWENTY-NINE

E ntry 5:

Many people told me that the first couple years of marriage would be the hardest, and Ava and I discovered that there was some truth to that. She was stressed with her dissertation, and when she graduated, she had trouble finding a job. I was still at Stanford, researching and developing new nano-technologies for the medical field. I loved my work, but it would be several years before I made enough money for us to move out of our small apartment. We weren't unhappy exactly, just a bit overwhelmed.

Life got better when Ava landed a job as an educational psychologist. It wasn't her specialty, but she liked the work and felt that she was making a difference. The extra income eased our stress. We moved into a better neighborhood and a bigger apartment that was fully furnished. We had an extra room for Ava to sew and paint, and the Dish foothills were only a short drive away. Lin would stay with us whenever she wasn't traveling, and Omar was only a few miles away.

We learned to enjoy the small things in life, and I believe that if we hadn't had those years, we would not have enjoyed the following years so thoroughly.

"Another loss," Omar said miserably. He had come over straight from work to watch the general election results of 2032. "This country is going to the dogs."

He cracked opened his eighth beer of the night.

"Don't you have to work tomorrow?" I said.

Omar shrugged. "You're worried about my hangover after this oaf has just become our leader? Your priorities are flawed, my friend."

Omar slumped back into the couch, his eyes bloodshot. Ava and I glanced between each other, uncomfortable. Omar had been drinking more and more ever since his brother had been deployed to North Africa.

"You heard from Tim or Lin lately?" Omar said.

"Tim's still trucking along in residency," I said, "and I can't keep track of Lin."

"She's in London," Ava said, her eyes on the screen.

Omar nodded in approval. "Good for her, getting out there and seeing the world. I'd like to go to London sometime..."

Omar often talked like this, mentioning things he'd like to do but never could afford.

Jessica, Omar's girlfriend, entered the room from the kitchen, carrying a tray of finger foods. She was one of the most bubbly people I had ever met, but I liked her very much. Ava and I thought she was good for Omar.

The news anchor on the screen repeated the president elect's name, seemingly for the millionth time that evening.

"Can we turn this off now?" I said. "It's driving me nuts."

Ava raised her hand. "I second this notion."

"I third it," Jessica said.

Omar rolled his eyes. "Fine. Can we at least play *Everstone Four*?"

"Excellent idea," I said.

I used the remote and switched the television so that the gaming computer turned on. I slipped the mask over my eyes and was instantly transported to another world.

"Now, where was I? Right, I was about to slay the beast and steal his treasure."

I made my character run, and the others watched what I was doing on the screen.

"To the left," Omar said. "No moron—your other left."

I waved him off. "I thought I saw some loot in that dungeon to the right. Love me some loot."

"It's a trap, noob. Keep going."

I didn't see Ava come and sit next to me, but I felt someone rest a hand on my shoulder. "You realize that you both look like morons when you have that thing on, right?"

"You'll address me by my proper name—Sir Lord Dragon Slayer 2000—or not at all. Silly peasant."

My projected character went to the right and the ground opened up, swallowing him whole.

"Damn it."

While Ava didn't share Omar's interest in gaming, they exchanged a look of mutual understanding, silently agreeing that I was indeed a moron.

"You'll get 'em next time, Sir Lord Dragon Slayer 2000!" Jessica said.

"Thank you, Princess Jess, that's very kind of you to say. I believe it's your turn?"

Jessica sat down and slipped on the headset. "If you could please speak quietly while I slay these usurping orcs, that would be much appreciated."

Omar laughed and kissed her on the cheek. "Good luck, Princess Jess. May your blade strike true."

We were watching Jessica kill what seemed like the thousandth orc when Ava's phone rang. She looked down at it.

"It's my dad." She stood up and walked out of the room.

I was still watching Jess play when Ava reappeared in the hallway door holding her phone to her shoulder. She motioned for me to follow her.

"What's up?" I said when we were out of earshot.

"Dad wants to know if we'd have dinner with him tomorrow night? He sounds really excited for some reason."

"Warren is acting excited?" I said. "Are you sure it's him?"

"Do you want to go?"

"Yeah, of course!" I said in a raised whisper. "If Warren is excited, then I'm excited."

Ever since we got married, Ava and I always had dinner with Warren on the last Friday of every month. However, we did force him to learn how to cook other delicacies beyond spaghetti and toasted peanut butter and jelly. His favorite meal to cook was chicken enchiladas, but he only made them for special occasions, which is why I was so surprised to see him making them at an unscheduled dinner the next night.

"What is this?" I said. "Your birthday isn't for another two months."

"Who says I can't make enchiladas whenever I want?"

"Nobody," Ava said, "it's just that you don't ever make them whenever you want. What's the occasion?"

"I have an announcement of sorts. It's rather important."

"Did you get that research grant you were hoping for?" I asked.

He tsked. "Dinner first."

We ate our enchiladas and spoke of daily life like we always did. Warren gave Ava a hard time about being a mystic mind healer, and she poked fun of his severely outdated fashion sense. When we finished our meal, we took our wine to the back porch and sat in three identical white rocking chairs. Winter had not fully reared its head, and it was still nice enough outside to sit without a jacket.

"So are you going to tell us your big news or what?" Ava asked.

Warren sipped his wine and stared out at the meadow beyond his backyard. "I've imagined this moment for so long, but now I don't know how to start."

"Hey," I said gently, "is everything all right?"

He nodded. "Quite." He took a deep breath. "Six years ago, I made a breakthrough in my research. It was so unprecedented, so unexpected, that I didn't believe it at first. I've spent the last five years testing and refining it. Making sure..."

"What did you find?" I asked.

Warren sat up straight and looked us each in the eye. "I successfully developed a one-time gene therapy that halts the deterioration of telomeres that take place during cell replication."

I laughed; I think anyone in my position would have. "Come on, Warren. What is it really?"

"I'm serious," he said. "I've taken it myself."

I frowned, worried about his sanity.

"What are you two talking about?" Ava said. "Plain English, please."

Warren blinked several times behind his large glasses. "I've discovered the secret to immortality."

"Are you sure you're feeling all right?" I asked.

"Yes," he said. "The only thing bothering me is your placating condescension."

"I'm sorry, Warren, but that's quite a claim."

"It's been reviewed by three separate committees. I took the pill myself a year ago and have watched closely. It's real, Jon. I've halted the aging process."

Ava and I sat back, dumbfounded. This couldn't be real. It was far easier to believe that Warren had developed a spontaneous form of schizophrenia. He went inside briefly and brought back a laptop and several papers. He handed them to Ava and me. The more I read, the harder my heart pounded. I saw the review-board signatures, full of names I recognized. I examined the evidence and tests that were performed on mice and chimpanzees. The data firmly pointed to what Warren claimed. But I still couldn't swallow it.

"It's real," Warren said. "I know it's hard to believe, but it's real. I've done it."

Ava looked to me, worried. She didn't have the scientific background to understand everything, but she wasn't an idiot either. She saw the results, and when I nodded at her, she sat back in her chair with a thump, deciding to believe her father.

"Holy shit."

"But how did... Why was it...Who approved..." I stumbled.

Warren laughed. "I have mountains of more data and evidence for you. But for now, please accept that I'm telling you the truth. Think about the possibilities!"

The full force of his revelation finally hit me. I jumped out of my chair. "Holy crap! Holy mind-blowing shit, Warren! You genius!"

He laughed. "Do you have the rings I gave you?"

Ava and I looked down at the infinity rings that Warren had given us on our wedding night, understanding bubbling to the surface.

"I said that the rings were your first present," Warren said. "I'm now ready to give you the second and third." Warren reached into his pocket and pulled out an envelope. "This is for you," he said, handing it to Ava.

Ava opened it and gasped. Her hand shook as she showed it to me. It was a check for twenty million dollars.

"Warren..." I said. "How..."

Warren held up a hand and pulled out a sleek metal box. He opened it to reveal two blue pills sitting inside. "This is it," he said. "You take this, and you'll remain the age you are now. Forever young. You can enjoy life like no human being ever has before."

Ava and I sat there, completely overwhelmed. We looked at one another, not knowing what to do.

"We'll never grow old together..." Ava said.

I considered her point for a moment. "Yes, we will; we just won't look it."

"And besides," Warren said, "having your body deteriorate isn't as good as it sounds. Trust me."

Ava and I sat for a while longer, trying to think of any reason why we shouldn't do this. Ava looked up at me.

"What about everyone we know and love? We'd have to watch them all die. I couldn't do that. Not with Tim, Omar, and Lin."

Their faces came to my mind, but in this vision, they were old and lying in a coffin. It made me sick to think about it. "You're right," I said. "That would be horrible." I turned to Warren. "What are your plans for distribution? Will everyone be able to take the pill?"

"No," he said. "Only a select few."

"Dad," Ava said, "you have to give it to Lin, Omar, and Tim."

Warren eyed her, shaking his head. "No, absolutely not. Do you have any idea what this pill means? I can't just go handing it out to everyone."

"We're not asking you to hand it out to everyone," Ava said. "Just Lin, Omar, and Tim."

"An irresponsible girl who lives off her parents' money, a drunk, and a man who has seen a psychiatrist for more than half his life! You really don't understand how powerful this is, Ava!" He took a calming breath. "This is going to change everything."

Ava closed her eyes in frustration. "We can't imagine going on without them."

Warren looked at the ceiling. "Friends come and go."

"They're not friends, Dad," Ava said. "They're family."

Warren sat back and thought for a while. "I'll make you a deal. I will give them a version of the pill, but it won't be the full thing."

Ava opened her mouth to protest.

"No, hear me out," Warren said. "You need to understand that I can't just go giving out this pill. I won't. If I do this, it will be for you, but I won't keep doing it for everyone you become close to. It's too dangerous. Imagine if someone like Hitler or Stalin got hold of this pill? The damage could they do. People will use you to get to immortality."

Warren sighed heavily. "But I understand what they mean to you. I'll give you a version of the pill, but it will only extend their life for three hundred years. We'll see how things are then and we can revisit it."

Ava and I looked at each other and nodded. It was the best we could do.

"Take it," Warren said to Ava. "Please take it. I can't lose you like I lost your mother."

Ava glanced at me, and I stared into her eyes. I imagined everything we could do. Everything we could explore. Everything we would see and accomplish. The possibilities were as endless as they were alluring, and my desire began to overwhelm my hesitance. The entirety of my imagination must have been written across my face, because Ava was shaking her head now too, grinning in disbelief.

"You remember that Fitzgerald quote we love?" I asked, breathless with excitement.

Ava's smile broadened and she nodded. "I wish I had done everything on Earth with you."

"Now we can."

Warren wasn't lying. He wasn't mistaken. I was thirty-four years old the night I swallowed eternity, and now, 638 years later, I still look it.

For the first time in over two years, we were all together again. Lin had just come back from London; Omar had taken the day off from his second job; and Tim had begrudgingly driven over to our side of town, even though he was on call at the hospital. It had been three days since Warren had given us his gifts.

"This better be good," Tim said as he walked in the front door and sat down.

Tim always looked tired, but I just then noticed how much older he looked. The first lines of age were etched into his face, and there were a few spots of gray in his stubble.

"Aren't you peachy," Lin said. "Did you just successfully lobotomize a baby or something?"

"We don't lobotomize people," Tim said, annoyed.

"But could you?" Omar asked. "Could you put your brain in my body and my brain in your body?"

"How could he put his own brain in your body?" Ava said. "He'd have to have an assistant. A brain carrier, so to speak. And he'd have to put your brain on ice for a little while, wouldn't he?"

"Imagine the brain freeze you'd get," I said. "Are you really ready for that kind of pain, Omar?"

"Anything for science."

Tim rubbed his forehead. "I'm not sure why I put up with you people."

Omar laughed and slapped him hard on the back. "We love you too, buddy."

"Seriously, though," Lin said, "what's so pressing that it couldn't wait until we were all free?"

Ava and I looked at each other, took a breath, and then explained the situation as best we could. We showed Tim the data and charts. His eyes were wide in shock. He probably understood them better than I did.

"This is impossible..." he said shakily.

I nodded. "That's what I said at first."

Omar started to laugh. "Do we get to choose a superpower too? I call invisibility!"

Nobody laughed.

"We're serious, Omar," Ava said. "If you take this pill, you'll live for hundreds of years."

Omar kept chuckling. "Come on, guys!" He looked over at Lin and shook her shoulder. "You don't believe this, do you? Wait, is she in on this also? I mean, I'm not *that* gullible."

Tim finally looked away from the data I had given him and turned to Omar. "They're not joking. It's real."

Tim's expression was so serious and his tone so dire that Omar's laugh faded away.

"You're really serious?" Lin said.

"Yes," Ava and I said together.

"And you've taken it?" Lin asked.

Ava and I looked at each other and nodded.

"And we want you to take it too," Ava added. "We couldn't imagine life without you. My dad gave us money. We'll be free to do what we want! Imagine the possibilities!"

Lin's shocked expression finally broke. "If it's a joke, then you got me. If it's not, then I'm in."

"Tim?" I said.

He nodded vigorously. "Yes. Absolutely."

That left Omar, who had sat back against the couch. We were all looking at him.

"What?" he said.

"What do you mean, what?" Lin said.

Omar squirmed uncomfortably. He was sweating. A car horn went off somewhere nearby, and he jumped. "Don't you think we should think about this first? I mean, it's kind of a big decision, right?"

"Look," Lin said, "from what it sounds like, it's not like we can't die. If you get tired of life in a few hundred years, put the gun to your head and pull the trigger!"

It was disconcerting hearing Lin say that with a smile.

"Omar," Ava said more seriously, "Jon and I had the same thoughts when my dad first told us. Trust me, the possibilities far outweigh the potential consequences. And, as grim as it is, Lin is right. You can always opt out." She leaned forward and put a hand on Omar's knee. "We're talking about walking into a dream, Omar. We will have the most extraordinary lives!"

Those were the right words. I think Omar was tired of feeling like just another guy, especially compared to his friends. He hesitated for another minute but then nodded. "What do we do?"

It's hard to believe that we really thought it was that simple. That the worst thing that could happen was that we'd have to kill ourselves. I wish we had listened to Omar and considered things more carefully. Sometimes I wonder how different the world would be if we had.

During the Sphere War hundreds of years later, Omar and I sat together, watching the destruction of an entire world. So many souls, wiped from existence in an instant. He looked at me with unnaturally cold eyes that seemed utterly alien to the boy he'd been, and he said: "I hope you remember the whims of our youth—of the undiscussed path—and weep for the billion souls that just perished."

CHAPTER THIRTY

Saiph couldn't watch the destruction of the Fulgurian forest, so he sat huddled in the corner of their new cavern hideout with Ayanda instead. It was dark and damp, and several small streams ran downward into the depths of the cave. The space was so large that it was able to house the shuttles and all of the command pods. The Blackhawks and Fulgurians were interspersed throughout other caves nearby.

"Are we safe here?" Ayanda said.

Saiph shrugged. "I don't know."

Off in the distance, people were bustling around, securing the entrance to the cavern and unpacking equipment. Saiph probably should have been helping, but all he could think about was his failure. People were dead, and the trees and animals within the forest...he tried not to think of it. Everything was supposed to be better, now that he was a dynamic, but he couldn't get the blood and death and sheer destruction out of his head. Would he ever stop being so naive? Would he ever stop being a failure? Deep down, he was still that crippled little boy who nobody wanted.

"Would you rather have not fought?" Ayanda asked as if she were reading his mind. "Would it feel better if you had just given up and left the forest to defend itself?"

"Of course not," Saiph said.

"Then you've done the right thing. That is all anyone can ever strive to do."

Saiph took a deep breath, trying to will the sense of inadequacy away. He closed his eyes and leaned his head back against the hard stone of the cave. He had to get past this. He took a breath, then said, *"Have patience with all things, but chiefly have patience with yourself. Do not lose courage in considering your own imperfections but instantly set about remedying them—every day, begin the task anew."*

Silence for a moment.

"Seriously," Ayanda said, "how do you have so many Verses memorized? You realize you're a bit of a fanatic, right?"

Saiph still couldn't muster the energy to smile, but he did feel a bit better.

Ellie approached, her shirt spotted with blood and a look of exhaustion on her face. Saiph looked up at her eagerly.

"Amira will be fine," Ellie said. "Another scar, though, poor woman."

Saiph breathed out and felt himself slump against the cave wall. He was so worried that Amira would have a limp leg, like he used to have. He didn't wish that on anyone, and now that he knew she was all right, he let himself relax. Drops of cold water fell from the ceiling and occasionally landed on Saiph, but he barely noticed them.

Ellie peered at Saiph and then leaned down. "Are you all right?"

"Fine."

She kept staring at him. "You know that I've killed thousands of people?"

Saiph looked up at her with a frown.

"Thousands," she said again. Ellie took off her plastic white gloves and pushed them into her pocket. "I've made surgical mistakes that have left my patients dead. I've failed to save someone, only to later realize that there was something else I could have done. Sometimes I've failed to see what was truly wrong with a person, and they slipped away before I could figure it out."

"That's not the same," Saiph said.

"It's the same," Ellie said. "If you make mistakes, people die. But Saiph, I've saved twenty times as many people as I've killed. You must remember that you are fighting to save people and that you're not perfect. You've gotta learn that."

Saiph sighed. "I know that. I know that I know that. It's just difficult to accept."

"If you didn't feel sad about the destruction of the Fulgurian forest and the deaths of the people who fought, then there would be a more serious problem. If this feeling you're having gets worse, and you feel like there is no way out, then Sarah may be able to help you."

"Wait," Ayanda said, "does Sarah have a medicine that cures sadness?"

"Not exactly. But if either of you ever do need to talk to someone, go to her. Or Jon, of course."

Saiph was kicked awake the next morning.

"What the hell?"

"What?" Silvestre said. "You think one little forest gets destroyed and you can just curl up in a ball and sleep all day? Do you ever quit whining?"

"I..." Saiph began. "I wasn't whining! I was sleeping!"

"This sounds a lot like whining to me," Silvestre said, turning and walking away. "Let's go, we've got work to do."

Saiph reluctantly rolled off his sleeping pad and followed her, rubbing his eyes as he did so. Silvestre walked down the slope of the cave and deeper into the darkness. It was becoming so dark that Silvestre reached out her prosthetic hand and created a ball of light to guide them. Once she deemed them far enough away from the encampment, Silvestre set up a few small lights and sat down on the ground.

"Tell me about your fight with Aulan and the Andhaka," she said.

Saiph went over every detail, and they watched video that was captured from Tokomoto's drones. Silvestre critiqued him mercilessly, but for once Saiph didn't argue with her. If he was better, then maybe he could have bought Amira enough time to disable the pulse cannon and they'd be back in the forest, smiling and celebrating. While Silvestre's criticisms numbered in the hundreds, there were two she kept focusing on.

"Look here," she said, pointing at the screen. "Aulan barrels right into you without you having any idea what is coming. You have to be more aware than that. Your senses are incredibly acute, practice filtering out unnecessary sounds. Focus on the noises that are dangerous. You see how the Andhaka dodged bullets and lasers from behind? You should be able to do that too."

"Can you do it?" he asked.

Silvestre shook her head. "I don't have the speed or reaction time to pull that off, but that lack of power has forced me to develop other skills. I'm able to hear the difference between a 35 mm and 45 mm bullet that's coming at me. If there are only a few people nearby, I'm able to hear and see them start to pull the trigger before they fire."

"That's a good idea," he said.

"It came out of my mouth, didn't it?"

Silvestre spent most of the morning lecturing Saiph on hand-to-hand combat and berating him for not once taking out his swords. She explained that best way to kill an Andhaka was to block its blades with his swords and shield and dodge the lasers. Getting close to the Andhaka was key to defeating its preposterous computational reaction time.

After a quick meal that Silvestre had stowed away in her backpack, they spent the afternoon sparring with their weapons. Though Saiph was much faster and stronger, he had a hard time catching her. He always did in the end, though. She moved in strange ways and used her knives to keep him at bay. She attacked unexpectedly and then would abruptly turn and run deeper into the cavern. With each bout, Saiph got better. He could sense it, and it helped him cope with the crushing sadness.

When they returned to camp at the mouth of the cavern, Saiph was feeling mentally well enough to find Jon and ask what was happening outside of their dark world. Jon was just leaving the command pod as he walked up.

"Saiph," he said, "how are you?"

"Fine. I was hoping to talk to you for a minute."

"Of course," Jon said, "I was just heading over to see Tokomoto. Join me?"

Saiph fell in beside Jon, and they walked through the camp. Soldiers were sleeping in random spaces on the rocky floor of the cave. Makeshift tents and beds had been set up and technical gear was strewn about as if a tornado had just passed through.

"What happened out there?" Saiph asked. "How did they know we were coming?"

Jon glanced around to make sure they couldn't be overheard. "Either we were betrayed," he said, "or they predicted that we would somehow know about the cannons. Treyges thinks they were told, but I'm not convinced. It happened too fast."

"How could they have guessed?" Saiph asked. "Like you said, it was fast."

"There's more to this than you know," Jon said. "Elean and Aulan are the muscle, not the brain. Someone else predicted our move."

"Where was Elean, by the way?"

A secretary came running up to Jon and handed him a tablet. Jon looked it over, scanned his fingerprint, and handed it back to him. "She was at the other pulse cannon, which also tells us that they didn't know which cannon you were going to. When she realized you weren't there, she went to help her brother. You were gone by the time she got there. It seems they wanted you as much as they wanted to protect the pulse cannons."

Saiph considered this while he walked, rubbing his temples as if they could sooth his thoughts. "What happens now?" Saiph asked. "Are we safe here?"

"For the moment. Tokomoto and Russ have booby-trapped the mountain and have set up a strong defense."

"So what's the difference between here and the forest, then?" Saiph asked as he tripped over a sleeping soldier's leg. He apologized quickly and sped up to catch Jon.

"Well, we can't exactly leave the mountains at the moment. Not like we could the forest." Saiph frowned, goading Jon to elaborate. "The forest was too big for the capital to set up an enclosure, but they have been able to do it with the mountains. We're able to sneak out drones and maybe a shuttle, but moving the bulk of our forces would be suicidal."

"So we're trapped here?" Saiph asked, unable to keep the panic from his voice.

"For now," Jon said, "but I've made contact with Khumbuza. I think that I can offer them a better deal than House Harain can."

They reached Tokomoto's command pod, and Jon knocked lightly on the door. It slid open and they stepped inside, grabbing dark goggles to put over their eyes. Tokomoto was moving his fingers like he was trying to get feeling back into them after they'd fallen asleep. The view screens flickered between the eyes of his drones.

"Just a minute," he said. "Almost done."

Saiph studied the maps that Tokomoto had up. The mountain range they were camped in wasn't very long, but they were in the middle of a series of tall mountains. Moving red and blue dots indicated enemy and friendly drones that circled the air above them. Tokomoto's fingers calmed down and he swiveled his wheelchair to face them.

Jon didn't look away from the screens. "Everything calm out there?"

Tokomoto nodded. "We will be safe until the other Houses arrive."

"Good. Where's Russ? Can we get him in on a conference call?"

"He is in the mountains, setting up sentry guns and scouting posts.

I will ping him." Tokomoto tapped a few buttons and waited for Russ to answer.

"Tokohamarama-san, you've reached Russ Henson, King of the Mountain Trolls and Lord of Fire, please proceed with your conversation."

"Russ, it's Jon, Toko, and Saiph," Jon said. "What's it looking like out there?"

"Oh, hello boys! Well my friends, I'm sorry to say it ain't exactly pretty. Been a few skirmishes on the edge of the perimeter, but haven't lost anyone yet. Things are starting to settle down. What the hell is Chet doing, by the way?"

Jon frowned and rubbed his chin. "What do you mean?"

"I just saw the crazy old bastard wandering around out here like he was going for his evening stroll."

Jon shook his head. "If you see him again, tell him to get back here, please."

"Aye, will do. Heading back to the cavern soon. Anything else?"

"No, but ping me if anything changes."

"Roger that. Russ out."

Jon took a few steps and leaned against the wall. "I've made contact with Khumbuza," he said to Tokomoto.

"And?"

"I think we have a real chance of getting them on our side."

"Khumbuza?" Tokomoto said, surprised. "That would be an enormous help."

"Why is that?" Saiph asked.

Tokomoto flicked the control on his wheelchair and turned to face Saiph. "Khumbuza is the second most powerful House. Only Harain is stronger. If they added their force to ours, we would be in a very good position."

"If they come with us," Jon said, "then the Grecian contingent and Asura may band together and form a third force."

Tokomoto and Jon spoke a little longer about the tactical possibilities that each alliance would give them and tentative contingency plans for when they arrived. Saiph listened intently, trying to keep up, but he mostly failed. After they left Tokomoto's pod, Jon stopped Saiph a short distance away where no one could hear them.

"The head of House Khumbuza is a woman named Aoko. She and her people will be visiting us in the mountains when they arrive in a few days. I'd like you to come to the meeting."

"Me?" Saiph said. "I haven't the slightest clue how these sorts of things work."

"There's only one way to learn," Jon said. "Besides, I want them to see you. They need to realize that you are a person and not some glorified battery. Aoko can be ruthless, but she's got a heart somewhere in there. I think she'll take a liking to you. Just be yourself."

"I suppose I can do that. Nothing more, nothing less, though."

"Good man."

Jon was called away by an engineer who needed approval of something or another. Where did he find the energy to deal with everyone else's problems? He was like a parent, teacher, and boss to everyone here:

What do I do?

Who should I see?

What's this?

Saiph walked through the maze of camped soldiers and suddenly felt thankful that Jon always made time for him. He wouldn't let him down again. He had to be better next time. *Begin the task anew.*

"Saiph!"

Charlotte was stepping over soldiers ahead and looking up every few seconds to keep an eye on Saiph, as if he were going to run away when he saw her. She pointed at him. "Don't move!"

"Am I moving?"

Charlotte reached him and grabbed his arm, pulling him to the side. When they reached the far end of the cavern wall, she stopped to face him. "I know your time is ever important, but you made a promise to me."

Saiph flushed guiltily. It's not that he didn't want to take Charlotte home. He wanted to see what was inside the forbidden building of the Old Gods, but there was always so much to do.

"I'm sorry," he said. "When do you want to go?"

"Now?"

Saiph closed his eyes and rubbed his forehead. "How about tonight?"

She looked at him suspiciously. "Fine. I won't make you promise, because I know how that goes, but I'll have you know that I have very high expectations."

"We'll go tonight," Saiph said, exasperated. What had gotten in to her? Where was the timid Charlotte from camp sixty-two? He supposed freedom had been good to her. "Meet me at the mouth of the cave at midnight."

"Saiph!"

He turned to see Roe was waving him over. What now?

"You're going to want to see this!"

Her expression sparked concern. "I'll see you tonight," he said to Charlotte, then ran over to Roe. She was already walking toward a crowd of people huddled around a table.

"What's going on?" Saiph asked.

"See for yourself."

When they arrived, a few people looked at Saiph and his burning blue eyes and moved aside for him to get a better view. Vincent sat in the center, his tablet lying flat on the table. On the screen, a very clean and accomplished-looking man was sitting and talking very seriously.

"Reports are still coming in, but the breaking news has now been verified by three separate Sphere Astronomy Association members: Another star has gone dark, and it is within the Sphere of humanity's outer boundary. I repeat, another star has been consumed by the Essens, and it is *within* the Sphere's outer boundary. More concerning than that, however, is that it is not on the eastern edge of the Sphere, where the last star went dark, but in the south. Does this mean any star could be consumed at any moment? What is our leadership doing about the crisis? What can you do to stay safe? All that and more, right after this."

Roe leaned over. "Didn't Jon say that another star going dark would eventually lead to a war?"

"Yeah, he did. I assume this is only going to speed things up."

The man on the screen reappeared. "This just in, Empress Euphraise of the Askan Empire has released a statement providing details about the organization of a State of the Sphere Summit to discuss recent events. This summit was put into motion over a year ago, when the last star was surrounded, and is set to begin within the next month in the Askani capital. It will be the largest gathering of Sphere leaders in over a century. She pleaded for people to stay calm until the crisis has been addressed. The full statement is available through Askani Communications Company."

Saiph and Roe watched awhile longer, but the man kept repeating the same things over and over again in slightly different ways. They wandered over to a giant water container that had been set up in the middle of a large clearing and poured themselves a cup.

"This is bad," Roe said.

Saiph nodded. "Sarah told me that there are 38 billion people alive. Can you imagine all those people in a war?"

"What?" Roe said, confused. "I guess it's bad for them too, but I meant it's bad for us."

"How so?" They found a spot away from the crowd waiting for water and stopped.

"The way I see it, people are going to flee from either the war or the dark stars. Where do you think they'll go? A planet that already has too many people or a planet that has barely anyone living on it, like Jangali?"

Saiph frowned. Why hadn't he thought of that? "You're right. But we're not there yet. Who knows what will happen?"

A chime came from Roe's person, and she looked down at a thin band wrapped around her wrist. "Shit! Stupid Skyfaller time. They're so prickly about it." She placed her cup in Saiph's hand and jogged away.

"Where are you going?" Saiph called out.

"Training!"

Charlotte was already waiting for him when he got to the entrance of the cave. There was a large sack on the ground next to her along with snoring lumps all around. It reminded Saiph of their grand escape plan from camp sixty-two. Hopefully this would go better.

"How am I supposed to carry you and that huge thing?" Saiph whispered, pointing to the bag.

"I'm sure you'll manage," Charlotte said. "You're a sort of star god now, right?"

"Star god? No, I—"

"Look, we should be going before someone starts asking questions. Can you carry the bag or not?"

Saiph sighed. "Yes, give it here. What's in all this anyways?"

Charlotte bent down and heaved the bag off the ground. "Supplies. In case we find anyone."

Saiph strapped the sack to his back and they set off. They both agreed that it would be best to put some distance between them and the cave before Saiph summoned his aura. The slope was steep, and it was very dark, but Saiph was perfectly capable of navigating his way down the slope. Charlotte put a hand on his shoulder to steady herself, just in case. When they reached the bottom, the jungle grew thick, and with it came light. There were thousands of tiny floating insects glowing a soft green. They gently swirled around one another, as if they were in water. Saiph had never seen anything like this back home.

"I wonder what they are." Saiph said.

"They're insects." Charlotte gave him a flat stare. "Now, how are we doing this? Aren't we trapped in these mountains?"

Saiph's gaze lingered on the light for a moment longer before he turned to Charlotte. "Right. So we can't fly out of here. We're going to have to run. Once we're outside the perimeter of drones, we'll fly the rest of the way."

"I can't *run* out of here. It's dark, and we have no idea how far it is." Saiph smiled at her. "Oh gods, what?"

"See this sack?" Saiph said. "That's where you'll go. I'll be doing all the running."

"No. No way. Not going to happen."

Ten minutes later, Saiph had his aura activated and Charlotte was securely strapped to his back. He was sure that they looked ridiculous, and he was glad no one else was there to see it.

"Ready?" he asked.

"As I'll ever be."

Saiph flexed the energy in his body and then broke into a jog. Going slow at first, then faster. Faster. Faster.

"Ohhhh gods!" Charlotte yelled. "Ohhh gods. Too fast! Toooo fast!"

It was incredible. In some ways, it was even better than flying. Everything was unnaturally smooth in the air, but running was more primal. Saiph's body reveled in the effort and the synchronized movement of his legs and arms. There was no pain in his leg and his breathing was flawless. The trees flew past, and Saiph actually laughed out loud.

"You're insane!" Charlotte yelled.

Saiph ran for over an hour. He could hear and see the drones up in the sky, but they were only dark specs to him. When he'd gone forty miles without hearing anything, he jumped and lifted into the air. Charlotte made quite a fuss about it, but she eventually relaxed.

"Please don't drop me," she kept saying.

"I'm not going to drop you. Relax. Now, how are we going to find your home?"

Charlotte squirmed on his back. "I looked at some maps before we left. I think my village is at the other end of the mountain range. There were two lakes on either side, and the shape of them looked right. Just keep heading north."

The flight was peaceful and quiet. The only sound was the soothing pulse of energy that came from Saiph's aura. He felt like he could have slept but thought that Charlotte might not appreciate that. *Charlotte*. She must be freezing. He stuck out a palm and let a sphere of energy form above it.

"Thank you."

To stay awake, Saiph thought of his father. He had to still be out there somewhere, alone and worried. What if he tried to escape, like Saiph had? Would they send him to the coliseum too? He'd have to remember to ask Tokomoto to sneak a drone in there or something. Maybe they had suspended the matches with everything else going on, though.

"There!" Charlotte yelled.

Saiph looked down and saw the two lakes Charlotte had described. One was long and curved, and the other was nearly perfect circle. They shone brightly from the reflected moonlight, the only light in an otherwise dark landscape. There was no way they could have missed them.

Charlotte directed him from there. As they got closer, Saiph could see the remnants of buildings on the land between the lakes. There weren't any structures standing properly. It was mostly large piles of burned wood. Had Altai looked like this? The thought was depressing.

They touched down, and Charlotte quickly unstrapped herself and jogged toward the center. She held a hand over her mouth, like the was holding in a scream. There wasn't anyone else around. Saiph grimaced as his aura retracted into his body.

"I'm sorry," Saiph said.

Charlotte shook her head. "I knew there was a good chance it would look like this. It's still hard to see, though."

They stood together in silence for a while, soaking it in. Even the sounds of wildlife were muted, as if they, too, mourned the destruction.

"Do you want to head back?" Saiph asked.

"Head back?" Charlotte asked. "No. I'm staying here."

Saiph spoke gently. "No one is out here. You can't stay."

"This is my home. I *know* some survived or avoided capture. They're out there somewhere. And when you free more camps, others will come back."

"But—"

"I've already made my decision," Charlotte said. "You might have a new life, but not all of us do."

She said it with a bitterness that surprised Saiph. "You think I wanted all this to happen? You think I wanted my family enslaved and my village destroyed?"

Charlotte breathed out and shifted her weight. "No, of course not. I'm just saying that you've got something else now. I mean, look at you. When I met you, you were so self-conscious about your leg and breathing. We could tell you were hiding the pain from us during the day, but you would moan in your sleep from it. That person is gone. Haven't you noticed the way people look at you now?"

How could he have not noticed? In his old life, he'd gotten so used to being ignored. Now, every time he caught someone staring at his eyes, he thought that there was dirt on his face or something. He really did think of it as his old life, though, didn't he? Yes, he had suffered, but he didn't want to go back to who he was before. He liked being strong. He liked not being in a constant state of pain. It was time to accept that. He wasn't the crippled boy nobody wanted anymore, and he wouldn't go back to being him, now that he knew what it was like to be someone else.

He didn't respond to Charlotte for a minute. He might had gone through at least some form of positive transformation out of their suffering, but had she? What did she have now?

"Do you have everything you need?" he asked.

She nodded. "More than enough. Some of the Skyfaller tools will make everything easier."

"Do you have a comm to reach us?"

She reached into her pocket and pulled out a small earpiece. "I'll let you know if I need anything."

Saiph turned to face her. "I'm sorry for not getting Alistair out of there."

He hadn't understood why he'd been so reticent around Charlotte until that moment. It was because she reminded him of Alistair. Saiph had become what he now was because of what had happened to Alistair. It felt too much like a sacrifice. He didn't want a gift tainted in the blood of his friend.

"It's not your fault," Charlotte said. "You know Al. He would have quoted some obscure Verse and told you to move on. I do miss him, though."

"Me too."

Saiph took a deep breath. *Another day, another life.* His aura ejected from his body, and Charlotte took a step back in alarm. The last pieces slid together neatly, and he rolled his shoulders. "Where is the building of the Old Gods?"

CHAPTER THIRTY-ONE

E ntry 6:

Historians often argue whether Warren had it planned from the beginning or if he improvised as he went. Personally, I think that he had a plan before he even finished his anti-aging pill, Boundless.

Warren was shrewd in the way he released it. He understood that he had a product that fell within the realm of inelastic demand—meaning that people, no matter how much a certain item cost, would find a way to pay for it. It was like purchasing a life-saving medical procedure. If you needed that surgery to stay alive, a doctor could essentially charge whatever they'd like; it wasn't as if that person could refuse because he or she thought it was too pricey or wanted to wait until a coupon was available. Warren knew that money would never be an issue for him again. He foresaw other problems, though, such as overpopulation and a strain on natural resources. So Warren sold Boundless for one billion dollars a pill, with an additional payment of eight percent of all the buyer's future income.

It seemed absurd, but it sold. And why wouldn't it? Who wouldn't pay for immortality if they had the means? In five years' time, Warren was the richest man in the world. He built schools, roads, and hospitals. He funded memorials and research grants. He subsidized universities and health care. It was all very altruistic on the surface, but he had other motives. He had a vision.

Warren started small, choosing to run for mayor of Palo Alto. He lost his first election but succeeded in the next term. Then he ran for the governorship of California and won, his popularity high from his charitable acts and successful businesses. After turning California's economy around and solving its ever-present drought issues, Warren ran for the US Senate. He won easily and served for fifteen years, learning the system and biding his time. He waited for a crisis, and when the super flu epidemic of 2048 began killing people by the scores, he saw his chance. He ran for president that year and won by the narrowest of margins. At eighty-two, Warren Winters was the oldest president to ever be elected.

The super flu subsided, and the economy began booming from a technology surge in automation. Warren initiated a fixed income in the United States, put an emphasis on education, and was a champion for both the poor and rich. His approval ratings were among the highest in US history. When his two terms were up, Warren stepped down and retired to private life. But when the next crisis emerged, Warren was asked to run once again, despite the illegality of it. He condemned it at first, saying he would never violate the constitution and the American people's trust. This only fueled his supporters further, and they begged him to reconsider.

He made his announcement three months before the first primary vote. He would run for president of the United States again if Congress introduced a constitutional amendment that allowed him to do so. He elegantly said that our forebears could not have foreseen a leader who had conquered age and who could, hypothetically, live forever. He promised that, if allowed, he would forever serve the American people if that was what they wished. Congress changed the Constitution and the "election" was held, but Warren won by such a large margin that it could barely be called that. He won again and again and again. His power and influence were so great that the elections were mostly a sham by the time he won for the seventh consecutive time.

Ava and I always managed to watch his reelection speeches no matter where we were. And we were everywhere. I could write a million pages describing our adventures during those thirty years, and it wouldn't be enough. But this is not the time for those tales. For now, I will only say this: They were the best thirty years of my long life. We explored all that Earth had to offer. We saw the northern lights with Tim during a six-month stay in Iceland. We ate and drank the finest delicacies with Lin. Wine from the south of France, sushi in Japan, gazpacho in Spain, and Peking roasted duck from China. Omar, Ava, and I rode the Trans-Siberian Railway across the Eurasian Steppe and then decided to stay for two years in Moscow. For six years, Ava and I lived on Watamu beach in Kenya, exploring the coral reefs and studying the hawksbill turtles. We took courses in philosophy, wrote books, and speculated on what new technologies we might one day see.

But most importantly, Ava and I explored one another to depths we could never have imagined. I thought I knew her when I married her, that, because I was her husband, I understood her completely. But it took me a lifetime to even break the surface of her. She was more complicated than I'd ever imagined. She would have years of exaggerated enthusiasm followed by months of hidden depression, and I never knew which it was going to be or exactly why she was feeling the way she was. There were times of hardship and apathy for us, but we were mostly living in an extended state of bliss. The memories of these years are like magnets to my attention, and I find myself dwelling on them more often than is probably wise.

One of our last extended trips was to New Zealand in 2064. Lin, Omar, Ava, and myself had been living there for four months, spending our days hiking the mountains and swimming the lakes. We were in our hammock beds late at night, when, surprisingly, Lin spoke up.

"I think I'm done," she said softly.

She had just gone through the worst breakup of her life and had been very unlike herself ever since. The wildlife sang outside our little house, but it was still very quiet. A breeze blew in through the window and swayed our hammocks.

"What do you mean?" I asked, looking up from my book.

"Thirty years," Lin said. "Thirty years I've been traveling. I'm tired. I want to do something else with my life. I want to go home."

Those words hit me hard. Home. Ava and I had discussed settling down several times over the last few years, but there was always one more stop, one more thing to see, one more place to visit.

"We've talked about going back to work," Ava said, pointing to me. "What would you do?"

"I don't know. Maybe start a business of some sort?"

Omar chuckled from the corner. "My flight leaves in three days, but I didn't know how to tell you guys. I'm going back. I'm starting a school."

We all laughed.

"So we're all going back, then?" I said, looking at Ava.

She nodded at me. "About time we started giving back a bit, don't you think?"

I smiled at her. "That workaholic Tim has always been one step ahead of us, right? He'll probably laugh at us and say it's about time."

"I am going to miss this, though," Lin said, looking around at our simple bungalow.

We were all silent, thinking of all the places we'd seen.

"It's not an ending," I said, "just the turning of the page. Who knows how the story will go?"

After my great adventures with Ava, I found myself as the secretary of science in Warren's cabinet, overseeing projects and developments all across the country. It was exciting and challenging work, and I enjoyed it very much. The only downside was Warren's micromanagement.

"How's the moon resupply mission going?" Warren asked.

We were sitting on the porch of Camp David, looking out at the woods. I was still baffled at how I'd gotten to that point, but more astonishing were the changes in Warren. He carried himself in such a different manner than the sometimes awkward, almost reclusive man I'd met so long ago.

"As planned," I said. "This may be the last supply mission they'll need for a long time. They're becoming more self-sufficient with every year that passes."

"Yes, but they will always need help from Earth," Warren said. He leaned forward and rested his elbows on his knees. "And it will never be like Earth, the way we're doing it now. We need more."

"What else are you hoping for? The terraforming department has all the theoretical ideas for accomplishing what you're saying, but we simply don't have the technology and resources to pull it off."

"Yes, I know that," Warren said. "That's what I wanted to talk to you about. What is the core problem behind why we can't accomplish this? What has stopped us from initiating all the grand theoretical plans we've developed over the last fifty years? What has plagued Earth since the industrial revolution?"

"Um, not enough low-income housing?"

"Energy," he said. "We are limited by the energy that we can harness. Nuclear fusion hasn't gone the way I'd hoped it would, but there has to be another way. I've given the matter a great deal of thought..."

Warren presented his plans to me. He wanted to create a machine that could travel to a star, surround it, capture its immense energy, and send it back to Earth. The idea was interesting, but he lacked the expertise to see it through. That's when I began my own great work.

I was twenty years into the project that would change the course of humanity when I began to have my doubts about Warren. In reality, it was Ava's worry, rather than my own. We were walking the mountains near our Santa Barbara home when Ava first brought up her concerns.

"Have you seen his latest proclamation?" Ava said. She was breathing heavily from the climb.

"Nope," I said. "What is it this time?"

"He released a statement that went something like: the growing tension between China and the US stems from a fundamental difference in ideology. That China's long history of jealousy toward the West is manifesting in aggressive ways and that he has no choice but to respond. He thinks that it's time for Europe and America to come closer together in this time of uncertainty. Blah, blah, blah."

I grabbed a root and pulled myself over a steep incline. "Sounds like bullshit to me," I said. "What's he getting at?"

Ava stopped in the middle of the trail and pulled her water bottle from her pack. She was glistening from exertion, her brown hair pulled back into a ponytail. She'd hardly changed at all over the years, and I could never seem to stop smiling at her. She handed me the water bottle.

"I don't know," she said, "but you know Dad, he's always got a plan. I'm worried, Jon. I think he's making a play for control outside of America. Maybe even trying to start a war."

"What!" I said. "Warren wouldn't start a war with China. The death and destruction from that would be catastrophic. He wouldn't."

"I don't know," Ava said. "He's become more and more detached from ordinary people over the years. He's got his sights set on something."

"That does sound like him," I admitted.

A pair of blue jays flew past, and I watched them chase each other.

"Could you try and talk some sense into him?" she asked. "He respects you."

I scoffed. "Try and talk to him? You know what he's like. He won't listen to me. You're the only one who might get through to him. Emphasis on 'might.'"

"Just try," she begged. "I'm afraid he's going down a path I can't follow. I don't want to lose him." Tears welled up in Ava's eyes, and the seriousness of her concern finally hit me.

"Yes," I said, "of course. I'll talk to him."

We continued on and reached the top of the mountain that overlooked the Pacific Ocean. Out of all the places we'd seen in the world, the view of the Santa Barbara coast from the heights was one of our favorites. We took our seats, scoring front-row tickets to the most beautiful of sunsets.

"How's Thomas doing? Is he still having nightmares?" I asked.

Ava had opened her own practice that specialized in treating gifted children who came from troubled homes. I was thoroughly disturbed at how many clients she had. I couldn't believe how many kids were still being abused.

"Yeah, but those may never go away. Not completely at least..."

She went on talking about the research behind trauma induced nightmares and I nodded along. I envied how dedicated she was for her patients, I don't think I could ever do what she did.

"What about you?" she eventually asked. "Are you going to keep with battering away at replication or put it on hold until energy transport is complete?"

"I'm starting to think we should just move on to energy transport," I said. "Maybe new replication technologies will develop while we do. We'll get there eventually, though."

I was trying to convince myself as much as I was Ava.

Ava's concerns about her father verged on prophetic. Two years later, China seized American assets in Asia and launched an attack on the Hawaiian Islands. While China may have fired the first shot, it was Warren who handed them the gun. It looked innocent enough from the outside, but everything was too coincidental, too structured. I didn't have any proof, but I knew that this was what Warren wanted. Ava and

I sat in the living room, watching the coverage of death and destruction taking place on Maui.

"I'm sorry," I said. "I mentioned that it was a bad idea in every way that I could, but I should have been more vocal. I should have tried harder."

"It's not your fault," Ava said, grabbing my hand. "This was his choice. Thousands of people are going to die. Millions, maybe."

We both let that sink in for a moment.

"What are we going to do, Jon?"

I shook my head. "I don't know."

We sat close together that night, holding hands and watching the news, scared and uncertain for the first time in many years.

CHAPTER THIRTY-TWO

The building of the Old Gods was more hidden than he thought something of its size could be. Saiph passed over it twice before he finally found it. He hadn't noticed it because it was built directly into the mountainside, like it had been carved and hollowed out by some divine sculptor. He had no idea how long it had been abandoned, but trees had sprouted up all around it, making it even more difficult to see. If Charlotte hadn't told him exactly where to look, then he wouldn't have found it at all.

Saiph supposed he could have flown to the top of the building and found some way in from there, but he wanted to go into the front. If something was happening to people who entered, then he wanted to find out what it was and stop it. People didn't deserve to die for their curiosity.

He landed among the trees and walked to the entrance. He knew it was the main entrance because there was no other side. There was only the mountain. The bottom of the structure was more narrow, while the top was long, giving it the shape of an upside-down triangle. He wondered how deep the interior went. Was the whole mountain hollowed out?

The wind was blowing fiercely this high up, and the trees swayed around him as he walked. Saiph saw no sign of any wildlife and didn't see anything glowing at all. It was strange and unnatural to him. As he approached, he noticed a dark, nearly pitch-black circle that caught his attention. He finally realized that it had to be an entrance to the building. He stopped a few feet from the threshold.

Saiph focused on the river of energy that always flowed through him and directed some of it upward. His vision and hearing immediately became more sensitive, but his eyes still couldn't penetrate the darkness inside.

Well, at least my hearing is good.

Saiph stuck out a palm and summoned a ball of energy. Its blue light pulsated quietly and hovered above his hand. He stepped inside. He entered a long tunnel that sloped slightly downward, and his footsteps echoed loudly off the walls. He walked for a quarter of a mile before he reached the first room. The ceilings were twice as high here, and the space was large and circular. Saiph took another step—

"Unauthorized personnel," an unnatural mechanical voice said. "Unauthorized personnel."

Two enormous guns dropped down from the ceiling, and Saiph was glad he hadn't retracted his aura. They sprayed bullets at him as thick as hunting knives. But before they had even begun to fire, Saiph had started to move. The surprise made him instinctively flare energy into his body, and he sprinted forward before jumping in the air and activating his flight systems. The guns were large and clumsy, so they struggled to track him. Saiph consolidated power into one palm, pointed it at one of the guns, and then released it. He reached the second gun as the first one exploded, and he grabbed it by the metal that attached it to the ceiling. He pulled downward, and the metal snapped. The gun fell the thirty feet to the ground and smashed with a fantastic crunch.

Saiph hovered back to the ground, breathing hard from alarm rather than effort. He scanned the room for any more threats but only noticed a handful of skeletons near the door. Saiph put a hand to his chest and tried to think of an appropriate death Verse for them.

"I'd rather get my brains blown out in the wild than wait in terror at the slaughter house."

It wasn't perfect, but it did seem to suit those who were willing to risk it all for their adventurous side. Saiph went to the other end of the circular room and walked through the next opening. Immediately, he could hear an odd cranking sound that repeated over and over again. It was still dark, but light would flicker from ceiling lamps every few breaths, allowing Saiph to see that the long room was lined with large tanks of water. Inside each one was a skeleton.

What the hell is this place?

Saiph's first instinct was to turn right back around and leave. He even started to move to do so, but he stopped himself. He had to know what this place was. He shook his head and chuckled nervously. It looked like the skeletons at the entrance weren't the only ones who had died for their curiosity. He walked forward.

There was a series of tables in the middle of the room. It looked like whatever had hollowed out the mountain had purposely left this material behind in the form of a slab. The only unnatural thing about it were the metal restraints that were at each corner.

Saiph came to another group of tanks where the skeletons inside were smaller than the previous ones. Slimy material floated around the edges of the mouths and eye sockets and most of their eyes were missing. He felt sick. Saiph retracted his aura as fast as he could and then threw up as soon as his face was free to the air.

Breathe in. Breathe out. Breathe in. Breathe out. Don't think. Breathe...

As soon as he recovered, Saiph put his aura back on. There was no way he was walking around this place without it. He moved on but didn't look at the line of tanks this time.

The end of the room led to a series of hallways that were lined with doors at seemingly random intervals. He chose a direction and began looking inside the rooms. Most of them were offices of some sort that all looked exactly the same. When he opened a tenth door and found it identical to the last nine, he stopped checking them. He'd been exploring for nearly a quarter hour when he heard a scream. Saiph broke into a sprint, heading in the direction of the sound.

Who else is here and why?

Moments later, Saiph found himself in a cavernous room. The sound of glass shattering was followed by the thud of running footsteps. The mechanical sound that followed was one he had heard before: the footstep of a battle droid. Saiph hurried forward, trying to spot what was happening, but towering shelves blocked his view.

He rounded a corner and saw the back of the battle droid. It was much smaller than any he'd previously seen, and he registered that it was covered with rust and was moving with jolting, rigid steps. It was facing three large cages. A figure on the other side of the bars popped its head up to get a look, and the battle droid fired, missing only because its movement was hindered.

Saiph hurried over, but the battle droid didn't even turn as he approached. He punched several holes through its back and started ripping its parts out. It fell over immediately, like it had been on death's doorstep anyway.

"Who's there?" Saiph called out. He could make out edgy movement through the cage bars.

"Saiph?" the figure said, walking around the cage to see him. "What the hell are you doing here?"

It was Sarah.

"Saving your life, it appears," Saiph said.

"What? From that?" Sarah said, pointing at the hunk of metal on the floor. "That thing is so old it couldn't kill a mouse."

"Are you saying I imagined that scream, then?" Saiph asked.

"I was just surprised. And hell, have you walked around this place at all yet? Gives me the creeps."

Saiph remember the tanks and the tiny floating skeletons within them and grew solemn. "What is this place?"

"I'm not sure," Sarah said, looking around, "but it's old. The technology here is from at least three hundred years ago."

Saiph's gaze passed over the cages. The floor was stained red, and there were old blades lying next to ragged clothes. He wondered if his ancestors were already here when this was built, or if they were a product of this place. He hoped for the former. He looked back at Sarah. "How did you come to be here?"

"I was about to ask you the same thing," she said, wiping sweat from her forehead.

"You first."

Sarah gestured for him to follow her, and they started toward a door. "Ever since we discovered Jangali—or rediscovered, I should say—I've been curious about it. The first samples of the fauna that reached me were...unbelievable. So unbelievable that I began to wonder if it was natural or not."

"What does that mean, exactly?" Saiph asked distractedly. While Sarah walked like she was in her own home, Saiph was constantly scanning the room for more surprises.

"Have you read about genetics yet?"

"No."

Sarah sighed. "Well, just know that we are capable of altering life and the way it forms through genetic manipulation. I wondered if someone had tampered with the way life formed here on Jangali." They crossed the threshold of another room and found a stairwell leading downward. "Ah, here we are."

Sarah started down, and Saiph shook his head before following. "And what did you find? Was life 'tampered with,' as you put it?"

"Yes and no," Sarah said. "It's difficult to explain. I'll let you know when I know."

Saiph nodded as they continued walking. Sarah passed several doors that led to another floor and kept heading downward. "You still haven't answered my question, though. How did you know about this place? I flew past it three times, and I knew where to look for it."

Sarah snorted. "Seriously, it was a bitch finding it. I've had a satellite running an algorithm to detect human settlement ever since we got here. It didn't find this place, but it found other signs of disturbance, and I was able to look for myself. I own a scouting drone that eventually noticed the windows."

Saiph shook his head, confused. "But why were you looking for *this* place?"

"Do you get to ask all the questions?" Sarah asked, turning around on the steps and looking up at him. "How did *you* find this place?"

"A woman I was enslaved with used to live in a village nearby, and she told me of this place. My friend Alistair and I started to become curious about where the walls of our camp had come from. We knew that we didn't build them and that they were old. Yet the Skyfallers we were with didn't seem to know what they were either. I decided to try and find out for myself."

Sarah smiled then, a bright, playful smile. "Very clever, Saiph Calthari. You'd think more people would have been concerned about those very details. They've been distracted, I suppose." She turned and kept walking. "If people from Earth once lived here, then they had a base of some sort. I believe that this may be it, but I could be wrong."

"What are you hoping to find?" Saiph asked.

"Records. An account of what was happening here and what they were trying to accomplish."

"And you think they'll be down there?"

Sarah chuckled. "If you wanted to keep something safe and hidden, would you bury it in the ground or hang it in a tree?"

Saiph rolled his eyes. "I suppose you're right."

They reached the very bottom of the complex twenty minutes later. At the end was a sealed double door made of metal. Sarah walked up and tried to pry it open, but it didn't budge. She knocked on the door three times, as if someone might answer.

"It's thick," she said. She turned around and smiled at Saiph. "Mind helping a girl out here?"

Saiph motioned for her to step back and then he put his hands in the slight crack between the doors. He pulled and the metal started to budge, but it was *heavy*. Saiph flared the energy within him, and the doors came flying open, kicking dust up everywhere.

Sarah coughed into the arm she was using to cover her mouth. "You really need to practice your control!"

"Sorry."

"Don't be. It's better than not being able to get in at all."

They walked into the room through falling dust, and Saiph physically jumped when the lights overhead illuminated automatically.

Sarah laughed in amazement. "The Cynic Corp sensors *still* work. I bet they'd love to make an ad campaign out of this."

The center of the room was dominated by an enormous circular table. It appeared to be made out of thick black glass and had at least twenty chairs around its circumference. There were notebooks and papers scattered across it, but the table itself also flickered with small squares of black and white light. Beyond the table were other computer stations, large displays, and sturdy-looking metal boxes.

"This is it," Sarah said.

"It is?"

"If we're going to find anything, it'll be in the table data set or in the locked vaults." She looked over at Saiph. "I'll try and access the table, you open all the vaults?"

Saiph nodded as Sarah pulled out her tablet and started manipulating it. All of the metal boxes were black and were nearly six feet tall. Saiph was just starting to gather energy into his arms so that he could try and pull the door of one of the boxes straight off, but then he noticed that it was cracked open slightly. He reached out and opened it. Inside were shelves of small glass bottles. Instead of investigating, he went to the next vault and then the next, making sure they were all unlocked. The last one he came to was smaller than the rest. It looked like it had been forcibly blown opened, but it was still intact.

"Damn it," Sarah said. "Damn it, damn it, damn it. This thing is fried. I guess it was too much to hope for. You find anything?"

Saiph gestured at the small lockbox. "They were all open, but this one looks like it was forced. See how the lock is crumpled inward and blackened?"

Sarah walked over and studied it before gingerly opening the door. Inside was a single sheet of thin digital paper. It was still solid with light. As she looked at it, her expression changed from curious to downright shocked.

"No. Way."

"What is it?" Saiph asked.

Sarah was clutching the thin sheet of light, shaking her head and smiling. "I knew it! I knew it had to be him!"

Saiph held up a calming hand. "What did you know? What's happening?"

"See this here," Sarah said, holding out the paper for him to see. She was pointing at a line at the bottom of the page, which had messy, flowing hand writing above it. "That's the signature of Warren Winters. He knew about this place. Maybe even created it."

"Who is Warren Winters?" Saiph asked. He really needed to get through *The Bing Bang to Boundless* so that he could avoid moments like this.

Sarah chuckled, walking over to one of the chairs and sitting down. "It's hard to believe that someone doesn't know who Warren Winters is."

"I find it hard to believe how condescending people are," Saiph snapped. He was tired. It was the middle of the night, and his adrenaline had been turned off and on like the glow of a firefly.

Sarah scowled. "Fine. Sorry. You'll hear about him soon enough, I'm sure." She looked at the device on her wrist. "We need to be getting back. It'll be light soon."

"But this place," Saiph protested, "we've barely begun to see what's here."

"We'll have to come back some other time."

Saiph closed his eyes and tried to blink the sleepiness away. "You go, then. I'll stay a bit longer."

Sarah raised her eyebrows. "Saiph, you're exhausted."

"I'm fine."

"Look," Sarah said sternly, "they need you back there. What if there's an attack and you're not there to help? What if it comes when you've been awake for more than forty hours straight?"

Saiph hadn't thought of that. He was suddenly worried about everyone in the caves. They had to get back right now. He could see skeletons on the ground of the cave floor, piled high. Which ones were his family? He shook his head, trying to shake himself awake. He really was tired, wasn't he?

"Okay," he finally said, calming down. "You're right. Let's go."

Sarah gathered a few more things from the other vaults, and then they set out. It was still dark when they reached the small vehicle she'd used to escape the drone perimeter around the mountains.

"Get in," she said, "you're in no state to fly back right now."

Saiph was too tired to argue. He climbed into the passenger seat and relaxed into it. How could they make seats so comfortable? He sank deeper into it, and the cushions seemed to embrace him. He sighed with gratification.

"Hold these," Sarah said, getting into the driver's seat. She passed him the items she had taken and the sheet of paper that had gotten her so excited. Saiph placed them near his feet and then looked at the sheet of paper again. He swiped it to one side, like he would with the Book of Light, and another page came up.

It was a list of names. He swiped again, and there were more names. He scanned a few of them, and something familiar struck him. Maybe if he were more awake, he would have placed it, but it escaped him in that moment.

Still, it nagged at him. He swiped again, and the list of names went into the Cs. He used his finger so that he could keep his place and scrolled down. At the very bottom of the list, a name stood out to him like a streak of lightning in the night:

Lola Calthari.

CHAPTER THIRTY-THREE

E ntry 7:

World War III was only six months shorter than the last World War, but it was even more destructive. The sheer mass of military might scarred the Earth so badly that it took a hundred years of restoration to make it look right again. The people suffered even more than the land did. Experts estimate that the death toll exceeded 120 million.

Ava and I were safe, of course, stashed away in Colorado, but we took no part in the war effort. I resigned from my position despite Warren's protest that he needed me to help design the increasingly deadly combat drones. This was the first war in which the outliers did more fighting than big, strong men on the ground. Instead, it was the small, smart, quick-reflexed men and women who sat miles away from the action, controlling the deadly machines.

Even so, most countries participated in the war but were too poor to afford fleets of drones and bulky battle bots. They fought the old-fashioned way, and it was bloody and brutal. The long-held tradition of the rich starting a war and the poor suffering for it continued.

Ava and I were horrified at the slaughter and loss of life, but we couldn't bring ourselves to go against her father. He was the man who had given us everlasting youth and the means to enjoy it. We knew that he was still a good man. Sometimes, I wonder what would have happened if we did stand against him. I don't think it would have affected the outcome of the war itself, but it would have made Ava feel better.

Though we didn't protest the war, others did. Three years in and with no sight of victory, many were fed up with the expense and death. They couldn't remember why we were fighting in the first place. There were riots so intense in Chicago, Berlin, and Oslo that a few thought Warren's whole regime would collapse.

From the beginning, Warren had only sold Boundless as an all-or-nothing pill, but we knew he could tailor the amount of years given because of what he gave Lin, Omar, and Tim. With the crisis mounting, Warren decided to release the limited version. Anyone who joined the armed forces was given fifteen extra years of youth. Political opponents suddenly changed their minds.

The war continued.

"Don't let the dumplings burn again!" Ava called out over the thunder.

The rain pounded down on our Rocky Mountain home so intensely that it was hard to hear myself think.

"I burn the dumplings one time, and after that it's like I'm going to burn them from now unto eternity!" I yelled back.

Ava came down the stairs and slipped behind me, wrapping her arms around my chest. Beneath her flowery perfume was a scent that was unmistakably her, and I breathed it in.

"Two times," she said, kissing me on the cheek.

I rolled my eyes. "Two times I burn the dumplings, and it's like I'm going to burn them from now unto eternity."

"Do you want some wine?" she asked. "We just got the Cabernet from Santa Barbara."

"Yes, please. I doubt Tim is going to show up anyway. Not in this mountainous tropical depression."

Because God hates me, the doorbell rang immediately after I stopped talking, and Ava gave me a look that emphasized that I shouldn't burn the dumplings. I heard her chatting with Tim while I cooked, barely taking my eyes off the warming dough.

Ava came back to the kitchen. I looked past her and at Tim. I hadn't seen him in five years, and he looked slightly different. He was still spindly with light-brown hair and an attractive face, but his eyes were more confident. He smiled.

"Hi, Jon."

I shook his hand. "Hey, Tim. Thanks for coming."

We left the kitchen and went into the living room. An enormous glass window overlooked the mountain edge, but it was only visible when lightning lit up the sky.

"Want a drink?" I asked.

Tim raised a hand and shook his head. He sat down.

"So what have you been up to?" I asked.

He shrugged. "Not much. Work. Research. Nothing new. What about you two?"

Ava put down her wineglass. "Work. Waiting for the war to end."

"Are you still talking to your father? Do you know anything else about all that's happening?"

Ava shook her head. "We have an unspoken agreement not to interact until all this is over. You know how Jon and I feel about it."

Tim nodded politely, but I had a feeling he didn't agree with our attitude toward the war.

"Look, Tim," I said, "I hate to jump right in on this, but I need your help."

"Really?" he said, looking surprised. "Mr. Likes to Work Alone needs help? Well, I'm all ears, then."

"Do we have to get into this already?" Ava said. "Can't we just talk for a little while longer?"

I smiled guilty at Ava. "But he already knows that I need his help now. We can't keep him hanging like this. It would be rude."

She rolled her eyes. "Fine. Let's get it over with."

I explained the work I was doing in as much detail as I could without the accompanying data. Tim listened intently. When I had finished, he leaned back into the sofa, thoughtful. It was so hard to tell what he was thinking sometimes. It made me nervous. I really needed his help; no one else was capable enough.

Finally, Tim looked up at me. "I'll do it. Give me a few days to wrap up my other affairs, then I'll come."

I sighed and bowed my head. "Thank you. Seriously.

He nodded.

"Oh shit!" I said, hopping from my seat and running to the kitchen.

I looked down at the pan full of darkened lumps, and the smell of burned food wafted into my nostrils.

"Damn it."

"Honey?" Ava called from the other room. "What's wrong?"

"Nothing..." I yelled back, thinking fast. "You know, I don't really feel like dumplings tonight. Mind if we have a frozen pizza instead?"

I quickly turned off the heat and waved my hand in the air to push the bad air away.

"You burned the dumplings, didn't you?"

"What? No, of course not," I said, tossing the black balls of dough into the trash.

Ava and Tim walked into the kitchen, their faces scrunched from the unpleasant smell. Ava looked at me with one eyebrow raised. "What's the smell, Jon? Don't lie."

"Burned dumplings..." I said, chin on chest.

Despite the great dumpling fiasco, we had a wonderful evening. I was elated to have convinced Tim of my cause. If I was being honest with myself, I hadn't thought that he would agree. Tim had his own work, and when he was absorbed in something, it was difficult to see him for dinner, let alone get him to leave his research all together, move, and come help me for an indefinite amount of time. I should have thought about his willingness more at the time, but I was so pleased, I didn't give it a second thought.

The war ended when the second Greater East Asia Coprosperity Sphere surrendered to the North Atlantic Treaty Organization in a small courthouse in Bangladesh on November 29, 2100. It's still celebrated as a world holiday on Earth, but I don't think anyone celebrated it quite as much as Warren Winters did. His first and biggest hurdle was almost complete.

At this point, Warren spoke fluent Mandarin (the Chinese national language at the time), and he went to accept their surrender himself. The Chinese people were impressed at how well he spoke their tongue and his abiding respect for their history and culture—a miraculous change of heart from the years leading up to the war. He eased them into it, but in the end, he told them that, to prevent further warfare, they would be joining the newly formed World Republic, which cemented the relationship between America, Europe, and Asia. In the eyes of the law, these massive regions were essentially one nation with very different cultural backgrounds.

The fog of war evaporated in the dawn of a new era of human progress. Warren would later justify the millions of casualties in the war by pointing to the unbelievable feats humankind made in the twenty-second century. Sometimes the leaps and bounds were so amazing that it was hard to argue with him. But then I would remember that those who would argue were dead and gone, and that most of the time, the end does not justify the means.

CHAPTER THIRTY-FOUR

The information they'd taken from the building of the Old Gods didn't have any more information on Lola Calthari, but Saiph wasn't wholly enthusiastic to discover more. She must have been his great-great-great-great-grandmother, or something, and she had likely been in that horrible place. There hadn't been a good time to go back to the building of the Old Gods, so Saiph distracted himself until he could return and find out more.

For most of the next week, Saiph split his time training with Silvestre and reading *The Big Bang to Boundless*. As much as he loved his aura, he found that he was enjoying the book more than Silvestre's teaching methods, which relied heavily on condescension and insults.

He had made it to the industrial revolution and read the stories of how the first industrial machines were built. The book was complete with schematics and diagrams, and many of the inventions were explained in full detail. It often took him several hours to fully understand a new machine, but when he did, he felt like he had climbed another step up the tower of enlightenment. He knew from that vantage, he would understand the world in a way that would have been inconceivable in his old life. He couldn't wait to share it with his father and explain how technology wasn't magic after all.

He was at the entrance to the cavern, reading about the invention of the internal combustion engine, when Darakai and Roe sauntered out, dressed in their army greens. He hadn't seen much of them over the past couple of weeks because they'd been so busy with their training and conditioning.

"Hey!" Saiph called to them. "Where are you off to? I thought no one was supposed to leave the cavern?"

"Got special permission," Roe said, with uncharacteristic excitement. "Russ is teaching us how to shoot."

"I don't think it's very polite to show that much enthusiasm for learning how to blow somebody's brains out."

Darakai grunted. "This coming from potentially the most destructive person alive? I'm not buying your bullshit, sorry to say."

"You've killed plenty of people," Roe said. "And they deserve it, whether it's from one of your lasers or one of my bullets. It's not like we're going to be wandering around and putting down the elderly."

"Well, I'm glad we cleared that up," Saiph said. "Never know with you homicidal maniacs. Can I come with you?"

"You need permission," Darakai said.

"Didn't you just say I was a significant force of destructive power? I think I'll come. Unlike you, I don't have a superior officer."

They carefully made their way down the steep path that snaked through the trees. Russ was waiting for them near the river a mile away from camp. Saiph pitied the soldiers who were forced to bring water up to the others.

Saiph noticed that the trees were different from the ones in the Fulgurian forest and Altai. They were smaller and they had more brown in their coloring than the bright-green vegetation at lower altitudes, but they were much more numerous. There weren't as many volt animals or glowing vines either. Just thinking of his current surroundings reminded him of what had happened to the Fulgurian forest, and he decided not to think about it. Instead, he tried to enjoy the feeling of being out of the cavern and in the rays of sunshine that beamed through the canopy. It was a springweek, and the sun was bright without it being too warm.

Russ sat with two other soldiers by the river, his signature white cowboy hat easy to spot among the green and brown. Roe and Darakai reached him first, jittery and bouncing on their feet.

"Howdy, Saiph. Didn't know you were coming," Russ said.

"Decided to tag along, if that's all right?"

"Hell yeah! You ever fire a rifle before? Ain't nothing like it. Gives me a warm and fuzzy feeling inside. Come on down a bit, me and the boys set up a little shooting range."

Russ led them downstream for a few minutes and then crossed the small river by jumping from rock to rock. The forest became lighter, and Saiph assumed there was a clearing up ahead.

"I know you live here and all, but even you three won't believe this," Russ said.

They walked past the tree line and into a huge clearing. A lake was surrounded by an enormous semicircle cliff that rose at least a quarter of a mile high. Water poured down over the entire arc, but it concentrated in four spots, where a series of majestic waterfalls stood out like gods among ants.

"Would you look at that..." Darakai said.

Saiph shook his head in disbelief. "How have we never heard of something so wonderful?"

"So what?" Roe said. "Are we going to be shooting at the waterfalls or something?"

Everyone managed to turn away from the waterfall and look at Roe.

"Only joking," she said. Saiph suspected she was only half joking.

Russ let them take in the sight for another moment before he led them to another clearing on the east side of the lake. Tin cans were propped up on logs and branches.

"Now," Russ said, taking a rifle off his shoulder, "before we get started, there are several rules you need to follow. Rule number one is knowing that guns are toys. They're fun and quite useful. Rule number two is that, even though they're toys, they are toys that will blow your fucking face off if not handled properly. I want you to repeat that last part to me."

Darakai and Roe looked at each other uncomfortably. "Go on now," Russ said, "say it back to me. Guns are what?"

"Guns are toys that will blow your fucking face off," Darakai and Roe said together.

"Again."

"Guns are toys that will blow your fucking face off."

"Good," Russ said. "Very good. Now pay close attention, this shit is serious."

Russ went on to explain every function of the rifle in front of him. He even went into detail about how it was built and how it generated enough force to sling a metal bullet several miles through the air. After he talked to them for an hour, he started from the beginning. After that, he made them repeat everything he had said. Only when they had gotten it all correct did he let them hold an unloaded rifle. He made them take it apart and put it back together again. Once he was satisfied that they weren't going to blow their fucking faces off, he loaded the weapon.

"Be sure to put the butt of the rifle against your shoulder, real firm like. Don't put your finger on the trigger until you're ready to fire. Keep your eye directly down the sight and your arm steady."

Roe, Darakai, and Saiph did as they were told. Roe shot first and missed terribly.

"Damn it!" she yelled. "Erlik's ass!"

"Whoa," Russ said, "calm down there, honey. This is supposed to be fun, remember?"

Darakai fired, and his shot was even farther from the target than Roe's. "Fun isn't exactly Roe's forte," he said.

Saiph held out the rifle with one fully extended arm and pulled the trigger. The can farthest from them exploded off the branch it was sitting on. Saiph smiled.

"Hah!" Russ spit to the side. "You dynamics...always showing off. I could do that, obviously, but I'm of a shy and humble disposition myself."

They spent the rest of the afternoon firing their rifles. Everyone cheered when Roe and Darakai hit their first cans. After that, they were hitting them every few shots or so. They laughed and joked around just like they had back in Altai. Saiph hadn't realized how much he'd needed to laugh.

Roe had just hit her third can in a row when a tremendous shriek filled the air above them. "What the hell was that?" one of the soldiers said.

"Quiet, Parvati, I don't want whatever that was coming closer," Russ said. "Hey, why are you three smiling?"

"Because that," Darakai said, "was a sytin."

Roe and Darakai broke away at nearly the same time, and Saiph followed them.

"Whoa, what's going on?" Russ said. "Why are you running toward the screeching roar of an unknowable beast? I order you to retreat! Hey! Ah, damn it." Russ ran after them into the woods.

They heard the screech again, and Saiph adjusted their course in the right direction. The branches were getting thicker and the incline steeper, but Saiph pushed his way through. Darakai and Roe followed closely behind him. Half an hour later, they saw the monstrous bird as it sat in its nest on the edge of a rocky cliff. Its long neck was connected to a slim brown-feathered body. Its wingspan was over forty feet in length. Saiph and Roe looked at each other in amazement but kept quiet. Russ, Private Parvati, and Private Chase came stumbling up behind them.

"Holy sh—"

Saiph slapped a hand over Chase's mouth and eyed him. Chase held up a hand and nodded his understanding. They gazed at the bird for a long while, taking in the rare close-up view. When it finally extended its great wings and jumped off the cliff, they hopped onto the ledge and watched it fly away. They stood in silence, taking in the sight until the bird had completely disappeared from sight.

Russ broke the silence. "That was King Kong crazy!"

"It's like something out of dinosaur age," Parvati said.

Darakai shook his head in wonder. "Never thought I'd get so close. Won't be forgetting that anytime soon."

Saiph was tempted to summon his aura and fly after it, but why fly off alone when he could enjoy this moment with his friends?

After the Sytin disappeared, Russ said, "Well, that's enough excitement for one day, I think. Let's head back."

They returned to the cavern as a group, and several times they saw Fulgurians off in the trees, collecting firewood and berries. They found Ayanda talking to Vincent in the meal area. Saiph introduced Ayanda to Russ and then Vincent to Roe and Darakai.

"How do you know each other?" Saiph asked Ayanda and Vincent.

They looked at each other and shrugged. "It's boring as hell in this cave," Vincent said. "So I've been showing Ayanda how coding and authoring software works."

"I ain't ever been that bored," Russ said.

"Oh," Vincent said, "and what do you suggest we do, then? We're not allowed out of here!"

Russ thought for a moment. "Say, have you Altainians ever heard of something called whiskey?"

A few hours later, Saiph found himself spectacularly drunk. He couldn't remember how the whole thing had started, but he was now deep in the cave, one arm around Vincent and the other around Russ, swaying back and forth and singing his favorite harvest song.

"No, no, no," Saiph said, "you're getting it all wrong, Vinny! It goes, 'the harvest feast what a beautiful sky, forget about the yokai, the ola wine makes me feel so fine, cheers to the harvest'!"

"I barely go outside!" Vincent yelled, even though Saiph was right next to him. "I've never farmed in my life, let alone sang...plowing songs!"

Ayanda and Roe giggled, and Darakai roared with laughter. "What is your musical preference, then, Vincent?" Ayanda asked.

"Hold on, hold on," Vincent whispered, the exact opposite of his yelling a moment before. "I'll show you." Vincent pulled out a small device and switched it on. He squinted at the screen and pushed a few buttons. "Quiet everyone, it's about to start!"

Their conversation reduced to a whisper. It was silent for a moment before a cacophony of sound erupted from Vincent's device. The rest of the group fell back, clutching their ears.

"It's called heavy death techno!" Vincent yelled over the sound. "It's straight from the Askani underworld. Blood pumping, right?"

"More like blood curdling," Roe yelled.

"Gods, this is awful!" Ayanda said. "It sounds like Erlik's own ballad."

Russ took his hands away from his ears long enough to slap the device out of Vincent's hand. "Make it stop!"

Vincent picked up the device and switch the music off while the rest of the group rolled around in drunken laughter.

"Russ," Darakai said. "Russsssel. Russel. Why don't you tell us a story, eh? I bet you've got a few good ones."

Russ squinted at Darakai suspiciously and took a generous gulp of whiskey. "Who told you?"

"What?" Darakai asked. "No one told me anything! I swear!"

"Good," Russ said, sitting down, "I'd rather tell you myself. Gather round."

They walked over to Russ and formed a close circle. Ayanda sat down next to Saiph. Russ let them get settled and paused to look them each in the eye before he started speaking. Saiph could hear drips of water from farther down the cave.

"So this is the story of how I met the famous, infamous, savvy, dashing...Jon Foster."

The circle contracted in anticipation.

"I've fought in a lot of wars," Russ began. "War ain't pretty, but it can be a way of life. For better or worse, it suits me. It's in my blood, you could say. Anyway...I had just gotten back to Mars from Tau Ceti, working a job for the Oligarchy, when I got a very strange and mysterious message. It said: Fifty million credits. One life. DNA sample needed to seal contract."

Russ took another swig and shrugged his shoulders. "What the hell, I thought. What is this? I mean, I'm no dummy, I definitely wanted fifty million credits, but it sounded like this person wanted me to assassinate someone. And they wanted my DNA for it? This individual had obviously misread Russ Henson. They thought me a drunken hillbilly who was good at killing things! The nerve! What was I supposed to do, just leave my blood on the note and walk away? Then it dawned on me. Yes, that was exactly what I was supposed to do. So I left my blood and walked away. Lost my tail, lost my second tail, then circled back to the note. Sure enough, five minutes later, I was the one tailing my own blood!"

Saiph had no idea where this story was going, but he was entranced. He barely noticed that Ayanda was squeezing his hand.

"As you might have guessed, I was pretty drunk at this point," Russ continued. "But I really wanted to know what was going on! So I tailed this fella all night long. After three hours, I got fed up and kidnapped the guy. Had to lose a few more tails and pull a tracker out from under his foot, but I got him. And would you believe it, this guy is absolutely crazy! I mean out-of-his-mind nuts!"

Saiph suspected that Russ had a skewed view of insanity.

"He was talking of plots to destroy Mars and that my target would've been Jon Foster. Jon Foster, I thought. I love that guy! He saved my kin back on Earth. Not knowingly, mind you, but he took in a hundred thousand refugees, including my family. That guy was number two in my mind—I'm number one, by the way—so I decided to repay him for doing right by me and mine."

"So you went and told him?" Vincent asked.

"What!" Russ said. "Of course not! You think I had his phone number lying around?" Russ put his pinky to his mouth and his thumb to his ear. "Hey, Jon, it's Russ Henson. You don't know me, but I believe there's an intricate plot to kill you! Nah, I handled it my own way."

"What did you do?" Ayanda asked.

"What any reasonable person would do. I infiltrated the group, stole some incriminating documents, planted some false evidence, contacted the attorney general through nefarious means, and had the whole organization collapse in on itself."

They stared at Russ, baffled.

"Of course," Russ said, "Jon found out that it was me. He called me into his office, and I went because I knew that he knew. I explained the whole situation to him. He probably could have arrested me on the spot for doing some of the things I did, and for a moment, that's what I thought he was going to do. But no, he stood up, laughed, shook my hand, and offered me a job. That's when I met Tokomoto. Fifteen years ago to the day." Russ raised his glass. "God bless that little Asian. I love him. Don't tell him I said that, though!" he said, pointing an accusing finger at them. They nodded placatingly. "And Jon Foster too. God bless him." Russ took another long swig. "So what about you guys! Any good stories?"

The circle looked among themselves, knowing that they didn't have any stories that fell within the same vicinity as the one Russ had just told.

"I've got one, if we're telling Jon stories," Silvestre said as she walked up.

"Hey!" Russ yelled. "How long you been there!"

"Long enough," Silvestre said. She gestured for Roe to scoot over and sat on Saiph's other side.

"Don't you go tellin' Toko what I said, now."

"Don't worry, I won't tell Toko of your deep affection for him. Besides, you're not allowed to repeat my story either, got it?"

Russ clapped his hands together. "Why, Silvestre, I would never have thought you'd be a storyteller."

Silvestre motioned for the bottle of whiskey, and Russ handed it to her, an impressed look on his face. She drank deeply and wiped her mouth.

"So most people, like Saiph, have something trigger their dynamic state. Something dramatic, stressful, or dangerous. But my mother had a hard, stressful birth, and I came out like this." She gestured to her eyes. "Have never known the color of my eyes underneath the red. Have always been curious to find out, though..." She took another long drink.

"So my mom died in childbirth, and I came from a very religious community in South America on Earth. Being born with red eyes was not good for me. They thought I was a child of the devil."

"Who's the devil?" Roe asked.

"An evil god," Russ said.

Silvestre nodded. "I was a freak. An outcast. My father tried to keep me for a while, for my mother's sake, but he was eventually pressured to give me up. No one for a thousand miles wanted me."

Saiph thought about how he had considered himself a freak when he'd first found out. Maybe he wasn't any better than the father who had given Silvestre up. She wasn't a monster. A little rough around the edges, maybe, but good underneath it all. Beautiful too.

"I'll never know how Jon found out about it," Silvestre continued, "but he did. He came to Earth himself, picked me up, and brought me back to Mars. He placed me in a family of very nice and supportive people, but I've always been a bit of a rebel. I wanted to travel and see the Sphere, so I started working for him. I think he was glad to have me."

"Did you know Jon very well growing up?" Saiph asked.

"Not really. I only saw him a handful of times during my childhood. He always sent me a birthday present, though. I've only gotten to know him better over the last few years."

"How do you know Jon, Vincent?" Ayanda asked.

"It's not quite as exciting as their stories. He sent me an e-mail with an offer of money and years to work with him on an aura suit. I accepted, and a shuttle came and picked me up."

"You're right," Roe said, "that wasn't very exciting. You should lie about your story, like Russ."

"Hey, that story is, like, seventy-three-percent true!" Russ said.

Roe and Russ were arguing about which parts were true and which weren't when nearly simultaneous notification chimes sounded from Russ's, Silvestre's, and Vincent's devices. They frowned at each other as Silvestre pulled out her device.

"Oh wow," she said, "Harmonia Jones has passed away."

Russ sighed sadly. "She was getting up there, wasn't she?"

"She was two hundred, I think," Silvestre said.

Saiph eyed Ayanda and Roe and then said, "I'm sorry for your loss. How did you all know Harmonia?"

Vincent scoffed. "Know her? We wish. She was one of the most famous singers in the Sphere. We'd be lucky just to have an autograph."

"I loved that one about oceans of Bao Haiyang and how she mixed the languages," Silvestre said with a faraway look. "I still don't know what it means, but it's so soothing."

"Hey, Vin, you got 'Below the Grave and Above the Stars' on your player?" Russ asked.

Vincent nodded. "Who doesn't?"

"Play it, will ya?"

They were quiet as Vincent pulled back out his device and navigated to the song. A moment later, an instrument Saiph had never heard before began to play—slow and beautiful.

"What is that?" Saiph whispered to Silvestre. He had to know.

"It's a piano."

Saiph listened intently. He thought it was both lovely and haunting, and that was before Harmonia Jones ever said a word. Then she started to sing, and Saiph immediately felt something stir inside of him. That voice. He'd never heard anything like it, never even imagined something so lovely was possible. He could hardly take in what she was saying, but when he finally did, he wanted to weep. It was about the death of her mother, whose love for her seeped through everything, from the deepest grave, to the farthest star. Had Saiph ever felt emotions as powerful as what Harmonia felt?

When the song ended, Saiph looked up and saw that he wasn't the only one who was deeply moved. This woman had just died? Was gone from the world, never to be heard again? It was a terrible tragedy, and they all knew it.

Russ raised the glass in his hand. "To Harmonia." He looked as if he wanted to say more, but he only took a sip of his drink instead. Saiph raised his glass with the others and drank.

Saiph stumbled back toward the entrance, leaving the others to listen to some of Harmonia's more upbeat and optimistic songs. He didn't want to listen to them, though. Not yet anyway. The encampment was mostly quiet now, but he was still startled when Silvestre caught up with him.

"Oy! Gods, you surprised me."

"Still not very good at those listening exercises, I see," she said.

"You're quite mean, you know," Saiph said. "Quite mean indeed. And sneaky too."

"And you're quite drunk."

"Ah yes," Saiph said. "So you agree that we both speak the truth, then? Excellent. Our first agreement. How grand."

Silvestre gave him a rare smile. "How you doing?"

Saiph shrugged. "That song did a bit of a number on me, I think. Sort of made everything hit all at once."

Footsteps on rock. Water dripping. Distant snores.

"Tell me another Verse," Silvestre said. "What Verse would your father say to you right now?"

Saiph thought of his father—his perpetual calm, large stature, and gentle smile. What would he say?

"*Courage is the art of being the only one who knows you're scared to death.*"

"But now I know too," Silvestre said.

"Then maybe it can be our secret?"

She smiled warmly and nodded. "You know, I've always hated religion. I've hated every Speaker I've ever met. I despise the old superstitious faiths. I can't stand the Purists." She paused and faced him. "But I like your Verses."

She turned and left without another word.

CHAPTER THIRTY-FIVE

Entry 8:

The Third World War is often considered the first hostility in what historians call the Wars of Unification. It took twenty more years to bring the smaller countries into the World Republic, though it caused nowhere near the same level of destruction. It's amusing that it's called a republic, since Warren was essentially its dictator. Benevolent dictator, sure, but dictator nonetheless.

One of Warren's first acts was to evenly distribute the food supply and make sure that every person in the world had access to clean water, an education, and the internet. This willful equality was undeniably the backbone of humanity's golden age. Every person, every mind, had the potential to break some scientific barrier. But first, one hole needed to be created before the dam of knowledge burst and the flood of progress was released.

I had moved my lab back to California after the war ended. I was enjoying the morning light and my habitual cup of coffee when Tim came rushing out.

"Jon!" he said breathlessly. "Jon! You. Come. Now."

"Are you finally going to go on a date, Tim? I'm proud of you if you are. It's been too long."

Tim ignored me, so I dropped the newspaper and followed him. He brought me to his workstation and pointed at the monitor and accompanying holograms. I started reading and analyzing the diagrams, photographs, and data. My heart pounded as I read.

"Shit, Tim," I said. "You've done it."

We launched the first Essens to six separate stars. They traveled at incredible speeds, but it still took fifteen years for them to get to their destinations. After that, it took them another five years to replicate enough to start seeing results. I'll be the first to admit that they were some of the longest years of my life.

"So these little things will eat a star or something?" Lin said.

The big night had finally arrived. The Essens were scheduled to send back the energy, and we would know whether our invention had worked or not. Everyone was at our lab for the reveal.

"They're called Essens," I told Lin. "And they won't eat the star, just absorb ninety-six percent of the energy it produces."

"Ah yes, I see..." Lin said. She was wearing an elegant black dress and held herself with an air of authority. She was still as beautiful as ever, but it was different somehow. She had changed so much.

I chuckled. "It's easier to understand the implications," I said. "If this works, we will never have to worry about energy again. We'll be able to try out new theories and create amazing technologies. It will change everything."

"I realize that," Lin said. "That's why I invested in it."

"You did?" I said, surprised.

"Of course I did. I own twelve percent of your company, Jon."

"Oh."

"You boys, so obsessed with your science. There's other interesting stuff out there, you know."

"Like clothes, perfumes, and purses?" I said, smiling.

"I sell more than that," Lin said briskly. "I own sixty percent of the drone delivery fleet. It's a thirty-billion-dollar industry."

"Seriously?" I said. "How did I not know this?"

She looked at me like I was a moron. "You are too brilliant to be this stupid."

I looked at her, thoughtful and confused, thinking that she might be right.

Lin looked up at the clock that was counting down. "If this works, though, you'll be richer than all of us. Except for Warren, of course."

"That's not why I'm doing this."

"I know," Lin said, "but that doesn't make it untrue."

I sighed, not wanting to think about my own finances, intent on focusing on what this invention would do for the world. The clock was under three minutes now.

"I'm going to find Ava."

I made my way through the crowded room, and an apprehensive buzz filled the space as the countdown ticked lower. I didn't realize that everyone else realized how important this was. I saw Ava standing by one of the control stations, looking thoughtful.

"This is goddamn nerve-racking," I whispered to her. "It feels amazing! How long has it been since I've been so excited?"

"I don't think you've ever been this excited. Except for maybe when you kissed me that first time on the boardwalk."

I looked at her, and my stomach filled with butterflies. I hadn't thought about that in so many years. I laughed quietly and hugged her.

"Not as excited as you were, I'm sure."

A beep filled the room, and I let go of Ava and turned to the projection hovering above. This was it. Another beep, and the room went deathly silent.

Beep...

Beep...

Beep.

I held my breath. The bar that showed the large battery readouts started flashing. They rose slowly at first but then shot upward. The global batteries that powered the world's cities rose hundreds of times faster than they normally did. The computer predicted that they would be fully charged within hours.

The room erupted into a chorus of celebration. I leapt in the air, my heart a tumultuous ball of elation. I grabbed Ava and held her close, then I took a step back, looked into her eyes, and shook my head in amazement. I turned and found Tim standing next to me; he wasn't much of a hugger, but I went for it anyway. He squirmed in discomfort. I shook the hands of a dozen people who had contributed to the project over the years. Warren walked down from his honorary seat.

"This changes everything," he said, a huge smile on his face.

I nodded, unable to speak.

"I am so very proud of you, Jon. A day for the history books."

I was surprised at how much I craved his approval, even after all these years. I was an old man in a young body, but I suppose many of us never really stop needing the blessings of our parents. Tears of joy filled my eyes as I thought how everything would change. The comfort that Ava and I so much enjoyed would be universally expanded.

We celebrated throughout the night, drinking champagne and congratulating ourselves for once again conquering the barriers that nature had set before us. I signed autographs for the first time and answered questions from famous reporters. It was an extraordinary night. As the party wound down and people finally began to disperse, I sat down at a workstation and began to analyze the data.

"There were times that I didn't think it would be possible," Tim said, taking a seat next to me.

I nodded. "I still can't believe we did it."

He rolled his chair a bit closer.

"We?" he said. "More like you."

"I couldn't have done it without you," I said. "I wouldn't have ever figured out the biomechanical links of mind and body."

"Fair enough," he said, raising his champagne flute. We clinked our glasses together. "Still, that was one thing. Everyone here knows that you did most of the work."

"It's been a dream I've had for a long time."

We sat in silence for a few minutes, staring at the large hologram readout above the room, watching the world power supply fly upward.

"Did you and Ava take the true Boundless pill?" Tim asked.

The question was so unexpected that I stared dumbly for a long few seconds.

"Yeah, that's what I thought," Tim said. "Why didn't you tell us? Why did you only give us a few hundred years compared to eternity?"

I was getting over my surprise. "Well," I said. "Well, we tried to convince Warren to let you, Lin, and Omar take the pill, but he wouldn't have it. He said he couldn't just give it out to everyone."

"I asked to purchase the real thing tonight," Tim said. "My stake in the Essens is more than enough to pay for it."

"Really? Tim, that's great, I—"

"He said no."

I sat back, confounded. "What? Why?"

"He wasn't even diplomatic about it. He just said that he didn't want to sell it to me. What irks me the most is that he's already sold it to Lin."

It hit me then that I had spent too much time working on the Essens and not enough time paying attention to the world around me. I had been so consumed with trying to change the world that I was left knowing next to nothing about its current state.

I took a breath. "I'll talk to him. Ava and I will talk to him. Surely, there's been some sort of mistake."

"And then us four will live forever and watch Omar wither away?" Tim said.

"What? No, no, I'll use my stake in the company to purchase Omar's pill. It will all work out."

Tim stood up abruptly with an all-consuming fire in his eyes. It was like all the emotion he had held back during his life was now released. "I don't want your fucking pity. Telling me you'll take care of it for me, like I'm a fucking child. You think you're so good, but you're blind. You don't see."

"Tim—"

"No," he said. He spun around, rubbing his forehead, not knowing what to do next. "Just...just don't tell Ava."

"But—"

"Promise me," he said, turning and staring into my eyes.

"Yes, okay, I promise. But just stay for a minute. Talk—"

But he turned his back to me and walked out. I thought myself old and wise, but Tim was right about me. I was blind. I've spent years thinking about what I could have said to him. I want to go back to that room, drop to my knees, and beg his forgiveness. But all the money in the world couldn't buy me a second chance.

It was astounding what people accomplished once we had harnessed the energy of the stars. An army of farming drones and machines were designed to do the manual labor of feeding the world. People were given an even greater fixed income and were free to do whatever they wanted. A renaissance in art, literature, and film swept the world. There were countless other discoveries, inventions, and projects in the early days, but my personal favorite was the terraforming of Mars. We were able to designate a star's power to heat the planet. This, combined with the release of certain gases, created an atmosphere similar to Earth's. Within another fifty years, a drone planting program succeeded in filling Mars with forests, rivers, and wildlife. Hundreds of millions of people migrated.

Warren was hailed as the greatest man to ever live. His power was absolute, and an entity called the Republican Guard was created with the sole intention of protecting him from accident or assassination.

Everyone was cared for, and only Warren had the vision to see this reality come true.

Humanity thrived on Earth and Mars for another thirty years before the third invention of 'the big four' was devised. The first two of the big four technologies were, of course, Boundless and the Essens. The third was the advent of quantum communication. Through the power of quantum physics and quantum entanglement, scientists were able to create devices that were linked to each other across space and time. They could communicate instantaneously from any distance. When combined with how much energy we had and the advances in three-dimensional printing, trade and exchange boomed to new heights.

Still, we were confined to our solar system, and measures would have to be put in place or overpopulation would become an issue. But it wasn't necessary. The fourth of the big four was created not long after, and in my mind, it was the most impressive. We simply called them "the gateways." They were a massive undertaking, requiring millions of people and trillions of credits to construct, but the effort and expenditure was well worth it. The first gate was created a hundred million miles from earth, about halfway to Mars, depending on the time of year. The gate required twenty fully devoted Essen stars to power it, but it was capable of ripping the fabric of space-time, allowing us to travel hundreds of trillions of miles in the blink of an eye.

"My god," Omar said, looking out the viewing window. "It's enormous."

He and I sat next to each other on the viewing ship floating thirty miles away from the gate.

"It's truly something, isn't it?" I said. "Did you ever think we would see something like this?"

Omar bit his lip. "I guess, intellectually, that I knew we might see something like this one day. But it never really sank in. You know what I mean?"

I nodded, smiling at Omar. At 272, he was looking quite the same, except for the eyes, which were often tired and oddly colored. His face was also more lined than a normal thirty-year-old's. I suppose mine was as well, at that point.

"How's everything at school going?"

"Great," he said. "We just opened our five thousandth school. This one is in the Galápagos."

"I read about that. Congratulations."

"Thank you."

At that moment, the gate began to power up. A hundred white lights flashed around its circumference before shooting out energy into the center and connecting.

"This is it," I said.

The beams of energy at the center formed a ball that grew brighter and brighter before erupting in a flash of light. Omar and I covered our eyes. When the light dimmed, we looked up to see a blanket of light within the interior of the gate's circumference. We were too speechless to say anything.

A tiny dot approached the gate. I knew the ship was enormous, but it looked like an insect next to the gate. It inched closer and closer, and then, suddenly, it was gone. I waited a moment, then picked up my readout, waiting to hear the results.

A minute later, a voice echoed through the device.

"Control, this is *Voyager I*, confirming that the jump has been successfully made. I repeat, we are here, and it is a beautiful sight."

I leaned over and showed the screen to Omar. It was a feed of the ship's view. Below, a green and blue planet glowed against the darkness of space, and it wasn't Earth.

"My god," Omar said with a laugh. "Incredible."

Humanity expanded. We terraformed new worlds and even found a couple that were already habitable. The world went wild with the discovery of alien life. For the first time, we knew that we weren't alone in the universe.

Our reach was limitless, our imagination unending. A universal feeling of optimism permeated everything. At least, that's what I assumed. I see now that people will always be people. Some want everything, despite the impossibility of having two opposing things at the same time. The fear and desire that drove our species to survive on the plains of Africa still lingers in our blood, driving us to senseless greed.

I wish I understood then, like I do now: more than anything, people want to be loved, often by people who do not feel the same. And unrequited love is something that no amount of abundance or ingenious technology can fix. The affection becomes infected, forging even the best person into a conductor of jealousy. And love, that most wondrous of emotions, quickly ebbs into something darker.

CHAPTER THIRTY-SIX

Saiph was sitting slumped over at the breakfast table covering his eyes. Ayanda, Roe, Nico, and Vincent all wore similar expressions of distress that were only exacerbated by Russ's unaltered enthusiasm.

"Wooooo-whee!" he said, slathering an unhealthy amount of butter over his toast. "Hell of a night last night. Nothing like a good cave party to ease the stress of being trapped in said cave."

The others chuckled and moaned ambiguously. Saiph's head was pounding, his mouth was parched, and he felt like his heart was beating out his chest. "I'm never drinking again."

"And you shouldn't!" Milla said, bouncing Landon on her knee. "Look at the state of you. And at a time like this."

"Look at the state of you!" Landon echoed.

"Have you been working on any new dance moves, Landon?" Saiph asked.

He nodded and smiled.

"When am I going to get to see them?"

"Soon," Landon said with a devious smile.

Saiph got as much breakfast into his stomach as he could and then thanked the gods that he didn't have to train with Silvestre today. He returned to the small area on the ground where he slept and retrieved the new Book of Light that Treyges had given him a few days earlier. It still had *The Big Bang to Boundless* on it, but the screen wasn't cracked and it contained loads of other information. He could even take notes and pictures with it. He reverently put it in its case and patted it like it was a newborn baby.

Saiph had an appointment with Sarah to talk about the Khumbuza delegation that would be arriving soon. They had both agreed that they wouldn't talk about what they'd found last week at the building of the Old Gods to anyone. They both wanted to keep it to themselves for the time being, and the risk of being overheard in such a crowded space was too great, or so Sarah thought.

Saiph found her in the conference-room pod. She sat alone at the enormous table surrounded by tablets and papers, a serious look of concentration on her face. Saiph stood in the doorway and waited for her to finish whatever it was she was doing that required such effort. After a few minutes, she leaned back in her chair but kept her eyes on her computer.

"Take a seat," she said, "we should get started."

Saiph sat across from her before a small space on the table that wasn't occupied by books and notes and pulled out his tablet. It seemed silly that he cherished it so much when Sarah had so many of them haphazardly lying around.

"What do you know about Khumbuza?" Sarah said.

"Um, not much. I know that they are the second most powerful House and that Aoko is the matriarch of the family."

"Yeah, of course," Sarah said, "but what else?"

Saiph shook his head. "That's it."

Sarah stopped and looked up at him. "That's it? What have you been doing this last week?" She looked at him more closely. "Are you hungover?"

Saiph looked down at his feet. "I've been trying. There's just so much to do and learn."

"Well your whiskey education is going to have to take a back seat to this, understand? Do you have any idea what will happen if Aoko decides not to join us? This cavern will become our crypt."

Saiph shifted uncomfortably in his seat. "I understand."

"Do you?" Sarah snapped.

"I understand," Saiph said more sharply.

Sarah sighed and stood up. She walked to the corner of the pod and poured a black liquid into her cup. It steamed and smelled delicious.

"Would you mind if we stopped verbally punching each other now?" Saiph said. "I want to try some of whatever it is you're drinking, but I'm too frightened of you at the moment."

Sarah shook her head, but a smile cracked through her tired eyes. "You're easy to pity and hard to stay mad at, Saiph Calthari. I can't believe you've never had coffee before. Get over here."

Saiph popped out of his chair and walked briskly to the corner of the pod while Sarah poured another cup of the black liquid. He took it in both hands and lifted it to his nose, breathing deeply. The aroma was intoxicating. He brought it to his lips and sipped. His smile instantly disappeared.

"This is disgusting!" he said.

Sarah laughed so hard that she had to put her cup down.

"How can something smell this good and taste so terrible! It shouldn't be possible." He took another sip to make sure he wasn't crazy but grimaced more than he had the first time.

When Sarah was able to calm herself, she asked, "Are you ever going to get some new clothes? Yours look filthy."

Saiph looked at himself, frowning. "What's wrong with my clothes? This is what I've always worn, or at least something like it."

"I'm fine with you wearing what you're comfortable in, but a shirt and pants with holes in them and dirt stains that seem to be permanent won't always be suitable. You might have to dress up for something one day."

"Bah, what for?"

Sarah smiled. "I guess we'll cross the bridge when we come to it.

You're lucky Jon wants you to wear your normal attire so that Aoko can see you for who you really are."

"Oh, and I'd be someone else if I wore something different?"

Sarah rolled her eyes. "Come on, let's get started."

They returned to the table and got organized. Sarah set up pictures and graphs for Saiph to see. He took pictures of her pictures so that he could study them later. The Khumbuza delegation could arrive at any time, but they wouldn't know for sure until a few hours before they got there.

"All right," Sarah said, "let's get you caught up. Before we talk about the rest of the delegation, let's talk about Aoko and House Khumbuza. It's important to understand that these two can't really be separated. Aoko Khumbuza is the founder and head of the family. Really, each of the Houses are just powerful families that have grown in size over the centuries. Only Aoko and her son Anwar are ageless, though."

Saiph listened to her while he wrote notes on his tablet with a special pen. Sarah took a sip of her coffee and let him catch up.

"Aoko purchased her immortality at the end of the twenty-first century in exchange for her military aid against Asia in the Wars of Unification. Her fortune came from the buying and selling of water during Africa's drought. She was able to expand her control over half of the continent and make vast economic and industrial gains by tapping into Africa's abundance of natural resources."

Sarah sat forward and presented a map to Saiph, showing the African continent on Earth. A small area of red was outlined in middle of the continent, and every few seconds, it would expand, reflecting Aoko's growing nation.

"To this day, Khumbuza still specializes in the buying and selling of resources. They were the first to capture and mine mineral rich asteroids, and they now have a near monopoly on the industry. They are one of the few political entities that still consistently travel the whole of the Sphere. Not even the Oligarchy worlds travel as much, even though their tech is much more advanced."

Sarah stopped and sat back, tapping her finger against her lips and staring at the ceiling. "More importantly than how Aoko acquired her wealth, though, is who she is and where she came from. The Congolese are a proud people, and a rejection of Western values in the generation before Aoko led to a resurgence in their indigenous religions. They believe in many nature spirits, but their religion is heavily influenced by ancestor worship. This is partly what makes Aoko so powerful, since her people see her as a walking, talking ancestor."

Saiph finished his writing. "Do not all the heads of Houses have as much power as Aoko?"

"Yes and no. Xiong House reigns from China on Earth, which has a strong cultural past of familial piety. Rather than a head of house, they have the First Family, which shares control. They have five members who are ageless—more than any other House."

Saiph whistled appreciatively.

"Aoko is different from the other leaders, though. She's worshipped and obeyed without question. The other founders like Evgeni Kozlov and Jeremiah Jackson are firmly in control, but they aren't worshipped. Close family members argue with them, and once, one of Kozlov's grandsons tried to wrest control from him. This would never happen to Aoko.

"Over the centuries, this worship has made her arrogant. She's used to getting her way. But at the same time, she still cares about what her ancestors think. She enjoys nature, which is why Jon thinks she might take a liking to you and the people of Jangali, especially the Fulgurians."

The lecture went on, and Sarah spoke further about how he should speak to Aoko and her people. She put a special emphasis on not lying to her. Aoko hated when she thought people were attempting to manipulate her, and she could usually tell.

"Be blunt," Sarah advised, "and if you can't do that, your usual sarcasm should suffice."

Sarah went over Khumbuza's customs of greetings and rituals, explaining that a few of them were used when striking a deal, which would hopefully happen at the upcoming talk. She showed him the various actions and words that were considered rude and offensive as well.

Saiph was glad he was writing it down, because his headache was making it hard to remember everything. Just when he thought he couldn't write anymore, Sarah told him that it was enough for one day. Saiph wrote a couple more notes and then dropped his pen like it was on fire and shook the pain out of his hand.

"You really need to learn how to type," Sarah said.

"I thought you said everything else needed be put aside so I can learn about Khumbuza? You think me a god, Sarah? I'm just a man! Emphasis on man, opposite of boy."

"The opposite of boy is girl," she said.

"Whatever."

The delegation arrived two days later on a drizzly fallweek morning. Saiph waited next to a specially set up command pod at the entrance of the cave with Jon and Sarah as the Khumbuza shuttle landed. The craft looked different from the ones Saiph was used to. It was larger and had an excess of weapons and other equipment mounted on its wings, cockpit, and fuselage.

"Remember," Sarah whispered to him, "Jon and I will be doing most of the talking, but if you're asked any questions, just do the best you can."

Saiph nodded as the shuttle touched down and the ramp lowered. Four soldiers exited first. Their weapons weren't drawn, but they looked around suspiciously before taking their places just beyond the shuttle entrance. They were followed by a small party of colorfully dressed individuals. Saiph recognized Aoko immediately. She was a dark-skinned woman of average height with a squat build, though she looked at least ten years older than Jon. She had large brown eyes and wore her hair up and wrapped in colorful yellow-and-orange dhuku. She strolled toward their party as if she'd been to this very Jangali cave a thousand times. Three others walked behind her. One was a girl of only twelve or thirteen with burning light-orange eyes. The two men were Aoko's advisors: Musimbwa and Amadou.

"*Bonjour*, Jon," Aoko said in an accent not unlike Amira's.

Jon bowed in greeting. "Hello, Aoko. Thank you for coming. It's nice to see you again."

"As you should be," she said. "You've put yourself...what do you Americans say, in between a rock and a hard place?" She turned and stared at Saiph. "Those eyes...they are *incroyable*. Maybe you are not as bad off as I first thought. This is good."

Without a word, Aoko pushed past their group and into the mountain forest, her subordinates following closely behind. Saiph looked sideways at Jon, who just shrugged and followed Aoko.

Everyone walked quietly as Aoko meandered around the vegetation, stopping every now and then to pick a flower or examine an insect. It was nearly half an hour before she selected a small clearing.

"We will speak here."

Jon sat down on a large stump, and the rest of the party awkwardly found seats wherever they could. Saiph was left with a mossy rock that was particularly jagged. As he sat, he stared at the young girl with flaming light-orange eyes. She was small for her age, but she didn't look nervous at all. In fact, she actually looked bored.

"So, Jon," Aoko said, "explain to me why we should join the losing side?"

"Do you really think I've made such a blunder?"

She shrugged and adjusted her dhuku. "All great men and women fall at some point. From what I've heard, you've had some rough decades recently."

"We all have," Jon said.

"Worse than most, I mean."

Jon stuck his hand out to catch droplets of rain falling from the leaves. "This is a battle I cannot afford to lose, and I won't. I have more options than your analysis suggests. But I would like to work with you, Aoko. I like Jangali, and I like its people. There is something innocent and pure about this place. You are one of the few that would give this planet the respect it deserves."

"You speak as if this planet would be mine."

"That's what I'm offering," Jon asked.

Saiph had already been told the conditions of their offer and therefore wasn't as surprised as the Khumbuza contingency. Still, he found the bargain uneasy. You couldn't trade a planet. Nobody *owned* it. But what did he know?

Aoko narrowed her eyes. "What are your conditions?" she said.

"You would gain control of the strategic locations and have the rights to build twelve other port cities across Jangali as a whole. The dynamic animals you harvest for energy are to be treated kindly while they provide energy and then released back into the wild after a year. No more than eighteen percent of the wildlife can be harvested at one time. The people already living here are to remain autonomous and receive fifteen percent of all total revenue."

Musimbwa leaned forward and whispered in her ear. Aoko listened and then nodded. "These terms are very favorable. Too favorable. What do you get out of this?"

Jon casually gestured to Saiph. Aoko turned her attention to him and fixed him with an oppressive stare. "And how do you feel about this, young man? Do you appreciate being bartered so?"

"I try to take it as a compliment," Saiph said. "Me in exchange for the entirety of the planet must mean you people hold me in high esteem."

Aoko smiled slightly.

"Saiph will be able to do whatever he wishes," Jon said, "but he is not to be forced into anything he doesn't want to do. And he is absolutely not to be harvested for his energy."

"Pah! You think I would harvest the boy?" Aoko said.

Jon raised his eyebrows. "Yes."

"Hah! Yes, I probably would. But fine, I will not harvest his power." Aoko sat back and crossed her legs, resting her elbows on her knees. "I still do not understand your terms," she said after a minute. "You have never been generous to the great Houses. You know we would accept a shared but majority control of the energy here. I will need to know why you are offering such terms."

Sarah scoffed. "Good luck with that. I don't even know why he's doing it." Jon considered Aoko's concern, and Saiph took the opportunity to try some of Silvestre's listening techniques. He closed his eyes and cyphered through the noises. After a moment, he was able to pick out heartbeats.

"I can't tell you exactly what I'm doing, but I'll explain the offer as best I can. First is that I do not have the time to stay on Jangali and set up a working government and economic system. The second reason has to do with the first, in that I have other very pressing issues that need my personal involvement. I can assure you that they have nothing to do with House Khumbuza. If anything, they will help your House. Lastly, I actually have more credits and energy than all of the other great Houses, the Askan Empire, and Tau Ceti combined. I don't need Jangali for its wealth."

Aoko, Musimbwa, Amadou went wide-eyed, and even Sarah looked surprised. To Saiph, this was a minor revelation compared to the other information he'd been presented in the last few months. He took a perverse joy in watching others reel for once.

Amadou leaned in and whispered to Aoko. This time, Saiph listened.

"He must by lying. If it were true, we would know about it."

Jon glanced furtively at Saiph, and Saiph gave the slightest of nods.

"I wouldn't lie to you about this," Jon said. "I need your help, Aoko. I'm trusting that your greed will be checked by your admiration of this planet and its people. The others would destroy this place as soon as I left it."

The Khumbuzas looked nervous; even Aoko looked tense. They were still processing the revelation about Jon's wealth and deciding whether they were being deceived or had stumbled across a wonderful opportunity. Saiph thought he saw the moment that Aoko decided. Her back straightened and her face became hard. "If you betray us, you will regret it. The Khumbuza memory is long. We will not forget."

"I've told you nothing but the truth," Jon said. "This is what is best."

Aoko relaxed. "Then you have a deal."

Jon held up a hand. "There is one more thing that I require."

"Of course there is," Amadou said. Saiph looked at Sarah and saw that she was as confused as he was. They had gotten what they'd wanted.

"When the time is right, I will need to enter Elean and Aulan's stronghold. There is something there I must have. It has no value to anyone but myself, but it is the primary reason I've come to Jangali."

Aoko looked amused. "What is it?" she asked.

Jon shook his head and smiled. "I'll need any dynamics you can spare for the extraction," he said.

Apara snapped out of her daydream and looked up, excited.

Jon held up a hand. "Not you, Apara. I'm sorry, but you're too young."

She deflated.

"I'm sorry," Aoko said, "but I cannot risk any dynamics without knowing what they are getting into. However, I will provide other assistance if you require it."

"I accept," Jon said, "but I will ask you to think on it and decide when the time comes."

"Fine," Aoko said, "but I am telling you now, I will not risk them. They are too valuable. Now, may we discuss how we are going to get you out of these caves?"

Saiph returned from the meeting mentally exhausted and with a sore backside. The negotiations, plans, and strategies had taken hours to develop. Jon and Aoko had done most of the talking, but others were constantly being consulted. Analysts on both sides were crunching numbers, Tokomoto and Khumbuza's outlier were pinged to give their insight, and both sides handed over their troop and resource statistics. Saiph was pleasantly surprised to hear that Khumbuza's army was larger than Jon's.

Saiph thought the plan was well conceived, and the more he understood, the more he began to respect Tokomoto's and Jon's insights. He had learned something of being a soldier, but by watching them, Saiph was also learning the bigger picture. It was fascinating, and he didn't have any trouble focusing on their conversation like he did with other subjects. Aoko and her advisors were nearly as capable, adding devious details to Jon and Tokomoto's outline.

After the contracts were signed and each party given multiple copies, both electronic and physical, Aoko and her delegation left the mountains and returned to their ship in orbit. Jon and Aoko would combine their encampments once Jon's forces broke out of their mountain prison. Jon and Sarah left Saiph and went to debrief the others and discuss the implications of their new alliance while Saiph made his way to the dining area. His hunger was enormous, and Saiph filled his plate with food. As he hunched over his plate, shoveling eggs and porridge into his mouth, Roe, Ayanda, and Darakai came running up to him.

"What happened?" Ayanda said, sitting down across from him. Roe and Darakai looked just as eager to hear. Saiph chewed his food exaggeratedly and held up a finger.

When he finished, he said, "Can't tell. Top secret." The three of them looked at him blankly and then erupted in outrage.

"You've got to be kidding me!" Ayanda yelled.

"I'm your sister!"

"We'll hurt you," Darakai warned.

Saiph laughed. "Only joking! I really can't tell you everything, though. But safe to say that we're getting out of this damn cave."

"When?" Roe said.

"Soon."

CHAPTER THIRTY-SEVEN

S aiph was in his aura, waiting for the word to fly out and start attacking the drones that swarmed above the mountains. He stalked like a voltlion through the large group of Blackhawks he was stationed with on the outskirts of the forest. The sun was rising and had just started to pierce the forest canopy, illuminating his armor. Many of the soldiers stared at him openmouthed and wide-eyed as he went by. He sometimes forgot how terrifying he looked to other people when encased in his aura. If his own allies were afraid of him, then his enemies must be truly frightened. He smiled beneath his mask, and a bit of a cocky swagger unconsciously entered his stride. He was going to find his father and make them pay for what they'd done. He was going to—

His internal monologue of revenge was interrupted by someone coming through the brush and into their clearing. It was Hekura.

"Gone," she said.

Saiph strode up to her. "What do you mean?" he said, hearing his own distorted voice through his mask.

"Gone," Hekura said again, her hand imitating a shuttle taking off. "Fly away."

Saiph frowned and then lifted into the air. He poked his head just above the tall trees to see a sky completely empty of the thousands of drones that had filled it the day before.

Tokomoto informed him that the Republican Guard and Harain forces had abruptly withdrawn half an hour before dawn. The bulk of their forces were back at their encampments, setting up a defensive perimeter. When Harain hadn't heard from Aoko Khumbuza, they'd deduced that she'd struck an alliance with Jon and that an attack was imminent. Saiph wondered, though, if the knowledge had been leaked to the enemy once again. If one of their own was betraying them, then they needed to find out who it was as quickly as possible. They couldn't keep being thwarted at every turn.

Saiph met up with the transport ships that were heading south to rendezvous with Khumbuza forces where they'd set up camp outside a small town thirty miles from the Harain city. The Khumbuza army was massive. It was one thing hearing their numbers in a report and completely another seeing the thousands of soldiers, drones, and battle droids milling about from the sky. From that high up, the army reminded Saiph of a colony of ants scurrying about before a storm, but as he got closer and each shape became a clearly visible droid, he shuttered.

Saiph saw two Andhaka striding about when he landed, and he unconsciously sent energy to his hands. When he realized that they were painted in traditional Khumbuza yellow and orange, he let the energy dissipate, feeling foolish. Just to be safe, he focused on his pass phrase, and his aura fell away and folded up. He grimaced in pain as it did so, wondering if he'd ever get used to it.

"How did you do that?" Apara said to him excitedly, her light-orange eyes bright in the morning light. She stood with another little boy who had red eyes similar to Silvestre's. He couldn't have been more than seven years old.

Saiph smiled at the irony that he was now explaining something to someone instead of the other way around. "My aura folds up and is stored inside my body," he said. "You see these small round scars on my arms and legs? Those are a few of the points of entry and exit for the aura."

"Cool!" the young boy said. "I want that!"

"Be careful what you wish for," Saiph said, "it's not the most pleasant of feelings. And look, I have these ten holes in all of my clothes!"

Apara and the boy smiled and ran off, moving much more quickly than normal children would have been able to. The land around them was all green grass and rolling hills. There were entire fields of grip vines, shuffling around slowly and jumping at anything that moved. There was no cover, and the sun beat down on Saiph, warming his already unnaturally warm body.

"That is quite a trick," a man said from behind him. Saiph turned and recognized the man but couldn't place his name. He was of average height with a shaved head and big round eyes. His smile was easy and engaging. The man picked up on Saiph's discomfort. "I don't believe we have been formally introduced," he said. "I am Anwar Khumbuza. Aoko is my mother."

"Of course!" Saiph said. "Yes, of course. You are...very old. Not that you're old, just that you are older than you look." Saiph dipped his chin, turning slightly red. "I'm Saiph Calthari."

The man laughed pleasantly. "It is all right, I am an old man! I have to admit, it is a bit refreshing coming to a place where someone does not know my name or station. That has not happened in a very long time. You'd not believe the amount of groveling that is done in my presence."

A woman approached Anwar and handed him a bowl of orange soup. He thanked her and she bowed slightly. As she walked away, she took a long glance into Saiph's eyes.

"Ah," Anwar said, "everyone is quite curious to see the man with eyes of a lost star. A miracle, they say."

Saiph shrugged, not knowing how to respond.

"You're not allergic to peanuts, are you?"

"What's a peanut?" Saiph asked.

"You are joking, yes? Do you not have peanuts on Jangali?" Saiph shook his head, and Anwar grabbed his arm. "Come with me."

Anwar led him into a large building off to the side. They walked passed a throng of Khumbuza, who all openly stared at Saiph. Anwar dragged him along like he was a child who had misbehaved.

"Suzy!" Anwar called out, the soup in his hands spilling over the side. "Suzy! Where is that woman? Suzy!"

A large woman yelled something back at Anwar in a language Saiph didn't understand, but from her tone, it was clear that she was not pleased to have Anwar calling for her. They argued for a moment, and then Anwar said, "Suzy, this is Saiph Calthari."

The woman tore her angry gaze from Anwar and turned to Saiph. Her expression changed from anger to surprise as she stared into his eyes. "Suzy," Anwar said, "Saiph Calthari has never had peanuts before."

Suzy's expression of surprise switched back to anger. "This cannot be! Surely you've had peanut soup?" Saiph shook his head. "Tell me you at least have had fufu?" Saiph shook his head again. "Sit!" Suzy ordered.

A few minutes later, Saiph was sitting at a table with an array of traditional Congolese cuisine in front of him. There was fufu, a sticky doughlike dish made of flour; ndakala, a dried fish drenched in a sweet sauce called moambe; a bowl full of rice and beans; and a cup of palm wine. And a crowd of people surrounded him, waiting for him to try each one. Whenever he took a mouthful of something, the crowd went silent. When his face lit up in delight from the new sensations assaulting his taste buds, everyone cheered loudly and pressed another plate in front of him.

At least an hour had passed when Saiph casually mentioned to Anwar that none of the others with him from Altai or Fulguria had ever tasted anything like this before. Anwar translated it into their native language, and the crowd broke out in alarm. They acted like the real war had just begun as General Suzy bellowed out orders. They brought her sacks of food and ingredients. Soon the room was full of a pleasant aroma.

That evening, they had a feast, and the two groups mingled under the influence of palm wine and full bellies. Saiph saw the Blackhawks talking with the Khumbuza ground troops and the Fulgurians questioning Suzy about her cooking. Russ was playing with a group of Khumbuza and Fulgurian children, who laughed as they tried to tackle him.

"Good job, Saiph," Sarah said, as she approached him. "A feast was an excellent idea. A perfect way for new allies to get to know each other and build trust."

"It wasn't my idea," Saiph said. "I didn't do anything."

"Don't be so modest, Saiph. We all heard how you walked into the kitchen and made friends with everyone."

Saiph sighed. "I was practically dragged into that kitchen. I—and I mean this quite literally—didn't even say a word. I just ate some food and smiled."

"Well, Jon is quite pleased. So am I. There hasn't always been a friendly tone between us and the Khumbuzas."

"Really?" Saiph said. "They seem quite friendly."

At that moment Amira limped into view. Every single Khumbuza stopped what they were doing and went silent. They stared at her like they had just made fun of their most revered ancestor. Amira stopped walking and scanned the gathering as if she dared anyone to say something. The party conversation slowly picked back up, but it was a little more subdued than it had been.

Before Saiph could ask Sarah what that was about, Silvestre walked up to them. "What the hell did Amira do to deserve that?"

"It's a long story," Sarah said.

"Give us the short version, then," Silvestre demanded, her eyes burning with curiosity.

Sarah sighed. "Amira was loved by one of Aoko's favorite great-

great-great-granddaughters. She was one of the most beautiful and promising talents to come from the Khumbuza family in a few generations. For whatever reason, she loved Amira. I can't see why, personally..."

Saiph glowered at her and Sarah shrugged and grabbed a cup of palm wine. She took a sip before continuing.

"Anyways, it was definitely a step up for someone of Amira's background. They dated for a year when Amira simply disappeared on them. Broke the girl's heart. I'm told that Aoko's anger was something to behold. She would have ruined Amira if Jon hadn't taken her in and protected her."

"Scandalous!" Saiph said.

Silvestre looked death at him. "You're such a gossip."

"A gossip!" Saiph said. "I haven't told anyone of your embarrassing indigestion issues, have I?"

"What embarrassing indigestion issues! I don't have any embarrassing indigestion issues?"

"See!" Saiph said. "A gossip would make something like that up and spread it all around."

"You're such a child."

"Oh, now I'm a child..."

Sarah groaned. "Jesus, will you two shut up. You act like an old bickering couple."

Saiph and Silvestre went quiet, properly chastised. Saiph spotted Ayanda, Darakai, and Roe speaking with a few Khumbuza teenagers, but he mostly watched the Khumbuza dancers. They jumped and spun in the firelight in lovely coordination. Saiph clapped when they finished.

"I know he was one of the most important people on Earth and the son of God and all that, but why do you say 'Jesus' when you're frustrated like that?" Saiph asked. "Can you do it with any important person? Like, could I say, 'Jon Foster, will you two shut up'?"

Silvestre and Sarah looked at each other and then burst out laughing.

"What? What did I say?"

The festivities escalated as the sun sank, and Saiph decided that he had spent too much time in a cave and not enough time out in the world. He left the crowds behind and headed toward the river two miles west of town. The warm fallweek weather and the smell of freshly blooming flowers made for a pleasant stroll. It reminded him of all the walks from the volt farm to his home after a long day of work. The moons hung on the horizon, facing each other like two sisters would over tea. All these years he'd looked up at Ay and Fay and wondered how the Ata gods had made them, never knowing that they also orbited Kayra and provided Jangali with a stable rotation. Without them, there could be no life on Jangali. It seemed fitting.

Once he was far enough form town, Saiph closed his eyes and concentrated. He could hear the distant sound of rushing water, of frog croaks, of the wind swaying across fields of long grass.

He crested the hill half an hour later and saw the river below—wide, calm, and peaceful. He could see tiny voltfrogs jumping around, their red glow illuminating the banks. Saiph was surprised to see a lone swimmer breaking the water. He squinted, and his unnaturally keen vision focused on Jon. Saiph walked quietly down the hill, not wanting to intrude upon his privacy. He went down the bank for a hundred paces and put his feet in the water, letting it flow smoothly around his ankles. He pressed his feet deeper into the ground and felt the mud between his toes.

He wondered how his mother and father were doing. Before his imprisonment, he had hardly gone more than a day without seeing at least one of them. They had taken care of him for more years than they'd probably bargained for. He missed them terribly. Had Saiph made a mistake, seeking answers at the Temple of the Old Gods rather than seeking out his father? He could have raided an entire camp by himself that night instead. But no, he knew he couldn't find him alone. He had to trust that Tokomoto would eventually pick up the scent of his presence. When he did, Saiph would be close behind.

"Do you mind if I join you?" Jon said. His hair dripped water and his clothes were soaked.

"Not at all. Sorry to disturb your swim, I tried to be inconspicuous."

Jon sat down. "You may need to put some sunglasses on to do that. I could see your eyes from a mile away."

"Right," Saiph said, putting his hand over his eyes to see the glow against them. "Still not used to that."

"I can imagine it taking some time," Jon said. "Have you gotten used to the stares yet?"

Saiph chuckled. "I constantly feel as if there is something on my face. No one ever looked at me in my old life."

"Your old life," Jon repeated. "I guess that's true of you if it's true of anyone. Not many go through such a change is such a short amount of time." He paused for a moment, then said, "What was your home like? Was it like this?" Jon gestured at the river as it flowed endlessly on. A fish broke the surface, but other than that, the night was still.

Saiph nodded and tossed a pebble into the river. "Sort of. It's lovely here, but Altai is a special place. There are volt trees hundreds of feet tall, wrapped in purple glowing vines or with bark etched with lines of light. Flowers bloom in orange and yellow and knip at your feet as you walk by. Voltbirds, voltbeetles, and voltfish are all over the place, giving light to even the darkest of places. I miss it very much."

"That sounds magical," Jon said. "Many would envy coming from a place like that."

"I suppose so," Saiph said, "but you have to remember that we didn't have air-conditioning or running water or electricity. People died young and often."

"Still," Jon said, "there is a certain appeal to it. You have to under-stand that, where I come from, we have forgotten the simpler joys of life. All of our lives, our entertainment and joy is...synthetic. Some-times I am sure that human cleverness has overtaken the rest of our nature, locking away our past beneath light and sound as it screams to get out."

Saiph thought about how they were from two different worlds, as alien to each other as two people could get. Yet, they were both human and they both shared a few core beliefs. Sometimes that's all it took.

"You may have a point," Saiph said, "and I can almost see where you're coming from or I wouldn't have left the feast to be out here. But you wouldn't find many Altainians who would agree with you. If you gave them enough food and wine, a warm bed and shower, a television for when they were bored, and medicine for when they were sick... Well, they would be overwhelmed with gratitude for comforts like that."

A bug crawled over Jon's leg, and he picked it up gently and placed it on the ground. "I've lived with those things for so long that maybe I do take them for granted. Even so, being here on Jangali has been very good for me—war and slavery aside." Jon took a deep breath and then looked seriously at Saiph. "Try not to forget where you came from. It's important to remember."

Saiph nodded obligingly, even though he was a bit confused. How could he forget where he'd come from? He scooped up water into his hands and splashed his face.

After a few minutes, Saiph made to get up and return to town, but Jon put a hand on his shoulder. "Wait just a minute? There's something I'd like to talk to you about." Saiph eased himself back down, curious. "You're not the only reason I'm here on Jangali. Not even the main reason, though I'm glad to have been a help to you so far, and I do desperately need your help in return. I'm here to stop something far, far worse than Elean and Aulan and the enslavement they brought."

Saiph nodded. "Is it the Essens that our swallowing up stars within the Sphere?"

"It's even worse than that," Jon said grimly, and the tense serious-ness that he usually wore came back to him.

"What is it?" Saiph asked. "What could be worse than that?"

"It is a very long and very complicated story. I haven't been able to tell anyone outside of Treyges because I haven't known who to trust, but I've watched you, Saiph. I know you're a good person and would try to do the right thing, but more importantly, I know he hasn't gotten to you yet."

"Who is he? You're scaring me a bit here."

"Trust me, you are not nearly frightened enough."

There was a rustling in the background, a wild animal or a falling branch. Saiph hardly noticed it. "Then explain to me what it is? I need answers if I'm to help."

Jon sighed but nodded. He handed him a small piece of plastic and metal. "I've written it all out for you. It is the story of my life and how it has intertwined with a man who threatens everything. That disc drive will tell you what you need—"

Saiph held up his hand and stopped Jon midsetence. It was that sound again. "Did you hear that?"

Jon shook his head. "What is it?"

Saiph closed his eyes and focused on isolating sounds as Silvestre had taught him. "There are...footsteps nearby. Many."

"Summon your aura."

Another day, another life.

Saiph made sure not to make a sound as pain and blackness enshrouded him. When he opened his eyes, the night seemed brighter. His vision could pierce his surroundings better than if it were midday. He could see soldiers in the forest. They didn't have the hawk emblem patched on their left arm like Russ's troops did.

"There are three dozen soldiers sneaking down the slope right now," Saiph said. "They'll be in firing range in less than a minute."

Jon tapped his side. "Treyges, it's Jon. Come in." He waited. "Treyges." No answer. "We need to get back to camp. Something's happening."

"What about the soldiers?"

"Take care of them and then come back to get me."

Saiph almost sent energy to his feet and back for flight, but he thought better of it. The approaching soldiers would see him and unleash everything they had on the pulsating blue energy that allowed him to fly. Instead, Saiph took off at a run, his mind processing every rock, stump, and ditch along the way. He was a black blur in the night, and though he was moving with incredible speed, he made barely a sound.

He made it more than halfway up the slope before the soldiers started calling out and pointing at him as he approached. The night lit up with flashes of gunshots and grenades. Saiph sent energy to his eyes and mind, and the world seemed to slow a bit. He could pick out individual bullets as they cut through the air, and he dodged them appropriately. When there were too many to dodge, he pulled out a sword and used it to block the bullets. Saiph was a ball of black armor, blue energy, and sparks from where the hundreds of bullets ricocheted off his weapon.

"Oh god!" one of the soldiers cried out. "It's him!"

In half a dozen heartbeats, he was among them. He fired lasers from his shoulders, but his enemies were hiding behind trees and wearing thick purple armor. Saiph kept dodging and blocking bullets. A portable laser cannon had been set up, and Saiph saw it at the last moment. He sent energy to his back and shot into the air. When he reached the top branches, he ceased his flight. He crawled and jumped quickly along the large branches and then dropped a hundred feet to the ground behind the two men with the cannon. He grabbed them and tossed them aside.

The firing recommenced, but Saiph was too fast. He went from soldier to soldier, either killing them with his sword or throwing them thirty feet into the air, leaving them to fall to broken bones or unconsciousness. He heard a distant boom coming from the camp, and he knew he had to be quick. He finished with the soldiers and returned to Jon not two minutes later.

"Any problems?" Jon asked. Saiph shook his head and Jon nodded. "I assume they weren't expecting you to be here or there would have been a lot more than regular ground troops." More distant booms filled the air.

"Are you hearing that? What's happening?" Saiph asked.

"We have to get back and help."

Saiph didn't hesitate; he picked Jon up and lifted into the air. He crested the ridge, and the higher he rose, the more his stomach sank. In the distance, a full-out battle was taking place just south of their camp. He held Jon tightly and rocketed toward it.

CHAPTER THIRTY-EIGHT

I t would have been the most beautiful and wondrous of firework shows if Saiph didn't know it was full of death. The sheer number of drones, battle droids, ships, and humanity battling each other left him panting like he'd just sprinted a mile. How could so many people want to kill one another? What had he become a part of? If he hadn't been so worried about his family, he might have stopped to consider it.

"Why are they attacking now?" he called out above the rush of air. "I thought they'd wait for the other Houses to arrive?"

Jon shook his head and spoke above the roar. "They aren't here for Jangali's energy! They're playing a different game than Khumbuza and the other Houses."

"What are they here for, then?"

"You!" Jon yelled. "And me!"

Saiph didn't know what he was talking about, but he knew that his friends and family were in danger. He increased his speed. A few moments later, he was among the first drones, weaving in and out and avoiding collisions. A comm came through; it was Tokomoto.

"Where have you been?" he yelled. "They have come with everything they have!"

"I'm here now," Saiph said. "Where are you? I have Jon."

"Thank god," Tokomoto said, "bring him to me. I am in a bunker pod just north of town."

Saiph dove down and turned left, skirting around the center of town. The main battle was taking place just to the south, toward the capital. A nav point appeared on his visor, indicating Tokomoto's position. They arrived a minute later, and Saiph set Jon down.

"What's happening?" Saiph asked for what felt like the hundredth time.

"House Harain and the Republican Guard are under control of a man named Sargas. They are his tools. Let's win the battle first, then we'll talk. They are going to be hunting for you out there. Whatever you do, do not get captured. Go. Help where you can."

That was enough for Saiph. He left the ground in a cloud of dust and reached for the sky. He flew even more quickly now that he didn't have to worry about another person, and he rose high above the ground, getting a feel for the fight. The battle lines stretched for nearly a mile, and thousands of drones filled the air above, raining down fire on the front line of battle bots and shooting each other out of the air.

"Talk to me, Toko. What do you need?"

"Russ is using a squad of Andhaka to hold off Elean and Aulan, but they are slowly dying off. One of House Harain's dynamics is wreaking havoc on our eastern flank."

Saiph took off in that direction. "Aura?"

It was a moment before Tokomoto answered. "Yellow," he said. "Take care of him, stabilize the left, and then head front and center. I'll call if you're needed elsewhere."

Saiph raced toward the left, and the distant battle came closer with every second. He saw the other dynamic in his red aura suit and yellow eyes, darting from the sky to the ground, shooting lasers and missiles as he did so. The dynamic moved faster than the rest of the battle, like an adult playing keep-away with small children. The only thing stopping him from simply wiping out the battle bots was Silvestre. She darted behind Tokomoto's bigger troops and drones, keeping the Harain dynamic away from the human snipers in the back line, who in turn fired armor-piercing rounds whenever he got too close. The drones were too busy firing their tiny lasers at incoming missiles and blowing them out of the sky to help engage.

Saiph didn't bother stopping to ask what he should do. He flew directly over the snipers in the back and heard them cheer. Silvestre was hiding behind one of the larger battle bots when she saw him. She turned and fired her missiles and lasers at the dynamic, unloading much of her arsenal to keep him distracted. As Saiph sped forward, he heard Silvestre's voice in his ear.

"I'm at fifteen percent. I'll be useless in another twenty minutes."

"Hang back for a bit, save yourself. Jump in if I really need you. Aim low."

"Roger."

Sil's lasers and missiles continued to fly low at the dynamic, forcing him up. He didn't see the black armor until it was too late. Saiph slammed into him, grabbing him around the waist and pouring energy into his flight system. He aimed downward and forced them to the ground, but Saiph had used too much power and overshot his mark. He was in the middle of the Harain battle droids, which loomed around him like towering demons in the night.

They started to turn on him, and Saiph began gathering energy into his core. He poured it into a single point, more energy than he had ever gathered before. Two Andhaka that had been hiding among the bigger bots were running away, their delicate sensors picking up the amount of energy he was collecting. The Harain dynamic was a few paces away, regaining his footing.

Saiph waited for the battle bots to turn on him as he sent more energy into his center. Right when they were about to fire, Saiph flung the energy he had built up away from him in a perfect sphere. The ground shook and then gave way, a small crater forming beneath him. The two-ton battle bots were flung back while others simply dropped, their electrical systems overloaded. The other dynamic screamed and frantically sent out energy of his own, but it wasn't enough to completely shield him, and he fell back. Saiph would later be told that it looked like a small, blue-hued bomb had gone off on the eastern flank. Every direction within a few hundred feet was clear of Harain troops.

"What the fuck!" Silvestre yelled into his ear. "That was nuts! What's your power level at after that?"

Saiph quickly glanced at his readouts. "Eighty-six percent."

"Damn," she said, "I couldn't do that even if I expended all of my power at once."

Saiph didn't have time to think about what he'd done. The battle bots outside the perimeter of his blast were turning to face him, and drones from the sky were reorienting to fire downward. The Harain and capital outliers had noticed him and were going to respond.

Saiph peered around and spotted the Harain dynamic stumbling away. He sent a surge of power to his legs and lunged into a sprint, pulling out his swords as he did so. The man heard him coming and turned around, firing lasers and missiles, unable to do anything else with his damaged aura. Saiph could have dodged, but he was short on time; the rest of the army was going to be firing on him at any moment. Instead, he sent out rapid shield bursts, one after the other, exploding the missiles and dissipating the lasers. He ran through their fire, letting his armor absorb the heat. At the same time, he started sending energy into his superconducting swords, and they began to glow, then shine.

The Harain dynamic gave a terrified screamed as Saiph ran forward, putting all his energy into his defense. It wasn't enough. He knew it wouldn't be, and Saiph could see the stark, animalistic terror in the man's one exposed eye. It nearly made Saiph stop in his tracks, but he felt himself swinging his swords anyway. A moment later, blood poured from a wound in the dynamic's side. He was dead before he hit the ground.

Saiph put away his swords and ascended high into the sky to get away from the enemy. Once he was high enough, he stopped and tried to compose himself. Had he really just cut down and killed a man who was so obviously terrified? Why hadn't Saiph knocked him out and taken him prisoner? He felt himself trembling and he closed his eyes and bit his lip. He didn't have time for this.

Hold on to your humanity. Come to terms with it later.

Saiph shook himself and forced his eyes opened. They were losing the battle. Their front line had large gaps that spilled inward and Harain troops surged through the holes. Saiph raced toward the center and pinged Tokomoto.

"The Harain dynamic is dead. What now?"

"Elean and Aulan have disengaged the center and moved back. They might be regrouping, but there's no telling. Help clear the skies."

"Will do."

Saiph plummeted to the level of the drones and started mowing them down. They were fast but fragile, so he sent hundreds of tiny pellets of energy streaking outward at them. Whenever one would fly by, he would catch it and rip it apart. Several crashed into him, whether by accident or on purpose, he couldn't tell. Each blow knocked him hard to the side, and he had to fight to regain control. He couldn't let his aura take so much damage before he fought another dynamic. Why hadn't he asked Jon or Tokomoto how many dynamics House Harain had?

Saiph heard a ping in his ear. "Saiph!" Russ said. "Three Andhaka down here. Need a little help!"

They weren't hard to find. A little way to the west, a section of the secondary line of human troops was in complete disarray. Saiph sent a slither of energy to his eyes and focused; the three Andhaka became clearer. He raced toward them, planning to slam into one like he had the Harain dynamic, but before he got there, the three Andhaka turned as if of one mind, and their drones, swarming around their hosts like flies around livestock, fired their deadly lasers at him. Saiph cut the engines and dropped the forty feet to the ground. As he fell, the Andhaka scurried across the ground like insects, converging on where he would drop.

Saiph powered his flight system back up, but all the firepower of the drones was raining down on him and his shield bursts weren't enough. One of the lasers nipped his left forearm and tore through his armor, taking a chunk of his skin with it. The light in the left hand of his aura blinked out as he was forced to cut his engines and drop into the mass of Andhaka. They were swinging their blades before he touched down, and Saiph twisted in the air to dodge as much as he could, but two of their blades were able to graze his left abdominal and right calf. He could feel the warmth of his blood, but there was no time to dwell on the seriousness of his injuries.

"Russ!" Saiph called out.

A series of thick shells and lasers rushed at the Andhaka, and they were forced to back off for a moment and dodge. They were so *fast*. Another burst of fire came, and they again had to move out of the way. One of the Andhaka broke off and dove toward Russ's company. Saiph whipped the sword from his aura and began heating it as he charged at the Andhaka that had broken away. He could hear the other two chasing after him as the drones struggled to target his moving body.

The third Andhaka turned quickly, abandoning his attack on the lesser targets, and whipped its blades at Saiph. Its drones consolidated near its core to shield its blades, but Saiph ignored them. He sent energy into his mind, and the world slowed by a fraction, allowing him to process the blades and respond. His swords cut through the air, not only blocking the Andhaka's blades but throwing them to the side. The Andhaka fell off-balance and Saiph spun, his glowing blue sword cutting the Andhaka down as he turned to face the other two.

The Andhaka behind him exploded, and he dashed for the others, firing two missiles from his shoulder and a series of lasers from his good hand. The drones shot down his missiles, and they exploded in a flash, but Saiph kept attacking and flaring shield bursts. The two Andhaka worked together, darting to his left and right to surround him. Saiph flared energy throughout his whole body and moved with a speed that even the Andhaka had trouble keeping up with. He was able to get inside the long blades of the Andhaka on the right, and he grabbed its slim torso, sending energy into his right arm, and then squeezed until the Andhaka broke in half.

Saiph turned to face the other Andhaka, expecting the blades to already be coming down, but pain flared throughout his body and he unwillingly dropped to one knee. It was that same burning pain he'd felt when they'd attacked the slave camp and freed his family, the one that made him feel as if his soul were being incinerated.

Not now!

Saiph thought he was going to die—from the pain, or the Andhaka blades, it didn't matter. After a moment, though, the pain passed and he was able to see that Russ had summoned one of his Andhaka, a painted hawk on the side. It was battling the other, their blades clanging in the air and their drones in a dogfight. Saiph rose to his feet to help, but there was no need. Russ's Andhaka dropped low to the ground, swinging its blades in an unnatural manner, and the other Andhaka buckled, then was sliced to pieces.

"Tengrii bless you, Russ Henson," Saiph said into his comm.

"Saiph!" Tokomoto yelled. "I am in need of immediate assistance!"

Saiph looked up to see a huge ball of plasma traveling through the sky. He gauged its trajectory and saw that it was arching over the battle and toward the camp—toward Tokomoto. And, Saiph realized, toward Jon.

"Why are they here, then?"

"For you! And for me!"

"They fired a plasma cannon! Isn't that a war crime during a battle?"

Saiph flew up and back into the air, trying to think of what to do. The enormous ball of plasma lit up the night sky and the battle below it, bathing every soldier, bot, and drone in light, like a third moon.

"Not concerned about the illegality!" Tokomoto yelled. "*Do something.*"

Saiph could hear the fear in Toko's voice. "What do I do?"

"Something!"

Saiph was flying higher into the sky, thinking furiously, when Silvestre's voice spoke into his ear.

"Gather energy into your hands," she said quickly, "then release the energy while at the same time continuing to feed it. It should create a continuous beam. Fire it at the plasma mass."

Saiph didn't question her. He fed energy into his right hand until it began to hurt. He aimed at the ball of plasma arcing across the sky and then released. An enormous blast erupted from his hand, throwing him back and almost making him lose his concentration and the flow of energy. It began to sputter out, but Saiph refocused and the beam grew in size. The large mass from the plasma cannon seemed to simply eat Saiph's beam like it was nothing. It didn't even slow. Saiph closed his eyes and inundated his hand with energy. The beam grew. Saiph gritted his teeth to keep from screaming out.

Night became day as the ball of energy exploded high above the battlefield. Drones were thrown from the sky, and every soldier and droid was knocked flat to the ground. Both sides were stunned into inaction, trying to recover from the enormous explosion. Jon's voice came over the group comm, speaking to every soldier on their side.

"All troops retreat north in small groups. Use this opportunity to disengage. I repeat, retreat north."

Saiph dropped to the ground, feeling physically exhausted for the first time since his eyes had turned blue. He looked at his power readout and saw that he was at fifty-eight percent. The beam of energy had taken a significant percentage away. He also noted that heating his swords also drained more energy than he had assumed.

Jon pinged him. "Saiph, Silvestre, Russ, Sarah, meet us at the river five miles north, near the eastward bend."

Saiph sat in the corner of the mobile command pod and waited for the others to arrive. His suit and body were repairing themselves quickly, but Ellie still fussed over him as she ran some device over his calf, forearm, and abdomen. Tokomoto wheeled up to him as Ellie worked.

"That plasma blast. I would have run, but..." He gestured at his wheelchair.

"Toko," Saiph said, "was that a joke? I'm so proud."

Tokomoto wheeled closer. "Thank you. I am not used to being the one in danger. Now I know how the others must feel when I come save them all the time."

"You're on fire!" Saiph said, laughing.

Russ came loudly through the door, a cold beer in his hand. Where he had gotten it, Saiph hadn't a clue. He plopped down on a chair, his hair damp with perspiration and his white cowboy hat smeared with dirt.

"Heard Saiph had to save your scrawny ass, Toko. Typical, you getting into a mess like that. If I wasn't so busy single-handedly holding the line, I would've done it myself."

Ellie stopped working for a moment and looked sideways at Russ. "You're telling us that you would have shot a beam of energy out of your hand, into the air, and exploded a ball of plasma eighty feet in diameter?"

Everyone turned and looked at Russ, eyebrows raised. He put his feet up on the table and took a sip of his beer.

"Yep."

Saiph, Tokomoto, and Ellie erupted in protest. They argued good-naturedly for a few minutes, and Saiph was laughing despite how much it hurt. He distantly realized that he might currently be depressed and wholly freaked out if he didn't have this to distract him.

After Ellie finished sewing Saiph up, she took Russ's chin in her hands and inspected a deep cut above his left eye. Russ protested, then let Ellie clean and seal it. Silvestre and Sarah entered a few minutes later, both looking haggard. To Saiph's surprise, Sarah was dressed in a combat suit and had a rifle on her back. He hadn't known she was a soldier too. The light atmosphere of before evaporated when they entered.

"What the hell!" Sarah said, her anger directed at Jon. He hadn't said a word since Saiph had gotten there. "What the hell!" Sarah yelled again. "What is going on here, Jon? We could have all been vaporized by that blast, yet they aimed it at two people in a bunker a mile away from the army. This is insane. A plasma cannon hasn't been used in a battle in over a hundred years. What else has changed? Is *Stargone* even safe in orbit?"

Saiph hadn't thought of any of that, and his good humor left him. Everyone was silent, the atmosphere as tense as a voltlion about to pounce.

Jon turned from a screen and looked at them. "There is something I must find inside Elean and Aulan's stronghold. I won't order you to come with me, but I could use your help."

Sarah stomped her foot. "Don't ignore me!"

"Saiph, do you have the drive I gave you?" Jon asked. Saiph nodded. "Will you please take it out?"

Saiph reached for his pocket. "You sure about this?"

"Yes," Jon said, rubbing his forehead. "If I can't trust the people in this room, then it's all for naught anyway.

Saiph reached for the small cube of metal and handed it to Jon, who inserted it into a computer nearby. He hit a few commands and typed in access codes. Everyone waited patiently, except for Sarah, whose face was a contortion of anger and fear.

"I need to consult with Aoko. Read the file. If you decide my cause is worthy, meet me outside in an hour. For any who refuse, I'll arrange to get you safely off Jangali. No hard feelings."

Jon left without another word. There was a long moment of silence as the six looked between each other and then at the computer. Saiph was first to act. He stood up and walked over to the table. He grabbed one of the tablets, resumed his seat, and began to read. Tokomoto wheeled over next. The others followed one by one.

For the next hour, they read, absorbed in Jon's letters. Though he was the first to start, Saiph was the last to finish. The others waited for him in silence. When Saiph set the tablet down, he looked around at his friends, but they could only shake their heads in disbelief, words not enough to convey their fear and worry. Past the terror, though, Saiph could tell a deep river of respect and sadness for Jon Foster flowed through them. The story humanized the man who had created the

Essens, the son-in-law to Warren Winters, but at the same time, it made Jon more unknowable, like a god watching from high above, his perspective too different to fully understand. His will, genius, patience, and compassion would have moved Saiph to tears if he hadn't been overwhelmed into a paralytic state of awe.

A beeping alarm shocked them back to reality. Their hour was up. Together, they stood and left the pod.

CHAPTER THIRTY-NINE

F orgive me, but I have to keep moving. We are leaving the safety of the caves soon. I will help you understand as best I can...

Entry 9:

Ava and I moved to Mars a decade before the first gateway was activated. Warren wanted us to govern the planet, but we chose a quiet life of exploration and new experiences instead. We climbed new mountains, swam in new rivers, and marveled at the slightly different curvature of the land. Mars was an exciting place to be and was forming its own culture of intellectualism, exploration, and traditional living. Since we were born in the so-called traditional times, we thought it appropriate.

I love Mars, and in many ways, I consider it my home. It was something totally new and beautiful, and it was as clean as Jangali is now—for a while, at least. I was endlessly entertained by the people, landscape, new technologies, movies, books, and games. I couldn't get enough. I swear, my psyche was built to live for eternity, but this wasn't true of everyone who'd taken Boundless. Many of the early billionaires who'd bought it had become...different. Some committed suicide, others attempted to erase their memories, and more than a few lost their minds. The human brain just hadn't evolved to live for centuries.

Doctors developed various remedies and rehab programs, but they always emphasized that early preventative care was key and how important it was to keep a looking for the signs. This stuck with me, and so I was worried when I returned from a fishing trip to find Ava balled up on the porch crying.

"Ava? Honey, what's wrong?" I said, stepping onto the balcony that overlooked the lake.

She shook her head and waved a hand at me. "It's nothing."

"But you're bawling..."

"I don't want to talk about it," she snapped.

"Okay," I said. "Okay."

I returned inside to shower and change, but I couldn't stop thinking about her. Just a week before, I had heard her sobbing in the office when she thought I wasn't home. She had gone through bouts of depression before, but it was never as emotionally overwhelming as this. In the past, it was more akin to a crippling apathy. That night, during dinner, I brought it up again.

"Hey," I said softly, "is everything all right? I'm worried about you."

She twirled her pasta around her fork and didn't make eye contact with me. She twisted it around and around for a long time.

"Don't you ever think of everyone else?" Her tone was accusatory and bitter. It stung. The change in her had happened so gradually that I don't think I took as much notice as I should have. You have to understand that this shift happened over decades, not a few pages.

"What?" I said. "Of course I do."

"Most people live and die in eighty years while we've lived a life of luxury for three centuries. And what about those who my father murdered during the wars? I did the math, you know. If those people had lived, their descendants would number over a billion right now."

I put my fork down and leaned back in my chair, taking a sip of water to buy time. "I...I didn't know that."

"That's my point, Jon. You know nearly everything, but not that. Tim says that the selfishness of confining Boundless to the rich is essentially a crime against humanity. To keep that sort of happiness to yourself while letting others feel the pain of loss as they watch their loved ones grow old and die—it's sick."

"Tim?" I asked. "Our Tim? He's been around here?"

"That's what you take out of what I just said? That Tim was here? What about watching loved ones grow old and die?"

"No," I said. "No, that's a good point. But that's not my decision. What do you think I should do about it?"

"You're telling me you've never even considered it before?"

I frowned, deeply hurt by her accusations. "Of course I have. I've seen people I care about come and go. Do you think that I didn't care for the friends we've lost along the way? I care. I promise I do."

Ava softened and rubbed her hands against her temples. The already soft sunlight of Mars was fading to dusk, darkening the room.

"I know you do," she said. "I just can't get these thoughts out of my head. I don't understand how you can enjoy *everything, all* the time. It bothers me."

The next few weeks were some of the most tense of our marriage. I thought that if she could just focus on the good in life, she would snap out of it. I shipped in rare foods she'd never tried, gave her tickets to an old-fashioned opera performance, ordered documentary films that celebrated the diversity of human culture. But these were all the wrong remedies. They only reminded her of our privilege. Desperate, I brought up adoption again for the first time since World War Three, but it only reminded her of our own inability to have children, and she drifted further away from me.

Months later, Ava was in the midst of what some researchers called a "fading." Still, I thought it might be just another episode of depression. Overwhelmed by worry, I tried something else: I called Warren.

"She'll snap out of it," he said, barely looking up from his papers.

I stared at the projection of him sitting in his office back on Earth and couldn't believe what I was hearing.

"Warren, I don't think this is one of her normal bouts. I think it's much more serious. Will you please come and see her? It's been a while."

He finally looked up from his papers. "Do you see all this?" he asked, gesturing at his desk. "I can't just jump up and leave the planet because Ava is having a bout of the sniffles. She'll snap out of it. She always does. Trust me."

I hung up the phone, furious. I was reaching my wit's end and felt like I was running out of time. But when Ava got home from a weekend away, she seemed better. We spent the next couple days going through old photographs and videos and reminiscing about old times. She was close with me again, hugging me and kissing me. That night, we made love for the first time in a while. I was happy, but mostly, I was relieved. My Ava was back. Life would be normal again.

It wasn't meant to last. Two days later, the AI Massacre of Alexandria sent her spiraling back down the black hole of her fading.

———

The summer air was thick with moisture and the heat was oppressive. Even the wildlife seemed to be taking shelter, resting beneath the trees or in the water, unaware of anything outside their body temperature. I envied them.

"An entire planet!" Ava yelled at the news anchor on the screen.

"No..." I said, unable to get anything else out.

Warren had unequivocally and harshly outlawed any kind of artificial intelligence throughout the years, more afraid of its consequences than intrigued by its benefits. Turns out, he had it right all along. Alexandria was a relatively new planet, and it was far enough away from Earth that the scientists and tech developers were able to get away with researching AI without Warren finding out. Much to their detriment, they succeeded.

The first and only artificial intelligence was created in a research basement far beneath the southernmost pole of the rocky planet. The researchers marveled at their achievement and spoke to the computer like it was a child, teaching it about the universe. The computer wanted to know more, but they refused, limiting it to information they saw fit. One researcher pitied the computer, though, and he gave it access to the planet's self-contained internet database. Immediately, the computer went to work. They had underestimated its computational power and learning speed. It hacked the military network and manipulated factories to build war machines. Within a few days, drones were flying about, killing citizens. The computer's objective wasn't the people; it only wanted access to the quantum network used to communicate between planets.

Luckily, one of the researchers had the foresight to predict the consequences of their research. Without hesitation, she sent a message to Earth and then self-destructed the station that was connected to the off-planet network. In my opinion, she saved absolutely everything and everyone. When Warren got the news a minute later, he also didn't hesitate. The Republican Guard came through the gate and pulverized Alexandria, burning it down to its foundations.

Teams were sent in to make sure the computer was dead, and ships stayed on standby for thirty years, ready to nuke it again if necessary. I was absolutely relieved when I heard that the threat had been contained, but Ava didn't see it that way.

"How many?" she asked after I got off the phone with Warren.

"How many what?"

She looked at me like I had completely lost my mind. "How many *people*, Jon. How many people did my father just murder with a thousand nuclear warheads?"

"I don't know. I think Alexandria had a population of about eighty million people? But, Ava, we could have lost everything."

She got up from the couch and paced back and forth. She didn't even notice when she spilled her juice all over the rug.

"Being a little bit dramatic, don't you think?" she said.

"I'm being dramatic?"

She spread her arms wide. "Eighty million people! Eighty! It's impossible to even comprehend that sort of slaughter. That's almost as much death as the five years of World War III but in mere moments."

I shook my head, trying to soak in that kind of tragedy, but it was impossible. Not only was it beyond my imagination, but I also didn't want to think about it. Maybe that made me a coward. Ava, on the other hand, sat for hours watching videos of the planet from before it was destroyed. Pictures scrolled endlessly of children and families that had moved to Alexandria to start a new life.

If I was a coward for not watching, then Ava was a masochist *for* watching. It was a choice between two sins. The progress I thought Ava had made over the last week evaporated like the oceans of Alexandria.

A few days later, I walked into our bedroom at ten o'clock in the morning and found Ava still asleep. I smiled, thinking the rest would be good for her—she hadn't slept properly in over a month. I gently closed the door to make sure she wouldn't be disturbed and went to catch up on some work. Later that morning, I went to check on her again, and she was still in the same position. I softly shook her shoulder.

Nothing.

I'll never know if the doctors could have done something if I'd checked in on her earlier. They say that she'd taken the pills hours before, in the middle of the night.

I'm honestly not sure what gets to me more, that she did it while I was sleeping next to her, not bothering to say goodbye, or that I rolled out of bed and brushed my teeth, not knowing that my wife of 350 years was lying dead beside me. She is never far from my thoughts, and I'm a living testament that time cannot heal all wounds.

I remember the first time I saw her, an angel dressed in black on the darkest of days. I was so hypnotized. Whenever I picture her face, I see the image of her shock and excitement as we swallowed eternity on a small porch in northern California. I remember the white of her wedding dress contrasting brilliantly with her almond-colored skin and the tears of joy in her eyes as she said "I do." The infinite number of tiny moments and experiences that made up my impression of *her*.

I can't write of it anymore. I just can't...

My Ava—my love—was gone.

I haven't told you this story to elicit your pity or sympathy. Maybe one day you'll learn more about who Ava really was. No, I've told you this story because Ava's death is what changed everything.

I called Warren from a private video conference room in the hospital to give him the news. It was early morning on the east coast of the United States, and I had to wait fifteen minutes before I was able to get through to him.

"Yes, what is it?" he said.

"Warren..." I began, but I couldn't get the words out. Saying it aloud would make it real, and that was unthinkable.

Warren looked up from whatever it was he was doing, suddenly serious. "Jon?" he said. "What's wrong?"

It took me a long moment and a long breath before I was finally able to spit it out. "Ava died," I said, voice cracking. "She committed suicide late last night."

Warren stared at me, confused. "No," he said. "No, that can't be right. Just let me speak to her. Tell her I will come to visit. I'll leave right now!"

"She's gone, Warren."

"Shut up!" His voice was manic. "Shut up! I know I've been absent, but a joke like this is beyond cruel. Put her on the phone. Right now."

I grabbed the sides of the monitor as if it were Warren's head and rattled it to shake some sense into him, to make him understand. "She faded! She's dead! Do you hear me? Dead! Gone! Forever!"

Warren blinked a few times, and then the anger left him and he deflated into the saddest creature I had ever seen. The anguish that rippled across his face and the groan that left his lungs showed me more than anything how much she meant to him. I knew that he loved her, but he hadn't been around in a while—too busy ruling his republic. For a long time, I just sat there, watching Warren as he stared vacantly at his desk.

Finally, he looked up. And in the most casual manner, he said, "Goodbye, Jon."

The screen flicked off.

"No!" I yelled. I tried calling him back but got nothing. I tried his secretary, but there was no answer. I called the head of the Republican Guard, but still, I was ignored. "Damn it!" I yelled, slamming my fists against the table.

At least he said goodbye.

I held Ava's funeral a week later in northern California, at the same graveyard as my parents'. It was a drizzly and dreary day. Ava would have preferred a small ceremony, and that is what she got.

I got to the site early and was staring down at the hole that would be her grave. I wasn't sure how long I had been there, but I was soaked through.

"Jon."

I knew that voice.

"Omar," I said in a whisper.

He took two giant steps forward, wrapped me in a hug, and began to weep. He sobbed uncontrollably. I patted him on the back until he calmed down.

"Sorry," he said. "I just can't stop thinking about her. Nearly four hundred years of memories is a lot to sort through."

I shook my head, not knowing what to say.

More people trickled in over the next hour. I was sitting on a bench when I saw Lin enter through the gates. Seeing her only brought more memories of Ava, but there was no escaping that. Ava was connected to everything in my life. She was my life.

Lin walked forward and sat down next to me. She said nothing but grabbed my hand and rested her head on my shoulder. I think we both knew that, if we spoke, we would lose it completely.

Ushers rolled in the casket, which was beautiful and intricate. Everyone gathered around, and I said a few words before the other attendees paid their respects. Lin, Omar, and I waited in the back, wanting to be the last ones to see her before she was put in the ground. I looked around for Warren, still hoping that he'd show up, but was only disappointed.

"Where's Tim?" Omar said. "He should be here with us."

We heard the screeching sound of a car suddenly braking near the entrance. A moment later, Tim came walking hurriedly down the path. Everyone stared at him and moved out of his way as he strode straight to the casket.

He stopped in front of it and looked down at Ava, his face like stone, unreadable and hard. Omar broke the frozen scene by taking a step forward, but Lin held him back. Tim continued to stare down at Ava before he reached into his pocket and pulled a chain of silver and placed it on her chest. He cocked his head to the side, and his mouth opened as if he were going to speak but had forgotten what to say. His mouth snapped shut, and he swallowed. His eyes finally left Ava and met mine. We stared at each other for a long moment before he turned on his heels and left.

Omar moved to go after him, and this time he didn't let Lin's grasp stop him. He pulled away and ran. Lin looked at me, and I nodded. She walked up to the casket, and when she saw Ava, she finally broke, letting a sob escape her. She fell onto the casket, letting it support her weight. She was whispering a song I couldn't hear.

When Lin stepped aside, I waited for Omar, but he never came back. I stepped forward. The silver chain that Tim had left sat on Ava's heart. The chain was connected to some sort of locket with complex writing on it.

I looked down at Ava one last time and said my goodbyes without making peace. It was the last time Lin, Omar, Tim, Ava, and I were ever in the same place.

My Reluctant Familiars.

Gone.

CHAPTER FORTY

E ntry 10:

Warren disappeared. There was no body, no trace that he had even stepped outside his office. He was simply...gone. The Republican Guard went into a frenzy and deployed their considerable power and resources trying to find him. But I knew it was pointless. If Warren didn't want to be found, then he wouldn't be. I waited with the rest of humanity for him to return. Thinking maybe he was just too shocked, too broken to think straight when he got the news. After two years, though, I concluded that he wasn't coming back, or that he was dead somewhere, his body turned to ash or launched to the stars.

The World Republic needed a new leader, and to my astonishment, the Republican Guard asked me if I'd like the position. I refused. I didn't feel capable of taking care of myself, let alone an entire empire. Instead, some bureaucrat from Washington stepped in as an interim president. For a few years, everything went smoothly, but without Warren, the republic began to deteriorate.

I didn't really realize how important Warren was until he was gone. Toward the end, Ava had genuinely thought he was a murderer, and maybe some of that feeling wore off on me. Looking back, I think he was a pretty benevolent leader, not unlike the idealized philosopher kings of old. Sure, he had his problems, and I didn't agree with a lot of his decisions, but he had created a peaceful and prosperous society among the stars. That had to count for something.

Without Warren, people became ambitious. The rich and powerful began to accumulate an increasing amount of wealth, hiding their credits in illegal accounts to avoid taxes. They bought elections, changed laws, and slowly, they altered the Essens energy flow from the public to themselves. The vast majority of people didn't even notice at first. How could they? Those who did accuse others of corruption were subject to smear campaigns, and the media spewed so much disinformation that nobody knew what was true or false anymore. I was probably the only one who could have possibly put a stop to it, but I didn't. I was too absorbed in my own self-loathing and depression to do anything. Once again, my cowardice shone through.

The Sphere of Humanity's economy collapsed and the thirty worlds that we had colonized fell into disarray. For the first time since the Wars of Unification, humanity fought each other. It was far more destructive and brutal than any war in human history, like we had forgotten what we were capable of during the long peace and were remembering it all at once. Billions of people died. These years in my life are like some unimaginable nightmare, and sometimes, when it's late at night and I'm nearly half asleep, I'm able to convince myself that it didn't happen—that I'd wake up, sigh in relief, and turn to find Ava sleeping next to me, her breathing soft and her hair a mess. But of course, I always wake up alone.

I was nearly killed several times during the war, and when I saw the things other boundless were doing, I seriously considered killing myself. How could they? What hope was there if they had turned away from goodness? It helped me understand why Ava had done what she had. I'm only glad that she wasn't there to see her friends go down that path and to witness the violence and death.

The Sphere War set humanity back at least two hundred years. Society had become so complex under Warren that it was like glass; one point of pressure, and the whole thing crumbled.

So much was lost during those seventy-six years of war. History was rewritten, records destroyed, and the best technologies were lost in battle, sabotage, and terrorism. The very foundations of our society fractured, then broke completely. Ideas of freedom, empathy, and progress became optional.

I spent most of the war leading the Mars-Earth alliance against the planets in the northern hemisphere of the Sphere. The space battles between dreadnoughts were horrific. Tens of thousands could die within seconds. That went on for thirty years. Over the next twenty, we fought a ground war on Bao Haiyang and finally took control of it. Fifty years of violence, and we had only managed to take a single planet.

The other battles across the Sphere were similar, and I realized that the fighting wasn't going to end until there weren't enough people left to keep going. I left the front and returned to Mars. For the next twenty-five years, I went back to researching my Essens. I designed a virus. I sent it out among the stars. My plan was to infect the Essens and make the entire power influx flow to me, on Mars. Without the energy to power the ships or gateways, the fighting would have to stop. I only half succeeded.

You see, the Essens are like living creatures; when they replicate, mistakes are made and different strains of Essens are created. My virus only worked for a certain type. It killed trillions of them, while some went completely rogue, sending energy all across the Sphere. Some went completely unaffected and continued to send power to the others. But it was enough to power down the gateways and to give me a signifi-cant percentage of the power influx. Energy became a rarity again, and machines weren't able to do all of our manual labor. The fighting was over, but so was the life of automation and ease. A new era began.

What emerged from the ashes of Warren's republic was a system of government that was almost medieval. Families that had bought Boundless in the past had acquired so much wealth and influence that they were able to subjugate their regions. Like the warlords of Africa in the twenty-first century or the Japanese daimyo in the Middle Ages, they brutally ruled their domains and took the wealth for themselves while leaving the people in poverty. We commonly call them the great Houses now. You can see why I dislike them...

These Houses formed along side new governments. People were scared, weary, and looking for some security. Strong men and women took advantage of this situation, and monarchies, empires, and oligarchies were created. Some stuck to the old ways and formed republics and democracies, but they were few and far between.

I hope you can forgive me for creating this situation, Saiph. It's my fault that everything is the way it is. I'm the one who created the Essens virus. I'm the reason Jangali is in danger, why you're a dynamic, why your village was destroyed and your family enslaved. I am so very and truly sorry. I never meant for it to happen this way. I meant for things to get better.

There is so much more to this story than you know. I've covered so much history in only a few pages, and you could read a thousand books about what happened and still have questions. You will know more, I promise. But it's time I tell you why I have written you these letters and why I need your help. Now, I will tell you the story of Timothy Sargas Elliot and how he destroyed everything I knew and loved.

———

Timothy Sargas Elliot. My shy, brilliant, and timid friend. We were never as close as he and Ava were, but we still had a friendship that was unlike any other in history. We shared the pain and joy of growing up together. We traveled the world. We changed it. But I guess that wasn't enough. I think, eventually, I could have forgiven him for betraying me, but I cannot forgive what he did to Ava. Not ever.

When the war ended, I returned to Mars, feeling lost and shocked, but also relieved that it was all finally over. I went back to the house where Ava and I had lived and started going through old pictures and mementos. During the process, I found something I had never seen before: Ava's journal. I sat and stared at it for a long time, not knowing what to do. I hadn't even known she had kept a journal. In the end, I read it. How could I not?

It brought back many emotions, and it was like reliving her death all over again. But what you need to know is that I found some very strange stories about her relationship with Tim. She had seen him much more often than I'd realized in the decade before her death. The weekends she had gone away for work or getaways, she'd actually spent with him. They had always been very close. Ava was, without a doubt, Tim's closest friend in the group. They had met in a hospital when both of their mothers were dying of cancer. If that doesn't bring two people together, I'm not sure what does.

Still, she hadn't told me she'd been seeing him so much. Why not bring me along? I hadn't met up with Tim in years and would have loved to catch up with him. I kept reading the journal, and things became clearer and more disconcerting.

There were countless entries from the last few years of Ava writing things like: *Tim says that it's wrong to deny people eternal youth and that my father is denying people the ultimate human happiness.* Along with: *Tim told me how Jon doesn't think about how other people grow old and die because he's too busy enjoying his infinitely privileged lifestyle.*

There were many similar entries. I saw phrases that Tim had told her that Ava had echoed to me during our arguments. Tim had put these ideas into her head. He was driving her toward the cliff while she was in the passenger seat, distracted by his conversation.

What's the point of living? Ava wrote. *Tim's right. How can I drink wine and play board games while children watch their parents die from old age? Jon's blissful happiness only makes it worse. Like he knows and is rubbing it in my face.*

I was heartbroken by her words, but I was also furious. How could

Tim do that to Ava? He *knew* that she was fading, and he fostered it—helped it grow. He killed her. I know that now.

I nearly dashed out of my house and tried to find him then and there. To confront him, to scream and rage, to tell him that he pushed our Ava, off the cliff. Instead, I started to research Tim's life. He was always private and busy with work and research, but now that I thought about it, I didn't really know what he'd been doing with his years.

I found that two things consumed his time: a new type of research and a dogged quest to acquire Boundless. He had been furious that Warren had sold Boundless to Lin, but not him. At the time, I thought he only felt hurt about being excluded—after all, he could have lived for hundreds, if not thousands, of years without the full version of Boundless. But now I think that it was something else.

I think he was scared that if people found out who he truly was, then he would never be allowed to take another anti-aging pill again. He wanted the true thing; to settle the question of his mortality once and for all. I found e-mail requests to Warren from Tim under a false name, requesting to purchase Boundless for ten times the normal price. There was even a raid on Warren's office, which I now suspect Tim was behind. Timothy, it seemed, was determined to live forever. I'm still not sure why Warren so fervently refused Tim the pill, but it wasn't unheard of. There were other billionaires that Warren had refused to sell it to. I suppose Warren knew something about Tim that the rest of us didn't.

Tim never did succeed in acquiring it. It must have been maddening, all those years of failure, the clock ticking in the back of his mind. He was desperate. What could he do? He couldn't get it while Warren was in control, and Warren didn't seem to be going anywhere. He couldn't fight him; no one could defeat the forces at Warren's disposal. So what could he do? How could he break Warren without ever getting near him? Sargas found his answer in Ava.

He manipulated her—and his job was only made easier by her predisposition to depression. She may have even been fading before he started talking to her. Either way, he succeeded in pushing her to the breaking point. It makes me sick to think about how he could do that to his best friend. I take some solace in the fact that he didn't get Boundless out of it.

Tim was in position, and when Warren left in the aftermath of his daughter's suicide, Tim raided the offices, laboratories, and vaults all over Earth while the Republican Guard searched for Warren. He never found a single pill of Boundless. All he found were a few more of the limited pills that would give him some extra years. His anger must have been something to behold. Sometimes, I wish he would have found it. Life might've been easier if he had.

Which brings me to his other pursuit: his research. It was incredibly difficult to find details on this aspect of his life. I probably couldn't have done it if it weren't for so much chaos during and after the war. Even so, the depths of Sargas's paranoia was breathtaking. He never stayed in one place for more than six months, and he always used a different name and different researchers for each location. He spent fortunes bribing officials into looking the other way. It took me years to get to the bottom of it, but I'm glad I persisted.

After he wasn't able to acquire Boundless, he abandoned the quest and focused solely on his research. He'd always been brilliant beyond measure, but even so, I was still impressed to discover what he had accomplished. Sargas was a born neurologist, and he knew more about the human brain than anyone else alive. In fact, the human brain was considered one of the final frontiers of research. We had ripped open the fabric of space-time, harnessed the energy of the stars, stopped the aging process, but so much was still unknown about the human mind. But what others could only dream of, Tim made a reality. About twenty years ago, he created true immortality, not just a stoppage of the aging process.

You see, Sargas is able to upload and download his consciousness into a machine and into other human bodies. With the quantum network, he is able to send his consciousness from body to body across the entirety of human colonization, something that is invaluable now that the gateways are gone. His consciousness is constantly streamed to machines in case something happens to him. I don't think he can inhabit more than one body at a time, but that's a small hindrance. He never sleeps—he never stops working toward his goals. For twenty years, I watched him, searching for a way to stop someone who couldn't be imprisoned or killed by conventional methods. I found out that he was planning something big. It scared me more than you could know, but I needed more information. So I quietly made preparations, consolidated my accounts, expanded my arsenal, and accumulated energy.

When I felt ready, I invited him to Mars and hinted that I had a secret store of Boundless. I think this is what convinced him to come in the end. Though he didn't really need it anymore, he probably would have still liked to keep his original body young. He arrived a few days later, unarmed and completely unaware that I knew all of his deepest secrets. Why would he suspect me now? He had hidden his psychosis from me for centuries.

I had my men grab him and knock him unconscious. They were rougher with him than I'd intended, but I had little sympathy for him. I chained him to a chair and was going to question him until he told me everything I needed to know to shut him down. I couldn't stop him from uploading his consciousness into another body, but I could find out how many bodies he had, where he kept the backup storages for his mind, and more about this massive plan that he'd been working so hard on.

I gave him a drug that lowers a person's inhibitions and encourages them to speak the truth. It didn't work out entirely like I had planned. Tim was aware enough to regain control and he was able to throw his original body off the cliff to escape my questions. I wonder if he mourns the loss of that body, the one he was born into.

Nevertheless, I had failed. That was my best chance to find out what was happening. At the same time, however, I had also found out about a Class G dynamic on a faraway world that had only recently been rediscovered. It was populated by people, too. How they came to be there, I don't know.

The Class G dynamic gave me a chance to redeem myself. Before Tim flung himself from the cliff, I was able to confirm my suspicions that he already had a body on the planet of Jangali. It was the one place I knew he had another body, and I had a good idea of where he was keeping it.

Not only could I try to redeem my mistake by recapturing Tim and extracting more information from him, but I could find you, Saiph. I'll be the first to admit that I need your help in fighting this war. Sargas has worked hard, and I'm not certain how much control he already has. I will also need your help to enter the capital palace, defeat Tim's dynamics, Elean and Aulan, and find the body Tim is keeping here on Jangali. But most importantly, I need you to help me find the one man capable of stopping this. The one man who might be able to bring back the days of peace and plenty. I need you to help me find Warren Winters.

My grand plan was to secretly find you and talk to you, to explain what was happening and to convince you that this was a worthy cause. I had no idea that you would be living out in the countryside, unaware of the larger universe. I had no idea that Elean and Aulan were enslaving people and that you were one of their captives. In the end, freeing you is what led you to trust me much sooner than would have otherwise been possible. Still, I felt uneasy asking you to do all this without you knowing the whole story. So I began writing you these letters. I wanted to say so much more, to fully explain everything that has led me here, but time has been extraordinarily short. Sargas has tried to kill me multiple times already. Treyges and I were the only ones that know his secret. Now you do too.

If something happens to me, I hope you will tell the right people. But be careful; I have not discovered who is betraying us. Sargas must have already gotten to someone in our group, but I have no idea who it could be. Whoever you tell will be in grave danger. He will not stop until his secret is his alone.

Lastly, I want to apologize for involving you in this. I feel that your suffering has been all my fault. I created the Essens virus that led these armies to seek energy on Jangali, resulting in the destruction of your village and the enslavement of your family, and turning you into a dynamic. You are a good man, and you did not deserve this in your life. I am truly sorry. If you decide to not help, know that I hold no resentment toward you and wish you a long and happy life.

———————

Your friend,

Jon

CHAPTER FORTY-ONE

The smell of blood and gasoline was mixed with an electricity in the air as Saiph, Tokomoto, Russ, Silvestre, Sarah, and Ellie approached the river. Saiph looked up at Ay and Fay, and they somehow seemed less beautiful than they had just a few hours before, though he knew that it was he who had changed.

Jon was waiting for them, his black hair and thin face as serene as they ever were. Treyges stood beside him, looking out of place in his black suit among the river reeds. Sarah increased the speed of her walk when she saw Jon.

"I thought you might not come," Jon said.

Sarah's stride turned into a jog, then a run. She threw her arms around him. "I never knew," she said. "I'm so sorry."

"You couldn't have. I should have told you sooner, but it has been very confusing. Even now, it's more tangled up than you realize."

Saiph stood a few paces back, waiting with the others. He examined Jon and tried to picture him at Saiph's age, studying in school and getting to know Ava Winters. Saiph knew the letters were true, but it was impossible to picture Jon differently from the way he stood before him now, centuries old, confident and unwavering.

"Thank you all for coming," Jon said. "It means more than you know. And I hope I've convinced you that this is the right thing to do."

"We are with you, Jon. As we always have been," Tokomoto said. "What is the plan?"

Saiph nodded, ready to act.

"Sargas's body is somewhere in Elean and Aulan's stronghold. It's some sort of palace. We can use these," Jon said, handing out several bulky handheld devices. "They are able to scan brain waves from up to two hundred feet away. We're looking for a readout that looks like this." Jon held up one of the devices that showed a line that was waving slightly. "In comparison, a normally functioning brain wave looks like this." He tapped a few buttons and showed it to them again. This time, the line was a true wave, undulating up and down, over and over.

"Wait," Silvestre said, "how does that work? Why is his brain like a flat line instead of like a normal person's?"

"He has multiple bodies," Jon said, "and when he is not actively using one of them, it looks like he is in a coma. Don't ask me how or why; I don't know exactly."

"There are hundreds if not thousands of people in the palace," Ellie said. "It will be like finding a needle in a haystack."

"I know," Jon said, "but this is our best chance. Besides, he wouldn't leave his body just anywhere. There are only a couple places it could be. We need to go in when Sargas is not expecting it. If he occupies the body and has normal brain waves, we'll never find him. He could look like anyone.

Russ took off his cowboy hat and waved a glowing fly from his face. "Wouldn't Sargas come back to Jangali once he hears that this palace is being infiltrated?"

"That's why we're going to sneak in while Aoko attacks the pulse cannons. She doesn't know why we're trying to infiltrate the castle, but for obvious reasons, she wants those weapons destroyed. I don't think Sargas will return for that. He must have other bodies that are important and which he has to spend time in. It will distract the Harain and Republican Guard forces, though."

"It's still not going to be easy getting into the—god, I can't believe I'm saying this—to get into the *palace stronghold*," Sarah said. "It's probably the most guarded building on the planet."

Jon sighed and looked uncomfortable. "I...have a way in."

Russ laughed. "Why ya looking so grim! That's good, ain't it?"

"You're not going to like it..." Jon said. The others waited, their expressions urging him to go on. "Chet has found us a way inside."

"Chet?" Silvestre said. "You didn't say this was a suicide mission!"

The others echoed similar sentiments, commenting on Chet's slippery grip on reality and his cavalier demeanor. Saiph didn't say anything; he only nodded his approval. Jon looked at Saiph. "What do you think, Saiph?"

Eyes turned to him.

"Well, Chet seemed to infiltrate the slave camp I was in easily enough. I had no idea he wasn't a slave. Maybe his eccentricities are what makes him so good at appearing like other people? If he says he has a way in, then I'm apt to believe him."

The others thought on this for a moment, then nodded hesitantly. All except for Silvestre.

"So we are really doing this?" she asked. "We are risking not only our lives but the lives of millions on Chet's word?"

Jon shrugged and nodded.

Silvestre scratched her jaw. "Fine. How are we even getting in?"

Treyges chuckled so softly that Saiph barely heard it. Jon glanced at him wryly, and Treyges cleared his throat and stood once more at attention.

"About that..." Jon said. "Well, you're not going to like that either."

Two hours later, Saiph was sitting in the bed of a covered truck between a pig and a large beetle barrel. The heat of the barrel made the smell of the pig pungent. Saiph had started sweating profusely, but it looked like he was enduring better than the others. Russ and four of his soldiers were sitting in crates nearby, and Saiph could only imagine the extra heat in that confined space. They hadn't made a sound since the trip started, and Saiph was tempted to check and make sure they weren't passed out, but Chet had been very clear that they shouldn't move.

Jon and Sarah sat next to each other between casks of wine and Saiph wondered if, during their many years, they had ever done anything like this before. Silvestre wasn't far from Saiph, a fat pig beside her. She had taken off her jacket, and her white tank top clung to her glistening skin. Several times Saiph found himself staring at her and forcibly made himself look away before she caught him. He'd never hear the end of it if she did. He went over the plan in his mind to help him keep his eyes off Sil.

Jon had explained that the body was most likely in one of two places: the vault next to the armory or in the throne room itself. They were to split into two groups to check the locations. Sarah, Russ, and Saiph were to investigate the throne room while Jon, Silvestre, Chet, and the soldiers searched the armory vault. If they were discovered, Tokomoto was standing by to launch an attack and help extract them. Ellie was back at camp, using one of the scanners to probe sleeping soldiers, just to make sure Sargas wasn't hiding among them. It was unlikely, but Treyges insisted that they should check anyway.

The truck rumbled on, and Saiph thought that they would be arriving within half an hour. He could hear Chet chatting with the guard in the passenger seat as he drove the truck, speaking in a manner that Saiph hardly recognized. The strange and nearly unintelligible accent that Chet had used when Saiph first met him was gone. Instead, he easily enunciated every syllable in an aristocratic manner, speaking frighteningly similar to the soldier he was in conversation with.

"I said to him, sir, I absolutely did not tell Private Simmons that beetle droppings were natural aphrodisiacs. That must have been Caraway. And the whole thing started again!"

The soldier laughed uproariously. "You did not! Chet, that is the damnedest story I've ever heard!"

The soldier continued to laugh, and Saiph decided that Chet was the most ridiculous person he had ever met. It took a particular force of will to keep himself from laughing too. He looked up to find Silvestre watching him, a small smile on her lips. Saiph gestured behind him toward the front seat and shook his head, mouth agape and eyes wide. Silvestre's smile widened, and she covered her mouth to hold in a laugh.

The truck came to a stop, and Chet spoke to someone outside. After a moment, the truck began moving again. Saiph closed his eyes and thought about his mother, father, Roe, and Landon. He would not fail. The truck's engine cut off, and Saiph heard two doors open and then slam shut. Footsteps echoed at the back of the truck.

"My Lord, Marshall, do my eyes deceive me or is that the queen of Nueva Belleza?" Chet said.

"By god, out here? Where?"

Saiph heard a muffled thud and then the sound of someone falling to the ground. The truck doors opened to a grinning Chet, who whispered excitedly, "We've arrived, my lords!"

Saiph stood and stretched his legs before climbing out of the truck. Silvestre unhinged the crates that Russ and his soldiers were in. Saiph thought that, as tall as Russ was, it would take him a few minutes to get his legs back, but the man jumped silently out of the box and quickly moved out of the truck. His soldiers followed him and then dragged the unconscious guard behind a few crates. Saiph looked around and saw that they were behind a large brick building with broken windows and only a few lights on inside.

"This way," Chet whispered. They left the truck and entered a small shack next to the main building. It was crowded, but they all fit.

"Remember," Jon said, "if you see Elean or Aulan, you run. If you find the body, ping me. If you get into trouble, ping Tokomoto." He looked at each of them for a moment. "Be very careful, please. Good luck."

Russ led the way, his steps light and silent and he moved with surprising grace for a man his size. Saiph tried to mimic his steps and motions, but even with his inhuman coordination, he still wasn't as muted. At least he was subtler than Sarah, whose footsteps seemed to echo like thunder down the street.

"Try and keep it down," Russ whispered. "First guards are coming up."

They turned the corner of the warehouse, and Saiph could finally see the palace. His mouth involuntarily dropped, and he nearly stopped in the middle of the street. It was enormous, like a building sculpted from a mountain. Its gray twin spires towered over the surrounding buildings and were adorned with statues of different people. The entire structure was made of indomitable-looking stone. He realized almost immediately that it was old.

They cleared the street and ducked behind a parked truck. Russ peered around, studying their route.

"What kind of psychopath builds a medieval castle using slave labor?" Sarah said.

"Not builds," Saiph said, looking at Sarah meaningfully. "Renovates."

Sarah looked at him curiously, then her eyes dawned with understanding. "Are you sure?"

"Yes."

"That can't be a coincidence," she said.

Russ turned from his spot and grabbed both of them by the shoulders. "Look, as interesting as your palace architecture lesson is, we're going to need to stay quiet for a while. Can you do that for me? Six-inch voices, yes? Excellent."

Sarah rolled her eyes. She was about to respond, but Russ held a finger to his lips. He looked questioningly at Saiph, who then closed his eyes and focused on the sound. He held up four fingers and then pointed. Russ put his hands out and raised his eyebrows in question. Saiph made another hand gesture to signal that the guards were a hundred feet away.

They waited behind the car, and two minutes later, the soldiers walked by and continued on their patrol. Russ took a moment to place an explosive underneath the car and then carried on. They continued in this manner, darting from building to building and having Saiph listen for patrols. His mind raced the entire time, trying to make sense of the fact that this palace was built by the Old Gods. Had Warren Winters been in this very building? What was its purpose before Elean and Aulan had moved in?

When they reached the palace lawns, they hid behind trees and bushes. Saiph was surprised how easy it was, but Chet had told them that most of the security lay outside the palace itself. Besides, the twins had never had to worry about infiltration before, and why would they? Jangali's native people weren't a threat to them in the slightest. That superior attitude had made the guards sloppy.

They reached one of the palace entrances and huddled in the bushes. Russ looked at his watch. "Two minutes," he said. "The throne room is in the center of the palace. We'll need to take the servants corridor if we want to reach it without being questioned. Just walk as if you belong there, and if we see a servant, act natural. I'll handle it."

"Handle it?" Sarah sneered. "You mean, kill the poor servant."

Russ frowned. "I'm not killing some poor soul forced to wipe Elean's and Aulan's bottoms."

"Sure, we'll see..." Sarah said.

"Hey," Russ said, "I'm not—" An explosion went off in the distance. "Oh shit," Russ said. He reached into his pocket and pulled out a handheld. He pushed a few buttons, and another explosion went off. The door they were next to burst opened a moment later.

"What the hell was that!" a man inside the palace said.

"Let's get a little closer," a woman beside him suggested. "Maybe we'll see something!"

She took off running, and the young man reluctantly followed. Russ popped out of the bushes and grabbed the door just before it swung shut. He opened it slightly and peeked inside.

"Nothing," he said. "Let's go."

They entered a small kitchen that was lit by a single light hanging overhead. It was dirty, and Saiph was uncomfortable at the sight of insects around so much food, but no one else was around, so he counted himself lucky.

"This way," Russ said. "It's not far."

They entered a hall that took them through a series of dorm rooms. Bunkbeds were stacked to the roof, and Saiph could hear snoring and the rustling of sleeping people. They must have entered through the slave quarters. Saiph briefly had a flash of terror at seeing the slave uniform, but he vigorously suppressed it.

At the end of the hall was an exit, but Russ turned left instead, opening a door to a steep and dark stairwell that led into the ground. Saiph peered down as a dank smell wafted up. Russ grabbed a lantern that hung on the wall and fiddled with it.

"How do I turn this damned thing on?" he whispered.

Saiph gestured for him to hand it over. He twisted a knob and pushed a button several times. The spark caught, and a small flame filled the glass container. Russ took the lantern back and began descending the stairwell. The passageway was short and narrow, and Russ had to bend down to keep his head from scraping the roof.

They had only walked thirty paces before Sarah took out her device and held it up to examine the reading.

"I thought Jon said we'd have to be close to Sargas's body and near a room that had relatively few people in it," Saiph whispered.

"I know," Sarah said. "Couldn't hurt to check, though."

"Oh yes, it could," Russ said. "Somebody sees that and all the sudden we're answering some questions that don't have any good answers."

"What, and explaining Saiph's eyes will be easier?"

Russ turned and kept walking. "Well, that there's a good point. Would have been helpful if you'd brought it up earlier."

They came to an intersection that forked in three directions. Russ closed his eyes for a moment and then pointed to the right. A few hundred yards later, they came to another intersection, and Russ turned left. Saiph tried to keep track of the turns, but he was distracted. This underground corridor looked like it had been carved straight out of the rock. He could faintly understand the purpose of the first Old Gods building he'd seen, but a palace? Why would they build such a thing? It didn't make sense. Saiph was contemplating the issue when he heard footsteps and saw a faint light coming around the corner. There was nowhere to go.

"Keep walking," Russ said. "Act normal."

The light got brighter, and Saiph made sure his face and eyes were concealed behind Russ's frame. A short woman rounded the corner at a brisk walk and came straight toward them. Saiph stepped to the side to allow enough room for the woman to pass. He kept his eyes down. As she walked by, Saiph risked a glance. The woman had brown hair and a clean, pretty face. She stared straight ahead, calm and unblinking. Without a word, she turned the corner. Saiph frowned in confusion. Had he seen her before? Was she from a town near Altai?

"See," Russ said, "no killing poor servants."

"We got lucky that she couldn't care less about us," Sarah said. "What if we run into someone who questions us?"

"That doesn't mean—"

Saiph's eyes went wide. "The woman from the forest!"

"What?" Sarah asked.

Saiph was already running back to where she had turned the corner. He reached it and looked left down a long, straight corridor. She was gone.

Russ and Sarah caught up to him. "What are you doing?" Sarah said. "We have to be quick and quiet."

Saiph frowned in confusion. "That woman...I think she was the one who helped me in the forest near the pulse cannons. She killed an Andhaka by running up and tapping it on its head."

Sarah looked at him like she often looked at Chet. "Are you feeling all right? Because we kind of need you on your A game right now."

Saiph had only seen her once before, and it was in the darkness of the forest. Maybe he was mistaken?

"Yeah," Saiph said. "Fine. Let's go."

They walked a few hundred yards, and then Russ led them up

another stairwell. He stopped at the top. "The throne room is out this stairwell and to the right. Chet has never actually been in the palace; all we've seen are floor plans. I expect we'll see someone we don't want to. Keep your head down and act like a slave. When we get close, help me deal with whatever it is we need to deal with. Yeah?"

Saiph nodded, and Russ took a breath before opening the door. He walked out with his head bowed. Saiph thought he looked ridiculous, a man of his size and physicality acting so demure, but hopefully it would buy them the few seconds they needed. Saiph glanced up and saw six guards wearing purple armor and pointed helmets.

"Republican Guards," Sarah said softly.

One of the men finally noticed them. "The lord and lady do not require anything at the moment," a guard said. Russ kept walking, his pace increasing ever so slightly. The guard turned back. "Did you not hear me? Go—"

Russ sprinted forward and slammed his fist into the man's neck. A sickening burble escaped his throat as he fell. Saiph couldn't wait the four seconds to summon his aura. He moved from behind Russ and sprinted at the three guards to the right. They were reaching for their weapons, but to Saiph's now energized mind, they moved at the speed of a passing cloud. Their faces were slowly dawning surprise as they looked at his burning blue eyes.

Saiph reached the first guard and threw an open-palmed hand into the man's chest. He flew ten feet through the air before crashing hard into the wall. Saiph dropped to a knee and kicked at the other man's leg. He heard the bone break, but he hit the man again as he spun toward the last guard. The man had his gun out and it was already half raised when Saiph grabbed the man's wrist and twisted it. The man screamed, and Saiph threw him hard against the adjacent wall, knocking him unconscious. Saiph turned and saw that Russ and Sarah had subdued the other two guards and taken their weapons.

"It won't be long before someone finds this mess," Russ said. "We're on the clock now."

The doors to the throne room were thirty feet high and intricately painted with portraits of two people who had glowing yellow eyes. Saiph marveled at the mural's beauty and at Elean's and Aulan's narcissism. How could they take something elegant due to its age and size, then paint themselves on top of it?

Surprisingly, the large doors opened easily and smoothly. They entered into a room that was even taller and grander than the entranceway. Huge stone pillars, each at least five feet in diameter, lined the hall. Stained-glass windows depicting scenes of battles were illuminated even though it was dark outside. At the front, two enormous chairs made of metal and glowing light sat empty.

"So they enslaved the people to live out their queer king and queen medieval fantasy," Sarah said. "How quaint."

"The Free Worlds sure do breed some odd folk," Russ said.

Even though they were in a hurry, the group walked slowly across the stone floor. The enormous chamber echoed with every step, giving it an ecclesiastical ambience. Saiph noticed that the twins hadn't changed everything; there were numerous intricate, rusting candelabras along the walls and paintings flecked with age.

"You got the scanner?" Russ said, his eyes darting around.

Sarah pulled it out, held it in the air, and spun slowly around, pushing buttons every few seconds.

"I don't like this," Russ whispered to Saiph.

Saiph felt it too. This was too easy, the throne room too empty. He started to focus his hearing when Sarah said, "I've got it. It's over there." She pointed to the back-right corner of the room behind the dual thrones, and something caught Saiph's eye. A woman draped in silver-and-yellow armor was falling from the ceiling and about to land directly next to Sarah.

Another day, another life.

But it was too late; he would never get there in time. Instead, he looked up. What he saw terrified him to the core.

CHAPTER FORTY-TWO

The last thought Saiph had before his aura sheathed his body was that he'd never get to see his father one last time. He would have liked to talk to him about Lola Calthari, show him how he could run now, and share all the new wonders he had experienced. But, really, all Saiph wanted to do was tell his dad that he loved him.

Above Saiph, Aulan hung on to one of the pillars, and he was surrounded by a swarm of at least a dozen Andhaka. What surprised Saiph the most was the presence of a third dynamic, one with yellow-green eyes. If Saiph was remembering his auras correctly, this third dynamic was even more powerful than Elean and Aulan.

"Stay behind me," Saiph said to Russ.

"Aye, I can do that."

Elean dropped next to Sarah and grabbed her from behind. Sarah let out a yelp of surprise, though she'd already known something was wrong when Saiph's aura burst from his body. Aulan and the Andhaka crawled down the stone pillars like cockroaches and surrounded the rest of their group.

"Take off the suit," Elean said playfully, "and no one gets hurt."

Saiph looked to Sarah, and she shook her head slightly. Elean laughed. "Got a hero here, Aulan!"

"Aw," he said, "the girl has read many fairy tales over her long life."

Saiph felt responsible for walking Russ and Sarah into this. It was supposed to be his responsibility to avoid this type of situation, but there was no chance that Saiph was taking off his aura. The third dynamic floated to the ground, flames from the surrounding torches reflecting off her green aura. Saiph was expecting her to speak, but she only stood quietly in the back.

"I," Russ announced, "am Russ Henson, Prophet of the Path of a Thousand Flames, High Druid of the Longwood Clan, and president of the amateur meteorology club of Jonesborough County. If you let the yellow-haired woman go, I promise to recommend a life sentence over execution to the judge."

Elean and Aulan stood in dumbfounded silence for a moment.

"I call him!" Elean said.

"You can't call him! I want him!"

Sarah squirmed and tried to pull away, but Elean barely noticed. The third dynamic dropped to one knee and waited patiently. She never took her eyes off Saiph. The Andhaka moved back and forth slightly, their metal feet clicking ominously against the stone. It was unnerving, and Saiph didn't know what to do.

He started to gather energy, and the Andhaka fell into battle stance immediately. Elean, Aulan, and the third dynamic's eyes all began to glow more intensely as they also started to gather energy into their auras' systems.

A door clicked open in the back of the room, and Saiph turned slightly to glance in that direction. A young man with red hair and a lanky frame strode into the room. There were fresh cuts and scars running up and down the length of his arms.

"Please," the man said quietly, "there is no need for this. Elean, Aulan, lower your energy. You too, Malin."

They did so, and the Andhaka relaxed as well. But Saiph kept his energy level high, and it buzzed excitedly through his body. He stared at the man who commanded them. He was good looking and couldn't be more than thirty-five years old, but his eyes spoke volumes. Oddly, he reminded Saiph of Jon. The man ambled forward and became more illuminated in the torchlight.

"Ah," he said, "you must be Saiph Calthari. It is a pleasure to meet you."

"Who are you?" Saiph said, trying to keep his eyes on everyone at once.

"Did Jon not tell you? Of course he didn't. That's Jon's way, always keeping secrets to himself. Only he knows best, after all." The room was quiet except for the man's footsteps. "I do not want to kill you, Sarah. You've done nothing to me. But I will if I have to, understand? Saiph here could destroy this whole building and then some if he got the time to gather the appropriate amount of energy. I can't have that."

"Who are you?" Sarah said, though Saiph suspected she knew perfectly well who he was.

"My name is Julien Thompson, and I've been charged as the guardian of Jangali."

"Yes, I see you've been doing a fine job too," Sarah said.

The man chuckled as an explosion erupted outside. Everyone turned at the noise. "It seems we are short on time," the man said. "I hate to be rude, having just met you all, but, Saiph, I am going to need you to take off your aura now."

"No."

"I understand your hesitance, truly. Why would you trust a total stranger? I wish I had more time to convince you that I mean you no harm, Saiph. As I said to Sarah, you've done nothing to me. But unfortunately, we are in a hurry, so I'll have to resort to threats and violence. I hate that, but my station requires it of me. Surely you can understand that I have responsibilities and that my people are depending on me? So now it comes down to a simple choice: either we kill Sarah and Russell and then subdue you by force, or you let your aura fall away and we peacefully take you into custody. Either they live or they die. I leave it up to you."

Saiph was suddenly considering taking his suit off. He couldn't fight his way out of this. Even if he tried, Sarah and Russ would certainly be killed in the crossfire. Saiph suspected that the man was Sargas, but how could he know for sure? What if he did mean to only capture them? Then Jon, Tokomoto, and Silvestre would have a chance to break them out.

"I'm sorry," the man said, "but like I said, time is short. Please decide within ten seconds, or I will have to decide for you."

Saiph started to focus on his pass phrase when the doors to the throne room slid open. Much to his surprise, Jon walked into the room, accompanied by Chet.

No, Saiph thought. *Not them too.*

The red-haired man clapped his hands together and laughed in delight. "Jon! How nice of you to join us. I was beginning to think you wouldn't come. And Chet! Welcome."

Jon strode confidently up to the first Andhaka in the circle and stopped, glancing at the red-haired man. "Hello, Timothy."

Sargas smiled and shook his head slightly, but Saiph could tell that the name irked him.

Chet suddenly let out a visceral moan of pain and started hitting himself in the face. Jon faced Chet and grabbed his arms, forcing them to Chet's side.

"Chet. Chet, what's wrong?"

Chet was mumbling and Saiph had to attune his hearing to make out what he was saying.

"Tim and Sargas. Tim is Sargas. Tim and Sargas."

An expression of understanding dawned on Jon's face, and he closed his eyes to gather himself. "Chet," Jon said, "it's not your fault. I should have told you more."

Jon whispered something else to Chet that Saiph couldn't make out, and the man calmed enough so that Jon could release his arms and face Sargas. "You took advantage of Chet's condition? How long have you been talking to him?"

Sargas's gaze was unfocused as he thought. "Did you know that I've actually known Chet for longer than you have? We met before he was even a billionaire."

"A blood feud of untold sorrow has begun!" Chet yelled through tears. "That forest didn't ever hurt no one!"

Sargas came back to the moment and laughed. "Look at what you've become, Chet. It's pathetic."

Gods, Chet, what have you done? Saiph knew he hadn't meant any harm, but harm was what had come from his actions. If he'd just kept everything a secret, maybe the Fulgurian forest would still be there.

Jon looked at Sarah. "Are you all right?" She nodded. "I know what you want, Tim. But you can't have it."

Another explosion boomed outside, rocking the walls. Dust fell from the ceiling.

"I doubt you know what I want, but either way, you're not in a position to tell me what I can and cannot have."

"I know you want his body," Jon said, gesturing at Saiph. "But if you erase his memory, he'll die."

Saiph frowned, but it was not nearly as dramatic as Sargas's expression. "What did you do to him?" Sargas asked.

"If his brain waves reach a coma-like state, a tiny bomb in his brain will go off. You can't have him."

Sargas closed his eyes, clenching and unclenching his fists in anger. He let out a piercing yell and slammed his fist on the throne next to him. The handsomeness of his young face contorted into a horrible weave of rage, petulance, and madness. It frightened Saiph more than anything else he had seen so far. Sargas was breathing heavily, his eyes still closed.

"No matter. It would have been nice being the most powerful dynamic in the Sphere, but that *was* secondary." Sargas was calm again, his quick change in moods disturbing. "Do you have any idea where we are right now?" he said, glancing around the room.

Jon was silent for stretch. Gauging. Thinking. "Only partly."

"A very small part, I'm sure." Sargas walked around to one of the glowing thrones and sat down. "This planet is full of secrets. Why don't you tell me what you know?"

Jon sighed. "There are structures on Jangali that are older and larger than what seems possible. Someone had been here before. I assume for reasons they wanted to hide."

Sargas looked taken aback. "That's it? That's all you know?"

"All I'm willing to share with you."

It was silent again, except for the titter-tattering of Andhaka legs and distant explosions. Saiph's mind raced as he tried to guess what was happening outside and what was happening in this very room. He kept the energy within him buzzing.

"I need your help, Jon," Sargas said. "It's why I'm glad you came."

Jon chuckled grimly. "What would you like help with, Tim?"

"Don't get me wrong, it will help you too. It's the question I'm sure you've been asking yourself for hundreds of years now."

"And what question is that?" Jon asked.

"What happened to Warren Winters?" Sargas's face lit up at Jon's skepticism. "Oh yes," he said, standing up and pulling out a small box, "it's right here. Warren was on this planet. He knew about it. Created it. And this is what he left."

The thin silver case that Sargas held was simple but elegant. Though it had probably sat in this castle for several centuries, it was unmarred. It even looked polished.

"I can't open it," Sargas said, "not without damaging what's inside. But you can."

Sargas made to open the box, and a robotic voice echoed from it. "Foster identification required." Sargas tried again. "Foster identification required."

"He left this for you," Sargas said.

Saiph peered at Jon, and though his face was still, his eyes gave him away. A storm of thought and emotion stirred within them. How could it not? How long had Jon wondered about his father-in-law, thinking he was dead or in hiding? Saiph wanted him to open the silver case and find out.

"This is the main reason you've come to Jangali?" Jon asked. "Why? Why do you care?"

Sargas shrugged and looked away. "There's only so much one can do in nearly seven hundred years. Curiosity is a hard thing to come by."

Jon shook his head. "You'll have to do better than that if you want me to cooperate."

Sargas's jaw clenched and his eye twitched before he said, "I don't like loose ends. I need to know what happened. Besides, that man is like an infection. If we don't completely get rid of it, it may come back stronger."

"Give it here, then," Jon said.

Sargas looked suspicious, but he walked over and then tossed the silver case to Jon before taking several steps back. "Why?"

"Because I think he's already dead and that you can't hurt him anymore."

Jon held the box gingerly for a long moment, simply staring at it. Saiph wondered about all the things that must have been racing through his mind. Eventually, he put his finger to the clasp. It unlocked.

Jon slowly opened it and pulled out a thin metal object that looked like a small coin, only it had very shallow holes poked into it. As soon as he held it in his hand, a steady, baritone voice emanated from it.

"Jon. It's Warren." There was a pause and heavy breathing in the recording. "I do not know how to say what it is I need to say, but I'll try my best. For you. For Ava. But first I must tell you—"

The recording cut off as Jon crushed the small coin in his hand.

Sargas's jaw dropped in pure shock and horror. "No. Why? What have you done?"

"A wise man once told me that forgiveness doesn't change the past, but it does enlarge the future," Jon said. "I've made my peace. I recommend you make yours."

Saiph could tell that Sargas hadn't heard a word Jon said. He simply stared off at nothing, a look of disgust and shock still on his face. He eventually brought his gaze up and looked around the room as if trying to remember where he was. Then he started to tremble with anger as he looked at Jon. He pointed at Sarah. "Kill her."

"Tim, no…" Jon said.

But Elean didn't hesitate. A small blade popped out of her glove, and she slid it across Sarah's throat. Sarah's eyes went wide with terror, as if she hadn't ever expected to die. Blood poured from the gash, drenching her dark shirt as it spilled to the ground. Saiph watched the life go out of Sarah's eyes and then felt an adrenaline spike of rage as Elean tossed Sarah's corpse to the side like it was garbage. Her body lay facedown on the stone floor as the pool of blood expanded like a wild-fire in a forest. Strands of her blonde hair were caught in the flood, and it broke Saiph's heart.

For the first time, Saiph saw Jon's perpetually calm bearing fall away. His gaze dropped to the ground, and he grimaced in pain. When he looked up, his pain was replaced with an anger that was terrible to behold. It was like gazing into Erlik's eyes and knowing you were about to suffer beyond reason. Electricity buzzed in the air around Jon like little bolts of lightning.

Sargas unconsciously took a step back. "I can't allow you to leave here alive."

Jon answered by walking resolutely toward the first line of Andhaka. Saiph readied himself to jump in the way.

"Take care of Elean, Aulan, and Malin," Jon said to Saiph. "Leave Sargas alive."

He kept walking forward as if the Andhaka wouldn't cut him down in an instant. The confidence of his stride somehow put fear into the others. It was as if Jon knew something they did not.

"Slaughter them," Sargas said. "Kill Jon first."

The ceiling exploded above, and boulders the size of trucks fell and landed on the first two Andhaka in front of Jon. Silvestre flew into the room, accompanied by three dozen drones.

Chaos.

Saiph let out a series of shield bursts as he grabbed Russ and sent energy to his feet, rocketing toward Jon and out of the circle of

Andhaka. Fortunately for Russ and Saiph, the Andhaka were focused on Jon. Russ fired his weapon even as Saiph carried him to the back of the room.

"You bastards!" Russ yelled, as Saiph put him down.

The first Andhaka reached Jon, its blade high in the air and ready to swing. Saiph engaged his systems and surged energy through his entire body. He ran, but he knew he would be too late. The blade came down, then...stopped.

The arm that held the blade sparked with electricity, and then the entire Andhaka fell to the ground, motionless. The other Andhaka attacked, their programming unable to recognize the threat. One by one, they swung their blades, but each one was stopped by an invisible wall. Jon walked inexorably forward as Andhaka fell around him.

Sargas screamed at the dynamics, who were dodging beams from Tokomoto's drones. "Kill Jon! Kill him!"

Elean and Aulan broke off from their evasive maneuvers and flew at Jon. They were about to hit him when Saiph stepped in front of them. Energy had been building in his systems ever since Sargas had appeared, and he used it now. He flooded his mind and limbs, and the world slowed. Aulan came at him from above while Elean hurtled at him from below, flying only a foot above the floor. He waited until the last second and then brought his legs up quickly and then smashed them back down. Elean's speed was halted immediately, and the force of his legs made her crash into the stone. Aulan reached for Saiph, attempting to get a hold of him, but Saiph batted his hand away and grabbed Aulan out of the air by the throat.

Adrenaline, sadness, energy, and rage coursed through Saiph's body. He squeezed Aulan's neck, making the man's legs kick frantically. Saiph could feel the dynamic's shield bursts hitting his armor, but he didn't care. All he wanted was to end this man's miserable life. If he'd had a second longer, Saiph would have crushed Aulan's armor into his throat, but a beam of yellow-green energy came at him, and Saiph was forced to throw Aulan's body at it. It hit and sent him flying across the room.

"I've got him!" Silvestre yelled, flying toward a hurt Aulan. "You take Malin and Elean!" Tokomoto controlled the drones and followed her.

Elean rolled hard to one side, and Saiph's legs came out from underneath him. He engaged his boosters and then flew backward to avoid a missile that shot up from Elean's shoulder. It hit the roof, and more stone fell from the ceiling. Elean popped to her feet and dodged out of the way of the falling stone. At that same moment, the wall next to her exploded inward, and she was once again thrown to the ground.

Saiph couldn't believe what he was seeing.

A thirty-foot, glowing orange voltyokai strode through the hole in the wall. Tasaday sat in some sort of harness on its shoulders, whispering in its ear.

"Yeah!" Russ yelled into the comm.

Saiph watched momentarily as Elean danced for her life. The voltyokai moved differently than anything he'd seen before. Elean rose into the air to try and get away, but the two-thousand-pound animal moved as nimbly as an insect, jumping from pillar to pillar and soaring through the air. It was a wonderful and terrifying sight.

Out of the corner of his eye, Saiph caught a flash of green, and he flung himself to the ground. He rolled to one knee and looked up in time to see Malin surging toward him. Saiph jumped in the air, spinning as he did so, firing lasers in multiple directions. One laser hit the roof and sent more stone crumbling down in front of Malin's flight path. She was forced to dodge left, where another laser was waiting for her. It hit her in the shoulder, and she lost control of her trajectory. Malin cut her engines and let her body fall to the ground, twisting to recenter herself. Saiph sprinted at her, then jumped into the air to intercept her falling body.

Malin turned to face him, and then she put her hands together, a green ball coalescing between them. A beam of energy flashed as Saiph approached. Saiph let out a shield burst and sent energy into his arms, readying himself to grab hold of her. The yellow-green beam burst through his shield and slammed into his chest, sending him crashing into the throne room doors twenty feet away. Saiph hit the wall and then slid to the ground, his chest armor melted slightly and smoking from the heat.

Saiph shook his head to dispel the dizziness and prepared to defend against another attack. None came. Saiph looked up to see that Malin had used the moment to escape through one of the holes in the ceiling. Saiph started to send energy to his back and legs, preparing to go after her, but he looked around the room and saw that his friends were in danger. He had to help them.

Aulan first.

Saiph got to his feet and ran to the left side of the room, where Aulan was simultaneously dodging Silvestre's attack while shooting down drones and ripping them apart. Once the drones were gone, Silvestre would be in serious danger. Saiph jumped into the air and then sent energy into his flight systems. He flew up behind Aulan firing thin but focused lasers from each of his fingers. Aulan sensed them and sent out a series of shield bursts, dissipating Saiph's attack.

"His right side is damaged and exposed," Silvestre said into the comm. "Try and hit him with something there."

Saiph fired a barrage of lasers and missiles at Aulan, trying to distract him. Aulan expertly dodged and shielded himself from each attack. Saiph loosed another volley and then unsheathed his swords. Saiph rushed toward Aulan, dodging lasers and missiles.

Aulan pulled out a metal staff and met Saiph in the air. He whirled the staff around himself, moving incredibly fast, even to Saiph's eyes. The staff knocked Saiph's swords away with ease, making him feel clumsy. He'd never been good with them, but he was so much faster and stronger than most that it usually didn't matter.

Aulan's staff flowed around his body like a shield, and whenever Saiph stabbed, the pole was there to knock it away. After a minute of this, the staff came down hard on Saiph's shoulder, and he lost control of his hovering and had to drop the ground. Aulan followed him, hitting the floor with a thud. He attacked, and Saiph was forced to dance back. Saiph frantically swung his swords, trying to block the pole that seemed to come from every direction. He sent energy into his right shoulder, thinking to shoot a missile and buy himself time, but the pole came down and bent the armor, jamming the release.

There were no taunts from Aulan now, just an intense focus. Saiph needed him to keep that focus for a little longer. Saiph let his mind relax, and he sent energy into his legs, feet, toes, and fingers. His movements quickened, and he was able to turn his defensive maneuvers into an attack. He stabbed, lunged, and flicked his sword at Aulan as fast as he could. Aulan parried every attempt, but he was forced to take a step back. Saiph screamed as his arms burned with the effort, but he kept pushing forward.

Just a little longer! Thrust, swing, stab. Thrust, swing, stab.

Aulan took another step back as Silvestre ever so quietly prowled toward him from behind. After another step, Silvestre pounced, driving her daggers into Aulan's exposed right side. He roared in pain and swung his staff behind him, but Silvestre had already retreated. His staff slowed its whirl, and he dropped to one knee. Blood came out of the mouth of his mask. Saiph was gathering energy to finish him off when Elean came flying in, her suit severely damaged from the voltyokai.

"No!" she screamed.

Saiph scrambled back, wary. The voltyokai followed Elean from behind but stopped when Tasaday told it to. Elean bent down over her twin brother, who was convulsing on the ground.

"Aulan!" she said. "Aulan, no...please, no." She took off her brother's mask and slapped him on the cheek. He looked up at her and smiled before the light left his eyes and his face slumped into her hand. Elean let out an animalistic scream, and Saiph felt a stab of guilt for her loss.

"Be ready," Toko said through the comm. Then he spoke aloud through one of the drones. "Surrender and you will be treated as a prisoner of war."

Elean looked around, as if she was trying to remember where she was.

Her eyes found Silvestre, and Saiph could see the rage underneath the yellow light of her eyes. She sprang at Silvestre with a bloodcurdling scream. Silvestre yelped and took a step back, but there was no need—Saiph was already there. He grabbed the armor around Elean's neck and slammed her back to the ground. He let loose a series of powerful punches, and Elean's face mask bent inward. After a half dozen hits, she fell still.

"I will remove her aura and secure her," Toko said.

Silvestre walked over. "Thanks. Are you all right?"

Saiph wasn't listening. His gaze wandered the room, and he found Jon and Sargas in the back. Saiph jogged toward them and attuned his hearing to their voices.

"...understood her," Sargas was saying.

"There is nothing you can say that can hurt me any deeper than you already have," Jon responded, taking another step forward.

Sargas lifted a gun out of his pocket and lifted it toward his own head. Before he could pull the trigger, Chet bear-hugged him from behind.

How did Chet get behind him? Sneaky bastard.

Saiph sent power to his legs, and he took three giants steps before lunging over Jon and landing directly in front of Sargas.

"I've got him, Chet," Saiph said.

Chet let him go and put his mouth to Sargas's ear. "Blood feud, buddo."

Saiph moved to stand behind Sargas and held him firmly to the spot.

Jon stalked forward and pulled out a small vial of clear liquid. "Let's try this again," he said. "Saiph, will you open his mouth for me, please?"

There was no need. Sargas opened his mouth willingly, a little smile there. Jon hesitated, but then shook his head and poured the liquid down his throat. Sargas swallowed it.

"Thank you," he said dreamily. "Shouldn't be long now..."

"How do you plan to take control?" Jon asked.

Sargas's chin drooped to his chest, and Saiph felt all the tension go out of then man's body. "Memory wipe," he mumbled.

"Explain," Jon said.

Sargas took a moment to answer. "I'm going to implant memories into all the important leaders. Make them think they owe fealty to me. Terrify them. Then take their bodies and implant my consciousness into their minds."

"Have you taken House Harain?" Jon asked.

"Yes..."

"Where are the hubs that store your consciousness?"

Sargas looked up at Jon, and Saiph could tell he was looking at his old friend with his eyes open. Then he started to convulse, and foam ran from his mouth.

"I didn't do anything!" Saiph yelled.

"He must have protected this body against the serum somehow," Jon said, coming closer. He grabbed Sargas by the chin and made him look into his eyes. "Where are the hubs?"

Sargas shook uncontrollably, but he still had that dreamy look in his eye.

"What are the hubs?" Jon repeated

"Nero," Sargas muttered, then fell still.

Jon reached up and put two fingers to Sargas's neck. "He's dead. Toko, will you take the body back to camp, please?"

Toko agreed, and Jon turned away and walked back to the center of the throne room. Sarah's body was still lying facedown, and the pool of blood had grown sickeningly large, but it didn't seem to be getting any bigger. Jon bent down and gently touched Sarah's hair. His hands were shaking.

"I can't..." he said. "Not like this. Russ..."

Russ strode over and put a hand on Jon's shoulder. "Go," he said. "I'll get her cleaned up. Don't worry. Just go."

Jon turned to leave the room, and Saiph made to go after him, but Silvestre put a hand on his shoulder. "Leave him be," she said.

Saiph looked at Sarah, but he had to turn away when Russ bent down to flip her over and pick her up.

"Harain forces are retreating to their dreadnought," Toko informed them. "Much of their force has surrendered, and Aoko has struck a deal with Cynix Corporation. They've joined our side."

Relief flowed through Saiph, rinsing him of the adrenaline built up during the fight. He leaned up against a pillar and slumped to the ground, exhausted in every possible way.

CHAPTER FORTY-THREE

It had only been a few hours since Sarah's death when Saiph received a message from her. After the trauma of the palace, Saiph had gone to a makeshift base outside the city to have his aura suit looked at. After a few repairs, he was able to get it back inside his body where it would finish healing on its own. Unfortunately, he needed it to go back out almost immediately after.

If you're reading this, then my death has been logged in Stargone's *database. I've left all my notes, research, and findings about Jangali in a hidden office pod in the wilderness. The location is linked below. Take care, Saiph. I hope the answers you find are the ones you're looking for. —Sarah*

The ejection of his damaged aura was more painful than it had ever been, but it worked. Someone yelled at him as he took a few running steps forward, but he was too busy sending the map of the hidden pod to his aura's system to listen. A few moments later, he was flying west. The computer confirmed his course and notified him that the flight at his current speed would take a little over an hour. Saiph settled in.

The night seemed extraordinarily quiet after the sounds of battle and the emotional turmoil he'd just been through. The events of the previous hours bubbled to the surface of his mind, even as he tried to suppress them.

Cutting down a screaming man.

The mortal fear of an incoming Andhaka blade.

Sarah, facedown on the floor, blood spreading beneath her.

The adrenaline had worn off, and Saiph felt as if his essence itself had been stretched thin. Alistair, Sarah, Gillums, Ayanda's mother, and countless more were dead. He suddenly had a strong desire to be crippled again, as if that would stop the chaos and bring back some sense of normalcy.

The energy drained from him as grief took hold, and he felt the energy of his flight systems sputter out for a moment. Only through force of will was he able to stir the energy within him and keep in the air. He took deep breaths to calm himself and looked down at the terrain. The plains below consisted of tall grass that was riddled with intermittent plants that pulsed with white light, reminding him of beetle barrels. In the distance, the sun was rising, lightening the sky without yet peeking above the horizon. It was serene and lovely, and he had trouble understanding how such beauty and such pain could coexist.

Pain makes man think. Thoughts make man wise. Wisdom makes life endurable.

The obscure Verse came to him in a flash. He needed to channel this pain into understanding. Only then could he come to grips with how the world was the way it was. Though the pain of his body and soul was still there, he flew on with a calm determination.

Saiph found the pod next to a small pond that had tiny voltminnows swimming near the surface. Short trees grew on the banks, but other than that, the pod was in plain sight. Apparently, Sarah thought this place we remote enough that she didn't need to hide it, and she was likely correct. There probably wasn't another soul for at least a hundred miles.

The sun had crested the horizon and was now shining brightly across green grass that glistened with mildew. Saiph steadied himself, then focused on his pass phrase:

Another day, another life.

His aura broke apart and clanged together as still-repairing pieces tried to knit themselves back into a whole. He grimaced as it retreated into his body. When it was all the way in, he collapsed to the ground and simply lay there for a time. He only wanted a moment to gather himself, but he fell asleep instead. He woke a few hours later, stiff from lying on the ground, but feeling much better overall. His mobile comm device had several new messages, and he sent a quick group reply to the others at the base, saying that he was okay and that he'd be back later.

Saiph walked into the office pod. The lights automatically came on and illuminated the cluttered, crescent-shaped desk. There was a large water container in the corner, and rather than going straight for the main computer terminal, Saiph put his face under the dispenser and drank greedily. After splashing more water onto his face, he went to the chair behind the desk and sat down. The computer powered on as he sat, and a bright light flashed several times.

"Access granted," the computer said.

There was an enormous amount of information on the next screen, and for a moment, Saiph felt a creeping despair. There was no need, though; he quickly found a meticulously well-kept main menu that linked to all the information that Sarah had compiled. Out of the list of twelve items, four caught his eye:

The Biology of Jangali
Catalogue of Potential Jangali Facilities
The Verses and Tenets
Lola Calthari

He clicked the last one first. Unfortunately, it didn't contain much, only old records that took Saiph half an hour to even understand. There was a certificate of some sort that showed when Lola Calthari was born: 2273. There was another official-looking paper from Saint Benedict Orphanage that described the release of Lola Calthari into the government's care to be placed in a new home.

New home? Saiph scoffed. *More like a whole new planet, to be experimented on and tortured. Poor girl had no one to protect her. No one to miss her.*

It made him terribly sad to think about. What had happened to her parents? What had happened to her on Jangali? There was no hint about Lola's fate. Not even a picture. It had only been a few days since they had discovered Lola's existence, and he was lucky to even have this, but still...he wanted more. He surmised that he would have to continue Sarah's research somehow.

This train of thought led him to the next category of information: *Catalog of Potential Jangali Facilities.* When he clicked on it, a large two-dimensional map appeared on the screen, with a side menu full of writing. Scattered across the map were dots of different colors. After some digging, Saiph discovered that the red dots were places Sarah had been, the yellow dots were possible facilities, and the blue dots indicated where she suspected facilities were likely to exist. There were dozens of them. At least forty in total. And it seemed as if Sarah was thinking the same thing he was—on the side panel, she had typed out: *I wonder how there are so many, but I'm more curious as to why. Why did Warren invest so much in this endeavor, and what was he doing here? I can't begin to imagine his motivations behind developing this place. There must be more information out there.*

Saiph navigated back to the main menu and clicked on the section on Verses and Tenets. It was short.

From the Verses I've compiled, it appears that the quotes the Jangalians use don't go past 2050. The Tenets, however, are mostly their own. They also don't use any of the quotes in the context of how they were said or who they were said by. From what Saiph knew of the outside world, this doesn't surprise me. It is fascinating how they chose these quotes and turned them into a powerful guiding force. I'm looking forward to surprising Saiph with a copy of the original book of famous quotes that I think his ancestors possessed. I've already had the replication machines on board Stargone *produce a copy of "The Thoughts We've Had" by Rachel Cas. Perhaps they already have them all written down somewhere, but I still think he'll enjoy having it.*

Saiph smiled sadly at the words before making his way back to the main menu. He clicked the link to *The Biology of Jangali* and was over-loaded by the complexity of the information. Nearly all of it was beyond Saiph's comprehension. He was just about to start scanning for words that made sense to him when his comm went off again. He looked down and saw a message from Tokomoto:

I found your father.

Saiph ran out the door of the pod, summoning his aura as he did so. He leapt into the air as it completed sheathing him and propelled himself into the sky. Rosh was six hundred miles to the south, but it only took Saiph half an hour to get there. It took all of his will and concentration to keep his energy levels high and flowing through his aura, but he didn't care. He needed to see his father.

Saiph landed on the ground and greeted the Khumbuza troops that were already at the camp providing food and medical treatment. He spoke with the colonel in charge, and the woman directed Saiph to the mass of tents that had been set up for refugees. Saiph found the quartermaster who told him which tent Rosh Calthari had been assigned. When Saiph found the tent, it was empty, and Saiph's anxiousness turned into anxiety. He stopped a man that came out of a tent nearby.

"Excuse me," Saiph said. "You wouldn't happen to know where Rosh Calthari is, would you?"

The man looked frightened of Saiph. "Um, yes, sir," he stumbled. "He spends most of his time at the volt farm. Said he couldn't just leave the animals now that we've been freed."

"Where's his volt farm?"

"Why, about three clicks west. Near the pond."

The man's face lit up in awe as Saiph lifted into the air in defiance of gravity. Saiph went higher and higher until he had an excellent vantage of the surrounding area. To the west, he spotted the pond the man had described and glided toward it. When it was directly below him, he descended, scanning the ground for his father. He was only a dot from this distance. As he got closer, he saw that Rosh was sitting on a log, throwing scraps to a caged voltguar. Saiph landed behind him, and Rosh turned around, surprised but calm.

"May I help you?" Rosh asked.

Saiph let his aura fall away, barely noticing the pain this time. Rosh's mouth fell open, and then he smiled in a way Saiph had never seen before.

"That's quite a trick, but what the hell has happened to your eyes?"

Saiph laughed and took two quick strides over to Rosh, gripping him in a tight embrace. Rosh returned the hug. "Your mother? Roe? Landon? Are they all right?"

Saiph nodded. "Yes. They're fine. Perfectly fine."

"Thank Tengrii," he said, unmitigated relief washing over him. Rosh took a step back from Saiph and looked him up and down. "Tell me everything."

Tokomoto dispatched a shuttle to come and chauffeur them back to the base, but it would take half the day to get there. Saiph took a seat on a makeshift bench across from his father and told him what had happened since they'd been separated nearly a year ago. The story came rushing out of him, as if he couldn't get it out fast enough. When Saiph reached the point of rescuing the rest of the family, Rosh stopped him.

"You've killed people?" he asked gently.

The stream of words died on Saiph's lips, and he nodded, feeling ashamed at how casually he had mentioned it.

"How does that make you feel?"

Saiph stared at the ground, drawing a circle with the toe of his boot. "You want to know what gets me? It's this expression they get the second before the end. They could be the cruelest person alive, but they still get the look of a terrified child when they face that last moment of life. Their eyes screaming that they're not ready to go."

Saiph involuntarily shuttered at his own words. "I once felt that way too, in the face of a yokai and a murdered friend. It's all so terrible. How did it all come to this?"

"You followed the Tenets," Rosh said. "Have they ever led you astray before?"

Saiph's breathing got heavier the more he thought about it. He was picturing the woman he'd thrown from the tower and her expression as she fell to her death. What if she was a mother? What if she were only trying to provide for her family?

"Roe said that the Tenets and the Verses are just words. Perhaps she's right. What are a few words compared to suffering and death?"

"You don't believe that," Rosh said. "We are what we say and what we think. It means everything."

The caged voltguar near them turned in its sleep and let out a little snore, but Saiph barely noticed the big cat. He needed this to be okay. "Can you just tell me that I did the right thing?" He felt tears well up in his eyes. "Tell me I didn't erase all those futures for nothing."

Rosh put a hand on his shoulder and waited for Saiph to look up at him. "It is hard to know the difference between right and wrong sometimes, but, Saiph, I know you're *trying* to do the right thing. I don't think there's anything more important than that. Hang on to your humanity." He squeezed Saiph's shoulder harder and got that faraway look he always got when a Verse was coming to him. Saiph smiled at the familiarity of it.

"*Do not be too moral. You may cheat yourself out of much life. Aim above morality. Be not simply good; be good for something.*"

Saiph took a deep breath and nodded. His father always knew what to say to make him feel better. "Did you know," Saiph said, "that the Verses are just famous quotes from those who came before us?"

"Well, of course they are," Rosh said, as if this were obvious. "What else would they be?"

Saiph laughed. "Yes, but they're not from Jangali. They're from another people on another *planet*."

Rosh shrugged. "Doesn't matter much to me."

"I suppose you're right."

Saiph continued with his story. The only thing he didn't mention was the name Lola Calthari. What was he to say? That their ancestor was likely tortured and experimented on? There was no point in that, and he'd rather not drive his father mad with curiosity.

Rosh had many questions during the story, and Saiph answered them all as best he could. He was amazed at how quickly Rosh accepted and absorbed the information.

"I searched for you when I got here," Rosh said after Saiph had finished. "I went out after hours, going from barracks to barracks, but it wasn't long until they caught me." Rosh lifted his shirt and showed him three long and grueling scars that stretched the length of his back.

"I was more careful after that. Still, after two months, I knew that you weren't here. I had a plan to escape with a few others, but we were caught stealing supplies. They hanged two of them and sent the other three to the coliseum, where they met their end, I suppose. They were good people. Brave. I was lucky that I had been called out to tend to a wounded voltmonkey, or else I'd be dead too."

It was dusk when the shuttle arrived. The ramp lowered and Roe, Milla, Landon, and Ayanda stepped out. They ran to Rosh and nearly knocked him over when they reached him. He laughed and hugged them all at once. Roe was wrapped around his waist and leaning her head against his chest. Milla kissed him on the cheek over and over again. Landon was jumping up and down. Ayanda grasped his hand and shook it.

Rosh looked at Ayanda. "Your mother?" he asked. Ayanda shook her head and began to tear up. Rosh withdrew from Roe and Milla and gave Ayanda a hug, cupping the back of her head against his shoulder. "You will always have a place with us, Ayanda. Not all your family is gone."

Ayanda sobbed and let her grief take hold. Saiph, Roe, and Milla came over and surrounded her like a shield, protecting her from the horrors of the world.

Saiph made it back in time to attend Sarah's funeral. It was small, and few words were spoken. There would be another ceremony held at Sarah's home on Mars, where they would lay her to rest next to her garden. After the service, Saiph stayed behind to offer his condolences.

"I'm so sorry," Saiph said to Jon. "I only knew her for a short time, but she meant a lot to me."

"Thank you. She lived a long life and she lived it the way she wanted, but that doesn't mean I'll miss her any less."

They stood in silence and watched the sun as it lowered toward the horizon.

"I'll be leaving tomorrow," Jon said.

"So soon? Where are you going?"

"Nero. One planet has already invaded another. It's beginning."

"What? When?"

"Yesterday afternoon. There is a gathering on Nero that I'll need to go to. It might be the last chance to avoid an all-out war. And Sargas will most certainly be there.

He looked Saiph squarely in the eye. "You've been through so much already, and I hate to ask more of you...but would you like to come with me? Would you like to see the stars, Saiph Calthari?"

Saiph looked up at the sky and spotted Kayra, misty in the sunset light. He thought about all he'd seen and learned over the last year and realized that, underneath all the strain and heartbreak, was a strong thread of wonder and awe. He had to know more. See more. Help more.

"Yes," Saiph said, "I believe I do."

Jon smiled and patted Saiph lightly on the shoulder before turning to walk away.

"Wait," Saiph said. "I know this may sound peculiar, but may I see a picture of Ava?"

Jon frowned but then nodded. He pulled out his handheld and

smiled sadly at the screen for a long moment, then lifted it into Saiph's view.

Saiph shook his head in unmitigated and perfect shock. It was impossible.

"What?" Jon said. "Saiph, what is it?"

Saiph stared at the photograph.

"I know her."

DID YOU ENJOY LOST STARS? READ THE FIRST CHAPTER OF BOOK 2!

Books live and die from Amazon reviews, so please consider leaving a review. If you'd like to find out how Saiph knows Ava, send me a screen shot of your Amazon review, and I'll send you back the first chapter of book 2 in the Lost Stars series!

If you'd like to be updated on Lost Stars news once a month, you can subscribe to the mailing list or visit www.donnyanguish.com. Thanks for reading!

ACKNOWLEDGMENTS

Lots of people to thank, so I'll jump right in. First I would like to thank the Winter Park Book Club for reading Lost Stars and giving invaluable feedback. Rachel, Matt, Katie, Aubrey, Robin, Alex, Wally, you all are amazing.

There are a few other early readers who gave their time and ridiculously good advice that I'd like to put here. Caroline Barnhill's take was so on point that I took nearly every bit of wisdom she had. Saiph changed for the better because of it. Thank you so much. Thanks to Patch Aiken, who heard I wrote a book and read it in a day. It came at a time when I needed to see that was possible. To John Moore, who has read all the early, not-so-good versions with minimal complaint. I appreciate it. Thank you Chris Morris, I appreciate it more than you know. Thanks to Hannah Kates for giving great advice about setting and for your encouragement!

To Kerrie Hiett, who read even when science fiction isn't really her thing. You're seriously the best sister in the world. I'd be remiss not to thank Jonathan Hiett. He caught a lot of grammatical mistakes and typos. More importantly, you're one of the most supportive people I know, and I am so happy to have you in my life. Of course I have an amazing friend in Jon Looke, who read Lost Stars and pointed out some pretty obvious technical flaws while always being courteous about it. Thanks bud. Another thank you to Alex Sooley, who read Lost Stars, asked how it was coming along, and has always been such a good friend.

Special shout out to Matt and Rachel Casscaddan, who would always stay up late talking about stories while laughing and drinking wine. More than anything, they encouraged me to keep writing and *always* made me feel good about Lost Stars. I will always love you all for that.

I'd also like to thank my copy editor Michelle Hope, who did an incredible job cleaning up Lost Stars and making it the best it could be. Also a thanks to Rafael Andres for the beautiful cover he created.

Thank you to my parents, Will and Kathy Anguish, for always supporting me no matter what I do. I always listen closely to their advice on Lost Stars and on everything else in life. They read *many* versions of the novel and gave opinions on nearly every step of the process. I simply can't imagine better parents than them.

Lastly, I'd like to thank Emily Loe. She not only reads everything I write, but listens to me complain, day dream out loud, and talk about my ideas. Lost Stars would not be the same without her input/support/overall awesomeness. You're the best, and I love you to the multiverse and back.

DID YOU ENJOY LOST STARS? READ THE FIRST CHAPTER OF BOOK 2!

Donny Anguish lives in Winter Park, FL with his Fianceé, Emily, and their two cats, Elodin and Daenerys. When he's not writing, running, or consuming an unhealthy amount of fried cheese on top of fried bread, he is usually lost in a novel, show, audio book, or some other form of story. He has a Master's degree in History with an emphasis on environmentalism and identity. While Anguish is indeed his real name and not a pen name, he does not actually suffer every moment of every day. Thank you for your concern.

CPSIA information can be obtained
at www.ICGtesting.com
Printed in the USA
BVHW031839191218
535889BV00010B/15/P

9 780578 424194